MIDNIGHT RESCUE

A KILLER INSTINCTS NOVEL

ELLE KENNEDY

A SIGNET ECLIPSE BOOK

SIGNET ECLIPSE
Published by New American Library, a division of
Penguin Group (USA) Inc., 375 Hudson Street,
New York, New York 10014, USA
Penguin Group (Canada), 90 Eglinton Avenue East, Suite 700, Toronto,
Ontario M4P 2Y3, Canada (a division of Pearson Penguin Canada Inc.)
Penguin Books Ltd., 80 Strand, London WC2R 0RL, England
Penguin Ireland, 25 St. Stephen's Green, Dublin 2,
Ireland (a division of Penguin Books Ltd.)
Penguin Group (Australia), 250 Camberwell Road, Camberwell, Victoria 3124,
Australia (a division of Pearson Australia Group Pty. Ltd.)
Penguin Books India Pvt. Ltd., 11 Community Centre, Panchsheel Park,
New Delhi - 110 017, India
Penguin Group (NZ), 67 Apollo Drive, Rosedale, Auckland 0632,
New Zealand (a division of Pearson New Zealand Ltd.)
Penguin Books (South Africa) (Pty.) Ltd., 24 Sturdee Avenue,
Rosebank, Johannesburg 2196, South Africa

Penguin Books Ltd., Registered Offices:
80 Strand, London WC2R 0RL, England

First published by Signet Eclipse, an imprint of New American Library,
a division of Penguin Group (USA) Inc.

First Printing, May 2012
10 9 8 7 6 5 4 3 2 1

PUBLISHER'S NOTE
This is a work of fiction. Names, characters, places, and incidents either are the
product of the author's imagination or are used fictitiously, and any resemblance
to actual persons, living or dead, business establishments, events, or locales is
entirely coincidental.

The publisher does not have any control over and does not assume any responsibility for author or third-party Web sites or their content.

ALWAYS LEARNING   **PEARSON**

ACKNOWLEDGMENTS

Writing a book is a solitary process, but I couldn't have done it without the support, guidance, and encouragement of some very wonderful people:

Jesse Feldman, my editor at NAL, whose advice is always spot-on and whose faith in this series is utterly contagious.

My agent, Don Fehr at Trident Media Group, for taking me under his wing and finding this series a good home.

And, of course, my family and friends, who continue to encourage me—and who don't take offense when I repeatedly cancel plans by giving my trademark excuse: I have to write!

Chapter 1

Corturo, Colombia

"Are you ready to talk?"

Abby cranked open her right eye—the left one was too swollen—and stared up at the harsh face of her captor. It was an unpleasant face, a menacing one. Pale blue eyes cold enough to freeze an ocean, hollow cheeks, a two-inch diagonal scar slicing his left cheek.

Devlin.

His thin lips curled in an angry frown. "Who are you? Who do you work for?"

She kept silent.

Gripping the whip in one hand, he crept closer, cat-like. "Still determined to stay quiet?" He smirked. "That will change. A few more visits with me and you'll reconsider."

He raised the whip high over his head. It sliced through the air with a hiss and connected with her bare stomach. Pain jolted through her.

Block it out. They can hurt you only if you let them.

The whip slapped her thighs. Her hands were bound,

tied to a rusty pipe over her head. Her feet suffered the same fate, attached to a metal peg protruding from the cold stone floor. The room smelled like sweat and blood.

Mind over matter.

He can't hurt you.

Abby repeated the mantra in her head, hoping to convince her aching, bleeding body that the whip couldn't hurt it. She didn't know how much longer she could take this.

"Turn her around," Devlin ordered the silent guard by the door. "No need to damage those breasts any further." He leaned closer, his faint British accent becoming more pronounced as he murmured, "Are they real, luv? I'd bet they are." He touched the bloody welt on her right breast, then pinched her nipple.

Abby spat in his face.

"Bitch." He retaliated with a vicious backhand.

The guard approached and turned her body around without untying any of the ropes. Her wrists twisted in an unnatural way, drawing a soundless yelp of pain from her swollen lips. One wrist was definitely sprained, if not broken.

"Who are you?" Devlin whispered in her ear. His hot breath fanned across her neck in a sadistic caress.

She mumbled something under her breath.

He pulled her hair. Hard. Almost tugging it out by the roots. "What was that?"

"I said I'm your worst nightmare."

He threw his head back and laughed. "Ah, I knew you weren't the pussycat Blanco claimed you were. I had your number the moment you spilled your drink in his lap at the bistro." He chuckled. "Clumsy, clumsy Erica, with her big blue eyes and fragile little body. What's your real name, luv? C'mon, tell me. It'll be our little secret."

She feigned boredom. "Call me whatever you want, Devlin."

Devlin dragged one finger along her spine. "I admit I liked you better when you were refusing to talk."

He made a *tsk*ing noise and stepped away. A second later the whip cut into her lower back.

Dizzying pain.

"Who are you?"

Another lash.

"Who sent you?"

The whip sliced her skin.

"It'll be better for both of us if you talk. I truly hate hurting you like this."

She fought a wave of nausea. Her ears started to buzz. "Liar," she said, wheezing. "You love every minute of what you're doing to me."

He gave a deep laugh. "Ah, but there might be some truth to that."

Another lash. Two more. Three. Water poured down her skin. No, not water. Blood. The stench of it filled the air. Oh God, her body hurt. Ted had really worked her over this time.

No, not Ted. That was a long time ago. Wasn't it? Her head started to spin. Nothing made sense anymore.

"I will break you," Devlin murmured. "Sooner or later, luv, I will break you."

She bit her lip. It bled.

He raised his fist and a second later it came crashing down on her jaw.

Then everything went black.

*   *   *

When she awoke, she was back in the cell. It was night. Or afternoon. Hard to tell. It was always dark in the cell. With a groan, Abby tried to sit up but failed.

Block it out. Sit up.

She tried again, this time managing to lift herself up. As she nearly keeled over, she braced her hand on the cold ground to steady herself. Bad idea. Her broken wrist objected to being put into use.

Head spinning again.

Blood drumming in her ears.

Blackness.

When she came to the second time, the faint sound of voices drifted from the end of the dark hall. They would come for her again. Soon. But she wasn't going to talk, no matter how many beatings they forced her to endure. It would get worse. She knew it would. Soon the beatings would become rapes and the rapes would become torture. But torture would not lead to death. Oh no. Blanco wanted her alive.

She drew in a breath, hoping the oxygen might clear her foggy head. She wiggled her right foot, tilting it to make sure the flesh-colored Band-Aid was still attached to her skin. It was, and she felt the tiny metal key digging into the sole of her foot. She'd swiped the key from one of the guards when they first brought her in here. Managed to get it off the key ring and everything—the moron hadn't even blinked. Picking pockets was just one of the many skills with which Jeremy had supplied her. She wouldn't use the key, though. Not yet.

Not until the time was right.

Chapter 2

A black Mercedes was approaching the fence. From the porch of the compound, Kane Woodland raised his beer to his lips and took a deep swig, narrowing his eyes on the vehicle. The windows were heavily tinted, which made it next to impossible to see the driver. Whoever it was, he or she obviously knew the drill. The sleek car stopped by the intercom box.

He watched as a long, slender arm emerged from the driver's-side window and reached for the keypad. One of Morgan's women? Nah, the guy never brought ladies home. Always drove into town to get his jollies. The compound was off-limits to everyone save members of the team and carefully screened staff.

And since Jim Morgan knew it the second anyone so much as looked at the compound from a distance, Kane wasn't surprised when the door behind him opened and Morgan stepped onto the porch. He was a commanding figure—six-three and all muscle, with intense blue eyes and a head of cropped dark hair. Women went wild for him. Men . . . Well, they usually kept their distance. Or at least the smart ones did. Morgan had *Don't fuck with me* written all over him.

"Fuck," the man muttered under his breath.

The radio poking out of Morgan's front pocket crackled. "Sure about this, boss?" The security man's voice was riddled with static.

Morgan radioed back. "Let her in."

Kane turned to study the frown creasing the other man's lips. Morgan's jaw was stiff, his teeth visibly clenched. Not unusual, though, since the boss was always stiff and frowning. Morgan was as prickly as they came, way too sarcastic for his own good, and God only knew if he ever laughed.

When Morgan had approached Kane after he'd left the SEALs nearly eight years ago, Kane had hesitated before accepting the job the other man dangled before him. Extraction had always given him the biggest rush when he'd been with the teams, but he wasn't sure he wanted to work for Morgan, mercenary extraordinaire, the man who never smiled. In the end, he'd decided working for the unsmiling merc was worth it, as long as he was able to continue playing G.I. Joe without being forced to adhere to the strict rules the navy loved oh so much.

Kane hated rules. The only reason he'd joined Morgan's team was because he'd been strapped for cash at the time; he'd figured it would be a temporary gig, a few fast jobs and then he'd move on. But he'd quickly come to respect Jim Morgan. The first mission out, Morgan had saved Kane's ass—big time. But gratitude wasn't the sole reason he'd stuck around. Morgan had a way of inspiring loyalty in his men. Treated them like equals rather than subordinates. With Morgan, it was no uniform and no rules; sure, the man barked orders at them, but it was easy to say *yes, sir* when you genuinely liked and respected the guy you were *yes, sir*-ing.

Still, it would've been nice if his boss weren't such a prickly bastard most of the time.

Right now, Morgan seemed extra prickly, his dark gaze fixed on the approaching vehicle. The guy looked . . . nervous? Nah, no way.

Kane arched one brow and said, "A friend of yours?"

"No."

The two men stood in silence as the gate creaked open, allowing the car to drive into the courtyard. The Mercedes' wheels slid over the red dirt, slowing as the vehicle pulled up next to Kane's silver Escalade.

Morgan looked like a volcano ready to erupt. A vein throbbed in his forehead, and he kept clenching and unclenching his fists at his side. Well. This was fucking weird. In the eight years they'd worked together, Kane had never seen his boss this agitated.

Curiosity sparked in his gut. Leaning against the railing, he waited for the driver to show her face.

And damn, what a face it was.

The woman who stepped out of the Mercedes belonged in a museum, in an exhibit called "The Most Beautiful Woman in the World."

She had the face of an angel—wide-set blue eyes, a delicate upturned nose, sensual red lips that other women would kill for. And that body. Petite and curvy, with full breasts hugged by a tight black tank and shapely legs encased in leather. Angel face and devil body. Damn, what a combo.

Next to him, Morgan didn't seem to appreciate the view. In fact, the other man's shoulders only stiffened again.

"Hello, Morgan," the woman called. Oh yeah, that throaty voice definitely suited her.

She sauntered toward the porch, the heels of her black leather boots snapping against the red dirt beneath them. Her blond hair shifted in the warm afternoon breeze. Great hair, Kane noted. Fell in waves almost down to her ass.

He felt his body stirring the closer she came, until Morgan uttered one word that killed every flicker of arousal and appreciation.

"Noelle."

Kane forced his mouth to stay closed. Noelle? *Noelle?* He supposed it could be a coincidence, just another woman with that terrifying name, but Morgan's next words confirmed Kane's suspicions.

"Here to kill me?" the boss said mockingly.

Holy shit. The queen of fucking assassins, standing on their freaking porch.

"Of course not—would I really do such a thing?" she drawled.

Morgan snorted.

"How've you been?" she added, her midnight blue eyes never leaving Morgan's face.

He didn't reply to the question, but posed one of his own. "What the hell are you doing here?"

Kane saw an indefinable glimmer flash across those fuck-me eyes. Anger? Annoyance?

Resting one delicate hand on her hip, she cocked her head thoughtfully. "Guess."

Morgan released a sharp laugh. "Well, you say you're not here to kill me. So . . ." He slanted his head in thought. "Hope it's not to fuck me, because we both know that's not gonna happen, baby."

Wow. Okay. Morgan might quite possibly be the only man in the world who would dare to call the queen of assassins *baby*. His balls were that big, apparently.

Kane wondered if he should discreetly disappear. This conversation had *personal* written all over it. But he was far too fascinated to leave. Besides, he couldn't quit staring at that dainty hand she had perched on her hip. Her fingers were long and slender, fingernails manicured and painted bloodred. Those hands were capable of killing men twice her size, or so the stories went.

Noelle—no last name, as far as he knew—was a legend. A private contractor, she sold her services to various government agencies and the occasional civilian, though rumor had it she only took out slime bags that deserved it. An assassin with a moral code, apparently. Rumor also said the women she employed were just as deadly. Kane's contact at the CIA had called them chameleons. You didn't see 'em until they were gunning for you, and by the time you realized the threat, you were dead.

So why the hell was she here to see Morgan?

"Sorry, *baby*," she returned dryly. "You're not my type." She glanced around, her shrewd eyes taking in the enormous ranch-style house in front of her, the high fence surrounding the property, and the long stretch of flat, barren land in the distance. "Nice digs you've got here, Jim. Very . . . open. What happened to the place in the mountains?"

Morgan shrugged. "Too easy to be ambushed. Here, I can see an enemy coming from miles away." He shot her a stony look.

Noelle laughed, the sound melodic and unusually warm, and then those eyes went all business. "Are you going to invite me in?"

"Are you going to tell me why you're here?"

After a long pause, she released a sigh. "I need your help."

Morgan laughed.

Her lips instantly tightened. "You think I enjoy asking, you son of a bitch? If there were any other option I'd take it. As it stands, I need you. So, are you going to invite me in?"

Still chuckling, Morgan took a step back and gestured to the open doorway behind them. "By all means, baby, come in. I cannot wait to hear this."

The other men were sitting out on the back terrace when Kane drifted onto the patio. He wondered what was going on in Morgan's study at the moment. Before disappearing with the sexy assassin, Morgan had told Kane to go outside and wait with the others. Kane shook his head, absently crossing the dusty tiles toward the table.

"Lloyd says we've got a visitor." Luke Dubois spoke up as he lifted a bottle of beer to his lips. A cigarette dangled from his other hand, the smoke curling in Kane's direction. The long-haired brown mutt lying by Luke's feet raised his head sharply at Kane's approach, then flopped back down, deciding that Kane was no threat. He had to wonder what the dog would do if he *was* a threat. Probably tear his throat out. A German shepherd and collie mix, Bear was enormous, and more skittish than an untamed horse. The mutt seemed to relax only when Luke was around.

"Oh, we sure as hell do," Kane replied with a grin. "Though I'm not sure *visitor* is the right word."

The sun was high in the sky, without a cloud in sight, and beads of sweat began to form at Kane's temples as he sank into the chair across from Luke. Man, he was sick of this heat. He'd grown up in Michigan, and in Michigan the month of November meant bitter-cold wind and shitloads of snow. Here in Tijuana, it meant baking in a sauna all day long. He supposed he could always find a place of his own, somewhere cooler, like some of the other guys who worked for Morgan, but fuck, what kind of life would he lead? Holden was married, so he had a woman to come home to when they finished a gig. Sullivan had always preferred his lazy no-mad lifestyle. And Trevor was still in mourning. The guy's condo in Aspen gave him plenty of space to deal with his loss.

But Kane had no woman and no reason to be alone. Hell, he couldn't stand his own company sometimes. Too many messed-up thoughts in his head, too much anger that always found a way out whenever he was alone. Here, at the compound, he had distractions. He could shoot the shit with Ethan Hayes and Luke, get drunk on fine Mexican rum, and when the anger found a way to the surface, all he had to do was head to the gym with D, where they could beat the crap out of each other.

He glanced at D, who stood by the railing, elbows resting on the sleek metal while his black eyes fixed on something in the distance.

"Pay attention, D," he called. "You're going to want to hear this."

D turned his broad shoulders. The snake tattoo that circled his neck rippled as he cocked his head with inter-est. Out of all the men in Morgan's service, Derek "D" Pratt was the most terrifying. Not just because he had ink all over that lean, muscular body. No, it was the eyes. Black as coal, hard as ice. He'd been with Delta for a while, then worked for a mysterious black ops agency nobody had ever heard of. Tough as nails, lethal as ever, and definitely a man you wanted by your side in a fight.

"So who is it? Feds?" Luke drawled over the rim of his beer bottle.

"CIA?" Ethan spoke up with typical boyish curiosity.

Ethan was the youngest of the team, a former marine who'd been orphaned as a teenager and tended to look at Morgan as a father figure. No matter how hard he tried, Kane couldn't view Ethan as anything but a kid. But the kid was good at his job, and Kane knew that despite his clean-cut, preppy good looks and gratingly polite personality, Ethan always had his back in the field. Same went for Luke, their resident Cajun bad boy. Luke could drink Kane under the table, and he hooked up with more women than Kane could keep track of, but like Ethan, he was a damn good soldier. Morgan had succeeded in putting together a team that functioned like a well-oiled machine—that was for sure.

Kane shook his head. "Guess again."

"The queen of fucking England?" D said in that gravelly rasp of his.

"Try the queen of assassins."

There was a stunned silence.

Luke raked his fingers through his dark hair. Kane could swear the man's hands were trembling. Look at that. Luke Dubois, smart-ass Lothario, scared speechless.

"Noelle?" Luke finally breathed, looking so impressed that Kane had to laugh.

"You're shitting us," D said. Those black eyes shifted uneasily. "Right?"

"Nope. She just drove up in a sexy little Mercedes."

"Why the hell didn't you get us?" Luke demanded.

"I was too absorbed. She and Morgan—they know each other. Fuck, I think they *know* each other."

Luke laughed. "No way."

"I'm serious, man. Sparks flying all over the place."

Before the others could press for more details, footsteps sounded from behind. Kane received a jolt of extreme satisfaction when he heard all three men hiss out their breath. He twisted his head just as Noelle, in all her leather-clad glory and shiny yellow hair, stepped onto the patio. Morgan appeared behind her, his back ramrod straight, like someone had shoved a poker up his ass. Didn't look happy, their boss.

The dog wasn't happy either. At Noelle's entrance, Bear got on all fours, pulled his lips over his teeth and snarled at the woman—maybe Luke's constant bragging about his dog's enemy radar wasn't *total* bullshit.

The enemy in question was completely unfazed. With a scowl, Noelle jabbed a manicured finger in the dog's direction and said, "Sit."

Bear sat. Just like that.

Kane wasn't sure if he was impressed or scared shitless.

"This your team?" Noelle asked in that husky, femme fatale voice as she turned away from the dog and coolly appraised the four men on the terrace.

Kane found that he couldn't hold her gaze for long. Her blue eyes were too astute, too eerie, as if she were looking right into his damn soul. Ethan and Luke also broke eye contact after a few seconds. But not D. Oh no, D eyed her right back, his black gaze as cool and calculated as her blue one. She seemed surprised by it, and oddly approving. Nodding, she glanced to Morgan for an answer.

"Part of the team," he said. "The others don't live on the compound."

"But these four do." She studied them once more, and her pouty lips curved slightly. "I bet you boys have barrels of fun here, don't you?"

Morgan made an irritated sound. "Sit the fuck down, Noelle. I told you, I won't agree to do this until I hear what my men think about it."

"So commanding, aren't you, Jim? I see power still gets you off."

"Just take a fucking seat."

"Very well." She offered a faint smile. "I've pushed your buttons enough today, haven't I?" Moving with the grace of a lioness, she pulled out one of the chairs and lowered her body into it.

Morgan moved toward the table, choosing a chair as far away as possible from the blonde. "Here's the deal. The package is being held at Luis Blanco's compound. She"—he gestured to Noelle—"wants us to extract it."

"Not *it. Her,*" Noelle cut in, steel in her voice. "God, Jim, still so fucking professional. You're not extracting a package. You're rescuing one of my girls."

Morgan glared at her. "You want to run this meeting, baby? Because I warn you, my men don't follow anyone's orders but mine."

She fell silent, but the frown never left her face.

"So, an extraction from Blanco's compound," Morgan repeated. He glanced around the table. "What do you think?"

Kane resisted a laugh. What did he think? Uh, not much to think about there, except *hell, no.* Luis Blanco was untouchable. Along with trafficking arms and drugs, the guy ruled the South American sex trade. The DEA hadn't had much luck in gathering evidence against Blanco. The bureau continually came up empty-handed too. The man was too smart and too calculating to allow himself to get caught. He was as shady as they came, and the current suspicions that he was smuggling Asian minors into South America and pimping them out weren't all that far-fetched. It would be just his style, in fact.

"What was the package doing tangling with Blanco?" Luke asked, sounding as unenthused as Kane felt.

"She was doing her job," Noelle answered in a frosty tone. "Blanco was her target."

"Who contracted her?" D inquired sharply.

"Let's just say the Colombian government is growing tired of Blanco," Noelle said vaguely. "They think he's giving the country a bad rep. My girl went in to remedy that."

Kane had to laugh. "She actually thought she could kill him?"

A pair of blue eyes pinned him down with a deadly glare. "What's your name?"

He gulped. "Kane."

"Well, *Kane*, not only was she perfectly capable of killing him—she had plenty of opportunities to do so. She infiltrated his organization two months ago. She gained his trust. Hell, she probably even got the bastard to fall in love with her."

"Then why didn't she off him?" he returned.

Noelle frowned. "I have no idea. Last time she checked in, I got the feeling she was stalling. I ordered her to do the job, and then she went off the radar. That's why I came to you," she added, her frown deepening as she glanced at Morgan. "The people who hired us are getting impatient, but me . . . Well, frankly, I'm just worried."

"How long since the last check-in?" Ethan asked without meeting Noelle's eyes. Not surprising. Ethan was shy enough as it was—put him next to a sexy assassin and he turned into a terrified bunny rabbit.

"Two days." Noelle let out a heavy sigh. "I tapped a source who told me Blanco's holding a woman in that makeshift jail of his. It's gotta be her."

"Some agent you've got there," D rasped, leaning against the railing and stretching his long, tattooed arms.

Noelle's head jerked toward him. "She's the second-best assassin in the world."

D raised one black eyebrow. "And the first?"

"Me, of course."

Kane watched with interest as the two locked gazes, and he could have sworn he heard the air begin to crackle. The lethal glint in Noelle's eyes rivaled the deadly glimmer in D's. Strange, but he got the feeling they were two peas in a pod. Dressed head to toe in black; cold, expressionless faces. Sexual tension streaked between them, and still they held the gaze.

Finally Morgan cleared his throat. "The woman in the jail—you sure it's your girl?"

Turning away from D, Noelle nodded. "Description matched Abby."

Morgan's blue eyes suddenly narrowed. "Wait a second—Abby *Sinclair*? Why the hell didn't you mention it was her?"

Kane glanced at Luke, then D, to see if either of them knew who this Sinclair chick was, or why Morgan had reacted to her name. Both men shrugged as if to say, "Fucked if I know."

"Would it have made a difference?" Noelle asked coolly.

"Jeremy was a friend. Of course it would've made a difference."

Kane's head was swimming with bewilderment. Abby. Jeremy. Who the hell were these people?

"Then you'll do it?" Noelle said, relief all over her angelic face.

Morgan swore under his breath, then turned to the men. "I'm gonna be straight here. Blanco's compound will be a bitch to get into. Getting the package out will be an even bigger bitch. This ain't gonna be easy."

Kane studied his boss. "You're going to try anyway."

Morgan nodded.

"And if we say no, you'll still do it. Alone."

Another nod.

Holy cow. What was going on? Morgan never took on suicide missions. And it was obvious he felt serious animosity toward the blond bombshell sitting at the table. So why was he agreeing to breach Luis Blanco's compound? Obviously, even after eight years of working together, Kane still knew shit-all about his boss.

But he did know there was no way in hell he'd let Morgan do this alone. Suicide mission or not, Morgan wasn't a man you said no to. He was the man you stood by until the bitter end.

"Okay, count me in," Kane murmured.

Luke nodded, while Ethan said, "Ditto."

Morgan glanced at D. "What about you?"

"I go where you go, boss."

Something that resembled relief flashed across Morgan's face. With a sigh, he got to his feet. "I'll call the others."

"Morgan," Noelle said.

He stopped at the terrace door, waiting for her to continue.

She leveled him with a dark look. "What's this going to cost me?"

Without answering, he left the terrace.

"Shit," Noelle muttered under her breath.

Kane's gaze drifted back to the blonde. At the moment, she didn't look like the most lethal woman in the world. She looked worried. Almost scared.

Before he could stop himself, he met her eyes and quietly asked, "Who is Abby Sinclair?"

Noelle slowly rose from the chair, her blond hair falling down her back like a silky curtain. At first he thought she wouldn't respond, but halfway to the door she stopped, that lithe body turning, those sexy blue eyes reaching his. "She's one of mine," Noelle said before stalking away.

Twelve more days.

Abby leaned against the cold stone wall of the cell, bringing her knees up so she could wrap her arms around them. Her wrist throbbed from the motion, and acid crept up her throat, threatening to gag her, choke her. She touched her chest and felt the welts, realizing the guards hadn't put her clothes back on this time. She was naked. Her entire body hurt, a dull, constant ache that pumped in her blood and sent tremors through her muscles. It was fine. *She* was fine. She only had to endure it for twelve more days. Not long at all. A lifetime.

Poor Noelle. Abby bit her lip, thinking about her boss. Only two people had ever given a damn about her. Jeremy was one. Noelle was the other. The woman had recruited Abby after Jeremy's death, taken her into her home, trained her, made her indestructible. The two women had forged a bond over the years. They'd both endured seriously shitty childhoods, and both had dragged themselves out of the gutter and given the finger to everyone who'd hurt them. But Noelle's experiences had inspired a craving for power. There was never enough power to be had, according to the dangerous blonde.

Abby—well, she wanted revenge. That was why she'd allowed herself to be captured by Blanco, deliberately blowing her cover. She could have killed the son of a bitch a hundred times over in the past two months. It had been so very easy finagling her way into his life. She'd researched him to no end before taking the assignment. He preferred redheads, so she became one. He liked meek little pussycats, so she became one. She allowed him to woo her. She moved into this empty, sterile compound. Hadn't fucked him, though. It had been a pleasant surprise, learning the mighty Luis Blanco couldn't get it up. Arm candy, that's all he wanted, and that she gave him.

She hated deep cover, but with this gig there hadn't been a choice. Half a dozen bodyguards surrounded Blanco day and night. When he left the estate, he and his men made sure a sniper couldn't get a clear shot, so straight-up bullet-in-the-brain had been out. His servants tasted his food before he ate it, so poison was a no-go. After she moved in, she decided a pill-induced heart attack might be the way to go, but then she'd gotten derailed.

If she came out of this alive, she was in for a long lecture from her boss. Hell, she'd probably get canned. But who cared? All it took was the memory of those girls in the bunker, those naked, bleeding, dirty girls, and the overwhelming need for revenge trumped everything else. Noelle, her job, her own freaking safety.

She was going to free those girls, even if she died trying.

Abby sat up, fighting the dizziness that came with the action. She blinked, cleared her head, and examined the cell for anything she might be able to use to defend herself. Although she could handle the beatings, the notion of sexual violation made her blood run cold. Using sex as a weapon was one thing. It was done on *her* terms, a tool she used when it was the only way to carry out her mission. But being sexually victimized? No fucking way. She'd been there, done that.

Blanco had told Devlin not to touch her. How sweet. He wanted to save her body for the scumbag who would purchase her at the auction.

But Devlin . . . Abby had seen the lust in his eyes during their last visit. And the fury, when she'd spat in his face. Rape was definitely on the bastard's agenda. So far, even the beatings were tame, compared to what she knew he must be craving to do to her. A broken wrist and some bruises weren't the end of the world. Devlin did enough to inflict pain, but not enough to kill or mutilate her. No, that wouldn't go over well with the perverts who attended the auction. Twelve more days of beatings—she could handle that. But even a second of rape? Never again.

No potential weapons in the cell. She would need to rely on her own skills to overpower Devlin, a difficult task considering one wrist felt broken and her entire body ached from the whipping.

You're stronger than you think, Abby.

Jeremy's voice again, accompanied by a memory of the drills and exercises her adoptive father had forced her to undergo. He'd maintained that every teenage girl should know how to defend herself. As a grown woman, she knew he'd been right. Because really, who knew when you might find yourself bloody and beaten in a sociopath's Colombian prison?

The guards returned nearly an hour later. The tall one, Rodriguez, approached the iron bars. "Did you get a nice rest?" he chortled, his accent sounding garbled in the stuffy hallway.

He unlocked the door and stepped inside. Bent down and unceremoniously hauled her up to her feet. Her head had cleared but she feigned a bout of light-headedness, lurching forward so the bulky dark-skinned man was forced to grab for her.

"Señor Devlin has a surprise for you," the guard said. The hard glint in his dark eyes belied the pleasant smile on his lips.

There would be nothing pleasant about this next encounter. Of that she was certain.

She was taken back into the interrogation room. This time the guards didn't tie her up. A cot was now set up in the corner of the room, boasting a mattress stained with fluids she never wanted to know about.

Rodriguez pushed her down on the mattress. It creaked as her weight hit it. The second guard stood by the open door, leering at her naked body like a lion hovering over a bloody carcass.

A moment later, Devlin stepped into the room. He wore a pair of khaki pants and a white button-down shirt, his brown hair slicked back from his face, emphasizing his harsh, angular features.

"Hello again," he said cheerfully. "Did you miss me?"

She didn't respond.

Anger flared in his soulless eyes. "Still not talking, are

we? That's fine. No words are required for what I have in mind." He nodded at Rodriguez, who promptly unzipped his trousers.

Devlin must have seen the glimmer of dread in her eyes because he laughed. "Don't be scared of Javier. He's only going to fuck you, not kill you. And when he's done, Sancho here will take his pleasure." He hooked his thumb at the second guard standing by the door. "And after Sancho's had his fun, it will be my turn."

Devlin licked his bottom lip and swept his gaze over her bare breasts. "I have to warn you, luv, that I probably won't be as gentle as my predecessors."

"Touch me and I'll rip your eyes out," she hissed.

She made a move to sit up but Rodriguez shoved her so that she was flat on her back. He glanced at Devlin as if asking for permission, and when the other man nodded he dropped his trousers and pulled out his cock. Chuckling, he wagged it in front of her face. As a rush of rage swept through her, Abby tried to bite at the tip but the guard slapped her hard across the face with one meaty hand. Her bottom lip snagged in her teeth. Blood filled her mouth.

"Let the games begin," she heard Devlin murmur.

Like hell they would.

She closed her eyes and waited for Rodriguez to lower his big body onto hers. His fingers dug into her sore thighs, attempting to pry her legs apart, his throbbing organ searching for her opening.

"You ready, señorita?" he muttered, his hot breath fanning against her ear.

"Yep."

Before he could blink, her arm soared upward. The

heel of her palm smashed into his face, breaking his nose, and as he grunted loudly, distracted by the pain, she wrapped her arms around his thick neck and twisted. He died instantly, his hand still on his cock. Ignoring the pain shooting through her wrist, she scissor-kicked herself onto her feet, lunging for Devlin, who looked stunned by the violence that had just transpired.

He reached for her but she delivered a well-placed kick to his balls and shoved him away. The guard at the door was drawing his gun but he was too slow. Her fist connected with his nose before he could act. Blood poured from his nostrils. She jammed her finger against his carotid artery and knocked him out cold. His eyes rolled to the back of his head as he dropped to the dirty floor like a stone, unconscious.

She was two steps from the doorway when a pair of hands encircled her neck and squeezed. She gasped, trying to kick Devlin away, but he was too strong, too enraged. "You little bitch," he hissed at her, his fingers tightening over her skin.

Her vision grew fuzzy, her windpipe quivering as it tried to suck in the oxygen this bastard was depriving her of.

"I'm going to kill you," he muttered angrily. He loosened his grip and she gulped in a gust of air, her brain struggling to function. "But first I'm going to fuck you. I'm going to fuck your cunt and your ass until I tear you open and you're bleeding all over my cock."

He dragged her by her hair and flung her back on the cot. Voices drifted into the room from the hallway. Three more guards appeared in the doorway, shouting at Devlin in Spanish.

He turned his head, just slightly, to bark out a few orders. The guards stepped back, wary, eyeing the two motionless bodies of the guards she'd taken care of.

Devlin glanced down at her, his eyes wild with fury and sexual excitement. He raised one arm over his head, then sent it smashing into her jaw. Abby grunted, spitting out blood.

"I told you I wouldn't be gentle," he taunted.

"And *I* said," she squeezed out, "that if you touch me, I will rip your eyes out."

Chapter 3

Either Blanco's security was slipping, or this was a fucking trap. Kane waited in the shadows, unmoving, unblinking, focusing on the small adobe structure that stood ten yards away. Breaching Blanco's compound had been too easy. Scary easy, seeing as Morgan had opted for a six-man team for the job rather than contacting all his men. Holden, using his techno voodoo, had disabled the electric fence and bypassed the alarm. D had snipped a nice little hole in the fence, and zero guards had stood sentry in the yard as the men crept onto the property.

Morgan had perched himself on the roof of the training facility across from the makeshift prison, rifle in his hands, eye on the scope. Luke and Ethan were back near the fence, covering the perimeter.

Kane and D had approached the jail from opposite ends, weapons drawn.

And still no guards.

Kane tightened his hold on the trigger. Fuck. He didn't like this. The compound was far too quiet, no sounds save for the soft hiss of the wind. According to their intel, there should've been five guards inside the prison, two at the entrance, but the steel door was unmanned. Why the hell was that? What were the two fuckers doing, making out in the bushes?

Hanging back, he wondered how Holden was faring with the power situation. Holden McCall was a genius when it came to technology—the guy could steal a damn car using nothing but his laptop. Quiet, intense, and ever focused, Holden could always be counted on, but at the moment he was taking his sweet-ass time. Kane and D were grounded until Holden killed the lights that illuminated the yard like a Christmas tree. They'd arranged for a neat power outage, something to throw the compound into a bit of chaos.

But apparently Blanco's men were perfectly capable of creating their own chaos.

He flinched as a primal cry rang out from the prison. A male shriek laced with pain, horror, and fury.

Kane's balls shriveled. Lord, any man who screamed like that had either been castrated or set on fire.

A few seconds later, the steel door of the prison was flung open and a stream of guards burst out. Kane did a quick count—one, two, three. Four and five were carrying a man in their arms. He didn't wear the navy blue uniform, so obviously a civilian. That left two guards.

Adrenaline pumping through his veins, he shot forward, nearly slamming into D. The two men stormed the jail, moving in opposite directions. Kane heard a startled male cry, a shout cut short by a sickening crack.

A familiar crack. A man's neck being snapped, aka D taking care of business.

Moving into the musty-smelling corridor, Kane raised

his assault rifle. Under the glow of the weak single bulb lighting the cell-lined hall, he caught a flash of movement. A guard was shoving a woman into one of the cells. The sound of Spanish expletives filled the air. Slamming the cell door, the guard cursed a final time, then turned. He froze when he caught sight of Kane.

Eyes flicking to the barrel pointed at him, the guard reached for the pistol holstered at his hip. He was a second too late. Kane's bullet hit the man between the eyes.

"Nice shot," D drawled, coming up behind him.

"She's down here," Kane said briskly, crossing the hall with three long strides.

He kicked the guard's lifeless body out of the way, glanced at the cell, and halted. When his gaze fell on the motionless woman lying on the floor, the blood in his veins turned to ice.

"Oh shit," D muttered.

As his heart thudded against his rib cage, Kane slid open the metal door and dropped to his knees. He reached for the battered woman, cursing wildly when he caught sight of all the blood.

"Fucking animals," D rasped.

Kane met the other man's eyes and the rage he saw in them mirrored his own. He glanced back at the woman. A redhead. Naked and bleeding and broken.

Swallowing, he lifted her into his arms and stumbled out of the cell.

"Cover us." He barked the order at D, then sprinted for the door.

Nothing and nobody encountered them when they stepped outside. No guards, no gunshots. Whatever happened in that jail just now, it had sent all of Blanco's men scurrying to the main house. And Holden had done his thing with the lights. The entire courtyard was bathed in darkness.

They rushed across the compound, Kane carrying the redhead, D covering them from behind. To his left, Kane caught sight of a guard sprawled in the dirt, neck twisted in an unnatural position. Dead. Morgan, as always, was efficient.

They stole across the grounds and headed for the hills at the edge of the compound. The barbed wire fence that surrounded Blanco's entire property boasted a jagged hole. Morgan and Holden waited there, swiftly bending down to help the new arrivals through.

"Go," Kane said to D, shifting the unconscious woman to his other shoulder.

D went first, then helped Kane pull the woman through. Finally, they were out.

They took off at a run, slicing through the trees and brush. Up ahead the brush widened into a large glade. The sound of a helicopter's rotors filled the night.

Kane tried hard not to look at the woman as he waited for the helicopter's descent, but he couldn't tear his gaze from her. Shit, she was in bad shape. Really bad shape. He shifted her to one arm, reaching out with the other to brush strands of red hair from her face.

Next to him, Morgan hissed. "Jesus, Abby," he muttered. "What did they do to you?"

Abby.

Kane stared at her, wondering who she was, what she meant to Morgan. There wasn't time to ask any questions though. The chopper set down, and seconds later they were all inside it, the woman still cradled in Kane's arms.

As their pilot, Sam, whisked them away from the compound, Kane was surprised to see moisture in his boss's eyes. Morgan's gaze was glued to the redhead, and the concern on his face was unmistakable.

"What did they do to you?" he murmured again.

Strong hands were clawing at his body, forcing him into the restraints. Devlin roared with fury as he felt the leather cuffs tighten around his wrists. "You bloody morons!" he screamed. "Let me go!"

"Stay still, Mr. Devlin," came a soothing Middle Eastern voice. "I need to examine the wound."

Frustration and rage seared up his spine and clamped around his throat. The doctor bent over him, his fingers prying, prodding, bringing a streak of pain that made the left side of Devlin's face throb with agony. Every muscle in his body shrieked in outrage. "Untie me," he roared as the doctor continued with his ungodly examination. "That bitch needs to pay for—"

"She's gone." A cold voice snapped from the doorway.

Devlin heard footsteps, and then Luis Blanco entered his line of vision. "Move away from him," Blanco barked at the doctor.

Zelig Hassan stepped aside, giving Blanco an unobstructed view of his patient. Blanco visibly cringed, but quickly recovered his composure. He observed the restraints shackling Devlin's wrists, then glanced at the doctor cowering in the corner of the room. "Are those necessary?"

Hassan nodded. "I've given him antibiotics intravenously to ward off infection. He has tried to escape twice already."

"Escape!" Devlin echoed in anger. "I'm not a prisoner." He glared at Blanco. "Release me. I have matters to take care of."

Blanco narrowed his eyes. "The woman did this to you?"

"Do you think I would have done this to myself?" Devlin tugged violently at the restraints. "Let me out so I can slit the bitch's throat."

"I'm afraid that won't be possible at the moment. Someone took the initiative to liberate her from the compound."

"How in bloody hell did that happen?" Devlin demanded.

Blanco's expression clouded over. "The fence was breached. Someone orchestrated a power outage and took advantage of your, uh, predicament to rescue the woman."

Devlin swallowed down a lump of fury. The pain dimmed, becoming a dull ache as he thought of Erica's innocent blue eyes and delicate red hair. Fucking bitch. He'd always prided himself on being extremely good at reading people. The woman's deception brought the vicious taste of bile to his mouth. He hadn't broken her. And now she was gone.

Devlin growled at Blanco. "Tell the bloody bastard to release me. Every second she's out there is one we can't afford to lose. We still don't know who she works for."

"You said you were confident she wasn't government."

"Confident, not certain. And if I'm wrong, your precious business venture is in jeopardy."

Blanco just laughed. "Government or not, the woman

can't hurt us. She learned nothing of value while she was here."

Cocky bastard. It still amazed Devlin how this half-brained idiot could have built such a nefarious empire. "Regardless, it's prudent that we find her," he snapped.

Blanco offered a humorless smile. "Don't fret. I already have people looking for her."

"Your people are imbeciles. I'll find the whore."

"When the doctor tells me it's safe to release you, I will." Blanco chortled. "You know, dear Devlin, it brings me a strange sense of pleasure, seeing you immobilized and chained to a bed."

Devlin's jaw tensed. He was about to remind Blanco of what he was capable of doing to him when he was no longer in restraints, but a hesitant knock came from the door. Devlin craned his head, squinted, and recognized Delgado, the guard who manned the security monitors. The young man's hands shook as he approached Blanco and held out a piece of paper. "The cameras caught one of the intruders. It's just a profile but—"

Blanco grabbed the photo and studied it. Then he dismissed Delgado and thrust the photo at Devlin. "Recognize him?"

There was a moment of silence, broken by Devlin's harsh chuckle. "Oh yes."

"A friend of yours?"

"Not quite." His lips tightened. "Tell your people to call off the search. They won't find the woman. These men don't leave a trail."

Blanco narrowed his eyes. "You know them?"

Devlin smirked. "Jim Morgan has her. The man in the security photo—that's Holden McCall, a colleague of Morgan's."

"Jim Morgan—the mercenary? You mean to tell me that Morgan's team of amateurs were the ones who breached my property?"

"Trust me, they're not amateurs."

Blanco seemed uncharacteristically flustered. With a frown, he turned to the doctor. "Release him. Mr. Devlin has a job to do."

Chapter 4

Kane stared at the unconscious redhead sprawled across the bed and cursed under his breath. Goddamn it. She was in bad shape. Her swollen face was various shades of purple, and the young doctor Morgan kept on the payroll had stitched up some of the deeper cuts along her stomach. A few ribs were bruised, her wrist was fractured, and the welts covering her entire body weren't pretty to look at.

But at least she was breathing.

A knock sounded on the bedroom door and D strode in. He let out a low whistle when he caught sight of their patient. "She looks dead," he remarked. "Devlin?"

Kane's jaw tightened. "Has to be, unless Blanco hired himself a new enforcer."

D shook his head. "Nah. Last I heard, Devlin was still employed by the son of a bitch."

His gaze drifted back to Abby. "Then this is Devlin's work. We both know how much he enjoys his whip."

"He also enjoys slitting throats. Why didn't he kill her?"

"No fucking clue."

"Has she woken up yet?"

"No." Kane paused. "Did Sam make arrangements with the airfield?"

"Everything's set. The jet's ready when we need it." D absently stroked the tattoo circling his wrist, a stream of tiny black text that Kane couldn't decipher. "The sooner we get this chick back to her assassin boss, the better."

Kane cocked his head. "Why's that?"

D shrugged, his gaze moving to the woman on the bed. "Got a bad feeling about this one, man. She's supposed to be a pro, right? So how the fuck did she wind up in Blanco's jail?"

"Even pros make mistakes."

D's black eyes narrowed. "Not this one, bro." He made for the door. "My advice? Don't let her out of your sight."

After D left the room, Kane gazed at the woman again. She was attractive. Well, probably. Once the swelling eased and the bruises faded he'd be able to make a better assessment. She didn't look dangerous though. Probably the jaw, too soft and delicate. But D was rarely wrong. The guy had a sixth sense about people.

He walked over and sat down at the edge of the bed. He didn't like this. What the hell had gone down in that prison tonight? The screams, the male body being lugged out. What had this woman gotten herself into?

A soft whimper.

Kane went on alert. He watched as the redhead stirred, her eyelids fluttering. With a sigh, he touched her cheek. Immediately, he withdrew his hand. Touching her felt . . . wrong. Or maybe it wasn't the contact itself, but the way he'd done it. Tenderly. Fuck. What was that about? He couldn't remember the last time he'd touched a woman with tenderness.

"Hey," he said gruffly. "Wake up."

No response.

He leaned closer.

The next thing he knew, he was caught in a headlock and a lethal little hand was gripping his neck. "Touch me again and I'll break your neck," came the hoarse mumble.

He was momentarily stunned. Christ, this woman was strong. But injured, which made it relatively easy to push out of her grasp.

Rubbing the back of his neck, Kane frowned. "Threaten me again and I'll break yours."

His warning fell on deaf ears. Whatever strength she'd managed to will up had promptly fizzled. She was unconscious again.

Shit. He didn't have the time to sit around and play nursemaid. Like D, he had a bad feeling about this woman. They'd all be better off after they deposited her in Noelle's hands and went back to the compound.

He swept his gaze over her face, noticing the rosy flush splotching her cheeks. Smothering a sigh, he gingerly placed his hand on her forehead, cursing again when he felt heat searing his palm. She was burning up. Not good. The doc had warned them about the dangers of infection, but they'd hoped the antibiotics they managed to shove down her throat would take effect. If anything, her temperature had only seemed to spike in the few minutes he sat by her side.

He dipped a washcloth into the bowl of cold water the doctor had left on the end table. Soaking the cloth, he moved it to the redhead's forehead and dragged it across her skin. She stirred restlessly. And then she spoke. Well, not so much spoke as mumbled. Soft, feverish words that had him leaning closer. He thought he made out the name *Blanco*. Then she muttered, "Save them."

His blood instantly went cold.

Save them.

Save who, for fuck's sake?

Kane tossed the cloth in the bowl and got to his feet. Screw this. He wasn't going to play nurse anymore.

With a frown, he marched out of the room. He found Morgan in the den, sitting in an armchair. D and Ethan were there too, the latter sprawled on the tattered leather couch, the former standing in front of the small window across the room. They'd used this safe house before, a spacious apartment in Usaquén, an upscale neighborhood in northern Bogotá. It was the perfect place to lie low, which Morgan's team frequently needed to do after a particularly hairy assignment. Not that this gig had been hairy. Too easy, more like it.

"Where's Holden and Luke?" Kane asked as he sank into the armchair across from Morgan's.

"Airstrip, hashing out details with Sam," Ethan replied.

Morgan's piercing blue eyes found Kane's. "How is she?"

"Unconscious. Woke up for a minute." He snorted. "She tried to snap my neck in two."

He could've sworn he saw the hint of a smile on his boss's face.

"Fuck," he burst out. "Who is she, Morgan? You've kept your trap shut about her since Noelle showed up at the compound. We went into this mission blind, but I'm not putting up with that shit anymore."

From the couch, Ethan shot Kane a surprised glance. Not many people had the balls to tongue-lash the mighty Jim Morgan. But hell, enough was enough. Kane had just spent the past three hours babysitting a woman he didn't fully trust. He hadn't slept in two days. He was tired, hungry, and pissed off. And he wanted answers.

"Who is she?" he repeated.

Morgan didn't even blink. "She's a killer."

"Yeah, way to state the obvious, boss. We know she works for Noelle, okay? Who is she to *you*?"

After a beat, Morgan released a heavy breath. "I knew her father."

"And . . ."

"And that's it. I knew her father."

"And?" Ethan chimed in.

Morgan swore under his breath. "Christ, it's like talking to children. That's all there is to it, kids. Jeremy Thomas was a good man. He saved my ass once, when I worked black ops for the Rangers."

Since it was rare to get any details about Morgan's past, Kane pressed on. "And the daughter? What's she to you?"

"I met her when I was twenty-seven. She was, shit, fifteen or something." Morgan shrugged. "Cute girl, but cold as ice. Had it tough before Jeremy adopted her. I saw her again a few times when I visited Jeremy, but after he died I lost touch with her. It's been three or four years since I last saw her."

"I don't trust her," D said, his tone flat.

"You don't trust anybody," Ethan shot back with a grin.

D smiled faintly. "Got that right." The smile promptly faded. "Something doesn't sit right. She's a fucking assassin. A trained killer. How'd she let herself get caught? And that boss of hers. I don't trust her either."

Morgan gave a sharp laugh. "And you shouldn't. Noelle doesn't inspire trust in many people."

Kane glanced at his boss thoughtfully. "Yet you agreed to help her."

Morgan shook his head. "Not her. Never her. This was a favor to an old friend."

The conversation halted as the young doctor they'd hired approached the open doorway. "She's regained consciousness," he said, his gaze hesitant as he looked around the room.

"How is she?" Morgan asked.

"For some reason she's still conscious despite the sedative. Oh, and she was beaten within an inch of her life."

Morgan ignored the remark. "What about the fever?"

"Still high." With a frown, the doctor added, "I found something on her body." Stepping into the room, he uncurled the fist he'd been making, revealing a small silver key. He handed it to D, who was closest to the door. "There was a Band-Aid on the sole of her right foot. This was beneath it."

"Thanks for everything you've done," Morgan said brusquely. "Now go home, Doc."

"I should really stay to monitor the fever—"

"No time. We're flying out tonight."

"I highly advise you don't move her for a couple of days."

"Noted." Morgan glanced pointedly at the door.

After a moment, the doctor walked through it.

"Ethan, escort the good doctor out," Morgan said.

As the two men left the room, D held up the key, studying it with a frown. "How much you wanna bet this opens the door to the cell we found her in?"

Kane experienced another jolt of confusion. Yeah, he'd take that bet. He voiced his perplexity aloud. "Why didn't she escape?"

"She's nuts?" D offered.

"Abby's not crazy," Morgan said quietly. "She's probably one of the sanest, toughest women I've ever met." He glanced at Kane. "Go check on her."

"Why the hell don't you do it?"

Morgan's lips tightened.

Kane sighed. "Fuck. Whatever."

He got to his feet and left the den, heading toward Abby's room. A pair of blue eyes pierced him when he walked into the room. Slightly glazed, but wary. "Where am I?" the woman on the bed demanded.

"Bogotá."

She slid up into a sitting position, then winced. She touched her ribs. "Shit," she murmured.

Kane watched as she ran her hands over her body, gauging her injuries. When her hand skimmed the bottom of her right foot, she frowned.

"We found the key," he said with a shrug. "Was it for the cell door?"

"You got me out of the compound?" she asked without answering his question.

He nodded.

"Why?" Suspicion flared in her eyes.

He couldn't help a soft laugh. "Because you needed rescuing. You know, other women would be grateful."

Her jaw tightened. "I'm not other women. And I didn't ask to be rescued."

Kane cocked one brow. "So you were enjoying the beatings?" *And rape,* he wanted to add, but the steel in her eyes told him not to go there.

"Who do you work for?" Suddenly she sighed. "Noelle sent you."

"Yes. But I don't work for her. I work for a mutual friend. He's in the other room actually. The name Jim Morgan ring a bell?"

To his surprise, those blue eyes softened. "Jim's here?"

"In the other room, like I said."

"I want to see him."

Annoyance prickled his skin at her insistent tone. What was Morgan's connection to this woman? Morgan said he had known her father—that's all there was to it, but Kane didn't like the way Abby's entire face relaxed when he'd said Morgan's name. Even more annoying was the fact that he was experiencing a spark of jealousy at the notion that Abby Sinclair and Morgan were somehow involved. He didn't even know this woman.

"He's busy right now," he said curtly. "He'll see you in a bit."

Abby watched as the handsome stranger crossed the room. Odd that she was even noticing his looks in her current condition. Hell, even if she was thinking clearly she probably wouldn't appreciate the view. Men didn't interest her. Not that she was into women. Neither sex appealed to her. She knew all too well what human beings, male or female, were capable of.

Her rescuer grabbed a pitcher of water from the table under the window and poured a glass. Turning back, he walked toward the bed. "Drink up. You're dehydrated." He held out the glass.

She stared at it.

"For God's sake, I didn't poison it."

And she was supposed to know that *because*? Opening your eyes and finding a man looming over you wasn't exactly supposed to inspire trust, was it? He might work for Morgan—or so he claimed—but until she laid eyes on Jim Morgan himself, she wasn't about to trust anyone.

But damn it, she was thirsty.

With a sigh, she raised the glass to her lips and downed the water in one long swig. Then she held the glass out to him. "More."

His lips twitched as if he was fighting back a laugh. "Yes, ma'am."

She studied him as he went to get more water. He was big. Six feet at least, but lean rather than bulky. Sandy-blond hair, somewhat unruly. Dark green eyes. And his face . . . jeez, he could easily pass for a movie star or model.

"I'm Kane," he said as he returned with another glass of water.

"Okay. Kane. Why did you rescue me from Blanco's prison?"

"Why were you in the prison to begin with?"

Say nothing. Always take care of yourself first, Abby.

She set the glass on the end table and discreetly studied the room. A bedroom, obviously. One window. No balcony. One exit—the door behind Kane. Getting out of here would be tricky.

"Forget it," he said as if reading her mind. "You're not going anywhere, not in your current condition."

His words proved prophetic when she tried to raise herself up into a standing position. Her head started spinning, causing her to sink back into the mattress. Damn.

Dehydrated, he'd said. It explained the wooziness. And her bruised ribs explained why breathing hurt so damn much.

At least she wasn't naked anymore. Someone—Kane?—had dressed her in a pair of loose sweatpants and a shirt that was three sizes too big. Her feet were bare but that would make it easier to scale the wall once she climbed out the window. Which she'd do, eventually. She needed to get out of here. As she'd told him, she hadn't asked to be rescued, and thanks to Kane's interference, she no longer had access to the girls she was determined to save.

She made another attempt at standing up, but the dizziness returned. She was starting to feel hot and the back of her neck was covered with sweat. She hated feeling this way. Trapped. Helpless. "Where is this place? Who lives here?" she demanded.

"It's a safe house. We've got 'em all over the world. Morgan insists on it."

"I might be comforted by that if I saw Morgan for myself." She frowned. "I'm not sure I believe you even work for him."

Morgan's voice came from the doorway. "He does. So quit being a pain in the ass and let him take care of you."

Abby's heart squeezed at the sight of Jim Morgan's familiar face. She hadn't seen him in at least four years, if not more, yet he looked exactly the same, save for a few new wrinkles around his mouth. He had to be in his late thirties by now, early forties perhaps, but his eyes were still shrewd, his dark hair still cropped in a no-nonsense military cut, and his body was charged with electricity as always. That always disturbed her, how wired he seemed, as if he could spring on you at any second, explode at the slightest provocation.

But Jeremy had trusted him, and she trusted Jeremy's judgment. Morgan might not be a close friend—she didn't have any of those—but he was, at the very least, an ally.

"I don't need to be taken care of," she grumbled, frowning at both men. "And I don't appreciate being pumped with sedatives. You know how I feel about drugs, Jim."

"Deal with it," he said, rolling his eyes. He moved toward the bed, his gaze sweeping over her bruised face. "How are you doing?"

"I'm peachy. You know a few cuts and bruises aren't going to keep me down for long."

He laughed. "No, I don't imagine they will. So . . . Noelle, huh? You didn't mention you worked for her the last time I saw you."

She gave a little shrug. "I know you don't like her. You would've just lectured me."

Kane watched the exchange with interest, his head swiveling back and forth to gauge her and Morgan's expressions.

"Yep, you'd have received a lecture. Like the one you're about to get now." He cocked his head. "Why were you in the prison, Abby? We both know you're too good at what you do to blow your cover."

She didn't answer. Force of habit. Both Jeremy and Noelle had drilled the importance of secrecy into her brain, and besides, she didn't want to involve Morgan in this potentially suicidal mission. She was the one who'd chosen to tangle with Blanco and Devlin, and she'd be the one to rescue those girls. She'd always worked best alone, and she might be a coldhearted bitch at times, but she refused to see anyone she cared about get killed because she'd decided—foolishly, probably—to undertake this crusade.

"Trust me, you don't want to know," she finally said, her voice soft. "I don't want you involved in this, Jim."

Morgan sighed. "I'm already involved." He paused, giving her another chance to open up. When she didn't, he frowned, then turned to Kane and said, "We're leaving in ten minutes. Get her ready."

Abby stared after Morgan in distress as he stalked out of the room. She shifted her gaze to Kane. "I'm not going anywhere," she insisted, panic rising up her spine.

"I don't think you have much choice in the matter," he answered wryly. He approached the bed, bent down and planted a hand on her waist. When she swatted it away he chuckled. "Don't worry. I'm not going to jump you."

"I don't want you touching me."

"Fine." He straightened his back. "Serves me right for trying to be a gentleman. Get up."

"What?"

"You obviously don't need my help to do it. So come on, on your feet. We're heading out."

"You say that as if I'm going somewhere."

"You are."

"I told you, I'm not going anywhere. I don't work for Morgan, so I don't have to follow his orders."

"Well, I do." He flashed a charming smile, which she suspected would make most women swoon. "So stop being so damn difficult and get up."

She stuck out her chin. "No."

He swore under his breath. "Come on, help me out here. I'd really hate to injure you any further by dragging you out of here by your hair."

She rubbed her swollen cheek, wondering if Kane would shoot her down if she tried to escape. Probably. Besides, getting out of this safe house would be a total bitch. Maybe she'd have better luck if she tried to bolt when they were on the move.

Yeah, probably a better plan. She'd play along with him. Get up. Follow him to wherever it was he was taking her. And grab any opportunity for escape before they reached their destination.

Drawing in a long breath, she swung her legs to the side of the bed and reached for the headboard again. She blinked, but the stars flashing in front of her eyes didn't dissipate.

No. Don't pass out. Stay alert, Abby.

Nausea scampered up her throat. She tried to take a step but her body protested wildly.

"Oh, for the love of God," Kane grumbled.

The last thing she saw before fainting into Kane's arms was his annoyed face.

Chapter 5

With a frown, Kane watched Luke carry Abby up the steps leading into the cabin of the small jet. He didn't particularly want to take her back to Tijuana with them, but she was in no condition to be left on her own. The fever had peaked when they'd left the safe house and she'd been in and out of consciousness since then. He'd shoved a couple more pills in her mouth and forced her to swallow, but it was too soon to tell if the antibiotics would do their job.

"All set," Morgan said as he entered the hangar. "When you get back to the compound, make sure she stays put, okay? Something's going on with her."

"You're not coming?"

Morgan shook his head. "Holden and I are sticking around here. I want to do some digging, figure out what the hell happened to land her in the prison. She's hiding something from us."

"No shit."

His boss sighed. "Look, I know you don't like this. I don't either. But you're the only one I trust to keep her in line."

"D would probably have better luck," Kane remarked dryly.

"D would badger her until she killed him, or vice versa." Morgan offered a cynical smile. "You've got more diplomacy."

"I don't like being a babysitter, Jim."

"And I don't like being kept in the dark. I can't have her running around until I know what the hell's going on. So keep an eye on her, and apply some pressure. See if you can get her to open up. I have a feeling she's got something up her sleeve."

"I'll do my best." Kane shrugged. "She's tough, though. I don't think she'll tell me anything she doesn't want us to know."

"Holden and I'll fly back in a day or two. Man the fort until I get back." With a nod, Morgan stalked off, heading to the Jeep parked at the edge of the dirt runway. Holden was behind the wheel, and he offered a brisk wave in Kane's direction before revving the engine.

The Jeep raised a cloud of dust as it sped off. Kane watched it for a moment, then sighed and turned back toward the hangar. When he stepped aboard the plane, he found Ethan kneeling next to Abby's seat, lifting a cup of water to her lips. Luke was next to her, looking slightly bored and impatient, while D sat on the other side of the small plane, scowling. Sam stood near the cockpit, silent as always.

"The fever hasn't gone down," Ethan said when he caught sight of Kane.

Ignoring the comment, Kane turned to Sam. "Get us in the air. Morgan and Holden aren't coming."

Sam nodded and headed for the cockpit, adding over his shoulder, "Buckle up. The runway hasn't been used in a while, so it could get bumpy." He disappeared into the cockpit, shutting the narrow door behind him. He'd worked as their pilot for four years now, and Kane appreciated his quiet efficiency and his ability to follow orders without question.

Moving into the cabin, Kane sank into the plush seat next to D. The plane's engine coming to life made the cabin shake, a high-pitched whine filling the air. The takeoff was indeed bumpy, but they were in the air a few minutes later and Kane was finally able to relax. It felt like a weight had been lifted off his chest. The three days they'd spent in this country had been a total irritation.

He glanced over at Abby. "How are your ribs?" he asked, unbuckling his seat belt once they'd reached the necessary altitude.

Her blue eyes looked glazed and weary as she answered, "They're fine. Don't hurt at all."

"You know, you're an amazing liar," he replied with a pleasant smile.

"Why isn't Morgan coming with us?" she asked, sounding uneasy.

"He had things to do."

An annoyed cloud floated across her face. "Checking up on me?"

"We're only trying to help you. There's no reason for you to be so antagonistic."

Next to Abby, Luke leaned forward, a lock of messy dark hair falling into his suddenly curious eyes. "What did you do to him?"

She spared Luke a glance. "What did I do to whom?"

"The dude in the prison. We all heard those screams. Sounded like someone getting their head ripped off."

"Close enough." She pushed a strand of red hair off

her forehead. In the dim lighting of the cabin the bruise on her left eye looked almost green. Her eyes closed and she continued speaking, her voice dull and emotionless, as if she were reciting a passage from a history textbook. "The man was William Devlin. He tried to rape me."

"Devlin?" Kane said in surprise. "*That* was who they carried out of the jail?"

She eyed him sharply. "You know him?"

"Yes." He eyed her right back. "And from what I know of the man, he prefers torture to rape."

"Is there a difference?" she asked mildly. Without letting him respond, she went on. "He tried to get the guards to do it first, but I took care of them. Then he stepped up to bat, climbed on top of me, rape definitely on his agenda."

Kane found himself oddly fascinated as he listened to her speak. "And what did you do, Abby?"

Her eyelids opened. Meeting his gaze, she set her jaw and said, "I ripped his eye out."

The four men just stared at her, this woman whose voice had suddenly become toxic, whose words shocked them into silence.

"You . . . ripped his eye out," Ethan finally sputtered, looking stunned.

"Right out of the socket." She turned her head and pressed her cheek against the leather seat.

Kane exchanged a look with D. Jesus Christ. Who was this woman? And damn, but he couldn't fight the rush of triumph knowing she'd stuck it to that sadistic bastard Devlin. It was something he'd wanted to do himself since the moment he'd met the son of a bitch. Morgan had actually been considering Devlin for the team, around the same time Kane came aboard. Devlin had gone on one of the early assignments, a test of sorts, and one he'd failed miserably. Kane could still remember the horror that swarmed his body when he'd watched Devlin slice off the head of a South African rebel with a machete. The bloodlust in Devlin's hollow eyes had been enough to convince Morgan that William Devlin had no part on their team.

Abby suddenly lifted her head and stared at him, bringing a flicker of discomfort to Kane's gut. From the moment he'd met her, her sharp, unwavering gaze had knocked him off balance. He had a thing for strong women, but Abby Sinclair . . . she was almost *too* strong, if that was possible. The woman was carved from a block of ice. She was cold, detached, so utterly composed that he was tempted to walk over and shake her a little, just to see if she'd flinch. Probably not. She was in full control of herself. Her words were carefully measured, her intelligent eyes in a constant state of alertness despite the sedatives administered by the doc. She didn't reveal a sliver of emotion.

She reminded him a lot of himself.

"Tell the pilot to land," she said, the pleading note in her voice coming as a total shock. "Please, Kane. I can't be here."

Next to him D stiffened. "You're in no position to give us orders," D barked. "So shut up, take a nap, and save the demands for your boss."

Abby's gaze landed on D. She looked extremely intrigued. "And you are?"

"Someone you don't want to mess with," he snapped, his black eyes burning.

"Derek Pratt." Ethan introduced his colleague hesitantly. "We call him D."

"D," she echoed. She pursed her lips. "You don't want me here, do you, D?"

He shot her a hard look. "Not really, no."

"And you didn't want to rescue me."

"Nope, can't say I did."

"Then get me off this plane," she said bluntly. "I didn't ask to be rescued either, and frankly, I have things to take care of, so for God's sake, just—"

"What things?" Kane demanded. "Tell us what you're up to and maybe we can help."

Help? The second the word exited his mouth he wanted to kick himself. The look of disgusted disbelief on D's face confirmed the error of his ways. What was he thinking, offering assistance? They'd been lucky to get in and out of Blanco's compound unharmed, though he knew now that it was thanks to Abby's violent assault on Blanco's second in command. If she hadn't thrown the entire compound into chaos, chances were they wouldn't have been able to manage such a smooth rescue.

But they *had* rescued her, and now it was time to wash their hands of it. Kane didn't mind a bit of danger, and most of the others took risks like they popped vitamins, but Luis Blanco wasn't a man you wanted to mess with. Blanco might not be on the same level as Devlin when it came to bloodlust, but the man was a power-hungry tyrant. Let his own government put him out of commission. As far as Kane was concerned, it wasn't his responsibility, or his problem.

"Forget it," Abby mumbled, closing her eyes again. "I'll figure something out."

Kane smothered a groan. Shit, getting answers out of this woman was like extracting teeth. They needed those answers, damn it. Morgan and Holden had stayed behind, risking their necks in order to figure out why Abby Sinclair had wound up in that prison, and Kane wasn't about to lose anyone he cared about because this woman liked to keep secrets.

A sprawling ranch house greeted them as the Jeep slowed at the end of the long dirt road. Acres of open land surrounded the area, as well as an ominous electric fence and a tall stone wall more suited for a medieval fortress than a ranch in Mexico. Or at least she thought it was Mexico. She'd heard one of Morgan's men mention the location after they'd landed on the dusty airstrip a dozen miles back, but she could've imagined it. The fever had ebbed but her brain still felt foggy. She just hoped she hadn't said something she shouldn't have when she'd been delirious.

Her entire body hurt. She didn't know what was worse—the constant irritation from her clothes rubbing against the welts on her body, or the fact that she was too damn weak to go off on her own. Each time the Jeep hit a pothole her head spun like a merry-go-round. Each time she moved an inch her ribs throbbed relentlessly. If she tried to run, she wouldn't make it three feet without passing out. That knowledge was the only thing that reined her in. She couldn't flee in her condition. Too weak. Too wounded.

You're strong. A day or two and you'll be back in Bogotá.

Jeremy's voice again. In her head. As always. She couldn't remember the last time she'd had a coherent thought that didn't manifest itself as Jeremy's voice.

The Jeep came to a stop in front of the large electric gate. From the driver's seat D stuck his arm out, punched a sequence of numbers into a keypad panel, and the gate swung open. She stared at his impressive biceps, studying the tattoo that covered his entire arm. Looked to be Japanese style, with a lethal samurai on his upper arm, fighting a snake coiled around the forearm. The background was filled in with black and gray wind bars and waves, giving the entire scene a turbulent feel.

Derek Pratt aka D wasn't happy with her presence—he'd made it clear on the plane that he wanted to be rid of her. There was something dark and dangerous rippling under his surface. He had a troubled past, as dark as hers, she suspected. In fact, out of all the men, she felt the biggest kinship toward D, despite his obvious hatred.

She could read the other two pretty well too. The young one, Ethan, seemed almost out of place on Morgan's team. He was handsome in a preppy sort of way, and way too polite for his own good. He'd told her on the jet that he'd served in the Marine Corps for four years before being recruited by Morgan. She couldn't picture the kid ever being in battle, but evidently Morgan saw a killer instinct in the guy, otherwise he wouldn't have taken him on.

Luke was the opposite of Ethan. Sexy as sin, most women would say. He'd been tapping his foot during the entire flight, as if he couldn't wait to go off and do something exciting. A bundle of energy, and though he'd barely said two words to her, she'd caught him checking her out several times. She suspected he was the ladies' man of the group.

And then there was Kane. The only one she hadn't gotten a handle on. He was obviously in charge in Morgan's absence, and seemed completely comfortable in the role of leader. Easygoing on the surface, but with a deadly air to him. Like D, there was anger in him, but he hid it with sarcastic remarks and dry grins, unlike D, who simply looked like he wanted to strangle someone all the time.

"This is Morgan's place?" Abby asked as D drove through the gate and parked the vehicle a few yards from the main house. The house was enormous but nondescript. Stucco and brick with a large flight of stairs leading to a pillared entrance.

"Yep," Ethan confirmed.

"Another safe house?"

Kane spared her a glance as he hopped out of the Jeep. "Actually, we live here."

Her mouth twisted in a sardonic smile. "Do you boys have slumber parties every night?"

"Funny. Morgan didn't tell us you were a comedian." Without a backward look, he strode toward the house, his faded jeans and navy blue T-shirt clinging to his lean frame. D marched after him, shaved head gleaming in the afternoon sun.

"Don't mind him," Ethan said. "Cute and cuddly isn't in Kane's nature."

"No, I don't suppose it is." She decided to take advantage of Kane's being out of sight and said, "How long have you worked for Morgan?"

"About two years." He smiled endearingly. "I'm the rookie." He swiftly changed the subject. "Can you walk?"

She took a tentative step forward and swallowed when her body ached in protest. "Probably not."

Infinitely gentle, he wrapped one muscular arm around her shoulder and helped her across the dusty earth toward the house, while Luke stayed behind to unload the Jeep. Ethan half carried her up the front steps, and she winced as her shirt brushed against the welts on her back. Her head was starting to clear, though. She didn't feel as light-headed as before, and that showed improvement. Now all she needed was for her ribs to stop feeling as if they'd been scraped raw. A few days of rest would help speed the healing process along, and then she could make plans to get back to Colombia to finish her mission. How long had she been in the safe house? One day, she figured. Which meant she had eleven days until the auction. Eleven days to find a way out of here, return to Colombia, and rescue those girls.

"Is Noelle here?" she asked, glancing around the front hall. She was surprised by the elegance of the space. Gorgeous landscapes covered the off-white walls, bringing an air of peace and charm, and a skylight above allowed sunshine to stream into the house.

"She went into town," came Kane's voice. "She left word with Lloyd that she'll be back in a few hours."

"Lloyd?" Abby echoed.

"Our housekeeper."

She raised one brow. "Your housekeeper is male?"

"Yep. He's a great guy," Ethan said. "You'll like him."

He was about to say more when a blur of brown and black burst into the hall and Abby found herself staring at a huge German shepherd with oddly floppy ears. Her gaze connected with the liquid brown eyes of the dog, who snarled when he saw her.

"And this is Bear," Kane said with a grin. "Don't be offended. He doesn't usually like strang—"

A loud whine interrupted. The dog was suddenly at Abby's side, rubbing his nose against her leg. Bear stared up at her, unblinking, then shifted his head toward Kane and Ethan and let out a deep growl.

Both men raised their eyebrows. "Why is he growling at us?" Ethan asked in a wary voice.

Kane let out a sigh. "He's protecting her."

I can protect myself, she almost grumbled at the dog.

Shaking his head, Kane turned to Ethan. "Take the mutt and go help Luke unload the gear. I'll show Abby to her room."

With a faint good-bye, Ethan slid out the front door, leaving her and Kane alone in the massive hall.

"Cute dog," she remarked wryly.

Kane looked a tad bewildered. "Uh, not usually." He shrugged and reached for her. "Come on—let's go upstairs."

She moved away before he could take her arm. For some reason, she didn't want him to touch her. When Ethan helped her inside, his touch had felt brotherly. The younger man wasn't attracted to her. Neither was D, or even Luke, despite his subtle flirting, which was why she felt reluctantly at ease with them. But Kane . . . He hadn't flirted with her, hadn't sent any suggestive looks in her direction, yet she sensed the sexual awareness simmering beneath the surface. He noticed her as a woman, and that was something that always made her distinctly uncomfortable.

"I can manage," she said coolly, walking toward the stairs on her left. Her ribs throbbed, but she breathed through the pain and forced her legs to carry her up the steps.

Kane trailed after her, and she could feel his dark green eyes boring into her back. On the second-floor landing, he took the lead, ushering her into a bedroom that was surprisingly cozy. Pale yellow curtains hung at a large window that overlooked the grounds. A tall cedar bookshelf rested against one wall, crammed with novels, from Dostoevsky to Stephen King, and the lovely stone fireplace with the leather armchair next to it offered a quiet niche to lose yourself in. The massive bed with its four posts and filmy canopy reminded her of something out of a Victorian-era painting.

"I see you're admiring the bed." Kane's voice came out slow and silky. "Most women seem to like it."

She whirled around in time to see a sensual glint fill his green eyes, and she immediately stiffened, confused by the fire that spread through her body. What the hell was that? Desire? She banished the thought. No, she didn't feel things like desire or sexual awareness. It was probably indignation, over the fact that he was flirting with her.

"I want to see Noelle," she said firmly.

"I told you, she's not back yet. So why don't you take a nap and I'll wake you when she gets here." He raked a hand through his blond hair. "It was a long flight. Get some rest."

She squared her shoulders. "I don't want to rest."

"Fine," he muttered. "Then how about a cup of tea? Lloyd's really into tea. He has these different kinds that are supposed to treat all types of ailments." He cocked his head. "Maybe he's got one with truth serum."

Her lips tightened. "I'll have coffee."

"Of course." He rolled his eyes. "Well, then, we're going back downstairs apparently."

He kept his hands to himself as they headed down the staircase. The kitchen was off the main hallway, an enormous room with granite counters and stainless-steel appliances. When they walked in, a giant of a man was pouring steaming coffee into two large mugs, as if he'd anticipated the request Kane hadn't even posed yet. The man had a head of curly red hair, a beard that seemed to devour his entire face, and a bulky frame that made him look like a linebacker.

"You must be Abby," the giant said with a cheerful smile. "I'm Lloyd."

"Nice to meet you." She was slightly taken aback by his gentle voice. It seemed out of place coming from such an intimidating, massive man.

"May I ask what happened to your face?" Lloyd inquired in a polite tone.

She met his eyes. "I walked into a door."

"Of course," he said with a nod. He glanced at Kane. "Sit out on the patio. It's a gorgeous day. Blue sky, yellow sun, singing birds—my three favorite things."

"Well, God forbid we miss out on such splendor," Kane said mockingly.

Lloyd shot him a disapproving look before turning to Abby. "Kane doesn't appreciate the simple things in life." He placed the coffee mugs on a steel tray. "He's also too sarcastic for his own good. Don't blame him for that, though. It's his nature."

Abby followed Lloyd through the sliding glass door that led out to a large stone terrace. She sank into one of the high-backed wicker chairs surrounding the white table, breathing in the fresh, balmy air. "You're right," she said to Lloyd as he handed her the coffee mug. "It's gorgeous out."

"At least one of you appreciates it," Lloyd responded. He set Kane's mug on the table and headed back to the kitchen.

"Where'd Morgan find that guy?" she asked, watching

as Lloyd ducked to avoid hitting his head on the doorframe. "The Dallas Cowboys?"

"Nothing so glamorous. He was working as a Mob enforcer in Boston when he and Morgan crossed paths." Kane lifted his cup to his lips and took a long sip. She couldn't help but be drawn to his mouth. It was far too sensual. Wide, with a bottom lip slightly fuller than the top one. His mouth was his only soft feature. Everything else about him was hard, rugged, piercing.

"Checking me out?" he quipped, eyeing her over the rim of the mug.

"Trying to figure you out," she corrected. "How'd you meet Jim?"

"He approached me after I left the SEALs. I've been working for him for eight years now."

"You were a SEAL?"

He nodded. "So was Luke, but he was with the East Coast teams. I was with the West. What about you? How did you end up working for Noelle?"

Abby sipped her coffee, letting the hot liquid slide down her throat. "She found me when I was doing contract work for the CIA. She made me a better offer and I took it."

Kane looked intrigued. "Did she train you, or was that Jeremy Thomas?"

Her throat clogged at the sound of Jeremy's name. She stayed quiet. She didn't like talking about Jeremy. He'd died seven years ago, yet the loss was still fresh, a painful vise that squeezed her heart.

"Tell me," Kane asked curiously, "why did an Army Ranger decide to adopt a fifteen-year-old foster kid?"

"You'd have to ask Jeremy that," she answered in a cool voice.

"I'd like to, but apparently he's dead," Kane said bluntly. "Want to fill in the blanks?"

"No."

"I thought so."

"On the plane you told me you knew Devlin," she said suddenly. "I want to know about him."

Kane narrowed his eyes. "Why? Are you planning on launching a second attack on him?"

"No, but I'm pretty sure he's going to try to come after me."

"Because you tore his eye out."

"Yeah, and because he couldn't break me. He seems like the type of man who doesn't handle failure very well."

Kane laughed. "You've got that right."

"I found only the bare details when I researched him before going undercover. I need to know more. What am I up against?"

"Take your definition of *sick bastard* and multiply it by ten thousand. That's Devlin."

She sighed. "That bad?"

"Oh yes."

"I know he was born in Liverpool, raised by his father. His mother was South African and died in childbirth. That's all I managed to find out." She took another sip of coffee. "Do you know more about his background?"

"More than I want to know," Kane said, letting out a breath. "He left England and moved to South Africa when he turned eighteen, wanted to learn more about where his mother came from. Turned out she came from a shady family that had been smuggling diamonds into Liberia for years. Devlin dabbled in smuggling for a while but decided the family business bored him. He found being a soldier for hire far more exciting."

"And you know all this how?"

"Morgan was considering hiring him. He came on an extraction gig with us, about eight years ago, but he had a violent streak none of us liked. So Morgan cut him loose. Devlin went to work for Blanco a couple years later."

"His dream job," she said, sarcastic. "He gets to beat and torture people all day long."

"Not many people survive his *interrogations*." His green eyes searched her face. "Why didn't he kill you, Abby?"

She shrugged. "Blanco had other plans in mind for me."

"I take it you're not going to share those plans with me."

"I can't." She curled her fingers over the handle of the mug, a wave of desperation rising in her chest. Damn it, she shouldn't be here. She needed to get back to Bogotá, needed to plan an attack. She'd been in perfect position before Kane and the men decided to rescue her, and now she'd be forced to start from scratch, figure out a new way to rescue those girls before Blanco sold them off like cattle.

Damn it.

"We can help," Kane said roughly. "Whatever you've gotten yourself into, you don't need to do it alone."

She met his gaze, startled by the intensity in his eyes, the sincerity of his voice. For a moment she was tempted to spill everything. Tell him about the girls she so desperately wanted to rescue. Tell him *why* it was so important to her. But in her entire twenty-eight years, she'd opened up to only two people. One was dead. The other didn't know the meaning of judgment.

Would Kane judge her if she told him about her past, the things she'd done to stay alive?

Maybe. Maybe not.

Either way, she couldn't trust him. He was a stranger to her. And a good-looking stranger to boot. Those movie star looks alone were reason not to trust him.

Lifting her mug, she took another long sip, then said, "Alone is the only way I know how to do things."

"I assure you, the festivities will go on as planned," Blanco was saying as Devlin marched outside.

Holding the phone with one hand, Blanco raised his other one when he noticed Devlin. An order for silence. Tightening his lips, Devlin drifted across the terrace to the iron railing overlooking the yard. He stared down at the lavish kidney-shaped swimming pool below, surrounded by healthy green foliage and colorful exotic flowers. Trying to control his impatience, he listened to Blanco's half of the conversation, battling the impulse to grab the bloody phone and whip it into the pool.

"There won't be a raid, Juan," Blanco told the caller in a reassuring tone. "The assault you're referring to has been highly overexaggerated. The men involved weren't government. I have everything taken care of." He paused. "I know you've invested a large amount of money in this invitation. Everything is under control . . . Yes, I know . . . My solicitor will be in touch with details by the end of the week."

Blanco was fuming as he hung up the phone.

"Will Juan Cortez be a problem?" Devlin asked with a pleasant smile.

"Damn that woman," Blanco said without responding to the question. "I ordered the guards not to speak of last night's activities, but word seems to have gotten out. The bidders are growing uneasy."

"You could always cancel the auction," Devlin said in a bored voice.

"Cancel it?" Blanco sounded outraged. "I will do no such thing. This is going to be something extraordinary, the festivities we've planned. Dear Devlin, we are offering a service no one else in the world would even dare advertise!"

Devlin didn't give a bloody rat's ass about Blanco's auction. As far as he was concerned, they had more pressing matters to deal with. He reached up to rub his eye, grimacing when he encountered the coarse material of the ridiculous eye patch one of the guards had brought back from the market. As his impatience spilled over, he twisted his mouth in a lethal scowl. "Why isn't the jet ready?" he snapped. "I told you I wanted to head out this morning."

Blanco's features hardened. "Don't speak to me that way. And to answer your question, the pilot reported engine trouble. It should be taken care of in a few hours."

"I don't have a few hours. I want to slit the woman's throat, Luis."

"And how will you do that?" Blanco said coldly. "You haven't even uncovered her true identity yet."

"No, but now that we know Morgan was involved, it shouldn't be hard to find her." He paused. "And I think you should consider my suggestion—postpone your main event, Luis. If Erica was working for the government—"

"Then agents would have attempted a raid days ago," Blanco said with a careless wave of his hand. "She must have been after me, and not the merchandise."

Devlin was about to argue, but then thought better of

it. Let Blanco have his misguided sense of invincibility. Devlin would recapture the woman before she could do any damage anyway.

"I shall take my leave, then," Devlin said, stalking toward the French doors leading into the house.

Blanco's voice stopped him. "And may I ask what you plan on doing to the woman when you find her?"

He turned and gave a humorless smile. "What I do best, of course."

Chapter 6

"What the hell were you thinking?" Noelle demanded, her beautiful face glittering with anger and disapproval.

Abby stood her ground. The fact that she was several inches taller than Noelle should've helped her cause, but Noelle had always seemed much larger than her five feet three inches. Especially when she was furious.

"I know. I fucked up." Abby sighed. "I had the chance to kill him but I chose not to, okay?"

"I don't care that you didn't kill him—I care that you nearly got *yourself* killed!" Noelle's blue eyes flashed, but the hand she laid on Abby's arm was oddly gentle.

When Noelle had stormed onto the terrace a few minutes ago, she'd looked ready to throttle someone. She'd coldly dismissed Kane, banishing him to the kitchen, yet Abby could feel his eyes watching them. Noelle had spun around, moved closer as if she wanted to embrace Abby, then stepped back and started tearing into her. Abby didn't blame her. The people who'd hired them had spent a great deal of money to ensure that Blanco would meet his demise, and she knew Noelle would need to do some serious ass-kissing to smooth out the situation.

That Noelle claimed not to care that Abby had failed in her mission came as a shock. They'd known each other for more than seven years, and this was the first time Noelle had come close to showing genuine concern for Abby's well-being. Abby knew she cared, but Noelle didn't wear her emotions on her sleeve. Never had.

"I was fine," Abby said defensively, leaning one elbow on the railing that ran around the stone terrace. "Blanco didn't want me dead."

"You don't look fine," Noelle snapped. "Your face is every color of the rainbow, and I can see you're having trouble breathing—don't bother denying it."

"Okay, I'm a little beat-up, but I'm alive, and I would've stayed alive."

Noelle leaned her lithe frame against the rail, her blond hair falling down her shoulders. "Why?" she asked sharply.

"Why what?"

"You blew your cover. I want to know why."

Abby let out a breath, wincing. Noelle was right—it hurt to breathe. Damn rib injuries. A bullet or knife wound she could handle, but taking a hit to the ribs was always a bitch. "About two weeks ago, Inez Alvaro, Blanco's housekeeper, stormed into the dining room screaming like a banshee, accusing Blanco of kidnapping her daughter."

Noelle frowned. "All right."

"Inez's husband, Rubio, is one of Blanco's drug runners. They live in a village a few miles from the compound. I went there a few times with one of the servants." Abby swallowed. "I met Lucia. She's a beautiful girl, thirteen years old and unbelievably smart. She wanted to learn English, so I offered to help and I swear, she picked up the language so fast—"

"I see where this is going," Noelle said with a groan. "Damn it, Abby. What is it with your need to play mommy to every fucking girl you meet?"

"He's *selling* her."

Noelle blinked. "What?"

"After Inez's outburst, I spoke to Luis and he actually gloated about it, saying he took Lucia because he found out Rubio was stealing from him, skimming from the drug profits. The daughter's suffering was the father's punishment." Her chest ached again, and this time it had nothing to do with her sore ribs. "At that point he trusted me, and he told me he had a surprise, something he thought I would enjoy. He took me to the prison, to a trapdoor that led to the tunnel system under the compound. There's a bunker down there."

"Where he's holding Lucia," Noelle finished.

Abby shook her head viciously. "Not just her. There were others. About a dozen of them, Noelle. Between eleven and sixteen years old." Bile clogged her throat. "He told me to pick one out. So we could play with her together."

"Oh fuck."

"Oh fuck is right. Blanco is impotent, but he gets off on power, and he wanted to see me screw one of the girls." She fought for breath. "I made a big thing about how I'm not into women, how they disgust me. So he locked up the bunker and took me back to the main house. Made me screw one of his guards instead."

She felt dirty just saying the words out loud, but it had to be done. Noelle needed the details—*all* the details—

before she agreed to get involved. And at this point Abby needed her boss on board.

"I did some snooping and managed to fill in the blanks," she continued. "Blanco's holding an auction. Apparently he's done it before, sold off young girls to interested bidders. They pay a price to attend, and the girls are paraded in front of them like pieces of meat."

"And you couldn't leave it alone, could you?" Noelle mumbled.

Abby stiffened. "No, I couldn't. I found out that the only way down to the bunker is through the prison, but I couldn't get Blanco to take me back there again. He had guards on me at all times. So I decided to get caught."

"God, Abby, that's the most insane thing I've ever heard. How could you be certain he wouldn't kill you outright?"

"I dropped enough hints to convince him I might be government and that I'd been checking in with my supervisor." She shrugged. "He wanted Devlin to interrogate me."

"And then?" Noelle asked darkly. "What did he plan for you?"

"He was going to put me up for auction." Abby gave a humorless smile. "He figured some of the prospective buyers might want a female with a bit more maturity." She paused. "I know you were worried about me and that's why you sent Morgan and his team, but damn it, I wish you'd given me more time."

"So Blanco and Devlin could slit your throat?"

"So I could rescue those girls." Desperation crept into her voice. "I have to go back, Noelle. Please, you need to help me find a way back."

A short silence fell between them. Abby could see

Noelle's shrewd brain working, going over all the information that had just been fed into it.

Abby waited patiently. Her boss didn't like to be rushed.

The nape of her neck suddenly tingled, and she slowly turned her head to find Kane standing by the glass door separating the kitchen from the terrace. His green eyes were stoic, his handsome jaw set in an uneasy line as he watched her.

Again, that burst of heat ignited in her belly. She couldn't seem to stop noticing how gorgeous he was. He was a big man, with a lean, muscular body that hadn't been sculpted in a gym. He radiated strength, and it wasn't hard to picture him soundlessly creeping through a jungle or hanging off a helicopter.

Why was her body responding to him? She had no problem using sex to achieve her goals, but she derived no pleasure from it. Sex was just another form of violence. And she already had enough of that in her life.

"I think this is a suicide mission," Noelle said frankly, jerking Abby out of her thoughts. "And I'm not a crusader, honey—you know that. Those girls . . . Fate has given them a bad deal."

"They're being sold as sex slaves," Abby said through clenched teeth.

"Luck of the draw. You can't save everyone, hon."

Somehow Noelle's callous attitude didn't surprise her. It did, however, annoy the shit out of her. Fine, so maybe those girls had been dealt a crappy hand, but if someone had the opportunity to save them, shouldn't they try to alter fate?

"What if Jeremy had decided not to save *me*?" she said softly.

"Then you would have saved yourself. You're a warrior, Abby."

"But Lucia and the other girls aren't like me. They're fragile and innocent and I can't let this happen to them." She curled her fingers over the edge of the railing, her body tight with desperation. "Please, help me save them. I know there's still some shred of humanity left in you, Noelle. You act tough, saunter around like a coldhearted bitch, but I know you remember what it's like to be helpless."

Noelle's shoulders tensed.

"You remember how it feels to be at the mercy of someone more powerful than you," Abby went on, her voice quiet. "So for fuck's sake, help me."

"She's pretty."

Kane turned his head as Lloyd came up beside him. Lloyd's gaze was focused on the two women on the terrace, though Kane wasn't sure which one the compliment had been directed at. Probably Noelle, who once again wore all black, with her golden hair streaming down her back. Abby was in the sweatpants and T-shirt Kane had dressed her in back in Bogotá. He'd thought about sending Ethan into town to buy her some clothes, but Noelle had beat him to it. She'd dropped three shopping bags jammed with clothing on the kitchen floor before marching out to the terrace to give Abby a piece of her mind.

The two women hadn't even embraced, he'd noticed with perplexity. Noelle had simply ordered Kane to leave, then unleashed what looked like a vicious reprimand on Abby. What kind of relationship did they have? Boss-employee? Nah—they looked a lot closer than that. Mother-daughter, maybe, though Noelle couldn't have been much older than Abby. But there was a definite bond between them—anyone could see that. Even now, with their eyes blazing at each other and the muffled angry voices he could make out from behind the glass, it was evident the two women respected—even cared about—each other.

"Abby," Lloyd clarified when Kane didn't answer. "She's very pretty."

Kane shifted his eyes. "Ex–Mafia thugs aren't supposed to use words like *pretty*, Lloyd."

The giant of a man gave a clumsy shrug. "Would you prefer I said *smokin' hot*?"

He laughed. "Don't let that red hair and sweet face fool you. The woman is a tiger."

"Probably awesome in bed, though," came Luke's drawl.

Luke entered the kitchen wearing a pair of faded jeans and a New Orleans Saints jersey with the sleeves cut off. Bear was scampering on Luke's heels, making a beeline for the door. The dog pressed his nose against the glass and began to whine, his gaze focused on Abby in such concentration that Kane shook his head in bewilderment. He'd never seen the mutt take such an immediate liking to a person.

Luke noticed it too, and frowned. "I think I need to teach him the word *assassin*," he remarked wryly. "Though he does have impeccable taste. Don't you, Bear?" Luke's dark eyes twinkled with pleasure as he zeroed in on the two women. "Who do you think is hotter?"

Kane rolled his eyes. "Are you serious?"

"I say the redhead," Luke announced as he went to the fridge to grab a beer. "Even with that black eye she's totally hot. And, like I said, probably crazy good in the sack."

Kane's eyes narrowed. "Don't be vulgar."

Luke hooted. "Oh, come on. We all know you were thinking the same thing."

Fine, so maybe he kind of was. It bugged him, this inexplicable attraction he was feeling toward Abby Sinclair. She wasn't even his type, damn it. Luke might be willing to screw anything in a skirt, but Kane was very specific about the women he chose to spend time with: bold, laid-back, and flirty—chicks he could have fun with, then walk away from without dealing with any clingy, please-love-me shit. Abby might be bold, in a scary, dangerous sort of way, but she sure as hell wasn't laid-back. She was wound tighter than a drum, and he had a feeling she could kill him without blinking an eye.

Oddly, that was kind of a turn-on.

"I want to meet the rest of them," Luke said as he twisted the cap off his beer bottle.

"The rest of who?"

"Noelle's chameleons. Think they all look like Abby?"

Kane sighed. "You have a one-track mind, Lucas. Do you ever *not* think about sex?"

The other man grinned. "Nope. And I don't just think about it—I *have* it too. Lots of it. Which is more than I can say for you." Luke slanted his head. "When was the last time *you* got laid?"

"What can I say? I'm pickier than you are," Kane said with a shrug. "I don't have sex just for the sake of having sex."

"Aw, isn't that sweet. You like *intimacy*."

Intimacy? Uh, no. The last thing he enjoyed doing was opening himself up to the women in his bed. He got off, and got out of there. Maybe he didn't share Luke's jubilant, anyone'll-do mentality, but he was on Luke's side when it came to commitment. Definitely overrated, in his opinion.

He opened his mouth, ready with a comeback, when his ass started vibrating. Reaching into his back pocket, he fished out his cell phone and glanced at the caller ID screen. Unknown number. Wrinkling his forehead, he flipped the phone open and said, "Yeah?"

A faint British accent greeted his ears. "Why, hello there, Kane. Did I catch you at a bad time?"

Every muscle in his body coiled tight. "Devlin," he said in a lethal voice.

Beside him, Luke's grin faded, his face hardening with menace.

"How did you get this number?" Kane asked.

Devlin chuckled. "Aren't you going to say hello to an old friend? No 'how are you'? No 'how's life been treating you'?"

"We're not friends."

"We were once."

Kane ignored the reminder. His fingers tightened over the phone. "What do you want, Devlin?" he demanded.

"I'd like to negotiate. You have something I want."

Kane's gaze drifted back to Abby. She and Noelle were still deep in conversation.

"She's with you right now, isn't she?" Devlin's voice rang with delight.

"I don't know what you're talking about."

The delight faded into annoyance. "Let's not play games. Give me what I want and I'll return the favor."

Kane laughed harshly. "I don't want any favors from

you, Devlin. You don't have anything I could ever want. And I'm not negotiating with you."

"I *want* her." Devlin's tone took on a petulant note. "So make this easy for both of us, and give her to me. Don't make me come after you, Kane."

"Go ahead and try," he taunted. "I'll be waiting."

He jammed his finger on the button to disconnect the call, but the anger streaming through his bloodstream refused to cease. He glanced over at Abby again. She looked small and delicate in that oversize T-shirt. As small and delicate as she'd looked when he'd carried her out of the prison cell, when he'd run a cold cloth along her forehead.

She'd been right. Devlin would come after her.

Fuck.

"What did he want?" Luke asked in a low voice. He set his beer bottle on the counter, all business now.

Kane jerked a thumb in Abby's direction. "Her."

Luke frowned. "Revenge."

"Yep."

"I told Morgan we should've killed the guy. He's a fucking sociopath."

"Yeah, well, hindsight."

"Should we let Morgan know?"

"Might as well wait till he gets back. Devlin might have gotten his hands on my cell number, but it'll take him a while to find the compound." That was a relief at least. The paperwork on this place was buried so deep it could take Devlin weeks, months even, to track it back to Morgan, so Kane wasn't worried about that. No, what worried him was Devlin's interest in Abby.

"Okay, then. I'll leave you to your babysitting duties," Luke said, the grin returning to his face. "Ethan and I are heading into town for a night of drinking and screwing. Well, I'll be screwing. Ethan will probably sit in the corner making googly eyes at that waitress he likes."

"Don't have too much fun," Kane said dryly.

As Luke and his mutt left the kitchen, Kane noticed that the heated discussion between Abby and her boss had wound down. Noelle was now heading toward the sliding door, her beautiful face expressionless.

"Everything all right?" Kane asked when she strode through the door.

"Nothing I can't handle," she said vaguely. She glanced outside to where Abby still stood, then back at Kane. "I've got a plane waiting for me at the airstrip. Make sure Abby stays put until I contact you."

He faltered. "Wait—you're not taking her with you?"

"Not yet. I have some things to take care of, and I want her somewhere secure. Don't let her leave, no matter what she says."

He cursed under his breath.

"What was that?" she said sharply.

"Nothing. Don't worry about it. I'll keep an eye on her."

"Good." Without uttering a good-bye, Noelle strolled out of the kitchen.

When she was gone, Kane swore again, this time a stream of obscenities that had Lloyd, who was wiping down the counters, raising his eyebrows in surprise.

"I take it you're not happy with this latest development," Lloyd remarked.

Kane didn't bother answering. Looked like he was going to be babysitting for a while longer. Shit. Abby Sinclair was an enigma wrapped in a fucking riddle, and he got the feeling she'd do anything in her power to protect whatever secrets she was keeping.

It should've pissed him off that Noelle hadn't whisked Abby away as he'd thought she would, yet for some fucked-up reason, a burst of pleasure went off in his chest at the thought of Abby sticking around.

Pleasure, and something that totally resembled anticipation.

Shit.

The mattress sagged as he slipped into bed with her, sliding under the thin cotton sheet and reaching for the hem of her nightgown. Her eyes flew open. She hadn't been asleep. No, she'd been waiting for this moment. Waiting for four nights now. Last time, he'd broken her nose.

Tonight she was ready for him.

"Don't fight it," he whispered in the darkness, one big hand latching onto her thigh. "Remember what happened the last time you fought?"

Oh, she remembered.

He'd hurt her so badly she hadn't been able to walk for days.

Tonight he'd be the one hurting.

"You're surprisingly docile," he murmured.

He mounted her.

She waited.

He was untying the drawstring at his waist.

Move your hand under the pillow.

That's it. Feel the knife? Good. Pull it out. Put it inside him.

"You fucking bitch!" he shrieked as the blade sliced into his fat stomach.

Hot liquid dripping onto her nightshirt. Blood.

"I'm going to kill you, you little bitch. You hear that, I'm going to fucking kill you."

And then his fists were pounding her face.
No.
This was wrong. He wasn't supposed to win this time.
You didn't stick the knife in deep enough.
Pain flashed in front of her eyes. She screamed, loud enough to wake the entire neighborhood. His hand clapped over her mouth, efficiently shutting her up. She flailed and writhed under his relentless fists, choking on the smell of blood in the air. His blood. Hers.

Her pulse buzzed in her ears. Walls closing in around her.
It hurt. Everything hurt—
Then it didn't.
He was off her. Where had he gone?
She suddenly saw the shadow at the foot of the bed. The gleaming silver chain around a thick, corded neck.
"No," she murmured, spitting blood from her mouth. "No, please . . ."
The shadow cast over her, bending down, reaching for her.
She slapped away the hands. "Please . . . don't . . . no . . . no!" She clawed at him, spat at him, ripped that chain off his neck. She clasped the tiny medal attached to the chain, trying to jam it into the shadow's eyes. His hands gripped her waist. He was carrying her away.
"Abby."
"Ted, no! Please don't—"
A sharp sting in her cheek. "For Christ's sake, Abby, wake the fuck up."

Her eyelids flew open, but the nightmare followed her into consciousness. A shadow over her bed. She instinctively released a right hook.

Kane easily deflected the blow.

"Don't make me slap you again," he said roughly.

She struggled for breath. *Inhale. Exhale. Breathe, Abby.*

"Kane?" she finally whispered.

"At your service." He sank down at the edge of the bed. "That must have been some nightmare. I heard you screaming all the way from my bedroom."

It took a few more seconds to orient herself. She was in one of the guest bedrooms in Morgan's compound. She'd come up here after Noelle left, to lie down for a bit. She remembered Lloyd bringing her some soup, which she'd dutifully eaten since she needed to regain her strength. And then she must have passed out, seeing as how the red numerals on the bedside alarm clock told her it was past midnight.

"I . . ." She sucked in another lungful of oxygen. "I'm sorry I disturbed you."

"I'm not the one who's disturbed here." He paused. "You called out the name Ted."

"I did?" Damn it. She hadn't said Ted's name out loud in years.

"Was he one of your foster fathers?"

"How . . . how did you know that?"

"Morgan mentioned you were in foster care before you were adopted."

"Oh." She swallowed, desperate to bring some moisture back to her throat. God, that dream had come out of left field. She never dreamed about Ted anymore.

Not since Jeremy had killed the son of a bitch.

"Come on, let's go downstairs and get you something to drink." He reached for the sheet covering her body, then cursed under his breath. "Shit. You must have torn a stitch with all that flailing around."

She glanced down and saw the dark stain on the front of her T-shirt. The coppery odor stung her nostrils, but when she took a deep breath, she noticed another scent. A masculine one. Spicy, bold, and erotic. Kane.

The heat returned to her body. Damn it. She wanted that warm flicker of desire to go away already.

Kane's hands were suddenly on her stomach, lifting the shirt up to her breasts. She held her breath as his fingers trailed over her exposed skin. "You're in luck. It wasn't the stitches. One of the scabs ripped open a little. I'll get a first-aid kit and we'll clean it right up—" His words halted when he felt her stiffen. "For God's sake, I'm not going to have my way with you."

She met his gaze. "No?"

"No." He looked ready to say something more, but then cursed again and stood up. "Stay here. I'll be back."

She took another deep breath, this time to calm the strange rush swelling inside her. By the time he returned with a small first-aid kit in his hands, she'd managed to get her hormones under control. This time when he touched her, she remained calm.

"The doctor in Bogotá gave us some ointment for you," Kane said gruffly, cleaning the cut on her stomach with rubbing alcohol and gauze. "It's for the welts. He said they might get itchy once they scab over. I'll bring you the ointment in the morning."

"Thank you."

"You're welcome."

He finished tending to the welt in silence, dressing it with a thin piece of gauze and taping it down. Shoving the supplies back into the case, he swiftly pulled her shirt down and said, "There. All done."

"Thanks," she said again.

He tucked the case under his arm and drifted to the doorway. A flash of light from the hallway illuminated his face, making his features look softer, kinder. "I'm taking a shower. If you need me, I'm two doors down, okay?"

"Okay," she whispered.

Again he opened his mouth, his green eyes glimmering with indecision. Then he shrugged and said, "Good night, Abby."

After the door closed behind him, she sat up in bed, ignoring the sharp pain in her ribs. Goddamn it. She needed to be in Colombia. Not here, in a strange bed, with a sexy man watching over her.

Damn Noelle.

"I'll think about it." Those had been her parting words when she'd left Abby in Morgan's compound to go God knows where.

What the hell was there to think about? Those girls needed to be rescued, period. They couldn't just leave them in Blanco's dirty clutches.

But she couldn't do this alone. She'd had the perfect in already, at least before Morgan's team of super-soldiers had decided to pull her out. She couldn't infiltrate Blanco's life again. Noelle could, though. Noelle, or Isabel, or Juliet, or any one of the women Noelle employed.

You don't need to do it alone.

Kane's deep, seductive voice slid into her head. She pursed her lips, wincing when the motion caused the bruise on her cheek to stretch and a jolt of pain shot through her face. No, alone wasn't going to cut it, was it? She was covered in bruises, her chest felt ravaged, and her fractured wrist still throbbed.

Could she trust him? With Noelle reluctant to come

on board, maybe Kane was a smart alternative. His team did rescues. They were trained, qualified. And Jeremy had held Morgan in such high regard. Maybe . . . maybe she should take Kane up on his offer.

Two doors down, he'd said. Slowly, Abby slid out from under the covers and stumbled to her feet, forcing herself not to second-guess her actions. She worked solo, always had, but circumstances had changed. She no longer had access to Blanco's compound, was no longer positioned in a location that put her close to Lucia and the girls. If Kane could get her close again, then why the hell was she hesitating?

She stepped out into the hallway, her bare feet padding against the hardwood floor toward Kane's bedroom. She paused in the open doorway, listening to the sound of running water. The door to the private bath was ajar and she could see steam floating out of the transparent shower stall. She crept toward the bed, where the faded jeans Kane had been wearing were tossed on the patterned bedspread. His bedroom was not what she'd expected. Masculine, yes, with the black and gray color scheme, but the antique furniture and cheerful landscapes hanging on the walls added warmth to the room.

She glanced at the bathroom door once more, her cheeks growing warm as the glass door slid open and Kane emerged from the steamy shower stall.

Naked.

She swallowed, unable to tear her eyes away from his nude, dripping-wet body. He had the kind of rock-hard physique that would make other women drool. His broad chest tapered to a trim waist, and his legs were thick and dusted with golden hair. He was lean, not bulky, with perfectly sculpted muscles that looked like they'd been carved out of marble. He was hard. Everywhere.

"I'm afraid it's too late for you to join me in the shower," he said in a silky voice. "Though we could still make good use of the bed."

Her cheeks grew even hotter. Damn it. He was taunting her, and looked quite amused by it too.

She cleared her throat, deciding to ignore the teasing remark. "I've changed my mind. I think . . . I think I want your help."

The corner of his mouth lifted in a smile. He glanced down, briefly, at the erection currently gracing his groin, then locked his gaze with hers. "Let me grab a towel."

He returned to the bathroom and came out a moment later with a white towel wrapped around his waist. "So, you suddenly want my help. Your boss shut you down, huh?"

She bristled. "Noelle has nothing to do with this. You offered to help, I'm taking you up on it."

"Who says the offer's still on the table?"

Panic rocketed through her. "I'll tell you everything, okay? I'll answer any question you have, as long as you agree to take me back to Colombia."

Holding on to the top of his towel, he sat down on the edge of the bed, his green eyes flickering with indifference. "I'm not sure I want to know anymore, Abby. No offense, but you've been nothing but trouble since we extracted you from the prison. And I have a feeling that whatever you're up to, it's just gonna land us in more trouble."

Her panic intensified. No. No, she couldn't let him turn her down. If Noelle wasn't willing to help, then she needed Kane. She might have stood a better chance of persuading Morgan—he seemed to have a soft spot for her—but Morgan wasn't here. Kane was, and he was obviously in charge in Morgan's absence. If she convinced Kane to help, he could convince the others. Maybe not D, but Luke was a good bet. He seemed to have an adventurous streak, so maybe he'd view this rescue as another adventure.

But first . . . win over Kane.

A heavy silence stretched between them. Leaning forward, Kane rested his palms on his bare knees. Her gaze dropped to his muscular legs, to the bulge in his groin that the thin towel couldn't hide.

She met his eyes, confidence gathering inside her. Her throat went dry as her mind kicked into business mode. She'd handled men like Kane before. He was strong, yes. Smart. Completely in control. But all men had one weakness, a weakness she'd exploited before and needed to exploit now.

Taking a breath, she took a step toward him and murmured, "What'll it take to change your mind?"

Chapter 7

Abby Sinclair had completely transformed in front of him. Kane's mouth went drier than a desert as the redhead moved toward the bed, her blue eyes darkening with sinful promise. The nightshirt she wore stopped just above her knees, revealing a pair of shapely legs, smooth and sexy despite the bruises marring her skin. She was a beautiful woman, and the closer she got, the more his body reacted.

"You're attracted to me," she said in a throaty voice. "I've seen the way you look at me, Kane."

She edged closer.

"I want your help. You want me." Raising one delicate eyebrow, she sank to her knees in front of him. "So give me what I want, and I'll return the favor."

His skin scorched when her soft, warm hands reached for the bottom of his towel. He couldn't breathe. Beads of sweat popped up on his forehead, his temperature spiking as if he'd just entered a sweltering sauna. Luke had hit pretty close to home earlier—Kane couldn't remember the last time he'd gotten laid. Probably a few months, maybe longer. And the moment Abby parted his towel, his cock sprang up, hard and thick and eager to remedy that statistic.

A dose of pure lust shot through him as Abby circled her fingers around him. She stroked him slowly, her red hair falling over her shoulder to tickle his stiff shaft. Shit. He had to stop this. He knew exactly what she was doing and he wasn't in the mood for games. He couldn't—oh *fuck*. Her lips brushed over his tip.

Kane clenched his fists, gathering willpower. His heart thudded like a drum, his pulse shrieking in his ears like an alarm. Abby took his cock in her hot, wet mouth, sucking gently, and for the life of him, he couldn't stop himself from arching his hips and pushing himself deeper into that warm recess. Screw it. Why couldn't he play this game? Why couldn't he let her do this, lose himself in these out-of-this-world sensations, come inside her mouth, and then—

"*No.*"

With a groan, he pulled out and stumbled to his feet, his hands clumsily trying to get his towel back in place.

Abby stayed on her knees, looking up at him wearily. Her lips were red and swollen, covered by a sexy sheen of moisture.

The arousal pumping through his veins was joined by the toxic rush of cold fury. "You're good," he said roughly. "How many times have you used sex as a weapon, Abby?"

Her shuttered expression was all the answer he needed.

"Fuck," he burst out. "Jesus, did you even feel *any-thing* when you had my cock in your mouth?"

Slowly, she moved to sit up on the bed, long silky tresses of hair falling into her face. Her throat bobbed as she swallowed, and when she met his gaze, the expressionless look in her eyes nearly tore him apart. "No," she said quietly. "I didn't feel anything."

Disgust crept up his throat. At her, for her complete indifference. At himself, for almost letting her do it.

"Sex . . ." She released a wobbly breath. "It doesn't mean anything to me. It never has."

The raw emotion in her voice—the first sign that she actually gave a damn—made him want to march over and pull her into his arms. He resisted the urge, keeping his hands pressed to his sides. Who was this woman? It annoyed him that he was so incredibly compelled to learn everything he could about her. Why did sex mean nothing to her? What had happened in her life to make her use basic human contact as a weapon?

"I don't . . . like it," she burst out when he still didn't respond. "Okay? It's nothing against you. I'm sure other women would cut off their left arms to go to bed with you, Kane."

"But not you," he said, a touch of bitterness in his voice.

She shook her head, looking anguished. Then, with another shaky breath, she stood up, suddenly seeming ridiculously small and fragile under that baggy T-shirt. "I'm sorry," she said softly. "I shouldn't have done that. You don't want to help me. I get that. I'll just . . . go."

He watched as she headed for the door, but before she could slide through it, he let out a groan. "Abby. Wait."

She turned around.

"Just . . . sit the fuck down, okay?" He moved toward the chair next to the bed and grabbed a pair of jeans. "Let me get dressed and then you can tell me what you want me to do."

*   *   *

"I think I might have a name. I'm faxing you the details now."

A wide smile stretched across Devlin's face as the voice on the other end of the line gave him the news he'd hoped to hear. He'd been hitting brick wall after brick wall for the past two days, ever since he'd flown to Colorado and discovered that Morgan's previous headquarters now stood abandoned. He'd been hoping for a trail, a way to find the bastards who'd stolen Erica from him, but Morgan was too bloody good to leave a trail. In the end, he'd returned to Blanco's compound, determined to tap every source imaginable in his search for the bitch.

Now he finally had a lead. He rose from Blanco's desk chair and drifted over to the fax machine to wait for the pages from his contact. Luis had been surprisingly accommodating, letting Devlin use his study as he hunted down Erica's true identity. Poor Luis. The man was getting mighty worried that his big event wouldn't go as planned.

Devlin, on the other hand, didn't give a damn about the auction. He wanted the woman.

The fax machine whirred to life, spitting out a dozen pages that Devlin hoped would get him exactly what he wanted.

"Is she government?" he said into the phone.

"Not exactly," answered Kerry Purdue, his contact in the CIA. "Apparently she did some contract work for us, but that was before my time. I couldn't get my hands on her agency file, but I put together a small dossier on what I could find of her background. So, about the money . . ."

Devlin rolled his eyes. Greedy Americans. It amazed him how bloody easy it was to buy information these days, particularly from agencies that swore to uphold secrecy and preached about national security.

"Being wired to you as we speak," Devlin said. "I'll be in touch if I need anything else."

He hung up the phone, anticipation building in his gut as he removed the stack of papers from the fax tray. He returned to the desk and glanced at the first page.

Abby Sinclair.

"Abby, Abby," he murmured under his breath. "I told you I'd find you."

He flipped through the pages, his excitement growing as he read. His Abby had been born in Los Angeles to a prostitute mother, who died of an overdose when Abby was eight. After that she'd been shuffled to various foster homes—thirteen altogether. The final home she'd lived at was run by a couple named Susan and Ted Hartford. In the five months she'd lived there, fifteen-year-old Abby had been brought to the emergency room eighteen times. Abuse, physical and sexual, was suspected, but no charges had been filed. Interestingly, Ted Hartford had disappeared six weeks after Abby was removed from his care.

The adoption papers caught his attention. A man named Jeremy Thomas had filed the papers. An ex-Ranger, no other background details. Interesting.

He picked up the phone and dialed Purdue's number. "There's no information about Jeremy Thomas," he barked when his contact picked up. "Can you get me more?"

"Not unless I want to get canned. Red flags were popping up all over the place when I typed in Thomas's name. The CIA and military databases refused me access."

"Keep trying," Devlin snapped, then hung up.

He skimmed through the file again, but the papers didn't tell him who his sweet Abby was currently working for. Government was highly unlikely; seemed like she preferred working independently. Private contractor, then.

A name suddenly caught his eye.

Dr. Amanda Silverton.

"Poor Abby," he clucked to himself. "Five years under the care of a shrink. What kind of baggage do you have, luv?"

The better question was, how could he use it against her?

He reached up to touch the patch covering his left eye. Fury spiraled through his body, followed by a rush of bloodlust that made his fingers tingle. That bitch had taken his fucking eye. He couldn't wait to wrap his fingers around her pretty neck and squeeze the life out of her.

But not right away. Oh no. First he'd ravage her body. Cut off her fingers and toes, one by one. Rip both her fucking eyes out.

Saliva pooled in his mouth, the images sliding through his brain so appealing that he felt himself growing hard.

Dr. Amanda Silverton. 2345 Sunset Terrace, Bakersfield, California.

He quickly dialed another number. "Get the plane ready," he said when Blanco's pilot answered the phone. "I have business in California."

"So what do you think?" Abby asked tentatively.

Kane didn't answer. Sitting in the chair near the bed, he'd been silent for nearly five minutes, his eyebrows drawn together, his green eyes revealing nothing. She'd told him everything she knew. About Blanco, Lucia, the auction. When she'd described how she'd purposely gotten caught, he'd frowned deeply, evidently displeased with what she'd done. But she wasn't about to defend herself to this man.

She also wasn't about to tell him how she'd lied to him just now.

Did you even feel anything?

She thought of the way he'd filled her mouth, the way his shaft throbbed against her tongue, and her entire body grew hot. God, she'd *felt* something. In that moment, her breasts had grown heavy, tingly, and there had been a dull ache between her legs. How was that possible? She'd performed oral sex on men before, spread her legs for them when the situation required it, and not once, not even *once*, had her body responded in any way.

Until tonight.

Maybe she was just tired. Or maybe her injuries were somehow creating these weird sensations in her body.

She couldn't be attracted to this man. She couldn't be.

"The only entrance to the bunker is through the prison," Kane finally said, sounding thoughtful.

"Yes." She paused. "Your team got into the prison once. You can do it again, right?"

He shook his head, a lock of blond hair falling onto his strong forehead. "We went in there to get you. One person, Abby. You said there's twelve, thirteen girls down there?"

She nodded. Tried desperately not to picture those dirty, terrified faces, but the image was burned in her mind.

"They're taken care of, though," she said. "The guards

give them food and water, so they're not starving or dehydrated. I think they can make it out without much help."

"It's too risky. We can't go in the same way we did last time. We'd have to lead a dozen girls across that compound, get them to the fence and then run to the clearing. I'm sure Blanco beefed up security after we got you out. The compound will be swarming with guards. Chances are, most if not all the girls will be shot down, not to mention me and my team."

He was right. Abby bit her lip, wincing when her teeth sank into a healing cut. Fortunately it didn't rip open. She ran her tongue along the cut, soothing the ache. "Damn it. I was *in* that prison, Kane. I could have—"

"Done nothing," he finished. A sharp laugh burst out of his chest. "I can't decide if you're the bravest woman I've ever met or the stupidest."

Her nostrils flared. "I had a chance to get them out."

"No, you didn't. In your condition, you'd have been lucky to get the girls out of the prison without fainting." When she tried to object again, he held up his hand to silence her. "We'd need to place someone on the inside."

"I *was* on the inside," she muttered.

Kane ignored the remark. "A bidder," he said suddenly, his eyes becoming animated.

"Huh?"

"We need someone to pose as a prospective bidder. Someone who can get an invitation to the auction."

She raised her eyebrows. "You want to pretend to be interested in buying a sex slave?"

"No, not me. It'll take more than a week to get the kind of cover in place that we'd need for this to work. Besides, Devlin knows me. We need someone he won't recognize." His forehead creased in thought. "I think I know who could do it."

"Who?" She couldn't hide the urgency in her tone.

Without answering, Kane got to his feet. "Let me make a few calls and talk to the guys, okay?" Moving toward the bedroom door, he tossed a glance over his shoulder. "Go down to the living room and read a book or something. I might be a while."

She shot up from the bed. "Wait—so you're going to help?"

He hesitated in the doorway, his broad shoulders sagging a little. "Maybe," he said, and then he was gone.

Maybe? Abby stared after him in dismay, that feeling of helplessness once again rising in her chest. She'd been hoping for a more solid commitment from him. Noelle hadn't seemed enthusiastic about the idea, which meant Kane and the men were her only option. She supposed she could call some of her colleagues, but Noelle's chameleons rarely took on assignments without approval from the boss. Isabel might do it, if Abby played her cards right. Other than Noelle, Isabel Roma was probably the closest thing Abby had to a friend, but again, her participation would rely on what Noelle said to her.

Damn.

She left Kane's bedroom and went back to her own, where she slid a pair of yoga pants up her legs, then changed into a loose yellow tank top. The welts caused by Devlin's whip still hurt and tight clothing probably wouldn't help them heal. Sleep might do the trick, but she was too wound up to go back to bed now. It was past one a.m. and she was wide-awake.

After pacing the guest room for a few minutes, she released a sigh and decided to follow Kane's advice. It took her a few moments of wandering the enormous main floor before she finally found the living room. The sheer size of it made her raise her eyebrows, but even she couldn't deny it was cozy. The ceiling was massive, a crisscross of wooden beams that looked as though they belonged in a hunting lodge or a fancy ski chalet. Plush leather couches, set up in an L shape, took up half of the room, while a large stone fireplace and a few comfortable-looking recliners filled the other half. Tall oak bookshelves and beautiful oil landscapes lined the walls, lending both warmth and elegance to the large space.

Abby approached one of the shelves and studied the titles, eventually selecting a hardcover edition of Hemingway's *The Sun Also Rises*. Hemingway had always intrigued her. She'd attended a lecture about him once, given by a feminist who admonished the author for portraying women as either castrators or love slaves, angels or demons. Which would she be? Abby had always wondered. She'd played the part of love slave. Castrator too. Maybe even a demon.

But never an angel.

Drawing in a breath, she got comfortable on one of the couches, pulling a dark blue wool afghan over her legs to keep warm. She opened the first page of the book and began to read.

Several hours passed—she could tell from the faint glow of light beginning to stream in from the large bay window overlooking the barren courtyard. Dawn was approaching. And Kane still hadn't returned.

When the sound of footsteps came from the hall, she lifted her head, anticipation gathering in her body. Finally.

"Do you have an answer for me—" Her words died in

her throat when D rather than Kane strode into the living room.

Wearing a pair of black track pants and a sleeveless black shirt that hugged his impressive chest, D leaned against the doorframe, his black eyes stormy. "Kane's on the phone." Sarcasm clung to his gravelly voice. "But I'm sure you'll be pleased to know he's decided to undertake this suicide mission of yours. Morgan's on board too. He and Holden are on their way back, and Trevor's already on a plane. He should be here in a few hours. Bet you're mighty pleased."

The hostility radiating from his lean, muscular body wasn't lost on her. "Who's Trevor?" she asked cautiously.

"One of the team. Just lost his fiancée too." D's lips tightened. "He'll probably be so distracted he'll get himself killed, which is probably why he's doing this."

Abby hid her confusion. She had no idea who Trevor was, or why he had a death wish, but she decided not to question it right now. D was evidently pissed off at her and looking to land a few cheap shots. Well, fine. She'd let him. As long as what he said was true, and Kane was truly on board, she wasn't complaining.

"Kane told you what's going on?"

D nodded, his eyes cold and relentless.

"And you don't think it's a good idea to help those girls?"

His big shoulders stiffened as he stepped into the living room. To her surprise, he sat down beside her on the sofa. Her eyes were instantly drawn to his tattoos, focusing on the lethal-looking dragon that looked like it was about to take flight off his shoulder.

"I don't like you," he said bluntly.

"Gee, and here I thought we were going to be BFFs."

"Do you want to know why I don't like you, Abby?"

She sighed. "Sure, D, go ahead and tell me."

"You're a loose fucking cannon."

Offense prickled her skin. A loose cannon? She was a professional, for God's sake. Cool under pressure, able to infiltrate any organization with careful planning and canny thinking. "I disagree," she said coldly.

He bared his teeth in a cheerless smile. "Oh, I know you're a pro," he said, as if reading her mind. "You're a warrior, aren't you, Abby?"

Wary, she waited for him to continue.

"But deep down . . ." He shrugged, the snake tattoo around his neck flexing ominously. "Deep down, you're just that scared little girl who got raped by her foster daddies."

"How—" She stopped abruptly, her voice too shaky to continue.

"How do I know?" he said, filling in the rest of her sentence. "Because I see it inside you. That ice-cold anger. The need for revenge."

"I got my revenge a long time ago," she murmured.

"No. You just got rid of *your* demon, Abby." He chuckled. "But you couldn't get rid of *all* the demons, could you? All the sick fucks out there victimizing young girls and young boys, getting away with whatever sick crimes they're committing."

"There's nothing wrong with wanting to help," she whispered. Steadying her voice, she met his eyes. "You're right. I was raped. Repeatedly, and for years. But I got over it. And if my own experience has made me determined to prevent it from happening to others, what the hell's wrong with that?"

D was quiet for a moment. Then he shook his head. "I

was like you, you know. Once." His voice softened. "Idealistic, driven, ready to dive headfirst into battle, any battle, as long as the bad guys lost and I won. Wanna know what happened?"

"What happened?" she echoed dully.

"I woke the fuck up. If I threw myself into every damn battle out there, I'd be fighting for the rest of my life. It became more practical to pick and choose. Fight when it was advantageous to me. You can't save the world, Abby. Want to know why?"

"I can't wait."

"Because as much as you want to save it, there will always be someone else who wants to destroy it. Better to back off. Pick your fights. And those girls in the bunker? They're not your fight." His face went hard. "And they're not our fight either."

"I take it that's your way of saying you won't help."

"Oh, I'll help," he said viciously. "Because somehow you managed to convince Kane to support your foolish crusade. And if Kane's on board, the others will follow like sheep. Which leaves me to make sure you don't get my fucking guys killed."

His words inspired a flicker of guilt. She quickly brushed it off. "Kane and the others are grown men. They know the risk, yet obviously they've decided it's worth it."

"Whatever." Cursing under his breath, he stood up, reverting back to his cold, impassive self. "I'm going to be watching you, Abby. If you do anything to endanger Kane, or any of the others, I will break your neck. Understand?"

"Perfectly," she replied, equally cool.

He marched toward the door.

"Who raped *you*, D?" she called after him.

He froze.

"Your father?" she guessed. "Mother? Both?"

Slowly, he turned to face her, his eyes flashing with fury.

"I see it in you too," she answered, with only a touch of sarcasm. "What is it they say? It takes one to know one."

Without a word, D left the room.

Abby stared after him. Was he right? Was this a battle better left unfought?

No. No, it couldn't be. It wasn't idealistic to want to save a bunch of innocent girls who were about to be sold off to rich, sadistic perverts, not if a successful rescue could be planned.

How could D—how could *anyone*—fault her for wanting to help?

"You have to eat, Sylvie." Lucia Alvaro spoke in a hushed, encouraging voice, but the small black-haired girl sitting beside her didn't even lift her head. In the doorway, the guard glanced over at the two girls in annoyance. She called him *halcón*—hawk—because he had a long beak of a nose. He also had the eyes of a hawk—sharp and cold—and he was always watching them.

"Please," Lucia urged in Spanish. "You heard what Señor Blanco said would happen if we didn't eat."

Sylvie shook her head ferociously. Her hands were wrapped around her bare knees, her long hair falling onto her dirt-covered face like a curtain. She was the youngest of the thirteen girls—only eleven. She had barely moved an inch since the *halcón* and the other guard, the one with the red scar next to his mouth, had thrown her into the cold, damp room.

Lucia didn't have an appetite either, but Señor Blanco's threat had scared her.

Sensing that all wasn't well, the *halcón* moved across the stone floor toward Lucia and Sylvie. "What's going on here?" he demanded.

"Nothing," Lucia said quickly. "We're . . . we're eating. See?" She lifted her fork to her mouth and bit into a piece of spicy chicken, hoping the sight of her chewing would distract him from the fact that Sylvie's plate still contained the rice, chicken, and vegetables it had entered the room with.

To her anguish, his black eyes didn't miss anything. "Why aren't you eating?" he barked.

Sylvie pressed her face to her knees. Tears squeezed out from the corners of her eyes like two fat raindrops, leaving streaks in the brown dirt clinging to her bare legs. Across the room, Adalia and Nita cowered against the wall, their eyes huge with fear. Lucia knew them from the village; they used to have picnic lunches by the creek while the village boys played in the water and tried to show off for the girls.

Lucia didn't know Sylvie. She'd met her only three days ago, when the *halcón* threw her into the room. She didn't know the others either, but the girls had begun to form a bond since they'd been locked up here together. Consuela and Valencia had become the leaders of the group, and it was Valencia who stood up now, her head held high.

"She's not hungry," Valencia said insolently. Valencia was fifteen years old, two years older than Lucia, and she had long brown hair and a thin body underneath her shabby clothes. She came from a village near Lucia's, but the girls had never met until now.

The *halcón*'s hand whipped out, striking Valencia's cheek. She stumbled a little, but didn't back down. "Please, her stomach isn't well. She—"

"She will eat when she's ordered to!" he snapped.

Lucia cringed at the vicious note in his voice. She bent her head toward Sylvie. "Please, eat the food, Sylvie, just—"

The *halcón* yanked Sylvie up to her feet. She gasped with fear, then moaned as the large hand that had just silenced Valencia came crashing down on her jaw. Blood spurted out of the corner of her mouth. "No!" she screamed. "Please, don't hurt me!"

Lucia tried not to look at the tears streaming down Sylvie's cheeks. Valencia was slowly moving away from them, sinking back onto the floor next to Consuela, looking small and defeated.

"You will eat," the *halcón* spat out, "or you will be punished."

The young girl screamed as the guard shoved his hand between her legs.

Sylvie cried. She let out an anguished, horrified wail, then sobbed, "Okay, I will eat. Please, just don't . . . don't . . ."

The guard pushed her away. He looked bored and annoyed, but Lucia had no doubt that he would have followed through on the threat. Unconsciously, she squeezed her legs together, a shiver of fear crawling up her spine. Was he going to do that to all of them?

Mamá, where are you?

The silent plea went unanswered. Lucia's mother had been visiting Aunt Maria in the city when the guards stormed their small house and threw Lucia in the back of their truck. Were her parents looking for her?

Would they find her before . . .

Before Señor Blanco did whatever it was he planned to do with them.

"That's a good *puta*," the guard rasped as Sylvie bent over her plate and shoveled food into her mouth. "Don't give me trouble again. You will not like the consequences."

The *halcón* stalked to the doorway. He glanced back once more to make sure Sylvie was still eating, then marched out the door. The girls all heard the lock clicking into place.

"You're going to get yourself killed," Valencia hissed when he was gone. "You're going to get all of us killed, you stupid brat!"

"Valencia," Lucia started.

Beside her, Sylvie was crying again, but still eating fervently.

"No!" Valencia said angrily. "You know I'm right! She's making everything worse!"

As Valencia continued to hiss at Sylvie, Lucia wrapped her arms around her knees and lowered her head.

Mamá, where are you?

Chapter 8

Isabel Roma got off the small airplane and into the beat-up taxi waiting at the edge of the private airfield. She wasn't surprised when the driver spun around with a look of shock and awe as she settled into the backseat. She still wore the trashy outfit she'd had on while tailing her target in Paris, a man whose tastes ran toward seedy strip joints. She hadn't had time to change her clothes before hopping onto the plane in France and then boarding the connecting flight in California. Noelle hadn't given her much notice, simply ordered her to get on a plane to Mexico. And Isabel had done it.

Abby's in trouble.

That was all Noelle needed to say to convince Isabel. She was thirty-one years old, had no children, no husband, no official place of residence. But what she did have was family. Granted, it was a slightly dysfunctional one made up mostly of assassins, but after her father went to prison and her mother killed herself, Isabel had been left with nothing. Until she'd met Noelle. And then Abby. Then Juliet, Paige, and Bailey. The five women were all she had. They were her sisters. And Isabel had no intention of ignoring the distress call of a sister.

Figured that it would be Abby. Damn that woman. Noelle had seemed extremely annoyed when she'd told Isabel about Abby's latest crusade. She'd called it a fool's errand, and Isabel was inclined to agree with the boss. Abby had no business snooping around in the sex trade. It was too damn risky, too many sick perverts willing to kill to stay in business.

Not that Isabel was one to judge. Her undercover work for Noelle was as risky as it came.

"Are you visiting Tijuana for business or pleasure?" the taxi driver asked in heavily accented English, his tanned face exuding sincere curiosity.

"Pleasure, of course." She flashed him a smile. "I'm here to surprise my boyfriend."

"*Sí.* I understand." He seemed to be fighting a laugh. "I am sure *su novio* will be *muy* surprised."

She pictured Abby's reaction when the cavalry arrived, and shrugged. "I hope so."

The taxi ride lasted the better part of an hour, as the driver sped along the bumpy dirt roads taking them to the outskirts of the city. When the fence surrounding Jim Morgan's compound finally came into view, Isabel was eager to get out of the car. The driver—Manuel, as he'd introduced himself—had been chattering on in both English and Spanish, his awkward tries at conversation hindering Isabel's attempt at a much-needed catnap.

Nevertheless, she gave Manuel a big tip—it was rare to meet truly decent people these days—and hopped out of the taxi, her small travel duffel slung over her shoulder. The cab did a U-turn, then sped off on the red dirt road leading away from the compound. Isabel walked toward the electric fence. She jammed a manicured finger on the intercom button, and when a crackly voice barked at her to identify herself, she said the three magic words: "Noelle sent me."

In less than five minutes she was walking up to the main house, admiring the beautiful Spanish-style architecture. She'd just climbed the wide front steps of the veranda when the front doors swung open and a very attractive man with suspicious green eyes stepped outside.

"Noelle sent you, huh?" he said, looking irritated.

"Yes. I'm—"

"Isabel!" came Abby's surprisingly delighted voice. A second later, Abby appeared on the porch, her blue eyes—blue?—shining with gratitude.

Isabel sucked in a breath at the sight of Abby's bruised face. "Shit. You look terrible," she said sympathetically. "You okay, Abs?"

"I'm fine. Better now that you're here." Abby grinned. "I knew she wouldn't make me do this alone."

"Of course she wouldn't. She told me you were in trouble and promptly ordered me to fly out here and help you out."

Abby looked touched. "Thanks for coming, Izzy."

"No problem." She tilted her head. "You're a redhead. It's weird."

Abby shrugged. "My natural color, if you'd believe it."

Isabel hid her surprise. It was extremely rare getting tight-lipped Abby to reveal any details about herself. And this particular detail was an even bigger privilege. Isabel hadn't had any idea what Abby's true eye and hair color were. Abby had always been flippant about what she really looked like. Almost as if she wanted to forget the woman she'd been before coming to work for Noelle.

The man on the porch cleared his throat, drawing Isabel's attention to his presence. "Sorry," she said with a smile, sticking out her hand. "I didn't properly introduce myself. I'm Isabel Roma."

"Kane," he said, leaning forward to take her hand.

His shake was firm, and the calluses on his palm told her he wasn't a man who sat around in an office all day. So did his ridiculously toned body. She noticed Abby sneak a brief look in Kane's direction, and resisted the urge to raise her eyebrows. Interesting.

"How much did Noelle tell you?" Abby asked.

"Everything."

Kane eyed her warily. "And she thought you could help?"

"She said the rescue is in Colombia." Isabel smiled again. "And I happen to have an incredibly solid cover in that part of the world."

Kane didn't answer for a moment. Instead, he studied her with those dark green eyes, his expression revealing exactly what he thought of her current appearance. "Okay," he finally said. "Come on in, then. Morgan just got here. So did Trev, and he happens to have a pretty good cover himself."

He turned and strode inside, leaving the two women alone on the porch.

"You really do look terrible," Isabel said softly, sweeping her gaze over Abby's purple eye and cut lip. "Did Blanco do that to you?"

"Devlin, his second in command," Abby said. She offered a small shrug. "I'm fine, Izzy, seriously. You know me—no one can keep me down for long. All I want to do now is rescue those girls."

Isabel tried not to frown. Noelle had warned her that

Abby was a little too intense about this plan of hers. *Obsessed* had been the word Noelle used. Isabel could figure out why. Over the years Abby had revealed a few details about her past, not many but enough for Isabel to deduce that she'd had it rough growing up. And no matter how tough she made herself out to be, Isabel knew that Abby was extremely fragile beneath the surface.

She wasn't sure *fragile* and *Colombian sex trade* were a good combo. Noelle hadn't been certain either, which was why she'd sent Isabel.

Shifting her duffel to her other shoulder, Isabel linked her arm through Abby's and headed to the door. "He's cute," she murmured as they walked into the house.

"Who?"

Isabel rolled her eyes. "Kane. I saw the way you looked at him. You must be aware of his hotness, Abs. He's sexy."

"If you say so," Abby said vaguely. She stopped in the massive front hall, shooting Isabel a suddenly amused look. "By the way, you don't look too good yourself. How many bottles of hair spray did it take to get your hair like that?"

"Gosh, you're funny. And here I thought you weren't capable of making jokes."

"I think there'd be something wrong with me if I *didn't* joke about that hair. Seriously, it's big."

Isabel experienced a rare flicker of insecurity. "It's not *that* big, is it?"

"It's enormous."

Great, and she was about to walk into a roomful of men who, judging by Kane's appearance, were probably really hot.

The things she did for her surrogate sister.

*   *   *

Isabel Roma had the worst hairdresser on the planet. Not only that, but her sense of style left something to be desired, Kane thought uneasily as he snuck a look at the blonde sitting on their terrace. She wasn't someone Kane would take a second or even third look at if he passed her on the street. Oh no. He'd look at her once, raise a brow at the hair, and dismiss her from his mind. He didn't dismiss her now, though, because one, she'd been sent by Noelle, who still kind of terrified him, and two, Abby's entire face had lit up in a joyful smile when Isabel Roma waltzed in.

What would it take, he wondered, for Abby to smile that way at him?

Probably quite a lot.

Pushing away his rueful thoughts, he glanced around the table, gauging everyone's expressions. It was an interesting group. Abby, with her intense blue eyes. D, whose expression revealed that he wanted to be anywhere but there. Luke and Ethan, who simply looked curious. Morgan, who'd come back from reconnaissance at Blanco's alone since Holden had gone home to his wife, all business as usual. And Isabel with that hair.

And Trevor, who looked absolutely ravaged.

Kane had been shocked when his old friend walked through the door. Trevor Callaghan was a different man from the one he remembered. The old Trevor had a buzz cut, a sharp sense of style, and a perpetual lopsided grin on his face. This Trevor looked . . . older. His hair had grown out, down to his collar. He wore a faded flannel shirt and pair of blue jeans with a hole in the knee. And sneakers on his feet. It was fucked up, seeing his friend dressed like a beach bum. Even more fucked was the complete emptiness in Trev's dark eyes. He was a man who didn't give a damn anymore, and it worried the hell out of Kane. This was the guy they were sending on a hazardous undercover op?

Kane shifted his gaze back to the newcomer at the table. Again he found himself thinking, *this* was who they were sending in?

Isabel Roma looked like she'd walked straight out of a trailer park, with all that big blond hair teased to oblivion, the gaudy eye makeup, and the rhinestone-studded jacket. She was also a little chubby, her cheeks round, her upper body slightly . . . padded. He had no clue what to make of her, and he suspected the others weren't sure either. At least the dog didn't seem to have a problem with her appearance. Bear was lying by Isabel's feet, gazing at her the way he gazed at those rawhide bones Luke lavished him with. No accounting for taste.

"Kane?"

He shot Morgan a quizzical look. "Sorry. What were you saying?"

"I wanted to know if you filled the guys in on the situation."

"Yeah, I did." He glanced at Luke, then Ethan. "You guys are still in?"

They both nodded. Luke offered a cocky grin, adding, "It sounds like fun."

Kane didn't bother asking D. He knew the man would come along, no matter how much he disliked it. Which he'd made exceptionally clear all afternoon.

"Okay, good. So," Morgan said briskly, "Noelle"—he said her name as if it carried the plague—"is lending us Isabel for this assignment." He focused on the blonde. "Tell me about the cover you've got in place."

"I'm Paloma Dominguez, a Brazilian heiress." Isabel leaned back in her chair. Kane was surprised that the weight of her hair didn't tip her over. "I'm a jet-setter. I like rich men and yachts and I'm spoiled rotten. I've been using Paloma for about five years now. She's a big hit in South America. European men love her too."

"Izzy's a chameleon," Abby piped up, sounding oddly gentle. "She can transform herself into anyone."

Kane gave Isabel another surreptitious once-over. He still couldn't figure her out. She was very personable, with a throaty, easygoing voice and an approachable demeanor. But he simply couldn't get past her appearance.

Neither could the others, apparently.

"Look." Luke spoke up in his lazy drawl. He turned to Isabel, holding his hands up like he was surrendering to an enemy. "I don't want you to take this the wrong way, but I can't see how your presence would benefit this assignment. You're . . . flashy. And, um, *frumpy* . . ."

It took all of Kane's willpower not to burst out laughing. Luke, tactful as always.

"I don't know how much you know about Luis Blanco," Luke continued, "but the man isn't impressed by chicks with flash. He goes for the fresh-faced, wide-eyed look. Not . . ." His voice drifted.

Isabel nodded knowingly. "Not the whore from the trailer park?"

Kane's peripheral vision caught Abby biting her lip as if she was trying not to smile.

"Um, yeah," Luke said awkwardly.

To Kane's surprise, Isabel began to laugh. "You actually think I dress like this?" she asked Luke.

"Uh . . ."

"Didn't you hear what Abby said? I'm a chameleon."

She cocked her head, as if to toss her hair over her shoulder, but the blond monstrosity didn't budge. Probably frozen in place with three cans of hair spray.

Kane was intrigued. Morgan had told him Noelle's women had the ability to transform themselves in the blink of an eye, but still ... How different could Isabel *really* look without the tacky getup?

"I just came from an assignment in Paris," Isabel added. "My target happens to like trashy women. Trust me, boys, this is all for show."

Luke cast Kane a look that revealed he couldn't possibly fathom how the chubby face and plump body could be a "show." Kane wasn't quite sure either. Across the table, Abby seemed to be fighting another grin.

Seeing the lingering doubt, Isabel chuckled again before getting to her feet. "Jeez, you obviously have no faith in my ability to transform."

"Izzy—" Abby began.

"Abs, these men aren't going to take me seriously unless I show them I'm perfectly capable of socializing with a man like Blanco," Isabel interrupted.

"Fine. Just make it fast."

With a hint of a smile, Isabel shrugged out of the jacket and tossed it aside. Instantly her arms looked thinner. The jacket obviously had hidden shoulder pads sewn into it.

"Undercover operatives can't survive if they don't know how to alter their appearance," Isabel explained. She shot Luke a pointed look. "As a former SEAL, you should know what I'm talking about. How many times did you have to disguise yourself when you were running around in the jungle or Afghanistan or whatever war zone you were assigned to?"

"A few," he admitted. "Though to be fair, SEALs don't do deep cover too often. Our job is to get in and out before anyone knows we were even there."

"A disguise is a disguise, no matter how short a time you use it." She stood at the head of the table, off to Morgan's side, and pointed to the tight baby tee she'd been wearing under the jacket. The top showed off her midriff, and nobody could miss the slight roll of cellulite at her belly. "Certain clothes can help, but unless you're willing to gain or lose thirty pounds for a gig you need to find ways around it. Makeup, for example."

Isabel bent down and rummaged around in the duffel bag she'd brought outside. She stood up a second later with a tiny packet of tissues. She proceeded to wipe her stomach, then her cheeks and chin, and when she finished, Kane was startled to see a dramatic change. Her cheekbones suddenly seemed higher, her chin more defined, and her stomach was as flat as they came.

"Subtle makeup," she continued, "designed to play with light and shadow, giving the impression of, say, cellulite." She rolled up the hem of her shirt to show the strategic—and like she'd said, subtle—padding sewn beneath it, padding that altered not only the garment but also the figure of the person wearing it.

"Oh, and my hair isn't this big, okay?" she said with an annoyed breath. To hammer the point home, she ran her fingers through the stiff beehive atop her head, finger-combed it for a few seconds, and suddenly her hair was cascading down her shoulders.

Kane was actually stunned speechless. The woman in front of them really had transformed. She was actually kind of beautiful, and he wasn't the only one to notice. Luke was all but gaping, his eyes darkening with appreciation. Ethan looked slightly amazed. D looked rattled. Morgan just seemed bored. And Trevor didn't even blink.

"See, I'm a chameleon," Isabel said with a pleased little smile before bending down to retrieve the jacket she'd carelessly dropped on the ground.

"She's also a trained sharpshooter and fluent in seven languages," Abby said wryly.

"Seven?" Ethan echoed in awe.

Even D looked impressed—and nothing impressed that smart-ass.

Isabel sank back into her seat and folded her hands in her lap. Casually, she glanced over at Trevor, who hadn't uttered a word during the entire exchange, and said, "So, what do you have to offer?"

It took a few seconds for it to register that the blonde was speaking to him. Trevor Callaghan lifted his head, fixing Isabel with an indifferent look. He'd watched her entire transformation without much interest, which wasn't a huge surprise. Nothing seemed to interest him these days.

The woman was attractive. He did notice that. Her skin, now devoid of that gaudy makeup, was smooth and tanned, and her body was slender with just the right amount of curves. Her eyes were her most dominant feature, though. Big and brown, with flecks of amber around the pupils. Could be contacts, but there was no hiding the intelligent gleam to them. He felt a distinct pang of discomfort under that shrewd gaze.

Fuck. He shouldn't have come back here. He'd been doing just fine in Aspen, in the small but cozy condo he and Gina had shared. The condo they'd bought themselves as an engagement present. Why had he let Kane talk him into coming back? Why the hell was he here?

Because you want to die.

The thought rushed into his head, bringing a peculiar sense of tranquillity. God, how soothing it was. Yes. Yes, he did want to die.

Though, really, was it possible to die when you were already dead inside?

"Are you going to answer me sometime this century?" Isabel asked, the corners of her mouth twitching.

"What did you want to know?" he asked gruffly. His voice sounded strange to his own ears. He hadn't spoken in a while. Couldn't even remember the last time he'd said a fucking word before Kane called him up and asked if he was willing to come back for a gig.

"What's your cover? Kane said we're going in together."

Trevor suddenly found it hard to speak. Everyone around the table was watching him, expectant. He was suddenly reminded of Gina's funeral. They'd all looked at him the same way. Expectant, waiting for him to fall apart, to explode.

God, the funeral.

Had it really been a year ago? It felt like yesterday.

As if sensing his sudden urge to flee, Morgan took pity on him and spoke up instead. "Trev's been using the alias Julian Martin for years. Julian dabbles in the arms trade, but he's also a part owner in a Brazilian brothel. He's an American who inherited a fortune from his folks, travels the world, and invests money in shady enterprises." Morgan turned to Isabel and let out a low laugh. "Congratulations, Paloma Dominguez. You're now married to Julian Martin."

Isabel looked intrigued. "And we're in the market for a sex slave?"

"Sure are." He glanced at Trevor. "You're still chummy with Felix Esposito, right?"

Trevor nodded, forcing some confidence into his voice. "I helped him out of a jam the last time I played Julian. He owes me one."

"Good. On the flight back, Holden used his computer voodoo and connected Esposito to Samir Bahar, who happens to be the solicitor for Luis Blanco. Bahar comes from Turkish royalty, but he's made his money working as the attorney for a handful of Middle Eastern and South American lowlifes."

Trevor grew thoughtful. His brain was beginning to function again. They'd done this so many times, he could do it on autopilot. "I get Esposito to set up an introduction with Bahar, then try to arrange for a meeting with Blanco."

"You probably won't get it," the redhead told him.

Trevor tried to remember her name. Annie? No, Abby. Abby Sinclair. When their eyes met, he was surprised by the jolt of connection he experienced. Her eyes . . . they were almost as empty as his own. Like looking into a mirror. She was dead inside too, he realized. Did she know it?

"Blanco gets Bahar and his other minions to do all his dirty work," Abby continued. "He'll have taken great pains to distance himself from the auction. Other than using his estate as the location, he probably hasn't done any of the legwork."

"All we need is an invitation," Morgan said briskly. "Trev, you and Isabel will pose as prospective bidders. Hopefully, if you throw enough money at Blanco, he'll let you join in the fun."

Morgan tapped his fingers against the table. "We just need you and Isabel to get an in. Once you've got it, we'll come up with an appropriate plan for extraction." He looked at Abby. "You know the layout of the compound, the interior, right?"

She nodded.

"Good. You'll need to go over it with Kane, draw us up some blueprints. As far as I know, you're the only agent who's ever managed to get inside there, so you'll have to provide every last detail." He frowned. "Make sure to label the positions of the guards, at least those that you remember. But we'll have to assume Blanco increased security after your escape."

She nodded again, then spoke hesitantly. "There's one other thing. Two, actually. If Blanco ends up wanting to meet with you"—she glanced at Trevor—"Devlin will probably be there. Kane said you worked with him before—will that be a problem? Will he recognize you?"

Trevor pursed his lips. "Honestly, I don't think he will. I didn't go on that mission with Devlin. I was at the airfield, though. Spoke to the guy for like two minutes."

"And you were rocking that mountain-man beard at the time," Kane said with a grin. "If I met you once, and eight years ago, I probably wouldn't recognize you now."

"Well, just be careful," Abby warned. "Do your best to stay out of his line of sight if you happen to meet."

"And the second thing?" Isabel prompted.

"If Blanco does invite you to the estate," Abby said, "you should be prepared."

Trevor narrowed his eyes. "For what?"

"Blanco has cameras installed in every room of the house. He claims it's a security precaution, but I think he's just a plain old pervert who gets his kicks watching other people screw. I did some snooping and confirmed there aren't any microphones, so conversations should be all right, but the cameras are definitely there."

"So what you're saying," Isabel said warily, "is if Trevor and I are invited to the house, the bastard will want us to put on a show?"

"Oh, he'll expect it," Abby replied matter-of-factly.

While Isabel looked unfazed, Trevor couldn't help but feel startled. He wasn't sure that was something he'd be able to do. Isabel was an attractive woman, yeah, but ...

She's not Gina.

Pain torpedoed into his gut. The black hole inside him widened another fraction of an inch. How could anyone expect him to touch another woman when the only woman he wanted to touch was buried under six feet of dirt?

"All I'm saying is be prepared," Abby said with a shrug. "If you two end up in one of those bedrooms, try to find a way around the sex part. But keep in mind that Blanco and his men will most likely be watching, so you need to stay in character every second you're in there."

Morgan shot Trevor a cautious look. "Trev, will that be a problem?"

Yes.

"No," he said, slowly shaking his head.

Fuck it. Who cared anyway? When Kane had said those three words over the phone—possible suicide mission—Trevor had experienced a wave of anticipation so great he'd nearly keeled over from it. If he wasn't such a pussy, he would've blown his brains out months ago. But he couldn't do that to his mother and his sister. They'd probably blame themselves, and he couldn't have that. His mother already blamed herself for canceling her dinner with Gina the night she was killed. Trevor couldn't add another serving of guilt onto his mom's plate. He wasn't a total bastard.

But if he died in the field . . . if he died trying to save a dozen innocent girls, then his family would be spared having to scrub his brains off the bathroom tiles. Win-win for everybody.

He set his jaw and added, "It won't be a problem at all."

Abby stared at her reflection in the mirror of the guest bathroom, assessing her appearance. The bruises were still purple, but some were starting to fade to a splotchy blue. In a few days they'd be green, then yellow, then disappear entirely. She wasn't usually prone to insecurity, but she couldn't quit thinking about the way all the men had ogled Isabel out there on the terrace. Not that she blamed them—Isabel was gorgeous, and her personality was just as appealing as her looks. Abby wasn't normally a jealous person, but over the years, as she'd watched men and women alike get lost in Isabel's laid-back charm, she'd wondered how it would feel, having people like you.

She pulled her gaze off her bruised face and took a breath. She wished she could erase the gleam of appreciation she'd glimpsed in Kane's eyes when Isabel had been putting on her show. Jeremy had taken her to a movie once, when she was sixteen or so, and Abby clearly remembered how puzzled she'd felt when the heroine on the screen rebuked her boyfriend for ogling some other woman. Abby had thought it weird that the heroine was angry rather than relieved. *I don't want anyone looking at me like that ever again,* she'd told Jeremy. *Let them picture someone else naked.*

For some reason, that memory came back to her now, as she pictured the look on Kane's face when Isabel started to undress. But so what if he found Izzy attractive? As long as he helped her save those girls, he could admire anyone he pleased.

Sighing, she stepped out of the washroom and headed to the living room, where Kane had said he'd wait for her. They were supposed to draw up blueprints of Blanco's compound, and she was eager to get started. The faster they planned this rescue, the faster they could be back in Colombia.

And the faster she could get away from Kane and the disturbing feelings he evoked in her.

Low male voices met her ears as she approached the doorway. When she recognized one of the voices as belonging to D, she instinctively ducked to the side and went still. Eavesdropping wasn't very polite, but when it came to the black-eyed man who'd confronted her last night, she needed all the ammo she could get. Especially since she had a hunch that D would do all he could to persuade the other men to abandon the rescue.

"I don't think we should do this."

Yep, she'd seen *this* coming.

"Seriously," D said. "I don't like anything about it. Isabel seems competent, but did you see Trevor's eyes? I don't know what Morgan was thinking. Trevor is in no shape to be part of something like this."

"I'm not sure I disagree." Kane's voice now, low and weary. "But Morgan wouldn't give Trevor the okay to get back in the field if he didn't think Trev was up to it."

"And Abby"—D went on as if Kane hadn't spoken— "she worries me the most, man. I don't trust her. And I don't like her either."

She clenched her teeth, though there was really no reason to be annoyed. D had made his feelings about her clear—to her face. She shouldn't be surprised that he was voicing those same suspicions to Kane behind her back.

"Bear likes her," Kane pointed out, his tone laced with humor.

"Bear is an idiot," D shot back. "And he isn't in danger of getting killed, not unless Luke decides to bring the mutt along on the extraction, which ain't gonna happen."

"So what do you suggest, D? We scrap the rescue and send Abby and Isabel on their merry way?"

"Fuck yes."

When Kane went silent, Abby's heart sank to the pit of her stomach like a block of concrete. *Damn him*. How could he let D sway him so easily? And to think she'd actually started to view him as an ally.

She was edging away from the doorframe, knots of bitterness forming in her gut, when Kane spoke again.

"I'm disappointed in you."

D sounded as shocked as Abby felt. "What the fuck is *that* supposed to mean?"

"It means that a dozen little girls are about to become sex slaves to a bunch of disgusting perverts, and you're perfectly content to let it happen." Kane made a sound of frustration. "I know you're an asshole, but this is bad even for you, man."

"Forgive me for wanting to stay alive," D spat out.

"Stay home, then. But me? I'm going to try to help those kids."

D swore loudly. "Abby—"

"Has nothing to do with this," Kane cut in, his voice growing hard. "You think *I* trust her? Well, I don't. She's done nothing to earn my trust—she won't even tell me where she grew up, for fuck's sake. I'm not doing this for her, I'm doing it for those girls. So you can help, or you can stay back. Frankly, I don't give a fuck."

Abby felt like someone had punched her in the stomach. Inhaling deeply, she crept away from the doorway, too shaken to enter the room and interrupt the heated argument between the two men. Kane's fierce declaration continued to blaze through her mind.

He didn't trust her.

Well, no kidding. She'd already figured that out, but hearing him say it was disconcerting.

You don't trust him either, Jeremy's voice reminded her.

No, she supposed she didn't, and the sad realization weighed on her chest. God, why couldn't she just be a normal woman? After everything Kane had done for her, rescuing her, agreeing to help her, defending her to a man he *did* trust . . . Other women would be throwing themselves at his feet in gratitude. But not her. Oh, no, she couldn't extend him even the tiniest olive branch of trust. What the hell was wrong with her?

People like us, we're not normal, Abby. We're warriors.

For the first time in her life, she was seriously tempted to slap Jeremy's voice right out of her head.

Chapter 9

"I like Isabel," Kane remarked as he walked Abby up to the guest room.

He sounded sincere, which didn't come as a surprise. Everyone liked Isabel. "Isabel's great," she answered honestly. "There's just something about her that draws people in." She paused. "I don't think it worked on Trevor, though. He was kind of cold to her."

Weariness clouded Kane's green eyes. "He's not himself," he admitted. "I'm wondering if maybe getting him involved in this wasn't such a good idea."

"He seems qualified."

"He is. But like I said, he's not himself."

"What happened to him?" she asked curiously.

Kane sighed. "Long story."

They reached the door of the guest room, and Abby hesitated before going in. It was only ten o'clock, but she was exhausted. She and Kane had spent the entire day drawing blueprints of Blanco's estate, trying to form an extraction plan that wouldn't get everyone killed. In the evening, she'd shared a quiet dinner with Isabel out on the terrace. Kane and the others had stayed out of sight, though Luke did join the women for dessert—and spent the entire time flirting shamelessly with Isabel, who just laughed it off. After dinner, Isabel and Trevor drove into town to make some arrangements for their respective cover roles, while Abby sat in the living room and read.

And now . . . now she was turning in, but for some reason, she wasn't so tired anymore, with Kane in her company again.

She couldn't stop thinking about the conversation she'd overheard, the determination in Kane's voice when he'd vowed to rescue those girls. And as they'd gone over the details of Blanco's compound tonight, she'd been unbelievably impressed by his intelligence, the sharp questions he asked, and the way he looked at every obstacle as a challenge rather than an impediment.

Was it possible to feel comfortable *and* uncomfortable in a person's presence? Kane somehow managed to inspire both in her. When she looked into his deep green eyes, something inside her . . . thawed. Just a little. For as long as she could remember, her emotions had been guarded by a thick layer of ice. Being around Kane made that ice melt.

Just a little.

She shifted, and the fabric of her shirt rubbed against her back, making the welts on her skin itch. Frowning, she rubbed her side, wishing the healing process would speed up already.

"The welts itching?"

"Yes," she admitted.

"Let me get that ointment the doc gave us. Maybe it'll help."

She tried to protest. "No, that's not—"

But he was already gone, heading downstairs with

long, easy strides. With a sigh, she walked into the bedroom and sat on the bed. Kane returned a few minutes later, holding the tube of ointment. He stood in front of her, the corner of his mouth lifting.

"Strip," he said casually.

Her heart did a little flip-flop. "What?"

"I'm pretty sure the ointment needs to be applied to the injuries, not the clothes."

Abby swallowed. "Just leave it here. I'll do it."

He raised both eyebrows. "You'll do your own back?"

Damn. He had a point. But she wasn't going to take her clothes off in front of this man, not when his mere proximity brought those disconcerting flashes of heat to her already tender skin.

"I've already seen you naked," he pointed out.

Another good point. She'd been nude when he carried her out of Blanco's prison.

But still . . .

"Fine," she finally grumbled, reaching for the hem of her shirt. Her fingers were oddly unsteady as she pulled the shirt over her head, leaving her in nothing but a black sports bra. At least she wasn't wearing naughty lingerie.

The mattress sagged as Kane put his weight on it, sitting cross-legged behind her. He unscrewed the tube's cap and a moment later, his warm hands were on her skin.

Abby's breath hitched.

"Cold?" he said, sounding concerned.

"No . . . it's all right."

She held her breath as he rubbed the soothing cream over the deep welts. When was the last time she'd let a man touch her? Without being on assignment, without wanting something from him? Jeremy was the only one she'd ever let get close, but even his fatherly embraces had been a strain sometimes.

"Can I ask you something?" Kane asked, his voice gruff.

She released the breath she'd been holding. "Yeah?"

"Have you ever come before?"

Abby twisted around in shock. "What?"

"You know, had an orgasm," he clarified, looking vaguely embarrassed.

Needles of indignation pricked at her skin. "I know what you meant. And I can't see how that's any of your business."

"I'll take that as a no, then." Gently, he turned her around and went back to work, his fingers skimming over the cuts. "It's just . . . you said you don't like sex, and I was just wondering if maybe that's because, you know, you've never gotten any pleasure from it."

Her cheeks were so hot she almost fanned herself. God, this was mortifying. Was this actually what men and women talked about? She hadn't had a lot of interaction with males, save for those she was ordered to kill. Maybe this was totally normal subject matter.

"It doesn't give me pleasure," she found herself revealing, grateful that he couldn't see the red flush staining her cheeks.

"Because you don't give yourself the chance to feel it?"

She frowned. "No, that's not it."

"Have you ever slept with a man you actually wanted to sleep with?"

"No," she admitted. She hesitated, then added, "I'm not attracted to men."

"Oh. *Ohhhh.*"

His startled reply made her laugh. "I'm not a lesbian, if that's what you think. I just have no interest in sex or relationships."

Kane made a *tsk*ing sound with his tongue. "Control issues."

"What's that supposed to mean?"

"Exactly what it sounds like. Turn around. Let me do your stomach."

Despite the irritation coursing inside her, she obeyed him, shifting so they were sitting cross-legged and face-to-face on the bed. He squeezed some more ointment on his hand, then dragged the pads of his fingers over the sensitive skin of her belly.

"What do you mean, control issues?" she pressed.

He shrugged. "You need to be in control twenty-four-seven. It makes sense you're not into sex. Sex is all about losing control."

His voice contained a hint of sensual heat. She wanted to look away, but she couldn't. Instead, her gaze rested on his mouth, noticing again how full his bottom lip was.

"Sex is about trust," he went on. "You have to give yourself to someone else completely. You have to open yourself up. But you can't do that, can you, Abby?"

His words brought little pinpricks of pain. She wanted to object, to tell him he was wrong, but she knew the truth when she heard it. Trust wasn't something she handed out freely. Scratch that—trust wasn't something she handed out at all.

"Have you ever trusted *anyone*?" he asked softly.

Her throat tightened, making it difficult to speak. "I trusted Jeremy. And I, uh . . . I trusted someone else too, a long time ago."

"Who, Abby?"

"My mother." The words squeezed out of her chest.

"And what happened to change that?"

The unbidden memories closed in on her so fast she nearly stopped breathing. She blinked a few times, trying to get rid of the sudden sting in her eyes. God, not tears. She couldn't cry in front of this man. She hadn't cried since she was eight years old. Hadn't thought crying was even possible anymore.

"We lived in this really seedy neighborhood, near Compton," she finally said. "My mom was a prostitute."

He visibly swallowed. "Why are you telling me this?"

"You asked," she said awkwardly.

"Yeah. But why now? Every other time I've asked, you shut down."

"I . . ." She drew air into her lungs. "I guess I figured we need to trust each other."

A knowing look crossed his face. "I knew it."

Abby bristled. "What are you talking about?"

"You were listening to my argument with D, weren't you?" He went on without letting her answer. "Yeah, I knew you were there." He paused. "So how did it feel, hearing that I don't trust you?"

"Shitty," she muttered.

A laugh rumbled out of his chest. "Yes, it *is* shitty. And now you know how I feel when you continue to hold back on me. I already said I'd help you extract those girls— there's no reason for you to continue to be secretive."

"So I'm supposed to tell you all of my secrets just because you've agreed to do this rescue?"

The humor in his eyes dissolved into a cloud of wariness. "Always on the offense, aren't you, Abby?" Sighing, he resumed the task of applying ointment on her stomach.

For some reason, his quick acceptance, the total indifference to the fact that she was prepared to shut down again, brought a jolt of irritation.

"She used to bring her johns home," Abby burst out. "There, is that a big enough secret for you? My prostitute mother brought her johns home."

His hand froze. "That's terrible."

"Yeah," she agreed dully. "And when I was seven, she got tangled up with this one man. He was Mexican, used to be some big-shot gang member but then he got into dealing. He liked little girls."

"Fuck," Kane murmured.

"One night, he was over and my mom left to pick something up at the store. It was just me and him, in the shitty one-bedroom apartment my mom and I lived in. She was gone for an hour." Abby abruptly quit talking. She couldn't do this. Twenty years had passed, and the pain was still so damn raw.

But Kane wouldn't let her stop. "Did he touch you, Abby?"

She met his eyes. "Yes."

"Did he hurt you? Rape you?"

"Yes."

Anger flashed across his handsome face. His hand dropped from her stomach, the other one clutching the tube of ointment so tightly he squeezed nearly half of it on the bedspread. "What happened when your mother got home that night?"

"I told her what happened. She didn't believe me," Abby said simply. "A year later, she OD'd on some bad heroin the Mexican sold her and social services took me away."

Kane slowly released the tube and tossed it on the nightstand. "Please tell me you killed the son of a bitch."

"Jeremy did. I was fifteen when he adopted me. He made me see this shrink—a really nice woman—and she encouraged me to tell Jeremy everything that had happened to me. So I did." She laughed softly. "And about a week later, I read in the newspaper that the Mexican had been found in an alley in Compton with a bullet in his forehead."

The satisfaction gleaming in Kane's eyes brought a smile to her face. Men and their protective instincts, always ready to save the damsel in distress.

"So the Mexican, that was Ted?" Kane asked cautiously.

Of course. He just *had* to remember the name she'd cried out during that nightmare. She supposed she could lie and say yes, but the thought of lying to this man brought a spark of guilt. "No," she said quietly. "Ted wasn't the Mexican."

A strangled breath flew out of his mouth. "It happened again?"

"Yes." Without elaborating, she reached for her shirt and slipped it on, officially putting an end to this heart-to-heart. Jeez, what was wrong with her? This sharing session with Kane was completely out of character. She'd extended her olive branch, though. What she'd given him tonight would have to be enough.

"I'm tired," she announced. "I think I'll turn in now."

Looking reluctant, he got up. "All right. Let me get something to clean up the mess." He walked into the bathroom and came out with a wad of toiler paper in his hand. She watched as he wiped the ointment off the bedspread, his broad shoulders hunched as he bent down to handle the task.

He really was a big man. More than six feet, easily.

She wondered why she wasn't afraid of him.

"Okay, I think that's the best I can do at the moment," Kane said briskly. "I'll ask Lloyd to change the bedding in the morning."

"Thank you."

"Sleep well, Abby." He looked at her briefly, indecision flashing across his face, and then he shrugged and headed for the door.

She watched him go, a tad confused about what had just happened.

Sex is about trust, he'd said. *You have to open yourself up.*

Alarm skittered up her spine. Was that what had happened right now? By opening up to him, had she taken some weird, scary step toward sex?

No. That was ridiculous. This strange encounter had been about showing him that he *could* trust her. But she wasn't going to sleep with Kane. She didn't know a thing about him. She didn't *want* to know him either. All she wanted to do was rescue Lucia and the others, and once those girls were out of Blanco's evil clutches, Abby would say good-bye to Kane Woodland and go back to what she did best—ridding the world of vermin.

And she would do it alone. The way she always did.

"Marriage certificate," Morgan announced the morning after Isabel's arrival, dropping a yellow manila folder on the kitchen counter in front of her.

She set aside the coffee Lloyd had prepared and looked up at Morgan's pleased face. "That was fast."

"Holden's good at his job," he replied.

He rounded the counter and sat on the stool next to hers, his blue eyes serious. "Look . . . Isabel . . . I need to speak to you about Trevor."

The topic didn't come as a surprise. She'd been waiting for Morgan to bring it up. From the moment she'd laid eyes on Trevor Callaghan, unease had spread through her.

Sure, Callaghan was unbelievably attractive, with that dark, scruffy hair and those intense brown eyes. The stubble dotting his defined jaw gave him a lethal air, and the sensual curve of his mouth was pretty damn hot. And sure, when Morgan announced that she and Trevor would be posing as husband and wife—as *lovers*—she may have been a little intrigued, maybe even turned on.

But Trevor Callaghan had self-destruction written all over his hard face. The man was a walking liability.

"He's had a tough year," Morgan began, sounding uncomfortable. "He, well, he lost his fiancée about eleven months ago. She was killed in an attempted burglary. Trevor was out of the country at the time, and I think he blames himself for not being home to protect Gina."

"That's rough," Isabel said sympathetically.

"Yeah, it is. He didn't handle Gina's death very well, I'm afraid. Started drinking, refused to leave his condo. Eventually I had to take him off rotation. I couldn't let him work in his condition."

"Should he really be back in action now?"

Morgan stiffened. "I wouldn't have told Kane to contact Trev if I didn't think he could do this job. If anything, I think it will be good for him. He needs a reason to live again, and this rescue might be just the thing to snap him out of his funk."

"He's got a death wish," Isabel said flatly.

Morgan looked alarmed. "No, I don't think it's that bad."

"It is. Yesterday I tried to go over security precautions with him and he totally brushed me off. He said we'd wing it." Her voice dripped with disbelief. "The lives of thirteen young girls are in our hands and he wants to wing it?"

Morgan sighed. "I'll talk to him."

"Your man wants to die," Isabel announced, blunt as always. "And if you don't talk some sense into him, he's going to compromise this entire operation."

Morgan slid off the stool, his features hardening. "I'll talk to him."

"Okay," she said, unenthusiastically.

With a nod, he marched out of the kitchen, leaving Isabel alone with her thoughts.

She knew Abby trusted Morgan—so did Noelle, seeing as she'd gone to him for help—but Isabel wasn't so sure about the man. Supposedly he was good at his job. Whatever the mission, he was rumored to be deadly but professional, and according to Noelle, when it came to rescues, Morgan and his men almost always managed to bring their target home alive. Apparently several government agencies employed Morgan's services more often than they'd admit, most likely because a civilian unit consisting of soldiers for hire could gain access to plenty of places and people that would otherwise be impossible to penetrate using proper government channels. Morgan's men were some of the world's top mercenaries, and they were obviously doing well, judging by the size of this compound.

Still, she'd never worked with Morgan before, and so far she wasn't too impressed. Mostly because she had a feeling that Trevor Callaghan could very well get her killed.

Picking up her mug, Isabel left the kitchen in search of Abby. In the hallway, she ran into Luke Dubois, the dark-haired Cajun who totally wanted to get in her pants. His trusty dog was at his side, letting out a whine when he spotted Isabel.

"Hey there, sharpshooter," Luke drawled, his eyes lighting up. "You lost?"

"Just trying to find Abby," she answered, resisting a grin as she bent down to pat the dog.

The man really was a charmer. Too bad she was so over that type. His confidence was sexy, sure, but confidence typically went hand in hand with arrogance, and she could see that in him too. Oh, he was definitely Mr. Cocky, a man who believed all he had to do was snap his fingers and a woman would rip off her clothes and hop into bed with him. It probably worked most of the time.

"She's upstairs," he said helpfully. "I heard her laying into Kane just now."

"They're arguing?"

"Sounds like it." Luke raked one hand through his hair. "Why don't you go up and play peacemaker? And when you're done, you can meet me in the courtyard."

She couldn't help but laugh. "And why would I do that?"

"To show off those shooting skills of yours, darlin'. D and I are going to do some target practice."

She was tempted to say no, but it did sound kind of fun. She hadn't gotten to the shooting range in a few months, having little opportunity while stuck in Paris following a man who liked trashy strippers. Fortunately, Noelle had taken over that assignment in order for Isabel to come here. She had no clue why Noelle simply hadn't helped Abby herself, but she suspected it had something to do with her boss's loathing of Jim Morgan. Noelle might trust the man, but it was evident she didn't like him.

"So what do you say?" Luke pressed, flashing another grin.

"What the hell?" she said, relenting. "I'll be down in ten."

They parted ways and Isabel climbed the enormous staircase to the second floor. Angry voices immediately greeted her on the landing. Huh. So Luke had been right.

When she reached Abby's door, she found the redhead facing off with Kane, who stood in front of her with his arms tightly crossed over his massive chest.

"Argue all you want," he grumbled. "But you're sidelined, sweetheart. Tough fucking luck."

"*Don't* call me sweetheart," Abby snapped, her blue eyes sizzling with anger. "This is *my* rescue. I asked for your help, damn it, not for you to completely take it over and—"

"What's going on?" Isabel interrupted quietly.

Abby's anger became relief when she laid eyes on Isabel. "Thank God you're here. I need you to tell him he's making a big mistake."

She entered the room, warily glancing from Abby to Kane. "Seriously, what's up?"

"*He*"—Abby hooked her thumb at Kane—"has decided to sideline me for the rescue."

Kane shot Isabel a help-me-out-here look. "Because

she isn't up to it. She's got four bruised ribs and a broken wrist. She's a liability."

It was the same word she'd used to describe Trevor, and Isabel knew Kane's point was as valid as hers. She examined Abby's rainbow-colored face, then glanced down at the Ace bandage covering the redhead's wrist.

Abby noticed where Isabel's gaze landed and made a frustrated sound. "I can breathe through the pain," she insisted, sounding surprisingly desperate.

Isabel faltered. It was so rare, seeing Abby drop that cold, aloof facade of hers. But as hard as it was to say it, Isabel had to agree with Kane. "You're hurt, Abs. What if you tangle with a guard and he hits you in the ribs? Or yanks on your wrist?" Isabel sighed. "You'd pass out like a light. We can't risk that."

Disbelief radiated from Abby's features. "I have to be there when you rescue the girls. I have to, Izzy."

A sigh lodged in her chest. She exchanged a look with Kane, whose green eyes told her exactly what he thought. "Then you can stay in the chopper," Isabel decided. "That way you'll be there when we bring the girls out."

Abby swore loudly. "This is ridiculous. You know my skills should be put to better use than sitting around in a helicopter." She stalked toward the door. "I'm going to talk to Jim about this. I'm sure he'll agree with me."

As Abby stormed out of the room, Isabel turned to Kane with a rueful smile. "She can be a handful. A really stubborn handful."

He let out a heavy breath. "Do you think I'm being unfair?"

"No. We both know she's not in any physical condition to be part of an extraction team. Abby knows it too. It'll just take her a while to admit it."

Kane laughed. "You have too much faith in her. I don't think she's capable of admitting she's wrong."

The note of tenderness in his gruff voice came as a bit of a surprise. Isabel looked at him with sharp eyes. "You like her," she said slowly.

"What? No." He seemed embarrassed. "I do respect her, though."

"And you also like her." A smile filled her face. "That's good. Abby needs someone like you in her life."

"I'm not in her life," he objected, sounding uncomfortable. "A set of circumstances may have thrown us together, but that doesn't mean we're going to become best friends."

"How about lovers?" She couldn't help teasing him.

His discomfort deepened. "Shouldn't you be going over details with Trev? You know, perfecting your cover stories or something?"

With a grin, Isabel headed for the doorway. "Message received. I'll stop prying into your business. If you need me, I'll be with Luke doing some target practice."

She left Kane in Abby's room, wondering if he would go after Abby and try to talk some sense into her. Probably. It didn't take a genius to figure out he had a thing for Abby. He might not want to admit it, but Isabel noticed the way his face softened when he tried to convince Abby she was too hurt to go out in the field. He seemed to genuinely care, and Isabel was touched by that.

It was very difficult caring for someone like Abby Sinclair. Hell, it had taken years for Isabel to form this tentative friendship, and even now Abby refused to fully open herself up. She shied away from affection. From any sort of human contact.

Isabel found it incredibly sad, but she also understood why the other woman acted the way she did. Life had thrown a lot of heartache at Abby, much more than Isabel had ever experienced. But Isabel suspected the damage that had been inflicted on her friend wasn't irreparable. Abby might be broken, but she could be fixed.

Chapter 10

It was almost midnight when Abby gave up on sleep and slid out of bed. Shadows danced in the bedroom, and a sultry breeze was drifting in from the open window. She'd hoped the humid Mexican air might lull her to sleep, but it had only succeeded in making her hot and uncomfortable. Scratch that—Kane was the reason she was hot and uncomfortable.

He was also the reason she was pissed off.

She couldn't believe he was sidelining her on a rescue that had been *her* idea. And Morgan had actually backed him up! A liability, her ass. She'd pulled off successful assignments in worse condition than she was in now. But there was no budging Morgan or Kane. The two men were as stubborn as mules. They refused to let her be part of the extraction team and there wasn't a damn thing she could do about it.

Sighing, she walked on bare feet toward the door. Her thin tank top and little cotton shorts stuck to her body. All that tossing and turning had given her a workout. A glass of milk might help her fall asleep, and if that failed, a shot of whiskey might do the trick.

The kitchen was dark, so when she heard Kane's voice she nearly fell over.

"Can't sleep?"

She let her eyes adjust to the darkness, frowning when she saw him on one of the stools by the counter. He had a bottle of bourbon in front of him, along with a half-finished glass.

"I just needed something to drink," she responded coldly, then walked over to the fridge.

She poured herself a cup of milk, sipping slowly, silently.

"Listen," he said in a rough voice, "I know you're pissed at me, but we both know I'm making the right call. You're in no shape to be part of the rescue."

"According to you."

"And Morgan. And Isabel, who happens to know you well." He slid off the stool.

Her heart did an involuntary jump. He was bare-chested, and the muscles of his abdomen rippled as he moved toward her. He wore gray sweatpants that hung low on his trim hips, drawing her gaze to the line of hair tapering down to his waistband.

"You can be angry," he continued, "but at least have the guts to admit I'm right."

"I won't admit to something I disagree with." The haughty pitch to her voice made her want to cringe. Jeez, she sounded like a spoiled teenager.

He must have agreed, because he offered a dry smile. "You're too damn stubborn—you know that?"

"Whatever you say."

He came up beside her and leaned against the sink. Their bare arms were inches from touching. Abby breathed deeply, only to inhale the spicy, masculine scent that Kane radiated. Her pulse accelerated, each loud thump of her heart bringing little sparks of irritation. For God's sake, what was happening to her? She didn't like it, whatever it was. Kane had been right earlier, when he'd accused her of needing to stay in control. She liked control. She *needed* control. It was the only reason she'd stayed alive all these years.

So why did the impenetrable shield she'd constructed around herself years ago seem to drop whenever Kane was around?

"Look, I get it. You're mad." His voice grew soft. "And I know you probably don't like sitting around while everyone else is getting all the action. It happened to me when Morgan forced a vacation down my throat a few months ago. The team did an extraction in Europe, and I was lying in a hotel room, pissed off and strategizing missions in my head."

"Poor Kane," she muttered.

He sighed. "Quit being a brat." Before she could blink, he'd swiped her glass from her hands and placed it in the sink. "A glass of milk isn't gonna put you to bed. Come on, follow me."

"No way—"

His hand was on her arm before she could object further. He pretty much dragged her out of the kitchen, leading her down the dark hallway toward the back of the house. Abby shrugged his arm off as they walked, but she kept following, now intrigued by his sudden burst of energy.

They reached a wide doorway. Kane stepped inside and flicked on the light, revealing an enormous space that housed both workout equipment and a small gymnasium. The gym featured a basketball hoop and a heap of blue mats piled against the wall. He strode toward the stack, grabbed a couple of mats, and laid them on the floor.

"Know what always puts me to sleep?" he said. "Physical activity. Gets you nice and tired."

She shot him a pointed look. "I'm not having sex with you."

"I was referring to working out, Abby. You sure do have a one-track mind." He grinned, his straight white teeth glimmering in the fluorescent lighting. There was something very predatory about that smile. Predatory and sexy as hell.

She forced herself to look away. "I'm not in the mood to lift weights."

"Who said anything about weights?"

His green eyes glinted devilishly as he walked over and grabbed hold of her arm again. She squeaked when he dragged her toward the mats he'd set up, his big, hard body inches from hers. "Hit me," he said in a lazy voice.

Her eyebrows soared north. "Pardon me?"

"Come on, Abby. Hit me. You know you want to. Expend some energy." He shot her an inviting smile. "I make a good sparring partner."

She started to laugh. "You want to *spar*? Hit me? What is this, *Fight Club*?"

"Trust me, the exercise will knock you right out." He wiggled his eyebrows. "That is, if I don't knock you out first."

"This is ridiculous."

"I'll avoid your wrist and ribs if you stay away from my face." He grinned again. "I can't have you marring my pretty features. I know you're capable of inflicting a lot of damage."

Warmth trickled through her at the confidence he seemed to possess in her skills. She appreciated that he didn't treat her like a fragile female who couldn't hold her own against a big man like him, but still, that didn't mean she was going to indulge him.

"Ridiculous," she said again. "I'm not sparring with—"

He came at her without warning, his fist slicing toward her face.

Her arm instinctively shot up to deflect the blow.

"Seriously, Kane—"

Another attack, this time a lightning kick that swept her legs from under her and had her falling onto the mat.

"What the *hell* is the matter with you?"

She was torn between cursing and laughing, but both impulses died as he pounced again. This time she was prepared for it. Exploding into action, she scissored her legs and locked his ankles together, bringing him down. He grunted as he fell, then laughed and shot up to his feet like an agile gymnast. She bounded up off her butt just as he retaliated with a string of impressive karate moves that left her gasping for air. She blocked each one, avoiding the use of her injured wrist, and surprised him with a roundhouse kick to his gut that made him groan.

He recovered quickly and attacked again, nearly landing a blow to her abdomen, which she stopped by latching onto his wrist and twisting.

"You're good," he said breathlessly.

"I know."

She twisted harder, but he got out of the hold, his foot connecting with her shin as he moved out of her reach.

She pounced on him with a kickboxing move she'd

perfected over the years. He caught her foot in midair and sent her stumbling backward.

"You're not so bad yourself," she admitted, sucking in oxygen.

"I know," he replied, mimicking her.

Their breath came out heavy, filling the room and heating the air around them. Adrenaline sizzled through her veins as she fought him off. God, this felt liberating. Kane was a formidable opponent, as well trained as she was, and like he'd promised, he stayed away from her wrist, as well as her bruised ribs, which were beginning to ache. But still she matched him move for move, brought him down again and jumped up, only to have him kick at her ankles and bring her down too.

Sharp gusts of air barreled out of her chest. Sweat coated her skin. It felt good, despite the pain in her ribs. *She* felt good. Alive. How had he known this was exactly what she needed?

"You're slacking," Kane taunted, wiping the sweat from his brow before charging forward again.

"Like hell I am." She landed an uppercut to his chin using her uninjured hand and, without letting him recover, executed a nifty little jujitsu move to send him crumpling to the ground.

He tried to roll away but she sank down and pinned him with her knees, her hand poised in a karate chop against his throat.

Kane released a panting chuckle. "Very nice."

Her heart nearly pounded straight through her rib cage from the strenuous workout. She sucked in a few deep breaths, ignoring the streak of pain that shot through her chest. As she allowed her pulse to slow and the adrenaline flooding her veins to dissipate, Abby suddenly became very aware that she was still straddling Kane. Then she became very aware of the hard bulge pressed against her core.

She quickly slid off him. "Control yourself," she grumbled, rolling onto her back. She was out of breath again, but this time for an entirely different reason.

"You and your control," he grumbled back, his voice raspy from their sparring session. "I'm really getting sick of it."

From the corner of her eye, she saw him shift over. She turned her head and met his gaze. Heat scorched her cheeks when she saw the glint of dark desire in his green eyes.

He stretched out on his side, inches from her. Without breaking eye contact, he rested one warm hand on her hip and stroked. She shivered, tried to slide away, but his hand curled over her waist and kept her in place.

"How long are you going to shut yourself off from the world?" he murmured, trailing his fingers up her hip toward the underside of her breast.

She swallowed. His fingers had nearly reached her breast when she finally found the courage to swat his hand away. She stumbled to her feet. "Thanks for the workout. I think I'll have no trouble falling aslee—"

He was on his feet before she could finish the sentence, both of his hands now tightening over her hips and pulling her toward him.

In a matter of seconds Abby's entire mouth went dry. Gulping down the lump of cotton in her throat was hard, but not as hard as stopping her body from sizzling the second it came into contact with Kane's. She could feel his rock-hard erection against her stomach and her brain screamed "betrayal" as the spot between her thighs pooled with moisture.

She hated this. Hated feeling so out of control. Not having any power over her hormones or the thoughts that kept floating into her head.

"You lied to me the other day," he said, pinning her down with a forceful stare. "You said you didn't feel anything when you were on your knees in front of me."

"I didn't," she whispered.

"You did," he corrected. "And I think you feel something now." He didn't loosen his grip on her waist, only strengthened it, and the warmth of his hands seared through her flimsy boxer shorts. "Your skin is hot to the touch, Abby. And I can see your pulse throbbing in your throat. You're turned on."

"I'm . . . not." The words awkwardly stumbled out of her mouth.

He took a long breath. "Control issues again."

"I *don't* have control issues."

He lifted one hand and placed it on her chin. Tipped it up so she had no choice but to look at him. "It makes you feel powerless, doesn't it? You want me, you can't fight it, and it makes you crazy."

The cotton returned to her mouth. She swallowed it down. "Maybe I just don't treat sex as casually as you do."

"Oh no, it's all about control." He dipped his head so that his breath tickled the bridge of her nose.

She didn't know where he was going with this, and she wasn't sure she wanted to. "Kane . . ."

"Control can be a very good thing to have, but sometimes you need to let go. Why don't we try to see if you can let go, Abby?"

A tremor of fear scurried through her. "I . . ."

"Please." His voice became rough. "Just close your eyes and let me make you feel good. Who will it hurt?"

Me! she wanted to shout.

"I won't hurt you," he said quietly. "For once in your life, lower your guard and let yourself feel something, damn it."

Before she could register what was happening, his mouth covered hers in a kiss.

Abby's body turned to jelly. Knees buckled. Heart pounded. Kane's mouth was hot and firm and terrifying.

He rubbed his lips over hers, once, twice, soft little brushes that sent shock waves sizzling through her nerve endings. The heat of his lips slithered into her mouth and down her chest, warming her breasts, hardening her nipples, settling into a pool of liquid between her thighs.

He deepened the kiss and she nearly burst into flames. His tongue coaxed her lips open. She tried to clamp her lips together, restrict his access, but her mouth wasn't responding to the furious orders of her brain. Kane's tongue slid inside with one sensual stroke. Her heart thudded. Her mind screamed for her to pull away, but she couldn't. She was helpless to stop this, and she felt herself drowning in his mouth, in his kiss, that greedy and wild and all-consuming kiss.

He caressed the small of her back, then moved lower to cup her bottom. His touch was electric. It burned, teased, drawing out her pleasure as his tongue explored her mouth. The attraction she felt for him transcended common sense. She felt dizzy. Powerless.

It was like nothing she'd ever experienced in her entire life.

And it scared the shit out of her.

Breathing hard, Abby wrenched her mouth away

from his and stumbled backward. "Why did you do that?" she stammered.

"Because I wanted to." He studied her face. "You liked it."

She wanted to utter an impassioned denial but the words refused to come out.

He went on, his voice hoarse. "I could feel your heart pounding against my chest. I could feel you trembling. I could taste your need. Let me kiss you again, Abby."

Yes.

"No," she blurted out. No, she couldn't let that happen again. Couldn't lose herself in that strange rush of pleasure again.

She thought he would push the issue, force another terrifying kiss on her, but to her surprise he didn't. He just exhaled a resigned breath, then bent down to gather up the mats before carrying them across the gym and placing them on top of the stack. Abby stared at him in bewilderment. Maybe he hadn't liked the kiss enough for a repeat performance. The thought brought a flicker of relief and a weird jolt of irritation.

As he walked back to her, a question she hadn't planned on asking—one she hadn't even considered before—flew out of her mouth. "Why don't you have a girlfriend?"

His eyes immediately became shuttered. "Relationships don't interest me," he said in a light tone.

Suspicion flooded her gut. "Why not?"

"Because they don't." He headed for the door. "Come on, let's go upstairs. I'm beat after that workout."

"No way." She marched after him, crossing her arms over her chest. "You've been trying to pry into my psyche since the day we met. And I—" She took a breath. "I told you about my mother, about the day I—" She forced aside the memory. "Don't I deserve some answers of my own?"

He didn't respond.

"You expect me to open up to you, yet you're not willing to return the favor."

"So we're back to that, exchanging favors?" Bitterness hardened his face. "What, you'll go to bed with me if I share my deep, dark secrets?"

Abby tightened her jaw. "Forget it," she muttered. "I don't want to know your secrets."

"You sure about that?"

"Yep." She gave him a sugary smile. "And I don't want to kiss you again either."

Without another word, she walked out of the gym.

It was a scorching-hot morning, the humidity suspended in the air like a thick fog. Abby drank her coffee out on the terrace, warily glancing over at Luke, who was devouring the plate of bacon and eggs Lloyd had prepared for him. With Isabel and Trevor in the living room coordinating cover stories, Ethan in town picking up some documents they'd need, and Kane, D, and Morgan off doing God knows what, Abby was alone with Luke, who'd popped a pair of iPod earphones into his ears and was bobbing his head as he ate.

Why weren't any of them sitting down to plan the extraction? She'd given Kane the entire layout of Blanco's compound yesterday and he hadn't done a damn thing with it. Was she the only one who actually cared about the well-being of those girls?

She looked at Luke's dark head, moving to the beat of his music, and let out an annoyed breath. "Seriously," she said loudly. "Don't you have a rescue to plan?"

He pulled out his earphones and shot her a quizzical look. "Huh?"

"I said, don't you have a rescue to plan?"

Luke grinned, his straight white teeth gleaming in the sunshine. "Izzy said you were impatient. Guess she was right."

Izzy? He was now on nickname basis with a woman he'd met only yesterday? The thought brought a flash of envy to her belly. How did Isabel do it, charm every man she met? Abby could charm too—when she was pretending to be someone else. But as herself, she was unable to form the kind of connections Isabel did.

"We can't do anything until Trev and Iz score an invite to the auction," Luke added, his voice oddly gentle. "We have no idea where the girls are going to be when it all goes down. We need our eyes on the inside giving us the proper details before we figure out the best way to extract."

His words made sense, but did nothing to alleviate her impatience.

"Don't worry. The second we finalize anything, you'll know," Luke assured her.

She offered a cool look. "Good."

Spearing some scrambled eggs onto his fork, he popped them in his mouth, chewed slowly, then said, "So, where'd you grow up?"

An alarm went off inside her. "Why do you want to know?"

He stared at her for a moment as if she'd grown horns. "Because that's what people do, ask each other things. *Where're you from, do you like your job, what's your family like . . .*" He trailed off, wrinkling his forehead. "Haven't you ever had a conversation with another person?"

Embarrassment crept through her. He was right. That *was* what people did. Normal people, anyway.

"California," she said reluctantly.

He looked pleased that she'd answered. "LA?"

"Until I was eight. Then all over the state before I was adopted. My adoptive father lived in Bakersfield."

"Jeremy Thomas," Luke said with a nod. "Morgan told us about him."

"He did?"

"Yeah, but not much. Morgan said he was an ex-Ranger, made him sound like a legend or something."

"He was good at what he did," she admitted.

Luke hesitated for a moment. "How did he die?"

A lump of pain lodged in her throat. "Lung cancer. I always told him he needed to quit smoking, but he thought he was invincible."

"Everyone thinks they're invincible."

"Yeah, I guess that's true."

A short silence fell, interrupted by a loud vibrating noise. Luke reached into his pocket and pulled out a cell phone, frowning. "Not mine."

He leaned over to the chair next to his, which Kane had occupied before heading off with Morgan. "Shit, Kane left his phone here," he said, reaching down and lifting a sleek Motorola flip phone from the chair. A glance at the screen deepened Luke's frown. Slowly, he opened the phone. "Kane's phone," he said curtly. A pause, then his frown twisted into a grimace. "Devlin."

Abby felt the color draining from her face. Devlin? Why the hell was Devlin calling Kane's phone? And why didn't Luke seem the least bit surprised?

"Kane already told you, there's no woman here."

Luke's voice had changed from careless and teasing to utterly frosty. "You've been misinformed."

Despite the sudden trembling of her body, Abby found herself reaching out her hand. "Let me talk to him," she said.

Luke shot her a *no way* look. "Stop calling us, Devlin. It's getting fucking annoying."

Abby raised her voice. "Let. Me. Talk to him."

"What? No," Luke said into the receiver. "That was just—"

She was on her feet and snatching the cell from Luke's hand before he could blink. Pressing the phone to her ear, she squared her shoulders and said, "What do you want, Devlin?"

The delight in his voice was unmistakable. "I knew they were hiding you away, luv. Tell me, how's my beautiful Erica doing? Or should I call you *Abby*?"

Shit. How had he found out her real name?

"What do you want?" she repeated.

"I just wanted to hear your lovely voice." He paused. "And I also had a question for you."

"Yeah, what's that?" she said sullenly.

"Did it hurt when Leon Garcia sodomized your seven-year-old virgin ass?"

All the air swept out of her lungs in one fast rush. Horror slammed into her, a tidal wave that had her sagging against the table. As her legs shook like trees in a windstorm, she collapsed into the nearest chair. Stunned. God, how did he know about Garcia?

"You still there, luv?"

She clenched her teeth. "I'm still here."

"Then answer the question."

"I don't know what you're talking about."

Beside her, Luke's dark eyes were swimming with concern. He tried to take the phone from her, but she swatted his hand away.

"See, I had the pleasure of paying a visit to an old friend of yours yesterday," Devlin said cheerfully. "Dr. Silverton—does the name ring a bell?"

Abby worked hard to keep her nausea at bay. "If you hurt her, I'll—"

"Don't you worry your pretty little head," he interrupted. "The doctor is safe and sound. I did, however, liberate some very interesting reading material from her office."

Her files. Dear God, he had her files.

"Now, this is what intrigues me. I listened to the first tape last night, luv. I heard all about Garcia and how he fucked you. Lord, you remembered every last detail, didn't you, Abby?"

Her fingers shook wildly against the phone.

"But you left out so many curious things," he went on. "Like how it felt. Why you didn't fight back."

"How do you think it felt?" she spat out, the vehemence in her tone making Luke jump.

Jumping to his feet, Luke stormed off the terrace, no doubt to find the cavalry. She barely noticed his departure. She was too focused on Devlin's merciless voice, the sheer pleasure he seemed to derive from this conversation.

"And you couldn't fight back, could you, luv? You were an innocent little girl, and he was a big bad rapist."

"What do you *want*?" she hissed out, determined not to let his words affect her. That part of her life was over. Buried. She refused to let him hurt her with the past.

"You. I want you."

"You'll never get me." She got great satisfaction saying the words. "You'll never find me."

"Sure I will." He suddenly sounded enraged. "And I will punish you for what you did to me."

"How's the eye?" she asked innocently.

"You fucking *bitch*." He was breathing heavily now. "Do you truly think I'm going to let you get away with that? I'm already tracking down Morgan's whereabouts as we speak. It's only a matter of time before I find him."

"Then I'll leave," she said, a laugh slipping out. "I'll leave here and disappear, and you won't find me."

"I *will* find you." His breathing steadied and when he spoke again, he sounded calm. "And until I do, I'm going to keep calling. I'm so very curious about your life, luv. Did all the foster fathers rape you the way Garcia did? Did Jeremy Thomas?"

She ignored that. "Call all you want. I won't pick up."

"But you will," he corrected. "Because if you don't, I'm going to pay another visit to Dr. Silverton. And this time I won't break into an empty office. I'll make sure the doctor is in."

Bile coated her throat. "Don't you touch her, Devlin."

"That all depends on you. You'll pick up the phone when I call again, won't you, Abby?"

Gulping down a wave of sickness, she thought of Amanda Silverton's kind gray eyes, the way she'd sat quietly and let Abby talk, without once pushing her to reveal more than she wanted. If anything happened to Dr. Silverton, she wouldn't be able to live with herself.

"What was that? I didn't quite catch what you said."

"Yes," she choked out. "I'll pick up."

"Wonderful. Let me tell you, I can't wait to delve

deeper into your past. I'm about to listen to the next session on the tape. Will it feature Garcia, or maybe Ted Hartford, the man who used to break your fingers when you refused to—"

The phone was ripped out of her hand. She blinked in surprise, shocked to see Kane looming over her, his green eyes flashing with unrestrained fury. "What the *hell* are you doing?"

It took her a couple of seconds to snap out of the panicked trance Devlin had sent her into. "W-what?"

"Why did you take the call?" he fumed. "William Devlin is a sick sociopath who gets off on tormenting others! How could you sit there and listen to his filth?"

She didn't answer.

Kane softened his tone. Kneeling at her feet, he looked up to meet her eyes. "What did he say to you? Are you all right?"

"I'm fine," she said. "And he didn't say anything I didn't already know."

"He's after revenge," Kane said darkly.

She stood up, her legs a tad rubbery. "Yep."

Kane eyed her in suspicion. "Anything else?"

"No," she lied. She headed toward the sliding door, then glanced over her shoulder. "If he calls again, let me talk to him."

"Abby—"

"Just let me talk to him."

"Why, for fuck's sake?"

She let out a weary breath. "Because Devlin and I have unfinished business."

Chapter 11

Trevor had barely said two words to her since they'd landed at Aeropuerto Internacional El Dorado, Bogotá's major airport. Hadn't helped carry her bags either. Before they'd left Mexico, Morgan assured her he'd spoken with Trevor and everything was fine, that Trevor understood exactly what was required of him for this gig.

Isabel wasn't as confident about that. She'd run into men like Trevor Callaghan before, men who'd lost everything they cared about, men who had nothing left to live for. And as much as she would've liked to view him as her partner in crime, she knew she was all alone in this mission. She couldn't trust Callaghan to have her back, which meant she needed to work extra hard to stay alive.

Trevor remained quiet as they walked out of the airport terminal and into the late-afternoon sunshine. He didn't speak as they got in line at the taxi stand, as they hopped a cab that took them to Morgan's uptown safe house. Still didn't utter a word even when he unlocked the door and led her into the modestly furnished living room.

Isabel gritted her teeth. Jeez. How much longer was

she supposed to put up with this crap? Yesterday he'd been more obliging, actually sitting down with her so they could learn everything they needed to know about each other's alternate personas. This morning, though, he'd turned into a mute. When Isabel had said good-bye to Abby back at Morgan's compound, the woman had reassured her that Callaghan was a pro, but Isabel wasn't so sure. He may have been a pro in his former life, but right now, with his disheveled hair and empty eyes, she couldn't see how he'd ever be an asset.

"Well." She cleared her throat. "When are you going to call Esposito?"

Trevor blinked as if emerging from some kind of hypnotic state. "What?" he said roughly.

"Esposito," she repeated, fighting back annoyance. "We need to set up a meeting with him, which means you need to call him."

"I have to make a few preparations first."

That was it. Without even looking her way, he slung the black duffel he'd carried on the plane over his shoulder and strode toward the narrow hallway that probably led to the bedrooms.

What the hell?

Isabel took a few deep breaths to steady the angry beating of her heart. Fine. If he wanted to act like a total asshole, let him. She might have to pretend to be married to the man, but that didn't mean she had to like him.

She headed for the corridor Trevor had disappeared into. She thought she heard the whir of an electric razor coming from behind one of the three doors in the hall. Hallelujah. She wondered how long it had been since Trevor had picked up a razor. Maybe he wasn't a total lost cause, if he'd decided to shave.

Tentatively pushing open one of the doors, she peeked into what looked like an empty bedroom and then headed inside. She set her bags down on the twin bed. Trevor was evidently getting into character. Time for her to transform too.

Transform. The story of her life, she thought ruefully as she unzipped one of her bags. She pulled out the two boxes of hair dye Ethan had picked up from the drugstore in Tijuana and walked into the tiny bathroom across from the bed.

She stripped off her clothes and then, in her bra and panties, stepped in front of the mirror and examined her reflection. Becoming Paloma would be hard work, but she'd played the part enough times that she could do the transformation in her sleep.

First came the dye, which she applied to her hair. While she waited for the chemicals to do their thing, she used the weaker dye on her eyebrows, then reached for a smaller box, read the label, and wrinkled her nose. Damn. She hated the pubic hair part. The memory of the last time slid into her head and she winced as she remembered the burning sensation. Oh, and the itching . . .

She tossed the box back into her bag. Screw it. She would just wax it all off. Not that anyone would get to see her handiwork. Chances were, she and Trevor wouldn't need to pay a visit to Blanco's estate, and unless Callaghan suddenly decided he'd fallen madly in love with her and proceeded to strip her naked, he wouldn't be getting a peek either.

The thought made her grin.

She sat on the closed toilet seat, waiting for the dye. Twenty minutes later, she was in the shower, washing the thick black goop off her scalp and watching as it swirled down the drain like sticky tar.

After she'd dried herself off and run a blow-dryer over her head, she proceeded to flat-iron her normally wavy tresses. And then it was time for the makeup.

By the time Isabel stepped out of the bedroom, more than an hour had passed, but she was pleased with her creation. Her hair, black and stick straight, cascaded down her back like a silk curtain. Thanks to the makeup, her skin was at least three shades darker, boasting of Paloma's Brazilian roots, and the dark green contacts she'd slipped into her eyes gave her an exotic air. She wore a short white sundress with a pair of white high-heeled sandals, adding at least four inches to her five-foot-six-inch frame. The entire look was so familiar she found herself falling right back into character, her normally easygoing gait becoming the hip-swaying sex walk Paloma had perfected.

Trevor was already in the living room when she walked in, and Isabel wasn't sure who gasped first, him or her.

The man she was looking at in no way resembled the man she'd boarded that plane with. His brown hair was now short and slicked back with gel, and his face was completely smooth, revealing a strong jaw and a cleft chin that his previous thick stubble had hidden. His right ear had a small diamond stud in it, his thick, corded neck was encircled by a silver chain, and the suit he wore . . . Isabel couldn't help but appreciate his tall, masculine body, covered in a tailored pin-striped number that hugged his muscular form.

She suddenly experienced a visceral jolt of arousal that left her speechless for a moment. Oh no, *not* a good idea. Just because Trevor Callaghan was a bona fide heartthrob when he cleaned himself up didn't mean she had to respond to it.

"You look . . . like Julian Martin, I guess," she said.

He shrugged. "I've pretended to be Julian for so long it's second nature to me."

"Me too." She found herself stammering. "I mean, being Paloma. Sometimes it feels like she's actually a real person."

"I know what you mean."

A silence descended over the room. Isabel swallowed to soothe her suddenly dry mouth. "Did you bring in a hairdresser when I was in the bathroom?" she asked with a hesitant smile.

"Nope, I'm my own hairdresser. I'm damn good at it too, not to brag or anything. If you ever need someone to cut your hair . . ."

To her extreme shock, he actually smiled. An honest-to-God smile, and boy, how it altered his face. He went from harsh and soulless to warm and inviting in a split second.

And then, to her disappointment, the smile faded as quickly as it had appeared, and Mr. Harsh and Soulless was back in full force.

"I'm going to call Esposito now." He moved toward the hallway. "Hopefully he'll be able to meet with us tonight."

Isabel stared after him, wondering if she'd imagined that smile. Maybe the contacts were just messing with her eyes. And maybe all the chemicals she'd rubbed on her scalp were creating these weird sensations of desire in her body.

Because she couldn't actually *want* Trevor Callaghan.

No, of course she didn't.

She didn't have a thing for dead men walking, after all.

Trevor could barely draw a breath as he barreled into the bedroom and shut the door behind him. Something had happened to him out there in the living room. He'd seen Isabel Roma's curvy body covered in that sexy dress, gazed into her smoky emerald gaze, and his body . . . shit, his body had actually *responded*.

For a moment, a barrage of forbidden images had flooded his mind. Images of him between Isabel's long, silky legs. Kissing her lush lips. Palming those firm breasts, bringing a nipple into his mouth and sucking on it until she—

No.

He squeezed his hands into fists and banished every traitorous image from his head. His cock, which had swelled at that first sight of Isabel's new look, now softened, retreating like a defeated soldier on the battlefield.

Gina . . . God, baby, I'm sorry.

He repeated the words over and over again in his head, disgusted and horrified with himself for betraying his fiancée's memory.

Yanking his cell phone from his duffel, he marched toward the window, focusing his gaze on the residential street two stories down. It took a few minutes to gather his composure. When a sense of calm finally filled his body, he scrolled through his contact list until he reached Felix Esposito's name. Last time he'd spoken to the guy, Esposito had taken an enforcer job for a drug runner in Bogotá. Hopefully he was still in town, but the private jet Trevor owned in Julian's name could easily take him and

Isabel to wherever Esposito was holed up. Though he hadn't used this cover in more than a year, Morgan made sure the jet continued to travel the world in order to keep Julian's passport nicely stamped. The jet now waited in a private airfield outside the city, where the filthy rich parked their expensive Lears and Gulfstreams when they came to town.

To Trevor's surprise, Esposito answered on the first ring. He'd obviously kept Julian Martin's number in his phone, because he answered with an elated, "Hello, Mr. Julian."

"Felix, it's been a long time," he replied in the faint Boston accent belonging to Julian. He was supposed to be an East Coast native, but Julian's frequent travels, in the States and abroad, had slowly eroded the thick Boston inflection.

"Too long," Esposito agreed.

"I've been busy. Got myself good and married, in fact," he added with a chuckle.

"*Felicitaciones!* And who is the lucky señorita?"

"Find out for yourself. My bride and I would like to take you to dinner. Are you still living in Bogotá? We just flew in this afternoon."

"*Sí*, still here. Business is very good."

"Glad to hear it." He turned away from the window. "So, tonight? Eight o'clock?"

"I would be honored. We will meet at my favorite establishment. La Mexicana. It is in Perdoma. You know it?"

"No, but my wife and I will find our way there." Another chuckle. "Looking forward to seeing you again, Felix. Like you said, it's been too long."

Esposito, proving he was as sharp as Trevor remembered, said, "And will this be business, or pleasure, Mr. Julian?"

"A little bit of both, actually."

"Interesting. I am looking forward to it, then."

"As am I."

Trevor hung up the phone and tossed it on the bed. Perfect. Phase one was in motion. Meet Esposito, chat over enchiladas and that god-awful watery Aquila Light beer Esposito preferred. Isabel would charm the pants off the man, Trevor would bring up Samir Bahar's name, and hopefully Esposito would set up a meeting with Blanco's solicitor.

He left the bedroom, squaring his shoulders in resolve and breathing deeply in preparation for seeing Isabel again. She was sitting on the living room couch, flipping through a fashion magazine. She must have brought it with her, because no way would big, bad Morgan stock his safe house with fashion magazines. Camo pants and muscle shirts made up the extent of his wardrobe.

"It's on," Trevor said stiffly, avoiding her eyes.

"Esposito's meeting with us?"

He gave a brisk nod. "Yeah. Eight o'clock."

Before she could say anything more, he spun on his heel and stalked back to the hallway, releasing a hoarse breath. There, he'd done it. Had a conversation with the woman without once looking in her direction. Gina would be proud of him.

And Esposito will only be suspicious, a little voice taunted.

Trevor faltered. Fuck. The voice was right. No way could he avoid looking at Isabel tonight when they met with Felix. She was supposed to be his wife. His brand-new, smoking-hot Brazilian bride. Felix would instantly know something was up if Trevor didn't have his hands all over her curvy body tonight.

He drew in a steadying breath. Fine. He could do this. Pretend he wanted to jump Isabel's bones. He could touch her, and kiss the soft-looking flesh of her delicate neck. Maybe he'd even squeeze that firm ass of hers.

It didn't mean he'd like it.

Kane found Luke, D, and Ethan in the small clearing a few hundred yards from the main house, where the team liked to do target practice and sometimes went just to chill out. Luke and Ethan were sitting on a couple of plastic lawn chairs, an open cooler filled with beer bottles wedged between them. No sign of Luke's mutt, which meant Bear was probably prowling in the bushes searching for something to attack.

D stood a few feet away from the other two, a beer in his hand and a rifle slung over his shoulder. Kane was surprised to see him. D had stayed out of sight since the arrival of Isabel and Trevor, and even now that they'd left for Bogotá, he'd barely shown his face. Kane would've taken it personally, if not for the fact that D had always been an ill-tempered loner.

Besides, it was Luke he had a beef with at the moment.

"Why the hell did you let her talk to him?" he demanded as he neared the three men.

Luke rolled his eyes, then took a deep drag on his cigarette. "She grabbed the phone out of my hands. What did you want me to do, knock her unconscious?"

"You shouldn't have picked up in the first place."

"Well, I did. And Abby seemed to handle the conversation pretty well." Luke shrugged, blowing out a careless cloud of smoke. "Wasn't like she burst into tears or anything."

But she'd been crying on the inside. Kane knew without a doubt that Devlin had shaken her to the core. Whatever that bastard said to Abby, it had gotten to her. She'd gone up to her room to take a nap, and he hadn't seen her since. It grated a little, that she didn't seem inclined to confide in him.

Bugged him even more that he wanted her to. He didn't do heart-to-hearts. Didn't like those mushy, annoying moments women tried to force on him. *Tell me how you feel.* Fuck, he didn't want to talk about how he felt, and he usually didn't give a damn how the women in his bed felt either. As long as he rocked their world and put a blissful post-orgasmic smile on their faces, he was perfectly content to get dressed and walk out the door.

So why did he care how Abby was feeling right now?

"Devlin spoke to Abby?" Ethan piped up, looking curious.

It took Kane a moment to remember that Ethan had been running errands in town all morning. "Yeah, earlier."

"What did he say?"

"I have no idea. She wouldn't tell me." With a sigh, he gestured to the cooler. "Toss me one of those."

Luke reached in and a beer bottle sailed in Kane's direction a second later. He caught it easily, then dropped into an empty chair. They used to have a poker table out here, but it had been smashed to smithereens by Sullivan Port, their Australian team member who hated to lose. The thought of Sullivan brought a frown to Kane's lips. Morgan had the annoying habit of forcing unwanted vacations on his men, so there were always a few faces missing on most jobs, taken off the rotation to avoid burning out. But Sullivan had been gone for a couple of months now, which was unlike him.

"Anyone heard from Sully lately?" he asked.

"I spoke to him a couple of weeks ago," Luke answered. He grinned. "He's on his yacht in the Caribbean. Said he's fallen in love."

Kane snorted. Right. Sullivan fell in love every other day. So far, he hadn't felt inclined to actually *stay* with any of the supposed loves of his life. Maybe it was an Australian thing.

"Ethan's in love too," Luke added, the grin widening.

"I'm not in love with her," Ethan protested, his preppy-handsome face flushing. "Maggie's just a friend."

"Sure," Luke mocked. "Because I go to a shitty bar every night, sit in the same corner booth, and gawk at my *friends* all night."

The younger guy's face turned a darker shade of red. "I don't gawk. I only go there to talk to her."

Kane wrinkled his forehead. "Really?"

"Yeah."

"What do you talk about?"

Ethan shrugged. "You know, stuff. I tell her funny stories about my hometown. She tells me about herself, how she hates working for her father and how she's saving up money to go to college in the States. She's a really nice girl," he said, sounding defensive. "She wants to be a doctor."

The kid's speech had Kane and Luke going silent. Seriously? That's the kind of shit he talked to women about? Kane couldn't remember the last time he'd had a real conversation with a female. His chats with women consisted of sentences like "Do you like that, babe?" or

"Roll over, I want to screw you from behind." He couldn't recall ever asking a woman what she wanted to be when she grew up.

"Wow, a doctor," Kane finally said, still at a loss for words.

Ethan drained his beer bottle, then tossed it into the milk crate they used for empties. "What do you talk with Abby about? You've been spending a lot of time with her since we rescued her from the prison."

He grew distinctly uncomfortable. Fortunately, he was spared from answering when D angrily grumbled something under his breath.

Kane glanced over. "What was that?"

Joining the conversation for the first time, D strode over, his rifle swinging against his hip. "I said, I think it's time we sent her packing."

Kane bristled. "That's kind of harsh, don't you think?"

"No, I don't think." D scowled. "I don't like her, and I sure as hell don't trust her."

Kane smothered a groan. "We've already been through this. I told you why this rescue is important to me. That hasn't changed."

"And neither has Abby. Do you honestly think she's just going to sit on the sidelines while we do the extraction?"

"She might not like it, but she's agreed to sit it out," Kane said grudgingly.

"And you fucking believed that? She's not planning on sitting out, man. She'll do everything she can to be part of that rescue, and it's going to get us all killed."

The vehemence in D's voice startled everyone. D wasn't afraid to vocalize his objections, but he'd never done so with such passion. Kane narrowed his eyes, studying the other man, but D's obsidian gaze revealed nothing.

"What the hell do you have against her?" Kane asked in a low voice.

"Nothing," D muttered. "Nothing at all."

There was another long silence, broken by the awkward clearing of Luke's throat. "So, your girl wants to be a doctor," he said to Ethan, his voice unnaturally cheerful.

"Her name was Emily."

Abby stirred, her eyelids fluttering open to find Kane perched on the edge of her bed. She sat up abruptly, annoyance swirling inside her. She hadn't even heard him come in, which pissed her off, since she'd always prided herself on possessing extremely sharp instincts. She could normally sense danger from miles away, the back of her neck tingling the moment she registered a threat. She'd once snapped out of a deep sleep at the sound of footsteps on the deserted street outside her New Orleans hotel.

She sank her teeth into her bottom lip. How had he been able to stroll right into her bedroom without so much as alerting her? Was it because deep down she didn't believe he posed any danger to her?

The troubling thought reminded her of the way he'd stood up to D, and she had to wonder if maybe that was the reason for her lowered guard. Kane's voice had been so fierce when he'd vowed to rescue those girls. Could a man who cared so deeply about a dozen innocent strangers really be a threat to her?

"Why are you here?" she murmured, her eyes quickly adjusting to the darkness. "Who's Emily?"

"She was my girlfriend in high school," he said hoarsely.

Abby slid up so she was leaning against the headboard. She wasn't quite sure what was going on here, but Kane looked incredibly uncomfortable. His chest was bare again, his defined pecs heaving as he sucked in a deep breath. And his hair looked tousled as hell, as if he'd been repeatedly running his fingers through it.

"It's late," she said when he didn't continue speaking. "Maybe we should talk about this in the morning."

"No." He cleared his throat. "I need to tell you this now."

"Why?"

"I . . . I guess I figured I should talk to you. Ethan has this girl he talks to all the time, and he knows all this stuff about her—" He stopped abruptly, something that looked like embarrassment reddening his cheeks. "Fuck, forget it. I don't know why I came in here. Just go back to sleep."

Abby blinked in surprise. Was he actually blushing? She'd gotten so used to his self-assured manner, his take-charge attitude, that she had trouble adapting to this sudden change in his behavior.

With visible discomfort, Kane made a move to get up, but she placed her hand on his shoulder. The heat of his skin instantly seared her palm, making her pulse race. She quickly dropped her hand back in her lap. Damn it. Why had she touched him? Why was she trying to keep him here when the smart thing to do was let him walk away? Far, far away.

"So Emily was your girlfriend," she repeated, urging him to go on.

"High school sweetheart. We started dating when we

were juniors. I was the running back for the school football team, and she was—"

"A cheerleader," Abby filled in.

"No." He corrected her, the corner of his mouth lifting. "The artsy girl. She was into painting, figures and
portraits mostly, and one day I got roped into posing for
her art class as a way to get out of detention."

She snorted. "Don't tell me you had to be naked."

"It was high school," he reiterated, rolling his eyes. "I
was fully clothed. Had to sit there on this stool for two
hours while fifteen kids sketched me. After class, Emily
came up to me and asked if I would pose for her after
school. She said my face had interesting lines."

"And you fell madly in love with each other."

"Not quite. We totally hit it off when she painted me,
but at school I was kind of an ass to her." Shame flickered
in his eyes. "You know how high school is—the jocks date
the popular cheerleaders, the art kids date other art kids,
geeks date geeks. I was embarrassed to be seen with her.
Fuck, I was such a jerk back then."

"So what happened?"

"She gave me an ultimatum. Said I could either be her
boyfriend in *and* out of school, or else she wouldn't see
me anymore." He paused. "I was disgustingly in love
with her. I didn't want to break up, so the next day at
school, I held her hand in front of everyone and asked
her to sit with me at the jock table for lunch."

Abby was oddly touched. She hadn't thought the
story would take that turn. *So I dumped her* was what
she'd been expecting.

"We went out for the next two years, and after gradu-
ation we both applied to the University of Michigan. I
landed a football scholarship, and Em was majoring in

art. We moved into this little apartment off campus." He released a breath. "We loved each other. Everything was really good. For a while."

"What changed?"

"Nothing, if I'm being honest. Em was always really insecure, ever since high school. Even though I chose to be with her, it was like she was waiting for the other shoe to drop, you know?" His face creased with frustration. "It got worse in college. I was the big man on campus, on the football team, and she was still the same quiet, artsy girl. And it didn't help that chicks were constantly throwing themselves at me. Em kept asking me when I would break up with her, why I was still with her."

"Why *were* you with her?"

"Because she was amazing. So fucking smart, and she had the most sarcastic sense of humor. Plus, she never let me get away with anything. If I was being an ass, she called me on it. She kept me real, you know." His tone darkened. "But no matter how hard I tried to convince her that I truly loved her, she refused to believe it."

Abby wasn't sure she wanted to hear the rest. She had a feeling it wouldn't be pretty, judging from the look in his eyes. But he kept going, each word coming out in a harsh burst. "She killed herself in sophomore year. I came home to find her hanging from the ceiling fan in our apartment."

She faltered. "Oh. Kane, I'm so sorry."

He didn't speak for a very long time, just sat there in the darkness of her bedroom, his chest rising and falling with each breath he took. "You asked why I'm not interested in relationships," he began gruffly. "That's why. Every time I get close to someone, I think of Em, and how it felt to lose her like that."

The revelation gave her pause. God, she knew exactly what he meant. The person closest to her had hurt her just as deeply, and she knew her inability to reach out to others had everything to do with her mother. Kane's words brought a strange sense of relief. Made her feel like she wasn't alone, that shutting down was something other people did too, not just her.

"Kane . . ." She hesitated. "I lied to you last night."

His green eyes searched her face. "What did you lie about?"

"When I said . . . when I said I didn't want to kiss you again." Her breath came out in an unsteady puff. "I lied."

Chapter 12

La Mexicana looked about as inviting as a crack house. Located in one of the seedier parts of the city, the restaurant was nothing more than single-story shack with a small brown sign that hung at an angle. A pair of skinny dark-skinned guys in their midtwenties were loitering out front, their shifty, uneasy gazes speaking of illegal activities. One of them let out a low whistle when he caught sight of Isabel. To her surprise, she felt Trevor's hand tighten protectively on her arm.

The restaurant was practically empty when they walked in. Dimly lit, it featured a scattering of small tables with no tablecloths and a narrow wooden bar off to one side. One of the three patrons in the place stood up at their arrival. She immediately recognized Felix Esposito from the photograph Trevor had shown her on the plane. The man was average height, with angular, rodent-like features and a thick black mustache that looked completely out of place on his thin face. His head was shaved, and his eyes were a dark brown and surprisingly warm. Trevor had told her Felix worked for one of the big drug honchos in the city, collecting payment and doling out punishment when necessary. She had trouble picturing this man, who couldn't be more than a hundred and twenty pounds, beating anyone up—that is, until he turned slightly and she noticed the butt of a small pistol poking out of his waistband. Ah, he preferred firepower to prove his points.

"Mr. Julian!" Felix exclaimed as he came up to greet them. He enthusiastically shook Trevor's hand, looking so happy that Isabel had to wonder exactly what Callaghan had done to earn Esposito's warmth and respect. "It is good to see you."

"Good to see you too, Felix," Trevor said in a Boston accent.

Esposito's eyes widened in appreciation as his gaze landed on Isabel. "And this must be your beautiful wife!" He took Isabel's hand without invitation and planted a sloppy kiss on her knuckles. "Señora, it is an honor."

She graced him with a cool smile. Paloma was very distrustful of strangers.

"Felix, this is Paloma Dominguez-Martin." Trevor chuckled. "But I like to think of her as the light of my life."

"Yes, I can see why." Felix stared at her with barely restrained lust, his gaze focused solely on the cleavage pouring out of the bodice of her dress. "Come, let's sit. I must know how Mr. Julian came to marry a beautiful creature such as yourself."

Isabel tried not to roll her eyes. Talk about laying it on thick. She and Trevor followed Felix to a table across the room. Esposito took the chair that faced the front door, and she noticed he was always aware of the entrance as well as the other patrons. She and Trevor sat side by side, and she immediately scooted closer and nuzzled his neck. She experienced a moment of light-headedness as the scent of his aftershave assaulted her. God, he smelled good.

Focus, Isabel.

Right. This was a crucial part of the plan, getting Felix to arrange a meeting with Blanco's representative.

"So how did you meet?" Felix asked after a sullen-faced waitress took their drink order.

Trevor offered a wide smile. "Paloma here knocked me off my feet. Literally." He proceeded to describe their first meeting, how Paloma had stumbled into him on the Saint-Tropez pier, where Julian's yacht had been docked. Love at first sight, of course.

"She was scheduled to return to Rio de Janeiro, but I convinced her to abandon the rest of her party and join me on the *Phoenix*, and that was it. I was a goner."

Isabel beamed at Esposito. "We sailed around Europe," she revealed in the Portuguese accent she'd mastered over the years. "It was the most romantic time of my life. Making love on the deck, looking up at the stars. And Julian is *so* generous!" She lifted the diamond pendant she'd slipped around her neck before leaving the safe house. "He bought me this on our one-week anniversary! Isn't it beautiful?"

Felix nodded, examining the pendant with the kind of approval that told her he knew his way around precious gems. "Mr. Julian has always been a generous benefactor."

The waitress returned with their drink orders, placing two glistening bottles of beer in front of the men and a glass of red wine before Isabel. She was surprised that this place even served wine. It was a total dump. The trio ordered their meals, and the waitress stalked off again, her face completely expressionless. Isabel suspected the girl was stoned.

During dinner, she made all the appropriate fawning noises, kissing Trevor's neck, nibbling on his earlobe. She played the part of a love-struck bride to a T, and Esposito bought into it, chuckling and commenting more than once how lucky Trevor was to have found such an enthusiastic woman.

"Brazilian women are very sensual, I find," Felix said, his eyes growing heavy-lidded as he admired Isabel's chest once more.

"We are," she confirmed. "I have never understood those silly Americans. So inhibited. All that second-guessing of themselves. Life should be *lived*. My late papa, God bless his soul, believed that enjoying yourself is the most important thing you can do." Her eyes twinkled. "And I must admit, I do so enjoy spending Papa's money."

Felix laughed loudly. "Money is there for us to spend it. It is no fun letting it sit in a bank."

Isabel cuddled close to Trevor, brushing her lips over his cheek in a sensual caress. "I like this man," she said with a beaming smile. "He is—what is the American expression? A man of my own heart?"

Trevor gave her an indulgent smile. "That's the one." He pushed away his plate and rested his elbows on the table. "Speaking of money, why don't we get to the business portion of this dinner?" he said to the other man, his voice light.

Interest flicked in Esposito's eyes. "I must admit, I am curious about how I may be of service. What is it you think I can do for you, Mr. Julian?"

"I'd like an introduction." The casual smile never left Trevor's face. "I believe you might be able to contact someone for me."

Felix's brow puckered. "Who?"

"Samir Bahar. He is the representative for Luis Blanco."

Isabel noticed the way Esposito's face paled, just a little, at the mention of Blanco. His curiosity had dissolved into sharp suspicion and his mustache twitched as he took a long swig of beer, growing quiet as if debating whether to let the discussion continue.

"Why do you need to speak to Bahar?"

Trevor slung his arm over Isabel's shoulder, planting a kiss on the top of her head. "I'm looking to buy my new bride a very special wedding gift, and I believe Blanco might be able to help." When Esposito didn't respond, Trevor lowered his voice. "I'm aware you've had dealings with him in the past, Felix. And I'd be willing to pay a handsome fee if you could arrange the introduction. Call it a middleman's bonus, if you will."

That got Esposito's attention. "How handsome?" he asked slowly.

"Fifty grand." Trevor arched a brow. "A lot of money for so little work, don't you think?"

Pretending to be uninterested, Isabel picked at the food on her plate. She hadn't eaten much of it—didn't trust the kitchen in the back to be any cleaner than the main room. She let the men discuss the matter for a while longer, growing inwardly frustrated as Esposito continued to insist he wasn't sure he could reach Bahar.

When the nape of her neck began to tingle in warning, Isabel lifted her head and found Esposito's brown eyes focused on her. "You're not eating, señora. Perhaps you are tired from all your travels?"

It took her a second to realize he had spoken to her in flawless Portuguese. "Actually, I enjoy traveling," she replied in her supposed native tongue. "I'm just not very hungry tonight."

"I suspect this meal is inferior compared to the Brazilian cuisine you are accustomed to. I had the pleasure of visiting São Paulo last spring—the city boasts many great restaurants."

Esposito was smart—she had to give him that. "I do miss the cuisine of my country," she admitted. With emphasis, she added, *"Mas eu sou de Rio de Janeiro, não São Paulo."*

"That's right," he said, switching back to English. "Mr. Julian said you were from Rio. I must have forgotten."

Must have been testing her, more like it. Despite his alleged loyalty to Julian Martin, Esposito had evidently been rattled by the mention of Bahar's name, and her presence probably added to his uneasiness. Julian's surprise marriage combined with his need for a sudden favor no doubt made Esposito extremely suspicious.

Better to let the man sit on it for a few hours, Isabel decided. Fifty grand for making a phone call. She had a feeling he wouldn't take long to weigh the matter, but she knew that continuing to push him now was a bad idea.

So she slid closer, lowering her hand into Trevor's lap with an impish little smile. He seemed startled, but didn't break character. Rather, he ran his tongue along his bottom lip and shot her a sensuous look. "Soon, baby," he murmured.

She stuck out her chin. "Now, *meu amor.*"

Without even blinking, Trevor scraped his chair back and stood up. Yanking his wallet out of his pocket, he dropped a handful of bills on the table. "I'm afraid my wife and I need to be going."

Esposito was all but leering as he watched them hurriedly get to their feet. "I see that," he said, his lips twitching.

"Call me when you make up your mind," Trevor added, carelessly resting his hand on Isabel's hip. "You know my cell number, but you can also reach me at Casa Medina. Honeymoon suite."

"I'll be in touch," was all Esposito said.

"The sooner the better, Felix. My wife isn't a very patient woman, in case you didn't notice."

Esposito grinned. Standing up, he extended his hand, and Trevor gave it a firm shake. "It was good to see you again, Mr. Julian." His dark eyes moved to Isabel, no doubt to mentally undress her. "And an honor to meet you, Paloma."

She held out her hand and he grasped it with both of his before lowering his head to kiss her knuckles. Used his tongue too, which made her want to vomit.

Her voice was low and husky as she said, "I hope we meet again, Señor Esposito."

"As do I."

They bade him good-bye and strolled arm in arm out of the restaurant. Outside, Isabel leaned her head against Trevor's shoulder, murmuring, "So far, so good."

The car was parked across the street, the driver looking bored as he got out to open their doors. As they settled into the plush backseat of the town car, Isabel glanced over at Trevor and said, "You think he bought it?"

He nodded. All the sensuality and teasing humor had drained from his face the moment they were alone, and he had reverted back to his usual expressionless self. "Yeah, he bought it."

"Good." She smiled grimly. "So now we wait."

"Now we wait," he confirmed.

*   *   *

Abby's pulse vibrated in her throat as Kane slid closer. His eyes had darkened to a smoky hunter green, thick with desire. "You lied," he echoed softly.

"Yes."

Saying that one little word took a lot out of her, but it seemed to please Kane. "Thank God," he muttered. And then his strong hand was cupping her chin and his mouth came down on hers.

This time Abby expected the rush of sensation that swamped her body. It was familiar now, not as terrifying. Her heart drummed relentlessly, while her limbs went warm and rubbery. Kane's tongue slid into her mouth, probing, searching. She hesitantly responded, touching his tongue with her own, and a shock wave of pleasure slammed into her.

She pulled back slightly. "Is it . . . is it supposed to feel this good?" she whispered against his mouth.

"Mmm-hmmm," he murmured, dragging his lips along the line of her jaw.

He kissed his way back to her mouth, eliciting a small whimper from her. The whimper became a yelp as he wrapped one arm around her and pulled her into his lap. The second she settled over him, she felt the hard ridge of his arousal pressing against her thigh. Her thin boxer shorts did nothing to protect her from the heat that scorched her at the intimate contact.

Her tank top had ridden up, and Kane's hands ran over her back, gently stroking her fevered skin as he kissed her. She suddenly felt awkward, uncertain. She'd never done this before. Kissed someone she wasn't trying to get information from. Touched someone she wasn't about to kill. Should she do something with her hands?

Yes, she needed to touch him. That's what women did to the men in their beds, right?

Kissing him deeper, she lowered one hand between them, seeking out his massive erection. As her fingers touched him over the material of his sweatpants, Kane let out a ragged moan.

And then he took her hand and moved it away.

"Is something wrong?" she said, a pang of anxiety tugging at her belly. It was followed by a sharp tug of self-reproach. Damn it. She didn't know what to do here. This wasn't *her*. She wasn't the kind of woman who sat in a man's lap and pushed her tongue in his mouth and—

"Nothing is wrong," he said huskily, reassurance ringing in his voice. "It's just . . . not time for that. I want this to be for you, Abby."

She faltered. "No, you don't have to—"

"I don't *have* to do anything," he said with a laugh. "But I sure as hell want to."

She made a startled sound as he rolled them over so she was lying on her back. He was on his side, hovering over her, and then his deft fingers moved to the waistband of her shorts and he slid them down her legs.

"Will you let me kiss you?" he asked gruffly.

A laugh squeaked out. "You already have."

"Yeah, but not here." He ran one finger along the top of her skimpy bikini panties. "And not here." Slowly, he lifted her tank top, baring her breasts.

A thrill of anticipation shot up her spine as the air met her exposed skin. When she saw the sexy glimmer in Kane's eyes, the thrill deepened into a throbbing pulse that snaked into her bloodstream. Oh God, who was this man? Why did her brain turn to mush every time he looked at her?

Kane dipped his head and pressed his lips on the swell of one breast.

Panic knotted inside her. What was she doing? Why did her skin feel like he'd set it on fire? The panic intensified. She fumbled with the bottom of her shirt, trying to cover herself. "I can't do this," she sputtered.

He looked up at her, his eyes gentle. "Yes, you can. It's okay to let yourself feel things. I think we both could use a lesson in that. At least try, and if you don't like what I'm doing, I'll stop. I promise you that."

She let out a pent-up breath. "Okay."

"You sure?"

Another slow exhale. "I'm sure."

Without giving her time to change her mind, he turned his attention back to her breasts, now healed from the whipping. He kissed each one softly, and her nipples tingled, hardened, demanding equal attention. His tongue licked its way up to one rigid bud. He sucked it gently. Another shock wave rocked her body.

"You like this?" His breath heated her skin.

"Yes."

He circled her nipple with his tongue, each raspy swirl bringing a jolt of pleasure that blazed down her body and settled between her legs.

"How about this?" He nipped at the side of her breast.

"Y-yes."

She found herself touching his hair as he played with her nipples, kissing and sucking, biting when it suited him. By the time his hand moved between her legs, she was clawing restlessly at the sheets. She needed . . . something. Something more.

"Let's get these off," he murmured, scrunching the side of her panties with one hand and pulling them down.

He touched her bare thighs. She shivered.

"Say the word and I'll stop, Abby."

"No. Keep going," she choked out.

He braced his hands against her skin and gently pushed her legs apart. "Has anyone ever gone down on you before?"

"You mean, like oral sex?"

He laughed at the dismay in her voice. "Yeah, like that."

"No." Abby shifted warily. "Nobody's ever done that. The ones I've been with didn't seem interested in—"

"No," he interrupted. "Don't bring anyone else into this." He softened his tone. "This is just about us, Abby."

"I'm sorry."

"Don't be sorry," he said gruffly. "I shouldn't have snapped at you. I just . . . I don't want you to think about anyone in your past. Not now, not ever again. You deserved a hell of a lot more than any of those bastards gave you."

"If it helps," she said with a faint smile, "I killed most of them."

A laugh choked out. "Oddly enough, that kind of does help."

Her smile widened. "See, my job does have its benefits."

Shaking his head, he shot her a grin. "If you don't like what I'm doing," he said awkwardly, "I'll stop. I promise I won't do anything you don't like."

She couldn't stop her eyelids from fluttering closed or her sharp intake of breath as he slid down her body, the rough hair on his chest scraping against her sensitive skin. She glanced down and what she saw made her quiver. Kane's blond head between her legs, his mouth inches from her most intimate place, was the most erotic visual she could have ever imagined.

Clasping his hands on her hips, he moved closer and slid his tongue over her already damp heat.

Each brush of his tongue brought on a new sensation that left her breathless. He licked her. Every inch of her body throbbed. Her core. Her breasts. That spot behind her ear. Even her knees began aching relentlessly. Her muscles went taut, tense from the sensations he evoked inside her. Slamming her eyes closed, she tried to ignore the spark starting to burn between her thighs.

"Don't fight it," he rasped against her hot flesh.

The spark crackled and hissed, until it became a flame that shot to every part of her body.

Her hands fisted in his hair, trying to push him away.

"Just let go, sweetheart. Let go for me."

The flame turned into a roaring fire.

His mouth moved over her wet slit, his index finger rubbing her opening. Then he pushed his finger deep inside her and she exploded.

The orgasm rocked her to the core, made her shudder and moan. Waves of ecstasy crashed over her, swelled inside her, their power endless and their force causing her body to thrash wildly until finally her limbs went numb with a satisfaction no words could describe.

When at last she found her breath and regained the ability to function, she found Kane looking up at her with a mixture of triumph and sheer desire.

He lifted a brow. "Well?"

"That . . . you . . . I don't think I can move."

With a laugh, he climbed up her body and pulled her close, kissing her neck. Another shiver shimmied up her spine.

"See, I told you losing control wouldn't kill you," he teased in a husky voice.

"That's never happened to me before," she admitted. Her lower body was still throbbing, vibrating from the aftereffects of that unbelievable and terrifying climax. It took her a second to realize that the vibrating was actually coming from Kane.

Cursing, he shoved his hand in his pocket and pulled out his phone, which was humming impatiently. Kane's frown told her exactly who the caller was, and all the pleasure flew out of her body like a sharp gust of wind. Abby's hands shook as she reached for the phone.

"No," Kane said severely. "No fucking way."

"I told you I wanted to talk to him if he called."

She disentangled herself from Kane's embrace, managing to seize the cell phone from his hand and flip it open. "Devlin," she said coldly.

Next to her, Kane hissed out a savage expletive.

Covering the mouthpiece, she looked at him, feeling the regret etch into her features. "I'd like some privacy," she whispered as her other hand fumbled on the bedspread in search of her underwear.

His face turned to ice. With another angry obscenity, he stumbled off the bed, looking so furious she felt a tremor of fear. His eyes were flashing, his shoulders stiff as a board as he stood over her.

"You still there, luv?" Devlin's voice chirped in her ears.

She took her hand off the mouthpiece. "I'm here," she said hoarsely.

Kane shot her a look loaded with fury and disbelief, and then he stalked out of the bedroom, slamming the door behind him.

Chapter 13

"Wake up."

Lucia slowly opened her eyes. Was it morning? One couldn't tell, not here in this cold, dark room.

She missed her mother. Was Mamá looking for her? Did she think Lucia was dead? Tears stung her eyelids. She didn't want to be here anymore. She wanted to see her mother, and put on her red and white school uniform, and play behind the church with her friends.

Across the room, Valencia was already awake, her long hair twisted in the messy braid she'd fixed for herself last night, when she and Consuela had tried to distract some of the younger girls by doing their hair. But nothing could distract Lucia. She was fully aware of where she was, though not so sure why she was here.

She got a niggling idea as the *halcón* snapped his fingers to get everyone's attention, then gestured to the burly man beside him.

The man holding a camera.

A tremor went through her as a third man entered the room, dragging in a green hose dripping water at its spout.

"You," the *halcón* barked, jabbing a finger at Emiliana. "Take off the clothes and stand against the wall."

When Emiliana hesitated, the guard held up his rifle and shook it ominously. Emiliana quickly ran to the wall and started to strip.

Lucia watched in horror as, one by one, the girls around her were forced to undress and stand in front of the hose. The *halcón* tossed them a bar of soap, ordering them to clean themselves. After each girl had been cleansed, the other guard gave her a towel to dry off with, then made her go to the other side of the room, where the man with the camera had set up a tripod.

Lucia flinched every time the *halcón* pointed at a girl. Soon he would point at her. Soon she would have to remove her clothes while the men ogled her naked body.

Vomit rose in the back of her throat. She swallowed it down as hard as she could, pushing the bad taste away.

The *halcón* flicked a finger at her. "Your turn. Get up."

Lucia trembled as she climbed unsteadily to her feet. Her fingers were numb, cold. She could barely undo the first button of her shirt.

"Faster," the *halcón* snapped.

She quickened her pace, wishing the entire time that she could disappear. That she was somewhere else. Anywhere else.

Just not here.

Isabel woke up feeling disoriented. It took her a few seconds to remember she was in the honeymoon suite at the hotel. Rubbing the sleep from her eyes, she sat up in bed and glanced at the thin shaft of sunlight streaming through the thick gold curtains hanging at the window that overlooked the city's business district. The king-size bed was covered with a dark yellow bedspread and a mountain of decorative pillows that she'd kicked off during the night onto the rich burgundy carpet. She hoped none of the pillows had conked Trevor in the head. When they'd returned from their meeting with Esposito last night, he'd promptly marched over to the closet, grabbed an extra blanket and pillow, and announced he was sleeping on the floor.

As if she'd really expected him to share the bed with her. The man could barely look her in the eye, for Pete's sake.

Stretching her arms high above her head, Isabel slid out from beneath the silk sheets. As she stood up, she snuck a peek at Trevor, who was lying on the floor with his eyes closed. She swallowed when she caught sight of his bare chest and long, muscular legs. He wore nothing but a pair of black boxer briefs that hugged his groin. He had a great body—tanned, toned, and totally drool-worthy.

Tearing her eyes away, she headed for the master bathroom to brush her teeth and wash up, all the while wishing Trevor Callaghan wasn't so damn attractive. It would have helped if his looks matched his less-than-desirable personality—that way she wouldn't have to be so aware of him all of the time. When she reentered the bedroom, Trevor was sitting up, yawning.

"Mornin'," he said gruffly.

"Good morning," she answered.

An awkward beat, broken by the clearing of his throat. "Did you sleep well?"

"Better than you, I suspect," she couldn't help but murmur.

His features tensed. "What is that supposed to mean?"

Isabel shrugged as she headed for the Louis Vuitton

suitcase she'd left in the small sitting area across the room. "You were tossing and turning all night," she said over her shoulder.

God, Gina, I'm sorry.

She kept that memory to herself, though his raspy, grief-stricken words continued to run through her mind. She was tempted to ask him about the dream, but didn't dare. Trevor was far too touchy, and always on guard whenever she raised a topic that didn't relate to this rescue.

"I always get restless on a mission," he said with a veiled expression. "I don't like waiting around, or relying on people like Esposito to get things done."

As if on cue, the cell phone he'd left on one of the love seats began to chime. Trevor sprang toward the ringing phone and glanced at the caller ID.

"Esposito?" Isabel asked sharply.

He nodded, then answered the call. "Felix," he said, his tone immediately transforming into one tinged with lighthearted pleasure. Trevor paused. "Yes, of course. No, we were already awake . . . He does? Well, that's very good to hear . . ."

Isabel listened intently to his side of the conversation, smiling to herself when she heard Trevor mention the fee he'd promised Esposito. Felix had done his job, then— Bahar had agreed to a meeting.

"Samir Bahar is willing to meet with us," Trevor confirmed after he hung up, his eyes glinting with satisfaction. "Today."

Her gaze flew to his. "Today?"

"You find it suspicious too, don't you? That he arranged such a hasty meeting."

"Do you think it's a trap?"

Trevor pursed his lips in thought, tilting his head to

the side. "I don't know. Could be, but Bahar really has no reason to suspect us. We've got a good cover in place, and I'm sure he did a thorough background check."

"There are no holes in Julian Martin's background?"

"None." He arched one brow. "And Paloma Dominguez?"

"Rock solid."

"Then we probably have nothing to worry about."

Isabel had to laugh. "Probably? That's very assuring."

She thought she glimpsed a hint of a smile on his handsome face. "Are there any reassurances when it comes to this kind of work?" he countered.

After a moment, she let out a sigh. "No, there aren't."

Trevor shrugged, then set down the phone and headed toward the bathroom. "So we go forward." He paused in the doorway and turned to shoot her a rueful look. "And if it's a trap, we'll know soon enough."

"Bahar agreed to the meeting," Morgan announced as he strode onto the terrace.

Kane lifted his gaze from the cards he was holding. "Trevor and Isabel convinced Esposito?"

Morgan nodded. "Yep. Bahar called Trev this morning. They're having lunch today."

"Good." Kane turned his attention to his poker hand, sliding two red poker chips into the heaping pile in the middle of the table. "I raise a hundred."

From her perch by the railing, Abby heard Luke curse softly. Apparently Kane had been kicking Luke and Ethan's asses for the past hour, but she hadn't been paying much attention. It was another disgustingly humid day, and the thin yellow sundress she wore clung to her skin like plastic wrap. Noelle must have been pretty angry with her when she'd gone shopping for clothes, or maybe Noelle was hoping her own femme fatale tastes would rub off on Abby. Either way, she was now the proud owner of several skirts, tight jeans, and skimpy dresses she normally wouldn't be caught dead in.

At least she wasn't the only one wearing next to nothing. The men were all bare-chested, sweat coating their muscled flesh, and Abby had been trying not to look in Kane's direction all morning.

He wasn't looking at her either.

He was pissed. Didn't take a rocket scientist to figure that one out. Ever since she'd banished him from her room last night in order to talk to Devlin, Kane had been speaking to her in two-word sentences, his green eyes pretty much screaming *I don't want to deal with you right now.*

"Abby?"

She turned at the sound of Morgan's voice. "Yeah?"

"Did you hear what I said? They got a meeting with Bahar." Morgan's face was unusually gentle. "We're halfway there."

She managed a halfhearted smile. "That's great."

He studied her. "You all right?"

"I'm fine." She noticed the way Kane's back tensed when she spoke. "Just distracted, that's all."

Although Morgan looked unconvinced, he simply nodded and left the terrace. Abby turned around again, breathing in the thick, almost unbearable heat.

"Why the fuck don't we have a swimming pool?" Luke demanded. "We have a gym, an indoor and outdoor shooting range, a security system that rivals the one in the White House, but no freaking pool."

"Maybe Morgan can't swim," Ethan piped up.

That remark set them off in a bout of loud laughter, but Abby noticed Kane didn't join in.

Damn it, she'd screwed up. She thought of the way he'd looked at her last night, when he'd brought her to her first honest-to-God orgasm. His eyes had sizzled with heat. Genuine warmth. And then Devlin had had to call and mess everything up.

Ribbons of uneasiness uncurled in her stomach as she remembered the main topic of discussion. Devlin had been talking about Ted. He'd even played a portion of the tape from Dr. Silverton's session, when Abby described the first time Ted hit her.

The memories Devlin had unearthed were ones she'd buried a long time ago. It sickened her that he could obtain so much joy from other people's pain. Several times last night she'd almost hung up on the bastard, but she'd forced herself to stay on the line. Truth was, she was learning as much about Devlin as he was learning about her. When he spoke to her, she heard his anger and resentment, but at the same time, his tone of voice was almost reverent, as if he might worship her as well as loathe her.

His obsession with her could be used to her advantage if she played her cards right. For the time being, though, she would allow him his sick games. Dr. Silverton's safety was in her hands and she knew Devlin wouldn't hesitate to snap the doctor's neck. From what she knew about the man, killing was a form of entertainment for him. He got off on it.

Well, Abby refused to give him a reason to indulge in his favorite sport. She knew Devlin wouldn't be satisfied with phone calls for very long, but for the moment they kept him occupied and gave her time to figure out her next move. If she attempted to step in and remove Amanda

Silverton from harm's way now, Devlin would simply find another way to get to her. Better to let him think he had the upper hand, that he was succeeding in tormenting her with the past. Let him believe she was weak. It would make it all the sweeter when she killed the bastard.

But not yet. The rescue mission was her top priority, which meant ridding the world of William Devlin would just have to wait.

"There's that pond on the other side of the property," Luke was saying. The chips on the table clinked as he added two more to the pile.

"Where D almost got mauled by the coyote?" Ethan hooted.

More laughter. Abby's ears perked up. Damn bastard deserved a good coyote mauling. She hadn't seen much of D since their disturbing conversation a few days ago, and she wasn't complaining. It made her too uncomfortable, being around the man. Especially since they had so much in common.

Luke stood up. "I fold." He dropped his cards on the table, faceup. Abby hid a grin when she noticed his hand—three of clubs and seven of hearts, with the five cards on the table doing nothing to help him out. She was surprised he'd stayed in for this long.

Kane groaned. "Seriously? But I'm having fun kicking your ass."

"Tough shit. I'm going swimming." Luke paused. "I'll take a gun just in case the coyote shows up. Anyone want to join me?"

Ethan got up without hesitation. Sweat dripped between his pecs. "Hell, yes."

Luke glanced over at her. "What about you, Sinclair?"

Her first instinct was to say no. Horsing around in a

pond with a couple of mercenaries wasn't exactly her idea of a good time, but this damn heat really was intolerable.

"What the hell?" she said with a shrug. "I think my ribs are up to it."

"Get changed, then." Luke headed for the sliding door. "I'll meet you guys at the Jeep in five."

As Ethan trailed after Luke, Abby approached the table, where Kane still sat in front of the abandoned poker game. "Are you coming?" she asked quietly.

He slowly met her eyes. "Should I?"

"I'd like it if you did." Her own words surprised the hell out of her.

Out of him too, apparently. "Interesting, because last night you couldn't wait to be rid of me."

"I'm . . . sorry." She took a breath. "I couldn't talk to him while you were in the room. It would've been too hard."

"Why?" His voice grew urgent. "Why are you spending time chatting with that sick fuck? What does he say to you?"

She shifted in discomfort. "It doesn't matter."

"Like hell it doesn't." He scraped back his chair, staggering to his feet, and before she knew it, his hands were on her waist, pulling her toward him. "We were getting somewhere last night, Abby. Before Devlin called, we were . . . connecting."

She swallowed. "I know."

"But you didn't think that connection was important enough to keep exploring. You preferred to speak to *Devlin*." Disbelief entered his face. "Why?"

"It doesn't matter," she said again. "Can we just put this aside, for now anyway? It's like a hundred degrees out. Let's go swimming, try to have some fun." She offered a self-deprecating look. "In case you haven't noticed, I don't usually do fun."

A reluctant smile tugged on his mouth. "I noticed." Dropping his hands from her hips, he let out a sigh. "Fine. We'll put it aside. For now. But don't think it's over, Abby. One way or another, you're going to tell me what you're doing with Devlin. You're going to tell me everything."

The restaurant Samir Bahar chose for their lunch meeting was considerably more tasteful than the one where they'd met Esposito. The establishment was small but quaint, with a beautiful garden in the rear that featured a cobblestone patio and secluded tables with pristine white tablecloths.

Trevor had a tough time staying in character as Isabel walked ahead of him. She wore an indecently short peach-colored dress that looked incredible with all that black hair sliding down her back. Her silver stilettos clicked against the cobblestones as she seductively made her way to Bahar's table. Trevor was tempted to turn around and get the hell out of there, but he forced himself to stay on course.

Still, it was incredibly difficult making sure his gaze rested on Isabel's round bottom, looking at her the way a smitten husband ought to look.

"You must be Mr. Bahar!" Isabel chirped as they reached the table.

Bahar, a thin man with chocolate brown skin, stood to greet them. He wore starched white slacks and a gray blazer, and he was incredibly short; Isabel towered over him in her stilettos, and Trevor had to angle his head down to meet the other man's wary dark eyes.

"Ms. Dominguez, I presume?" he said in a crisp, polished accent.

"Mrs. Martin," she corrected with a giggle. "But please, call me Paloma."

Bahar took her hand and squeezed it lightly, then turned to examine Trevor. "And you must be *Mr.* Martin."

"Julian."

The two men shook hands. "Please, have a seat," Bahar said, gesturing to the two empty chairs.

Trevor made sure Isabel was settled, then took the remaining chair. "Thank you for meeting with us on such short notice."

Bahar reached for the wineglass in front of him and took a small sip. "My employer and I were quite intrigued by the request." He set the glass down and clasped his hands. "So tell me, what is it you think we might be able to do for you?"

Right to the point. Trevor liked that. So many businessmen tended to dance around the issue. Julian Martin preferred a more direct approach.

"I was told your employer might be offering some merchandise my wife would very much like to purchase."

"And where did you hear that, if I may ask?"

This was the tricky part. The dossier they had on Blanco contained a list of known acquaintances and business associates, but Julian Martin hadn't actually spoken to any of them. In the end they picked a name they felt Blanco might confide in—Juan Cortez, a fellow arms dealer with a vast network that stretched across several continents. They'd researched the network, discovering that one of the men further down on Cortez's command ladder was a frequent visitor to the Brazilian brothel Julian Martin supposedly co-owned. Julian could've met

Abdul Farah any number of times, making him the perfect contact.

Didn't matter that Trevor had never met the guy, or that he probably never would. Chances were, if Cortez believed one of his men had spoken out of turn about his business, whether that business was real or not, he'd have the rat taken out. And Trevor didn't feel even an inkling of guilt. The world would be better off without the likes of Farah in it. The bastard liked young boys.

"An acquaintance by the name of Abdul Farah," Trevor said carelessly. "Farah works for Juan Cortez, who I'm sure you're familiar with."

"I am." Bahar's tone was cautious. "And what did this Farah have to say?"

"That your employer is in possession of some very unique merchandise."

Giggling, Isabel leaned forward. "Very young and alluring merchandise," she added.

"The likes of which my wife and I would be very interested in procuring," Trevor finished.

He could tell that Bahar was still extremely suspicious. The man reached for his wine again, this time draining the slender glass. He snapped his fingers to get their waiter's attention, and the young man hurried over to take their drink orders. Trevor was pleased that Bahar didn't make a move to pick up the menu in front of him. No let's-chat-over-some-delicious-food pretense. This was right to business, just the way Trevor liked it.

"Let's say that the information you've received is correct," Bahar began. "And mind you, I am being hypothetical here."

"Of course," Trevor said pleasantly.

"Hypothetically speaking, if the type of merchandise

you mentioned should exist, I believe there would be a high price to pay."

Yes.

Next to him, Isabel's expression didn't change, but he sensed that she felt the same burst of excitement. Always came down to money now, didn't it?

"No price is too high," Trevor replied with a cocky smile. He squeezed Isabel's bare shoulder, eliciting a girlish squeak from her lips, which were slathered with pink gloss that made them look lush and shiny. "I would pay anything to put a smile on my beautiful bride's face, and I can assure you, I have plenty of money to invest in just this sort of enterprise."

Bahar simply nodded. That he didn't question the remark told Trevor he'd had Julian Martin's financial statements thoroughly examined. Several of Julian's assets were completely bogus, the nature of the fraud buried under heaps of tiresome paperwork, but the cash in Martin's numerous bank accounts was no fraud. Morgan had used much of his personal fortune to finance the elaborate cover, and that fortune was pretty damn impressive. When Trevor first went to work for the legendary mercenary, he'd been shocked by the man's net worth. Apparently Morgan came from serious wealth. Why he'd decided to work as a merc rather than sit on his big pile of money was a fucking mystery to everyone.

"So, is this something your employer would be interested in?" Trevor asked, injecting a touch of pressure in his voice.

Bahar leaned back, his thin lips pursed. "Perhaps. If, of course, such merchandise was available."

"And let's say it is," Trevor pressed. "How would a transaction of that nature come about?"

"Hypothetically speaking—"

Oh, for fuck's sake.

"—it would happen in a secure location. The buyers would be taken to private rooms and be provided with a catalog showcasing the merchandise. If buyers request a closer look, the item would be brought to them for further examination."

Trevor felt sick. Fortunately, their waiter returned holding a tray of drinks, providing a brief respite from the revolting course this discussion had suddenly taken.

Thanking the waiter, he handed Isabel her martini glass. She took a delicate sip and smiled impishly. "Salty," she purred. "Just the way I like it."

Bahar coughed. He recovered quickly, downing half the wine in his glass. "As I was saying . . ."

"Yes," Trevor prompted. "The transaction."

"More of a silent auction, I would call it."

Bingo.

"After the merchandise has been examined, the buyers place their bids, funds exchange hands, and the merchandise is released to the successful bidders."

Isabel looked curious. "And the items that don't get sold? What would happen to them?" She smiled prettily. "Hypothetically, of course."

"The items would be shipped to Asia. We—" Bahar quickly corrected his slipup. "A *person* with such merchandise on hand would most likely have a standing business arrangement with Asia. They seem to enjoy these particular types of goods."

Disgust circled Trevor's gut like a hungry vulture. Jesus. These people were sick fucks. He couldn't believe he and Isabel were sitting here with this man, listening to his hypothetical bullshit, discussing the sale of human beings as if it were an everyday occurrence.

"Of course," Bahar continued, "an attendance fee would be required, in the event that the items aren't to the bidders' liking."

"Like I said, money isn't a problem."

"Yes, you did say that, didn't you?" Bahar tipped his head pensively. "What business are you in, Mr. Martin? You neglected to mention it."

"I dabble, do a little bit of everything. Most of my funds came from an inheritance, but I've invested wisely over the years. I own several businesses, including a very lucrative gentlemen's lounge in Rio." *Gentlemen's lounge* was just a fancy way to say whorehouse, but Bahar obviously got the drift.

"I see," Bahar said absently.

Trevor forced himself to maintain a relaxed posture. Bahar wasn't taking the bait. He was still wary of them. Guarded.

Prepared to launch into another pitch, Trevor opened his mouth, then snapped it shut when Isabel's manicured hand suddenly snaked into his lap, bloodred fingernails scraping against his zipper. Unlike the way she'd crotch-handled him in front of Esposito, she didn't hold back this time. He knew what she was doing. Bahar needed a show, needed to believe Julian Martin and his feisty Paloma were all about debauchery. A hand job in public would be no biggie for them. They wanted to buy a real-life sex toy, for Pete's sake.

Trevor smothered a wild groan. Jesus. Her hand rubbed his groin, which started to harden, to his dismay. Why couldn't his body remember he was dead inside? It wasn't supposed to come to life when Isabel Roma touched him.

"Have you ever been to Rio?" Isabel asked Bahar in a conversational tone, all the while continuing to stroke Trevor's growing erection.

Disapproval and arousal warred in the man's dark eyes. "Several times. It's a lovely city."

"Yes, very lovely," she agreed.

Trevor's mouth felt like someone had shoved a handful of sand in it. He couldn't get a word out. The traitorous heat of desire surged through his veins, combining with a dose of self-hatred that made him want to push Isabel away.

He hadn't thought about sex since Gina's death. That part of his life had ceased to exist once he'd lost the only woman he'd ever wanted in his bed.

He nearly fell off the chair when Isabel cupped his cock over his pants. He released a ragged breath and noticed Bahar's knowing gaze. Despite the long tablecloth covering Trevor's lap, it was hard to miss the movement of Isabel's hand.

Clearing his throat, Blanco's attorney put down his wineglass. "I'm afraid I must get going," he announced, smoothing the front of his gray wool blazer. "I'll pass along the details of this meeting to Mr. Blanco, and, if he's interested, we will contact you."

"Thank you again for taking the time to see us." Trevor didn't stand for a handshake. He simply leaned forward and extended his hand, forcing Bahar to step over and shake it. No way was he getting up in his condition. He probably wouldn't be able to walk with that rock between his legs.

Isabel rose, though, her heels snapping as she moved

toward Bahar. She bent down to kiss both of the man's cheeks, her voice practically purring as she said, "It was wonderful meeting you."

Bahar's dark eyes went a little glazed. He glanced down at Isabel's breasts, then said, "The pleasure was all mine."

With a nod, the small man left the patio, his strides surprisingly long and smooth despite his height. Isabel watched him go, then took the seat Bahar had occupied, putting much-needed distance between the two of them.

"What do you think?" she asked, sounding pensive.

Trevor finally found his voice. His erection, thankfully, had begun to subside the moment Isabel quit stroking it. "I'm sixty-forty on this one," he said roughly. "I think we piqued his interest."

A slow smile spread over her pretty face. "Yeah, I think we did."

He wanted to berate her for the borderline sex show she'd put on, but bit back the resentful words. She'd played her part perfectly, done precisely what she'd needed to do to ease some of Bahar's concerns.

Her small, delicate hand reached for the menu. "Should we stay and have some dinner?"

"No," he blurted out.

His abruptness caused her eyebrows to rise. "No need to snap at me, Callaghan."

Rather than apologizing, he stood up, his knees unusually wobbly. Fuck. This wasn't good. The need to get away from this woman came hard and fast. Why had she done that to him? How could she make him betray Gina like that?

"Let's go back to the hotel," he muttered. "I have some phone calls to make."

*   *   *

Luke whistled as Abby approached the edge of the pond to test the water with her big toe. She'd changed into a skimpy green bikini that left so little to the imagination she may as well have been naked, and Kane was valiantly trying not to leer at her like a horny teenager. The creamy expanse of her cleavage, her firm ass, the graceful curve of her spine, her long, shapely legs. He finally decided to focus on something that *wouldn't* give him a boner—her injuries. Some of the red welts on her stomach were beginning to fade, as were the bruises on her face, and she didn't seem to be struggling with breathing anymore either, a sign that her ribs were starting to heal. But damn, looking at her rib cage naturally lured his gaze to her breasts again, and he clenched his teeth to quell his rising desire. He couldn't look away. Neither could Luke and Ethan, which annoyed him.

"I can see why Blanco trusted her so easily," Luke remarked. "She does exude a certain charm."

She exuded a helluva lot more than charm. Sex appeal oozed out of her, which was ironic seeing as how she was completely indifferent to sex.

But she hadn't been indifferent yesterday . . .

He still couldn't wrap his mind around it. Walking back to his room last night had been somewhat of a struggle, considering how hard he'd been. His pulse had raced like a thoroughbred around a track and the heat flooding his stiff body made it difficult to breathe. He definitely hadn't been expecting it to be like that. He'd wanted to tease her a little, give her a taste of what he had to offer, and instead he was the one who felt teased. He was the one who wanted another taste.

He couldn't remember the last time a woman's release had turned him on so intensely. He'd been primed and hot and so ready to bury himself inside her he'd almost keeled over from the need.

And now she was standing five feet away, practically naked, and it was just as difficult to shake the fog of arousal from his brain. He couldn't stop picturing the way her face had looked last night. Taut with desire. Blue eyes smoky with passion. The soft moan slipping out of her throat as she toppled over the edge.

He inhaled, then released his breath slowly, trying to erase the image of Abby's flushed, aroused face from his mind. But then she turned her head toward him, and the breath he was in the process of releasing came out as a hiss. Her eyes. The pale blue he'd become accustomed to was now dark yellow, the color of warm honey. Surrounded by thick, dark lashes, her eyes seemed to glow in her face. Holy shit, they were incredible.

Abby caught his expression, and, with a dry smile, walked toward him, her bare feet padding across the grass that ringed the pond. "Noelle only brought enough contact solution to last a few days," she explained.

Luke's jaw went slack. "Is that actually your real eye color?"

"Afraid so."

"Don't look apologetic about it," Luke replied seriously. "It's incredible. I've never seen anything like it."

"Which is why I wear contacts on the job." She shrugged. "The real thing is too unforgettable."

She got that right. *Unforgettable* was definitely the word Kane would use to describe her eyes, not to mention last night's tryst. To his embarrassment, he found himself getting hard, and quickly forced a barrage of mundane images involving chairs and kitchen appliances into his brain before Luke had ammunition he could use to belittle Kane for months to come.

Shifting his gaze away from Abby, Luke shoved his thumb and forefinger into his mouth and let out a piercing whistle. A second later, his dog barreled through the brush and came to a stop at his master's feet.

"Feel like a swim, buddy?" Luke asked. He pointed to the water and said, "Go on."

Letting out an excited yip, Bear dashed across the grass and practically flung his four-legged body into the pond. His wet brown head popped out a second later and he proceeded to embark on an awkward-looking doggy paddle that made Kane laugh.

"Amateur," Luke announced as he observed the mutt. "This is how it's done, folks."

When they'd first moved to the compound, Luke and Ethan had built a long wooden dock at the edge of the pond, high enough so they could impress each other with ridiculously dangerous flips. As Kane and Abby watched, Luke took off running, then executed a scary-looking double back flip before landing in the water. He surfaced with a grin and began doing a lazy backstroke.

"Ladies first," Kane said.

"Yeah, I don't think I'm up for flips just yet." She moved to the water's edge, wading in slowly.

Kane watched as she ventured deeper, until the water was lapping beneath her breasts, and then she totally submerged herself, her shapely legs kicking as she moved through the water. He followed her in, grateful for the cold sensation against his crotch. Felt like his body was always hot when Abby was around.

"We had a pond like this near the house I grew up in," he said as he and Abby swam side by side. A few yards away, Luke was floating on his back with his eyes closed, while Ethan had channeled his inner fish and was doing underwater laps at the other end of the pond.

"In Michigan," she said, looking pleased that she'd remembered.

"Grand Rapids, if we're being more specific. In high school, my friends and I would hop into our respective pickups and drive to the pond. Mostly after dark, so we could coerce the girls to go skinny-dipping."

Abby's eyes twinkled. "Did it work?"

"Usually." He laughed. "Though somehow the guys wound up naked most of the time while the girls managed to keep their underwear on."

They neared the middle of the pond, treading water for a bit. Before she could protest, Kane placed his hands on her slender waist so that they were face-to-face. To his surprise, her arms looped around his neck. She was close enough to kiss, but he didn't dare. Not with Luke and Ethan nearby. He suspected Abby Sinclair was not a PDA sort of woman.

"God, you had such a normal life," she commented with a wry look. "Football and skinny-dipping and pickup trucks. I bet your parents are perfect too, huh?"

He thought about his mom's sprawling garden and the hockey rink his dad built in their backyard every winter, and had to smile. "Pretty much," he confessed.

"I didn't have a pond, but we did have a pool in our backyard," she said, surprising him with her candid revelation. "Jeremy had one built, so he could train me in underwater warfare."

Kane stared at her. "Seriously?"

A husky laugh left her mouth. "Seriously. He said I had to be prepared for anything, you know, because sometimes holding your breath for five minutes could come in handy."

"No way can you hold your breath for five minutes."

"I really can." She tilted her head. "How long can you hold yours, Mr. Navy SEAL?"

"Six," he said arrogantly.

Another laugh. Wow, two laughs in less than a minute. He wanted to comment, but forced himself to shut up. Abby was already prickly enough. One wrong word could turn her back into the tight-lipped professional she'd been when they'd first met.

"Your Jeremy sounds really interesting," Kane said tentatively. "How did he come into your life?"

She seemed to hesitate, as if deciding whether it was safe to tell him. Finally she said, "He was our neighbor. The Hartfords' neighbor, that is. He wasn't home very often, always off on some mission, but then he got shot and was in recovery for a while." She grew hesitant again. "He could hear me screaming." A sharp laugh. "Hell, the whole neighborhood could, but Jeremy was the only one who gave a damn. He broke into our house one night, during one of Ted's beatings, and he saved me."

Kane went speechless. He'd known that Thomas had adopted Abby, but her story painted a picture of a man with unbelievable honor. Not a lot of men had the balls to interfere with other people's domestic troubles. And to rescue a teenage girl he didn't even know, to whisk her out of an abusive foster home—that told Kane a lot about Jeremy Thomas. He suddenly felt a pang of regret as he remembered Thomas was dead. As he realized he'd never get the chance to thank the man for everything he'd done for Abby.

"He left the Rangers a couple of years after the adoption," Abby said in a faraway voice. "He said he didn't like leaving me alone. And then he got sick and—"

The sound of Kane's phone ringing carried over the water and Abby's mouth snapped shut.

Damn it. Annoyance thudded in his chest. Just when he was getting somewhere with her, they had to be interrupted.

Abby was already swimming off, and the exasperation in his body transformed into anger. No fucking way. He wasn't about to let that bastard Devlin ruin another moment with Abby.

Kane moved forward, his long, strong strokes quickly propelling him past Abby. He reached the water's edge before she did and, dripping wet, stalked across the warm grass toward the tree stump where he'd left his phone. He heard Abby running after him, protesting, but he ignored her. Enough. He'd had enough of Devlin's bullshit.

"She doesn't want to talk to you," he spat into the phone.

There was a moment of silence, then a hard chuckle. "Good," came Morgan's dry voice, "because I was calling to talk to you."

Kane stifled a groan. Shit. "Morgan?"

"Uh, yeah. Don't you have caller ID?"

"I didn't look at . . . Sorry. What's up?" Next to him, Abby's protests had died, and she was now warily listening to his side of the conversation.

"Trev just checked in. He thinks the meeting with Bahar was promising. I'm arranging for the jet to be ready in an hour."

"We're flying out?"

"Yep. So get your asses back here and gather your gear. We're leaving for the airfield in forty."

Chapter 14

By the time evening rolled around, Isabel had had enough of Trevor Callaghan's surly attitude. He'd been giving her the silent treatment since they'd returned to the hotel, and the distant look on his face was beginning to seriously annoy her.

She'd spent the last hour on her laptop, reading the dossier on Blanco that Morgan had e-mailed her, but it didn't contain anything she didn't already know. The man was a violent pervert. Big shock.

Closing the laptop, she glanced over at Trevor, who sat stone-faced on one of the love seats. She didn't think he'd even blinked in the last hour.

Bristling, she suppressed an irritated sigh and got to her feet. Moving with purpose, she crossed the room and flopped down on the love seat across from Trevor. "Do you plan on sulking all night?" she asked cheerfully.

He slowly met her gaze. "I'm not sulking."

"Okay, let's call it punishing yourself, then." She lifted her legs so she was sitting cross-legged. "Tell me—do you just say *It's my fault* over and over again in your head? Sort of like a meditation mantra?"

Shock filled his dark eyes. "Pardon me?"

"You heard me." She kept her voice casual, trying not to feel guilty about what she was doing. Fine, so maybe digging up painful memories wasn't a pleasant experience, but she couldn't put up with his pitiful attitude a second longer. "Morgan told me about your fiancée, you know."

The shock turned to cold anger. "I don't see how that's any of your business."

"Normally, it wouldn't be." Her lips tightened. "But since I'm supposed to be your wife, I find myself very concerned about this. Your demons are going to get us both killed, Callaghan."

His lips tightened too, a bitter slash across his face.

"Earlier, you were seconds away from breaking my hand so I'd stop touching you," she said with a scowl. "You could've blown everything."

"But I didn't."

She ignored his grumble. "What if Blanco wants to meet with us, Trevor? What if we have to spend the night at his estate? You heard what Abby said about the cameras. I can't have you pushing me away because you feel it's some ridiculous betrayal to your late girlfriend."

"Ridiculous?" he echoed, his voice so chilly she was tempted to shiver. "Gee, Isabel, I'm sorry it's hard for me to get over the *ridiculous* fact that the woman I was going to marry was shot to death."

"That's not what I said," she said calmly. "I just think you shouldn't be blaming yourself for something that was out of your control. And you shouldn't feel like it's a betrayal when your pretend wife touches your goddamn dick. It's not like you're the only one who's ever lost someone, Trevor."

"Yeah, and who'd you lose, Isabel?" he asked coolly.

"My mother." Her voice went soft. "She killed herself when I was ten. I was the one who found her body, okay? So I know all about blaming yourself for not being able to save someone you loved."

The ice in his voice thawed. "Shit. I'm sorry."

"It was a long time ago," she said lightly.

Silence stretched between them. She noticed his features were no longer rigid, and she could also see the reluctant curiosity in his eyes. He wanted to know more. She didn't blame him. The tidbit of information she'd provided barely scraped the tip of the iceberg. Her past wasn't something she spoke of often. She might have come to terms with it a long time ago, but that didn't mean it was her favorite topic of discussion.

He cleared his throat. "You were raised by your dad, then?"

"Not quite. My father sent me to live with my grandparents in Jersey. He and my brother stayed in Brooklyn. Dad couldn't leave the family business."

Trevor must have heard the derision in her tone, because he frowned. "What kind of business was he in?"

"He owned an Italian bistro. On paper."

"Mafia?" Trevor asked slowly.

"Number three man for one of the Five Families," she said in a clipped tone.

"Where is your father now?"

"Prison. Life without parole."

Trevor studied her. "And your brother?"

"Dead."

She dropped her gaze to the laptop balanced on her knees and traced the manufacturer's logo with one finger. The conversation had taken a wrong turn, leading her to a place she wanted no reminders of. Trevor must have picked up on her discomfort because he gave a harsh laugh.

"Not so fun, is it, talking about your past?" His voice was low and mocking.

"My past isn't hindering this mission," she retorted.

He ignored the barb and let out another laugh, this one incredulous. "So you're a Mafia princess, huh? I never would have guessed."

"Hardly," she said, her tone dry. "Actually, I was a Fed."

Trevor's eyebrows shot up. "You were with the FBI?"

"Noelle didn't tell you?"

"I never met Noelle, and Morgan didn't mention it."

She leaned back against the cushions. "I was with the bureau for five years. When I first joined, the director wasn't crazy about my Mob connection, but—"

"They decided to use you," Trevor finished.

"Yep. But I resigned after the third time they sent me undercover."

"Tired of playing with the Mob?"

"Hell, yes. When I signed up with the bureau, I was interested in violent crimes." She smiled faintly. "My dream was to track serial killers all over the country. But the director decided my background made me the ideal candidate for the organized-crime unit. I didn't like it, so I quit."

"And went to work for an assassin," Trevor finished ironically.

"I don't kill for Noelle," Isabel said, a little annoyed by the distaste in his voice. "I only do undercover work."

"But you've killed before."

"Yes," she admitted. "Then again, so have you."

"More times than I'd like." His face clouded. "And

sometimes you can kill someone without even pulling the trigger."

She knew he was talking about his fiancée, but again she suppressed the impulse to ask for details. Instead, she shook her head and said, "If there's one thing I've learned in my life, it's that shitty things happen. You can't always stop them. They just happen. And yeah, you can let them destroy you, but what's the point? Might as well learn to deal with all those shitty things and move on."

"Is that what you did?"

"Yes." She paused. "And you will too. You just have to accept your loss and try your best to live out the rest of your life without letting the loss destroy you."

"Easier said than done," he muttered.

She laughed. "Who said life was easy?"

They'd been in the air for about two hours when Morgan slid into the seat next to Abby's. Kane was across from them, his body still and eyes closed, but she wasn't so sure he was sleeping. More like waiting. Ever since they'd boarded the plane, he seemed to be waiting for her to open up about the phone calls with Devlin. Like she would actually tell him anything with everyone else around. Luke and Ethan might be across the narrow aisle, but they weren't out of earshot, and D had been glaring at her since the moment they'd boarded.

Maybe she shouldn't have goaded him that day in the living room. His private demons belonged to him. Dragging them out in the open hadn't been her best moment, or a very compassionate one, but then again, who ever said she was compassionate?

"I wanted to talk to you," Morgan said quietly.

"Huh—yet you've been staying out of sight since the

moment your team rescued me from the prison," she replied.

"I know." Regret flashed across his face. "Seeing you again brought some old memories to the surface."

"Of Jeremy?"

He nodded. "Among other things."

She shifted in her seat to look at him. "You know, I never quite understood your relationship with him. You didn't treat him like a father figure, but he kind of treated you like a son."

"He was my commanding officer, not my father," Morgan said curtly.

"Once, after you came to visit, he told me . . ." She hesitated.

"He told you what?"

"That you were looking for someone."

Morgan stiffened.

"But he didn't offer any specifics." She paused for another beat. "Did you ever find who you were looking for?"

He released a breath. "No, I didn't."

"Are you still looking?"

"I never stopped."

Curiosity rose inside her, but she forced it down. The expression in Morgan's eyes told her he didn't like where the conversation had gone.

So, of course, he quickly changed the subject. "Luke told me you spoke to Devlin."

"I did," she answered carefully.

"What did he want?"

"Nothing important." She grinned. "Just to remind me that it's become his mission in life to destroy me."

Morgan cursed under his breath. "You shouldn't have spoken to him."

"Why not? He can't hurt me over the telephone line."

That wasn't entirely true. Devlin was certainly succeeding in ripping open old wounds. Yet she knew that wouldn't satisfy him for long. New wounds were what he was ultimately after. He wanted her dead.

Unfortunately for him, that wasn't going to happen. She had her own plans for Devlin ... once she figured them out anyway. If there was one thing she'd learned from Jeremy, it was that a divided focus always led to disaster. One battle at a time, he'd constantly advised. And the only battle that mattered at the moment was rescuing Lucia and the other girls. Dr. Silverton would be safe as long as Abby answered Devlin's silly phone calls, but once the girls were free, all bets were off.

Maybe she'd take his other eye first, before she killed him ... The thought brought a rush of satisfaction to her belly.

"You're playing with fire here," Morgan muttered. "The only reason Devlin hasn't come after you yet is because my compound is virtually impossible to find. I wish you'd decided to stay there, Abby."

She crossed her arms over her chest. "Kane promised I could be on the chopper when the girls are rescued."

"So you can see with your own eyes that we got them out? Can't you just trust us to do our job?"

"I want to be there," she said firmly.

"And to hell with what anyone else wants, right? Fuck, you're still the same stubborn kid I met twelve years ago." Morgan cursed again. "You'll be much easier to track down in Bogotá. Devlin will sniff you out."

"Let him," she said coolly.

A second obscenity sliced through the air. She glanced

over and saw Kane scowling at her. "Let him?" he echoed, practically seething. "Are you fucking serious?"

Abby faltered for a moment. How was he surprised? There had never been any doubt in her mind that she and Devlin would face off again.

"Of course," she answered. "Devlin and I are going to finish what we started in that prison. It's always been an inevitability."

"He's a killer, goddamn it."

"So am I."

Morgan's head moved from her to Kane. He looked intrigued by the exchange. "Nobody is killing anyone," he said sternly. "At least not until this extraction is behind us."

"You're not going near Devlin," Kane grumbled, as if Morgan hadn't even spoken.

Abby glared at him. "Is that an order?"

"It sure as hell is."

From the other side of the cabin, Luke chuckled.

"You don't give me orders," she said to Kane, her hands curling into fists. "If I choose to go after Devlin, you can't do a damn thing to stop me."

"Wanna bet?"

"Is there a reason why you're acting like a caveman right now?"

Kane shot her a saccharine smile. "Is there a reason why you're acting like an idiot?"

Had he just called her an idiot? The soft whistle coming from Luke's direction confirmed that he had indeed. Lord, you let a man give you an orgasm and suddenly he decided he ruled your life? Well, screw that.

"The subject is closed, Kane," she snapped. "Seriously, this isn't open for discussion anymore."

She thought she heard him murmur, "That's what you think," but Morgan swiftly held up his hand to silence them both. "Enough. You're acting like fucking children. The only thing any of us should be worrying about right now is how to get those girls out of Blanco's compound safely. Understood?"

Abby sobered instantly. He was right. The whole reason Devlin had targeted her was because she'd risked everything to save Lucia Alvaro and those helpless girls. She cursed Kane for making her forget that.

"Understood," she echoed. She turned away from Kane's angry gaze. "I'm taking a nap. Wake me when we land."

"Where the hell are you?"

Devlin glanced around the cramped motel room and gave a dry laugh. "Bakersfield, California. A rather dull place, I'm afraid."

On the other end of the line, Blanco released a string of Spanish curses. "I don't give a damn if it's the most entertaining location on the planet. I need you back here. Now."

"I'm tracking the Sinclair woman," Devlin replied through gritted teeth. "As per your instructions, Luis."

"Is she in this Bakersfield?"

"Well, no, but—"

"Then get your ass back here. You can just as easily track her from the estate."

Devlin's fingers tightened around the phone. Goddamn useless bastard. It was a wonder Blanco had managed to stand at the helm of a successful empire for this long. His dependence on Devlin reeked of weakness, and weakness revolted Devlin. Always had.

"The pilot is waiting for you in the hangar," Blanco added briskly. "If you're not here by tonight, you can seek other employment."

"Don't you think you're being a tad overdramatic, Luis?"

"Tonight, Devlin."

A click sounded in his ear. Devlin growled with rage and tossed the cell phone on the bed. It landed next to the tape recorder he'd stolen from Amanda Silverton's office, which he'd been listening to before Blanco called and ruined all of his fun. Abby was in the midst of describing the last time Ted Hartford visited her bedroom. Poor thing. Tried to fight back and failed.

He allowed the anger to wash over him for a moment, then squared his shoulders and began gathering his things. So be it. He would indulge Blanco and return to Colombia, but he was nowhere near finished with his sweet Abby.

He tucked the psychiatric tapes into his duffel and zipped it up, the sound of Abby's young, hesitant voice still floating in his head like the lingering scent of perfume. Oh, how he enjoyed tormenting her. He absently reached up to rub the sickening patch covering the mutilated eye socket the doctor hadn't been able to repair, feeling himself grow hard as he imagined the punishment he would exact on that little bitch.

Slitting her throat would always be his endgame, but there were still so many moves he wanted to make before he reached that point.

Blanco may have sent him on a bit of a detour, but soon he'd be back on the right path.

The one that would lead him straight to Abby Sinclair.

Chapter 15

It was dark when they finally arrived at the safe house. Kane and Morgan went in first, weapons drawn as they moved stealthily through the house before determining it was clear. The rest of the team filed into the den, Luke mumbling something about finding the nearest bar. Abby didn't make a move to follow the men, so Kane stayed rooted in place too. He regretted his outburst on the plane, but not enough to drop the subject as Abby had demanded. He didn't like these phone calls between her and Devlin. Not a damn bit.

"We'll take the bedroom at the end of the hall," he said curtly. "Morgan usually commandeers the master bedroom, and the others can bunk in the third room."

Abby's yellow eyes narrowed. "I'm not sharing a room with you."

"No, I'm pretty sure you are." He set his jaw. "Tonight we're going to finish what we started, Abby."

"And if I don't want to?"

"Tough shit."

She glared at him again, then spun around and disappeared down the hallway. A moment later he heard a door slam. An involuntary smile sprang to his lips. Damn, he liked her. She was fiery and stubborn and unbelievably hot when she was angry. Cold as ice too, but he'd already proven he possessed the ability to make her melt.

Heading for the den, he poked his head in and said, "Abby and I are turning in."

Three pairs of eyebrows rose at his remark. D's wasn't one of them. He simply stood at his customary place by the fireplace, his black eyes unreadable.

"Kane . . ." Morgan sounded oddly gentle. For a second. Then he reverted back to his harsh, no-nonsense self. "What the hell are you doing?"

He leaned against the doorframe. "Like I said, turning in."

"You know exactly what I mean." Morgan looked frazzled. "Abby Sinclair isn't a woman you want to mess with, for fuck's sake."

"Who says I'm messing with her?" he replied in annoyance. "I happen to enjoy her company."

"Yeah, I got that. You've enjoyed a lot of female company over the years. But I'm warning you that Abby isn't like the others. She's dangerous."

"I think I can handle her, sir."

Morgan seemed unconvinced. "Just be careful."

"I appreciate the concern." In other words, back off.

Morgan got the hint. With a heavy sigh, he changed the subject. "There was a message waiting on my voice mail. Bahar contacted Trevor again. Apparently Blanco wants to meet them."

Kane gave a pleased nod. "He took the bait, then."

"Looks like it. They're visiting his estate tomorrow afternoon. Once we get word that it's a go, we'll start to think about the best way to do this extraction."

"Okay. Keep me posted."

Ignoring the scowl D sent in his direction, Kane turned and headed to the bedroom. He half expected the door to be locked, but when he twisted the knob, it opened easily. He found Abby sitting on the bed, staring at the wall.

"What exactly did you do to D?" Kane asked as he closed the door behind him.

Her head lifted. "I didn't do anything to him."

"Really? Because he's turned into a tight-lipped asshole since we brought you back to Morgan's compound. Not that he was Mr. Chatty before, but I've never seen him act like this."

Something flickered in Abby's eyes.

Guilt?

"He doesn't like me," was all she said. "He made that pretty clear the night we met, and then several times afterward."

Kane searched his brain, trying to remember if Abby and D had ever been alone since that first night. He couldn't think of a single instance, yet he knew they must have had a run-in. D was more volatile than ever, and his gut told him that Abby had everything to do with it.

"So you didn't say anything to him," Kane pressed.

"Nope," she said lightly.

She was lying. He could feel it in his bones, but he had nothing to go on, no solid evidence to throw at her. Whatever. At this point, D's mysterious rage was the least of his worries.

Kicking off his boots, he moved toward the bed. She flinched at his approach.

"Don't," he said harshly. "Don't look at me like I'm going to hurt you."

She ran a hand through her red hair. "You can't hurt me," she said, sounding so matter-of-fact he wanted to throttle her.

He yanked his shirttail out of his waistband and began unbuttoning. Peeling it off his shoulders, he tossed the button-down across the room, then undid his pants.

Abby looked alarmed. "What are you doing?"

"What people usually do before getting into bed. Undressing." Sarcasm dripped from his voice.

"We're really going to share this room?"

"That's what I said."

Now wearing only a pair of black boxer briefs, he strode to the bed, lowered his body onto it, and stretched out on his back. Next to him, Abby shifted slightly. "You're being childish."

"Me? I'm pretty sure I'm the most mature adult in this room at the moment. At least I'm not going out of my way to pretend there isn't anything between us."

"I'm not pretending anything," she said with a frown. "There *isn't* anything between us."

"You can lie to the targets you cozy up to, but don't lie to me."

Shoving a strand of hair out of her eyes, she looked down at him, her face harsh. "You think because you made me come that we've formed some kind of bond, Kane? That we're going to get married and live happily ever after?"

Her emotionless tone annoyed the hell out of him. "I'm not naive enough to think that, Abby. But whether you like it or not, we have chemistry, and yes, I think we've formed a bond."

She shook her head. "Whatever you're aiming to get out of this, you're going to be disappointed." Her voice cracked. "I don't do relationships. I don't *want* relation-ships."

"Fine." He shrugged. "Then I'll just have to be satis-fied with sex."

Her throat bobbed as she swallowed. "I won't . . . I don't want it."

"There you go, lying again."

"I'm *not* lying."

"Then why are your nipples so hard? And don't blame the cold. Morgan cranked up the heat when we got here." He propped himself up on his elbows, his gaze sweeping up and down her body. "And why are you breathing so hard, sweetheart? Your breasts are practically heaving."

Those exquisite yellow eyes burned with indignation. "You're acting like a total bastard right now."

"I don't give a damn. I'm tired of this one-step-for-ward, two-steps-back bullshit. Tonight I want it all."

He fisted his hand in her hair and brought her head down to his. Their mouths collided in a hard kiss, which he deepened instantly by pushing his tongue between her lips. She gasped, tried to move away, but he held her in place, holding her prisoner with the kiss.

"Go ahead," he rasped against her mouth. "Tell me you want me to stop. Just say the words and I'll back off."

She searched his face, her eyes clouding with confu-sion. "You'll really back off if I ask?"

"I'm not like one of those bastards from your past," he muttered. "If you say no, I'll walk right out of this room, Abby."

Her lips trembled, her pulse throbbing furiously in her throat. She didn't say a word, and a flicker of alarm went off in his chest. Damn it. He wanted so badly for her to say yes. And he knew that if he felt like it, he really *could* be a bastard. He could force the issue instead of giving her the opportunity to back out.

But ...

It has to be her choice.

Although the gentle reminder had his cock twitching with impatience, his brain conceded to it. Abby was not a woman who liked to be pushed. She would push back—and then run away. Christ, he didn't want her to run from him. He wanted her so badly he could taste her. He *craved* her.

And he wanted her to feel the same way about him.

Meeting her gaze, he saw the conflicting emotions in her eyes. Need and confusion. Anticipation and reluctance.

"I want to say no." Her voice shook desperately. "I want to say it so badly—why can't I do it?"

He brushed his lips over hers. "Because you want to see this through as much as I do."

"I ..."

"You know I'm right." He lifted his hand to her breast, cupping the firm mound. "You want me to touch you. And you"—he gripped her wrist with his other hand and dragged it down to his groin— "want to touch me."

Her palm rubbed over him in a featherlight caress.

He sucked in his breath. "You've spent your entire life holding back. Don't you want to feel what it's like to let go?"

Those lush lips trembled again. "When you let go, you fall."

His heart squeezed in his chest. He stared into those gorgeous yellow eyes and suddenly found himself looking at a different woman. One who'd been hurt repeatedly as a child, one who'd built those enormously high defenses, that impenetrable wall, in order to protect herself.

But the wall was down now. Her face was awash with vulnerability. She was scared.

A rush of emotion flooded his body. He hadn't felt anything like this since Emily died. Hadn't allowed himself to get close to anyone, especially not the women he slept with.

This was different. Abby was different. She was a killer, a cold, distant woman who'd spent years building that wall around herself, yet somehow she'd broken through *his* wall. *His* defenses.

Jesus.

"I won't let you fall," he murmured, rolling onto his side and pinning her down on her back.

She gazed up at him uneasily, her red hair fanned out beneath her like strands of silk. "I'm not sure this is going to end well, Kane."

"Why does anything have to end?" He lowered his head and pressed a kiss to her neck. "Right now, let's just focus on the beginning."

Her uneasiness seemed to fade. "Okay."

That was all he needed to hear. He swiftly moved in to kiss her, and this time she responded. Her arms twined around his neck, pulling him closer, and he could feel her heartbeat vibrating against his chest. She was so warm, so soft and beautiful. It took all of his willpower not to rip her clothes off and devour her. She must have showered after their swim in the pond, because she smelled distinctly like the fancy Swiss soap Lloyd kept stocked in every bathroom at the compound. But another aroma mingled with the soap, something flowery and feminine and unbelievably intoxicating.

He breathed her in, then tasted her with his tongue, licking his way up her neck so he could nibble on her earlobe. She made a contented sound and her lower body moved restlessly against his, a slow, lazy rhythm that turned his cock to granite.

He kissed her again, groaning as their tongues met and swirled together. Gripping her waist with both hands, he ground himself against her, desperate for any contact. He wanted inside her. Wanted it more than life itself. But he didn't want to rush.

With infinite gentleness he hadn't known he possessed, he moved one hand between her legs and stroked her, eliciting another soft sound of pleasure from her throat.

"That's nice," she whispered.

"Very nice," he murmured back. He slowly dragged the panties off her smooth legs, sliding down so that he knelt at the juncture of her thighs. Unable to resist, he dipped his head and gave her one long lick.

Abby cried out.

Kane grew dizzy. Jesus, she tasted like heaven. Sweet and feminine. Heaven. He lapped at her with his tongue, surprised by the violent wave of arousal that slammed into him like an eighteen-wheeler. If he died right this instant, then he'd die a happy man. He couldn't remember the last time going down on a woman had brought him such incredible pleasure, and the new sensation spurred him on.

Abby moaned as he feasted on her. He alternated between long licks and lazy kisses, then tongued her frantically, until she was clawing at the sheets and murmuring nonsensical things at him. When he slid a finger inside her, she bucked her hips off the bed, crying out. He felt her orgasm pulsing against his tongue, and he rode it out with her, his mouth pressed to her damp sex as she lost control. He was pretty close to losing control too. His cock was hot and heavy between his legs, begging for attention. The need to claim her was so freaking strong he barely gave her time to recover before he was moving up her body, one arm fumbling over the edge of the bed for his jeans so he could get the condom he'd stashed there.

Abby's hands dug into his shoulders, stilling him. "Not yet," she said softly. "It's my turn."

Before he could blink, she had him on his back and her long red hair tickled his pecs as she slithered down his body. When he felt her warm breath on the tip of his cock, he nearly exploded right then and there. Breathing deeply through his nose, he willed away the impending release. Abby's tongue darted out to lick his engorged head, summoning a low groan from his chest.

She rubbed her lips over him, then lifted her head to meet his eyes. "Tell me what you like."

"Everything," he choked out. "I like everything you're doing."

"Tell me," she insisted.

Kane was floored by what he saw on her face. Eyebrows drawn together, lips pursed, eyes shining with fortitude. She seemed determined to bring him pleasure and he could suddenly picture that same determination hardening her features on the field, as she threw her entire being into the task of accomplishing her goal.

Although it nearly killed him to say it, he mumbled, "Start slow. Make me beg for it."

With a hint of a smile, she bent down and proceeded to torture him into oblivion. She lavished all her attention on him, squeezing and kissing and worshiping his cock so thoroughly that his chest tightened with emotion. She licked him from base to tip with the lazy swipe of her tongue, again and again, breaking the rhythm every few seconds to suck him deep into her mouth. Groaning, he tangled his fingers in her hair and tried to thrust into her mouth, but she turned her cheek and pressed soft kisses to his inner thigh instead, refusing to give him what he wanted.

Kane's muscles loosened and turned to jelly, tiny pinpricks of pleasure making every inch of his skin tingle. "Abby," he said hoarsely. "Please."

Laughing, she brought him back to her mouth, wrapping her lips around his cock and sucking so hard he thought he might have a heart attack. She moved one hand to his balls, cupped them, kneaded them, and then her tongue was down there and he cried out in agony-laced ecstasy. He grasped her hair in his fist and yanked her up.

"Jesus Christ, Abby, *fuck me.*"

She laughed in what sounded like sheer delight, already fumbling for the condom. She rolled it onto his erection and positioned herself over him, her gaze locked with his as she seated herself on his throbbing dick.

They both moaned as he filled her. Abby arched her back, drawing his attention to her chest, to those dusky-red nipples that begged for attention. He cupped her breasts as she rode him, pinching her nipples and rolling them between his fingers. In response, her inner muscles clamped over him, squeezing so tight he knew he couldn't last long.

"It's going to be fast," he warned huskily. "I can't ..."

She undulated against him and he muttered a curse. "I can't hold back."

"I don't want you to," she whispered. "You said we're letting go, right?"

His pulse took off at a wild gallop as she ground her tight sex against him, her hips thrusting with reckless abandon. Fire consumed him, searing his skin and burning through his veins. He didn't want it to end. Ever. Yet he couldn't stop himself from racing to the finish line. She began to ride him hard, and he met her furious movements with his upward thrusts. He hit a spot deep inside her and she cried out so loudly he worried he might have hurt her, but one look at those yellow eyes, gleaming with raw passion, and he was reassured.

He felt her tightening around his shaft, squeezing him, milking him as she lost herself to another pounding climax. It was too much. With a groan, Kane exploded inside her, his cock throbbing with each endless wave of release. Every nerve ending in his body hissed with pleasure, crackling and sizzling and sending sparks of heat jolting through him.

"Jesus," he mumbled when they both grew still.

"Why do men always say that?" she teased, sounding breathless. "Jesus and sex don't really go hand in hand."

A laugh squeezed out of his chest. "Would you prefer I say, *Holy fuck, Abby, I can't move my fucking legs, that was so good*?"

She laughed. "I think I might like that better."

"Okay, then. Holy fuck, Abby, I can't move my fucking legs, that was so good."

Trevor liked Isabel Roma.

He actually *liked* Isabel Roma.

He wasn't sure if it happened during her confession about her background, or maybe at some other random time he couldn't pinpoint, but somehow, during the last few hours, he'd realized he was actually enjoying her company.

They'd shared a quiet dinner in the honeymoon suite of Casa Medina, then moved to the love seats by the fireplace and started talking. About this current assignment. About past assignments. Random childhood stories. And sure, he may have consumed several glasses of wine, but he didn't feel drunk. Only confused, that somehow his partnership with Isabel had gone from coldly impersonal to oddly comfortable.

The realization brought that familiar pang of guilt.

"I hope Abby's all right," Isabel was saying, twirling a lock of black hair around one slender finger.

Trevor pushed his disturbing thoughts away. "I'm sure she's fine. She seems like the type who can take care of herself."

"Oh, she is. To the extreme." Isabel smiled wryly. "What she needs to learn is how to let other people take care of her once in a while."

"Have you two known each other long?"

"Five or six years. She's a hard woman to get to know, but eventually she lowered her guard with me. Want to know a secret?"

Isabel's eyes twinkled playfully. Trevor had to force himself to remain unaffected. So what if Isabel Roma was drop-dead gorgeous? So what if her laid-back personality and innate charm had the power to put him at ease? Like Abby, he may have lowered his guard around Isabel, but this tentative friendship didn't mean . . . It didn't mean anything.

"What's the secret?" he said gruffly.

"Abby's my favorite." Isabel let out a little laugh. "I always say that I love them all equally, but I actually have a big soft spot for Abby."

"Who's *them*?" he asked quizzically.

"The other chameleons Noelle took under her wing," she clarified. "There's Abby, of course, Juliet, Paige, and then Bailey, who's been on some hush-hush undercover op for the past year. We all try to get together a few times a year. Really, they're my only family."

"Are they all as good as you at becoming a different person?" he asked in a wry voice.

"Bailey's even better. When she's in character, I could walk right past her on the street without even batting an eye."

"So you're all pretty close."

"Sure. Aren't you close with Morgan and the guys?"

"I used to be." He winced at the wistful note in his voice. Fuck, he'd definitely had too much wine if he was getting all sappy.

"I like them," Isabel said frankly. She grinned. "Even Luke, who thinks he actually stands a chance at seducing me."

Trevor couldn't help but laugh. "You mean you didn't fall for his Cajun charm?"

"Sure I did. Just not enough to go to bed with him."

"Wait until you meet Sullivan." Trevor snorted. "I've yet to come across a woman who can resist him."

"He's the Australian one, right?" When Trevor nodded, she said, "Yeah, Luke mentioned him when we were out shooting." She took a sip of her wine. "You've got a really diverse group there. Rangers, SEALs, Marines, Australian Defence Force. How'd you meet Morgan anyway?"

"He approached me after I left the army." Trevor ran a hand through his hair. "I was so tired of fighting wars I knew we could never win. Wars we shouldn't even have been fighting. I went back to Colorado and worked at a security firm, and one day Morgan showed up and told me it was a waste of my skills to be working as a security guard at a bank. I talked it over with Gi—" He stopped hastily.

Isabel sighed. "It's okay to say her name, you know."

"I know." He gulped, forced himself to continue. "I talked it over with Gina, and she agreed with Morgan. Said I was wasting away in all the *normalcy*." He smiled faintly. "Apparently I wasn't good at doing normal."

"Join the club." To prove her point, Isabel swept her hand over her newly transformed appearance.

"Just out of curiosity, what do you actually look like?"

"Boring old blond hair, boring old blue eyes. I'm the only blue-eyed blonde in my immediate family. They all look very Italian—dark hair, dark eyes, olive skin. My brother used to tease me when we were kids, said I must have been adopted. If I wasn't the spitting image of my maternal great-grandmother, I probably would have believed that."

Trevor laughed, and this time it didn't sound so rusty. He'd laughed a lot tonight. Too much, probably.

Fortunately, his cell phone began to ring before he could question his renewed capability for laughter. The ringing phone didn't belong to Julian; it was the one he used for work, and sure enough, Morgan's number flashed across the screen.

The conversation was short, and when he hung up, Isabel gave him a questioning look. "They're here?"

"Landed a half hour ago," he confirmed. "After our

meeting with Blanco tomorrow, he wants us at the safe house to go over the extraction."

For the first time all night, Isabel looked ill at ease. "Do you think Blanco will give us an invitation?"

"Yeah, I do." There was no hesitation on his part. "Bahar obviously gave his approval, and Blanco trusts the guy. I think this meeting is just a formality." His mouth twisted. "And I think he's going to demand a fortune from us for this attendance fee of his."

Isabel leaned over and set her wineglass on the little table between the two love seats. "Greed," she said, shaking her head. "I've never really understood it. So many lives destroyed, thanks to all those greedy people out there."

His throat tightened. "A television," he heard himself stammering.

She glanced over in confusion. "What?"

"That's what the man who robbed our condo got out of the deal. He took the television and Gina lost her life."

Too much. He'd said too fucking much, and now it felt like a huge weight was pressing down on his chest. Stumbling to his feet, he began gathering up their wineglasses and the now empty bottle, then stalked over to the meal cart by the door and dumped everything on it. He rolled the cart out of the suite, leaving it off to the side, then hesitated in the carpeted hallway.

He drew in a ragged breath. Enough. He was here because Morgan had asked him to take the lead on an extraction.

He was here because this was a suicide mission that probably wouldn't end the way Morgan desired. There were too many variables to contend with. Blanco's army of guards. William Devlin. A compound where security had undoubtedly been strengthened after the last breach, courtesy of Morgan. Thirteen girls in who-knew-what condition.

Chances were, there would be casualties.

And Trevor was perfectly content to be one of them.

Abby was out of her element. She and Kane were lying in bed, legs tangled together, her head nestled against his bare chest while one strong arm wrapped tightly around her. She'd never really shared a bed with a man before. The targets she'd been involved with hadn't wanted to sleep beside her. A lot of powerful men, she'd found, preferred sleeping alone. So had she, up until just now. Who would've guessed how nice it could be? Cuddling close to a warm male body, hearing his heart beating in her ear as his fingers absently stroked her hair.

She kind of liked it.

"You still awake?" he murmured in the darkness.

"Yeah," she murmured back.

"Abby . . ." He trailed off.

"What is it?"

"I don't want to push you." He sounded frustrated. "Normally I just make demands and get the other person to do what I want, to tell me what I want. But I don't feel right pushing you."

She sighed against his skin. "You want to know about Devlin?"

"Yes, damn it."

The impatience in his voice brought a smile to her lips. She suspected it had taken a lot out of him not to demand answers the moment the sex had ended.

"I don't like that you're speaking to him. I don't like knowing he wants to hurt you," he added hoarsely.

"It's not like I want to talk to the bastard." She hesitated, then opted for the truth. "He threatened someone I care about."

She could practically hear his brow furrowing. "Who?"

"The psychiatrist I saw after Jeremy adopted me. Her name is Dr. Silverton, and she was the one person I was able to talk to about my past."

"Okay. How the heck did Devlin track her down?"

"I don't know. I'm assuming he has a rat in the CIA — that's the only government agency with a file on me. He must have gotten his hands on it, then dug into my background until he found Dr. Silverton." Her voice shook. "He broke into her office and stole my session tapes. And he said he would kill her if I didn't take his calls."

Kane swore softly. "Why didn't you tell me?"

"In case you haven't noticed, I don't like to confide in people."

"So what, he calls you and . . . chats?"

"No. He makes me remember the past."

"What the hell does that mean?"

"He talks to me about my childhood. Last time he played a part of Dr. Silverton's tape."

Kane's arm tightened around her. "He makes you listen to yourself talk about . . . everything that happened? Makes you go through that over and over again?"

"Well, he's only called twice," she said lightly.

"That's more than enough. Jesus, Abby, how do you stand it?"

"I have to." She shrugged. "Besides, I need to make him think he's actually getting to me."

"But he's not?"

"Not as much as he thinks he is." She let out a sigh. "Look, I know you don't want to hear this, but I *will* eliminate Devlin. I can't be looking over my shoulder for the rest of my life. I'm going to have to kill him, but not yet. Right now I'm perfectly content with distracting him."

His jaw tensed. "You're playing games with a psychopath, Abby."

"I know how to handle men like Devlin. I've done it before, and I always win."

He seemed perturbed by her confidence. She tilted her head to see a frown marring his mouth. "It'll be fine, Kane. You don't have to worry about me."

With a frustrated sound, he tried to shift out from under the bedcovers.

"Where are you going?" she demanded.

"To tell Morgan about this. We can hire some guards for Silverton, someone to watch over her, make sure she's safe." He frowned again. "You should have told me earlier."

She slung an arm over his muscular chest, keeping him in place. "You can talk to Morgan in the morning. Devlin won't do anything, not unless I don't take his next call."

Kane relaxed slightly. "Fine," he conceded. "But we're taking care of this in the morning."

"Fine."

They lay in silence for a while. Abby's eyelids grew heavy. She was too sated, too exhausted to move, and at the moment there wasn't anywhere else she wanted to be.

"Falling asleep in each other's arms like normal people is nice," she whispered.

"Yes," he agreed roughly. "And stop saying you're not normal."

"But I'm not. I kill people for a living. How is that normal?"

"You also get yourself thrown in Colombian prisons in order to save the lives of innocent children," he pointed out.

She burst out laughing. "How is that normal?"

"I'm talking about the motive, not the method. You saw those girls and your first instinct was to save their lives. Know what that means?"

She smiled in the darkness. "What does it mean?"

"That you're a good person." He gave a mock gasp. "Can you believe it? You're actually a good person."

"Not as good as you." She slid her hand down his chest and rested it on his crotch. Almost immediately, she felt him swell beneath her palm.

"I thought you were tired." His voice was a sexy whisper.

"I'm suddenly really alert." She stroked him. "So are you, by the feel of it."

"Why, Abby, are you trying to seduce me?"

"Yes. Is it working?"

Before she could blink, he rolled on top of her, his thick hardness pressing into her thigh. "Yeah, I think it might be working."

Cupping the back of his head, she drew his mouth to hers and murmured, "Good."

Chapter 16

Devlin called early the next morning while Kane was out with Morgan to meet their helicopter guy. Abby was grateful Kane wasn't around for this phone call. He'd left his cell at the house, after she made it perfectly clear that if something happened to Amanda Silverton because Kane was too protective to let her handle Devlin on her own, she would cut his balls off.

Apparently he held his balls in high esteem because he handed the phone over without so much as a protest.

"I apologize for being out of touch," Devlin began cheerfully, "but I had to catch a flight back to Colombia."

Suspicion crept up her spine. He'd left California? Without touching Dr. Silverton? That couldn't be good.

"But don't think the threat to the lovely doctor is over," he added. "One phone call and Silverton will be the victim of an unfortunate mugging gone awry on her way home from the market."

"What is the point of all this?" she asked with a sigh. "What do you think these phone calls are going to achieve?"

"They bring me pleasure, luv. I enjoy hearing that

adorable crack in your voice when we speak about your appealing childhood."

"You're really screwed up—you know that?"

"Who isn't?" He laughed. "I finished listening to the last session on the plane. I enjoyed hearing you describe your plan of attack." Another laugh. "Did you honestly believe you could kill Ted Hartford?"

Tonight she was ready for him.

"Don't fight it," he whispered in the darkness, one big hand latching onto her thigh. "Remember what happened the last time you fought?"

Oh, she remembered.

She pushed the memory away and sank down at the edge of the bed. "I did at the time."

"But you were too weak, weren't you, Abby?"

"Yes." It hurt her to admit it, but there was no point in lying. "But I grew stronger. I grew very, very strong, Devlin."

"Jeremy Thomas." He paused. "Did you screw him too? Was that what he required in exchange for getting rid of Hartford?"

"Jeremy never touched me," she said through clenched teeth.

A shadow at the foot of the bed. The gleaming silver chain around a thick, corded neck.

"No," she murmured, spitting blood from her mouth. "No, please . . ."

But she'd thought Jeremy would touch her, hadn't she? When he'd pulled Ted off her, when he'd scooped her up into his arms. No matter how many soothing words he'd murmured in her ear, she hadn't seen him as her savior. Only a new enemy.

The memory of Jeremy's shaved head and gentle hazel eyes flashed in her mind. He hadn't been her enemy, though. He'd helped her become strong. Helped her put the past behind her. She could never repay him for everything he'd done.

"You know, you can't hurt me with this," she said before she could stop herself.

She immediately regretted the slipup, cursing her stupidity. No. She needed Devlin to think he *was* hurting her. She needed to keep him distracted until they managed to free the girls.

"I'm starting to think you're right," Devlin said slowly. He went quiet for a moment, while Abby resisted the urge to kick herself for her foolish error. "Drat. I guess I'll just have to find another way to hurt you."

A loud click sounded in her ear. He'd hung up.

She experienced a rush of self-reproach. She'd been supposed to play along, to let him think his little forays into her childhood were truly affecting her. Now he'd be searching for new ammunition, something else to hold over her head.

Damn it. She'd messed up.

With a sigh, she dropped the phone on the bed and left the room, heading for the small, tidy kitchen. Her stomach had been grumbling for the past hour, and she decided to quit ignoring it. Her body didn't feel as bruised and ravaged anymore, but her injuries weren't going to heal if she didn't give them any sustenance.

To her dismay, D was in the kitchen when she entered, leaning against the sink as he ate a bowl of cereal. A pair of black pants encased his long legs and the muscles of his chest rippled beneath his black muscle shirt. He truly was a formidable-looking man, every inch of him hard and radiating danger. His gaze darkened the moment he saw her.

Abby squared her shoulders. Might as well get this confrontation over with. Kane had already noticed the deep animosity between her and D. The others would eventually notice too.

"Mind if I join you?" she asked breezily.

He made an unintelligible sound, which she decided to take as *yes*. She opened a few cupboards until she found a stack of bowls, grabbed one, then swiped the cereal box he'd left on the counter and poured herself a bowl.

"Look," she said as she got a carton of milk from the fridge, "I don't do this often, but I'm going to apologize, okay? I'm sorry about what I said the other day. It's none of my business what may or may not have happened to you in your past."

D didn't respond.

She hopped up onto the counter and took a bite of cereal, then made a face. No sugary cereal in this house. Morgan apparently preferred tasteless lumps of bran. She chewed, then swallowed fast, trying to ignore the bland taste. "I get it," she said when he remained silent. "You don't like me. Most people don't."

D let out a harsh laugh. "Kane does."

Discomfort climbed up her spine. "And that bothers you."

"That you're fucking our second in command? Yes, it bothers me."

"And why is that?"

"Because you're distracting one of our best men." He scowled. "I've seen the way he looks at you. It's sad, really."

"Kane is a professional. Sex isn't going to cloud his judgment."

"It already has."

Annoyed, she gave up on trying to convince him otherwise. She ate quietly while he stood there on the other side of the kitchen, looking equally annoyed to be sharing the space with her.

Abby took one last bite, then jumped off the counter and proceeded to rinse her bowl in the sink. "I won't hurt him," she said softly, keeping her back turned.

"Whatever you say."

She spun around. "I don't care what you believe, D. I was planning on rescuing those girls on my own, but the plan changed, all right? You guys interfered and now I'm stuck on the sidelines. You think I like this? I could easily sneak away in the middle of the night and try to do this myself, but it's too late. You guys are involved now, and I won't do anything to jeopardize your lives."

He looked at her dubiously. "If you expect me to believe you're going to sit in this house twiddling your thumbs and miss out on all the action . . ."

"Believe what you want," she snapped. "You think I'm a loose cannon—I get it. But you're wrong."

"Am I?" he said coolly.

"You're wrong," she repeated. She shoved the clean bowl in the dish rack, dried her hands with the little towel hanging off the stove, and then walked out of the kitchen, leaving him to believe whatever the hell he wanted.

"Remember," Trevor said as the car neared the long driveway leading to Blanco's estate, "we'll be watched at all times. And just because Abby said there weren't any microphones doesn't mean she's right."

"This isn't the first time I've done something like this," Isabel replied, rolling her eyes. "In fact, I've probably done more undercover work than you."

"Probably," he agreed. His dark eyes studied her face. "I'm annoying you, aren't I?"

"Nope. Actually, I think the constant reminders are kind of cute."

Cute. Oh brother. Had she really said that? Funny, how a few days ago, *cute* would've been the last word she'd use to describe Trevor. *Asshole*, maybe. *Lifeless robot*, perhaps. But not *cute*.

She had no clue when it happened, but somehow, during the past couple of days, she'd actually started to like Trevor Callaghan.

Fortunately, Trevor's cell phone began to vibrate before Isabel could dwell on the troubling thought. Trevor looked at the caller ID screen and answered the phone with a gruff "Yeah?" He listened for several moments, then hung up with a frown.

"What's going on?" she asked.

Trevor glanced at the partition separating them from the driver to make sure it was up. "That was Abby," he said in a low voice. "She said Devlin is at the compound. She wanted to make sure I stayed out of his way."

Isabel felt uneasy. "You said he wouldn't recognize you if he saw you again."

"He probably won't. I look nothing like I did eight years ago, and I only met the guy once. I didn't even go along on the mission Morgan took him on."

"But there's a chance he'll remember you."

"There's a chance," he conceded. "But I don't think he will."

Isabel hoped he was right. They couldn't afford having

their covers blown. Not now, when they were so close. The car neared the guarded front gate of Blanco's property. Four dark-skinned men in navy blue uniforms promptly marched out of the security booth, signaling for the driver to halt. Four men—not the two Abby had warned them about. Security *had* been tightened, then.

After the car came to a stop, one of the guards tapped on the driver's window. "Out of car," the guard barked in broken English after the window rolled down.

"Here we go," Trevor murmured.

The two of them exited the vehicle along with their driver. The guards swarmed them, demanding to see ID, then patted down their clothing and mumbled to each other in Spanish.

One of the guards frowned as he discovered the handgun tucked into Trevor's waistband. He held it up in front of Trevor's face, demanding, *"¿Qué es este?"*

Trevor shrugged. "Protection."

The guards exchanged a look, and the one holding the gun disappeared into the booth with the weapon. Isabel saw him pick up the phone, his face expressionless as he informed the person on the other end of the line about the situation. A minute later the man returned, his eyes hard. "Gun stays here. You get back when leave."

Trevor looked annoyed. "If you insist."

The guard pointed to the car. "Drive. Park at house."

Isabel smothered a sigh of relief as they were allowed back into the vehicle. Their driver started the engine, and then they continued up the long driveway until the main house came into view. Isabel had seen pictures of it, but the elegance of the sprawling hacienda still surprised her. It had pale cream walls and a green roof, with a large plantation-style porch and an enormous pillared entrance.

Abby had told them the house boasted two large wings—the east belonged to Blanco, and the west featured guest suites and the servants' quarters. The prison was housed in a separate building at the other end of the compound, and beneath it would be the bunker where Blanco's "merchandise" was being held.

Most of Blanco's meetings took place on the rear terrace, according to Abby. Apparently the back of the property had a Playboy Mansion feel to it, the terrace overlooking a kidney-shaped pool surrounded by leafy palm fronds and a grotto that held a twelve-person hot tub. A tad over the top. Isabel preferred her surroundings to be cozy, simple.

Another uniformed guard greeted them at the end of the driveway. This one spoke English, and he was very polite as he informed them that his employer was waiting for them on the terrace. He was also very obvious as he scrutinized Isabel from head to toe, appearing very pleased with what he saw.

She'd chosen a skintight red dress for this meeting. The material barely covered her upper thighs, and her breasts practically popped out of the bodice. A pair of black stilettos completed the ensemble, and today she'd swept her hair up in a complicated twist. She barely glanced at the admiring guard as she linked her arm through Trevor's and headed toward the front steps.

The interior of the house was as elegant as its exterior. Antique furniture and modern art made for an interesting combination, and the floor beneath her high heels was smooth white marble. When they finally stepped onto the terrace, Blanco was indeed waiting for them, and she was surprised by how short he was. Couldn't have been taller than five-seven, yet he had a commanding air to him that made him seem larger. His skin had that leathery look, hinting at too many years in the sun, while his robust body boasted of at least a couple of sins—sloth and gluttony.

"Mr. and Mrs. Martin," he said in surprisingly smooth English. His voice held only a trace of an accent. "I thank you for driving all this way to come visit with me." He shook hands with Trevor, kissed Isabel on both cheeks, then gestured to the large glass table behind them. "Please, sit."

Surprisingly chivalrous, Blanco pulled out Isabel's chair for her before rounding the table to take his own seat. "I apologize for requesting that your weapon be confiscated," he added, looking over at Trevor with a regretful smile. "I can't be too careful. I hope you understand."

"Perfectly," Trevor answered.

"Rest assured, your property will be returned to you on your way out."

Smoothing out the hem of her dress, Isabel settled in her chair and reached for the starched napkin on the table. Blanco's cook had laid out a feast for them; the table was adorned with various dishes along with several bottles of wine. The aromas of grilled fish, rice, and a variety of vegetables filled her nostrils.

If she'd known lunch would be this elaborate she would've gone easy on breakfast.

Blanco gestured to the plate in front of her. "Eat. I know you Brazilian women are very particular about your food, but I am sure you'll find Pedro's cooking to your liking."

"I'm sure I will."

She hesitated only slightly before lifting the fork to

her lips. The chances of the food being poisoned were slim, but she still felt apprehensive taking that first bite. She noticed Blanco watching her mouth, his dark eyes flickering with arousal as she wrapped her lips around the fork. His gaze dropped to her neck, then lower, to her breasts.

"You have exquisite taste in women, Mr. Martin," Blanco said, smiling broadly at Trevor.

"Very exquisite," Trevor agreed, his gaze appreciative as he looked at her.

The two men chatted about business as lunch progressed. Abby had warned Isabel that Blanco wasn't fond of women joining in during business discussions, so she wisely kept quiet, eating the delicious food, which so far hadn't made her drop dead. Trevor gave Blanco the same details he'd offered Bahar, though this time he spoke in more detail about his gentlemen's lounge, which seemed to capture Blanco's interest.

"I have been looking to invest in such an establishment," Blanco admitted. "I've been told it's a very profitable market."

"It is," Trevor confirmed. "As long as one pays the authorities to look the other way, it can be very lucrative."

Blanco nodded fervently. "I would like to discuss this more, Mr. Martin. At a later time perhaps. As you know, I'm quite busy with other matters at the moment. Which brings us to the purpose of your visit."

Isabel lifted her head. Finally. She pushed her plate away and joined the discussion. As she and Trevor had planned, she pasted a look of uncertainty on her face. "I'm afraid my husband and I are having some second thoughts," she confessed.

Blanco's dark eyes met hers. "Is that so, señora?"

"We have discussed it," she went on, "and we are concerned about some of the details."

Blanco turned to Trevor. "What kind of details?"

Trevor laced his hands together. "Travel issues, for one. I suspect there might be individuals looking for your merchandise—stolen goods are often hunted, no? My wife and I are avid travelers, and if we were to purchase one of your items, we are worried it might affect our lifestyle."

"I can assure you, traveling will not be a problem. Passports and other identification papers have already been issued." Blanco smiled graciously. "Adoption papers can also be arranged if you'd prefer to pass the item off as your child. I feel that would appeal to you, as a couple, and make it far easier to explain the sudden presence of the item in your life, particularly since you two enjoy the limelight." He shrugged. "It is easier for the other buyers. Most of them are wealthy single men who prefer to stay in rather than socialize. But you and your wife . . . I believe adoption is a simple solution."

Isabel swallowed her horror. Was this man for real? She casually placed her hands in her lap—it was the only way to stop herself from strangling him.

Trevor pretended to be appeased by Blanco's speech. "That's reassuring. We were also worried about the . . . the *quality* of the goods, if you will."

Isabel wrinkled her nose in distaste. "I don't like dirty things," she said petulantly. "And strong odors irritate my sensitive nose."

Blanco gave her an indulgent smile. "Not to worry, señora. I've arranged for the goods to be taken into our servants' quarters before the sale. They will be in pristine condition."

She feigned relief. "Oh, that is wonderful. That was my main concern, I must admit."

"What about security?" Trevor said sharply. "A contact of mine informed me you had a little . . . *mishap* here about a week ago."

Blanco's face darkened. "Yes," he admitted. "That is true. But rest assured, my security is stronger than ever. My men will monitor the entire property, and I have a very close relationship with some very important government officials. They have assured me there will be no interference on their part."

"Good." Trevor leaned back in his chair. "I'd like to discuss payment now, if it suits you. Your solicitor was very vague about the actual cost of attendance."

Isabel didn't miss the brief smirk that graced Blanco's mouth. Oh yeah, he was totally going to bleed them dry here. She wouldn't be surprised if he demanded triple the regular fee from them.

"Because you expressed your interest at such short notice, the price will be higher, I'm afraid."

Isabel stifled a laugh.

"How much higher?" Trevor asked.

"Seven hundred and fifty thousand."

Trevor didn't even blink. "I believe that's fair."

Blanco looked momentarily surprised, but he recovered quickly, clearing his throat. "Very well, then. I will have Bahar contact you with the details for the wire transfer. The funds will need to be transferred tonight. The sale is in two days, after all, and I'd like the attendance fee to be received well before then."

"That won't be a problem."

The conversation came to a halt as a wiry man with a long scar slicing one cheek appeared on the terrace.

William Devlin.

Isabel didn't need the black eye patch for confirmation. Abby had given a detailed description of Devlin, emphasizing the cold, emotionless face. As usual, Abby was right. The man in front of them looked completely incapable of feeling. There was something dark and evil emanating from his lean, muscular frame.

From the corner of her eye, she noticed Trevor angle and bend his head slightly in a subtle attempt to shield himself from Devlin.

"Sorry to interrupt," Devlin said in a British accent. "I wanted to inform you I spoke to Cortez. He will be attending as planned."

Blanco picked up his wineglass, taking his sweet-ass time in answering. Panic jolted through her. The longer Blanco chugged on that wine, the better the chance that Devlin would pay closer attention to Blanco's guests. Swallowing, Isabel reached for the tall water glass by her plate and scooped out a wet ice cube with her manicured fingers.

"My, it's hot today," she exclaimed, sending a sexy giggle in Blanco's direction. Next to her, Trevor was chewing vigorously, as if the meal in front of him were the most interesting thing on the planet. Giggling again, Isabel brought the ice cube to her collarbone and moved it across her skin. A chill tingled her flesh.

Across the table, Blanco's eyes widened in appreciation. His gaze followed the movements of her hands, and her peripheral vision caught Devlin glancing her way too. His expression revealed a hint of disdain, though. Looking annoyed, he flicked his eyes to his boss, who dismissed him with the wave of his hand.

"If Cortez changes his mind again, please reassure

him. Now go check on the merchandise. I'll send for you later."

Annoyance hardened Devlin's jaw, but he simply nodded. Without even glancing in Trevor and Isabel's direction, he strode off.

Isabel slowly released the breath she'd been holding, continuing to drag the irritating ice cube over her cleavage. Damn, now the top of her dress was wet.

"I must apologize for Devlin," Blanco said pleasantly. "He's not particularly sociable." He pushed back his chair. "And I must also apologize for the brief nature of this meeting. My guests usually enjoy staying the night, but I'm afraid I must bid you good-bye now."

"Not a problem," Trevor said, helping Isabel to her feet. "We should get going anyway. I'll need to contact my banker to arrange the money."

They exchanged pleasantries, and then the guard that let them in walked them back to the car. After stopping yet again at the security booth and enduring another search—what, did Blanco think they'd steal the silverware?—they were in the car and on their way back to the city.

"That was close," Isabel breathed. "I don't know why, but I really thought Devlin was going to recognize you."

"For a moment there, so did I," he admitted. A rare smile lifted his mouth. "Nice move with the ice. Blanco's eyes nearly popped out of his head."

She offered a smile of her own. "That was the plan." The smile faded as she remembered the reason they'd met with Blanco in the first place. "Well, he seemed interested in taking our money, so now what? How do we save those girls?"

"We're seeing the others tomorrow morning," Trevor

reminded her. "We'll figure everything out then and decide what our next move will be."

Devlin barely noticed Blanco's guests as he left the patio. He didn't give a damn about the perverts attending this auction. His mind was a million miles away, mulling over ways he could lure Abby Sinclair to him. He'd had his fun torturing her about her childhood, but now it was time for a very different kind of fun.

Now he wanted his hands around her throat.

The guard standing outside the prison door blanched when he saw Devlin's face. The man had been there the night Abby Sinclair assaulted him, Devlin remembered.

"What the fuck are you looking at?" he snapped.

The guard stared down at the floor. "Nothing. Sorry if I offended you, Señor Devlin."

Devlin brushed past the man without another word. He entered the prison and stalked toward the cell at the far end of the block. The metal trapdoor in the corner of the cell squeaked as he thrust it open. Bloody Blanco and his bloody sex auction. Devlin cursed his employer as he climbed down the steel ladder leading to the underground tunnel that had been installed on the property long before Blanco purchased it from a retired arms dealer.

The tunnel was damp and musty, reeking of mold and stale urine. The overhead lights flickered relentlessly as Devlin charged toward the bunker. The sentry at the door—Corbacho was his name—had a big beak of a nose, beady black eyes, and an AK-47 tucked under his armpit.

"Blanco wants an update on the merchandise," Devlin snapped irritably, switching to Spanish. Most of Blanco's guards were dumb as shit, and spoke garbled broken English that grated on his nerves. Corbacho was one of them.

Corbacho's gaze rested briefly on the patch covering Devlin's eye before dropping down to his feet. "The merchandise has been fed, clothed, and photographed."

"No problems with any of the items?"

Corbacho shifted uneasily. "One has been refusing to eat, but I fixed the problem. Two are very insolent. I believe they might prove to be troublesome when they're being transported."

"I'm sure you'll be able to control them." Devlin glanced at the AK-47. "Though I must ask, is that really necessary? I would think a small pistol would do the job just as well. An assault rifle feels like overkill for a bunch of weak little girls, no?"

Corbacho looked insulted. "That is what the woman said, but I would disagree with both of you. This is a fine choice of weapon."

Devlin blinked. "What did you say?"

"I said, it is a fine—"

"No," he cut in impatiently. "You said something about a woman."

The guard looked confused. "Yes. Señorita Erica."

Devlin's pulse sped up. None of the guards save those who worked in the prison were aware of "Erica's" escape. Blanco—no doubt to save his silly pride—had ordered total secrecy on the matter, so it didn't surprise Devlin to hear Corbacho speak of her in such a respectful tone. The idiot probably thought Erica was still the boss's mistress.

But the guard's revelation . . . now that was a surprise. "Blanco brought her down here?" he asked sharply.

"Yes. He seemed very eager to let her see the merchandise."

"And how did she react?" Devlin demanded.

"Very excited. She asked a lot of questions." Corbacho smirked. "I was told she was a very sensual woman."

Devlin wasn't listening anymore. His mind was working over the implications of what the guard had told him. Abby Sinclair had been taken down to this bunker. She'd seen the scared little girls huddled in that dirty, cold room.

"Excited," he muttered to himself.

Oh no. His Abby had been enraged. She had looked into those huge, terrified eyes. She had looked into a mirror.

Turning swiftly on his heel, Devlin glanced over his shoulder and said, "Contact me if any problems arise." And then he marched down the tunnel, a wide smile stretching across his face.

Oh, Abby, you wanted to save them, didn't you?

Stupid little fool.

Chapter 17

"Wow," Isabel said when she and Trevor strode into the safe house the next morning. As Trevor drifted off to find the men, Isabel studied Abby intently. "You look so much better."

Abby felt herself blushing under Isabel's astute gaze. How much did Isabel see? The fading bruises and how breathing was less of a struggle? Or did she see more? Abby remembered the way Kane's strong hands had roamed her body yesterday, branding her with his intoxicating touch. Could Isabel tell that things had changed?

Like she always did when she felt cornered, Abby went on the offensive. "Enough to be part of the rescue?" she demanded. Not that it was Isabel's seal of approval she needed. No, it would be Morgan and Kane's call, but Isabel's recommendation would go a long way toward convincing them.

Tossing her newly black hair over her shoulder, Isabel fixed Abby with a shrewd look. "I don't know. Let's see."

Before Abby could react, the other woman grabbed her wrist and gave it a sharp twist.

Abby promptly saw stars.

Resigned, Isabel released her. "Not better at all, I see."

Her wrist throbbed relentlessly as she drew in a deep breath to clear her head. "Damn you," she hissed.

Her friend just smiled. "Imagine that was a two-hundred-pound guard whose touch certainly wouldn't be as gentle as mine."

Abby turned away before Isabel could see the flush of anger and frustration rising in her cheeks. A broken wrist. She couldn't believe that a stupid broken wrist was the only thing stopping her from carrying out *her own* mission.

"Come on," she said stiffly. "Everyone else is in the den."

"And I assume there's a plan in place?"

"Not quite," Abby admitted. Her irritation over Isabel's cheap shot began to fade as they walked across the soft living room carpet toward the den. "Morgan and Kane managed to get their hands on some crazy military chopper, and they haven't stopped talking about it since they got back."

"Men and their toys," Isabel said, rolling her eyes.

The room was crowded when they entered. Abby went to stand by the sofa near Kane, while Isabel moved toward Morgan's desk and hopped up on it. As Isabel crossed her legs, Abby noticed every man's gaze zero in on the sensual motion.

Isabel looked unbelievably hot as Paloma Dominguez-Martin. Even the way she moved was subtly different, and wholly sexual. Abby wasn't surprised that Isabel's appearance affected the males in her vicinity, but she experienced a flicker of annoyance when she noticed Kane had also turned his head.

"All right," Morgan began briskly. "How the fuck are we gonna do this?"

Trevor cleared his throat, and when Abby glanced at him, she almost raised her eyebrows in shock. He looked different too, with his sophisticated new haircut and the tailored suit clinging to his lean body, but it wasn't the hair or the clothes that gave her pause. It was the eyes. They looked a little more . . . alive.

"We sent the wire transfer before coming here." He turned to Morgan. "I know it's too late to ask, but are you sure you want to hand over that much money to that sick son of a bitch?"

Morgan shrugged. "We'll get it back eventually. Holden has yet to find a banking system he can't hack into. We'll let the money sit for a while, then steal it back when it suits us."

"If you say so." Trevor shrugged. "So, Bahar said the auction starts at seven tomorrow. Bids are placed at eight, and after money has exchanged hands, we take the girl or girls we purchased, and go on our merry way."

"Blanco's sending a car for us," Isabel added. "That same car is supposed to take us off the compound after the auction, but obviously we won't be needing the ride back."

"Isabel managed to find out where the girls will be held before the auction starts. They'll be in the servants' quarters." Trevor glanced at Morgan. "Do you have those blueprints handy?"

Morgan placed the blueprint they'd prepared on the table. He spread out the large sheet and glanced at Abby. "Why don't you talk us through it?"

Nodding, she went to the table and knelt in front of it, gesturing for everyone to take a look. "Okay, so this is the main house." She moved her finger. "The east wing here will most likely be off-limits. Those are Blanco's private quarters." She slid her finger to the other side of the map. "This is the west wing." She looked at Isabel. "Did he say if the bidders would be given private rooms?"

"Yes," Isabel confirmed.

"Then they'll most likely be here. There are about twelve bedrooms along this corridor. Now, this long corridor here leads to the servants' quarters. Kane and I marked all the exits I know about in red."

Luke's dark head nearly bumped hers as he bent to examine the page. "So this exit here is our best bet," he said, pointing to a red line in the servants' part of the house.

Abby nodded. "This door is located in the storage room, which is right next to the laundry room over here. To get there, you need to walk through the kitchen."

"Where does the door go?" Ethan asked.

Abby lifted her head at the sound of his voice. She tended to forget he was even part of the team. His gentle, polite nature caused him to get lost in the crowd, blend into his surroundings. "To the helipad," she said with a grim smile. "The perfect out, if it weren't for the dozen guards monitoring the area."

"We can handle the guards," Morgan said confidently. He focused on Isabel, then Trevor. "If you two can manage to get the girls to the storage room, Sam can land the chopper right on Blanco's damn helipad, and then you make a run for it."

Abby shot him a sharp look. "You want to land your aircraft in Blanco's *backyard*? What about the clearing you used last time?"

"Not an option," Morgan said flatly. "Last time we had the element of surprise on our side. Blanco wasn't expecting us. This time, he's bound to be doubling or tripling his security."

"He is," Trevor confirmed. "This auction is extremely important to him. He's going to make sure nothing goes wrong."

"A power outage won't work again," Kane noted, looking thoughtful. "That's how we managed to get in last time. Holden disabled the fence and cut the lights."

"We might be able to do it again," Luke said. He suddenly looked frustrated. "But not without Holden. Why the hell is he sitting this one out?"

"He's home with his wife," Morgan said firmly. "And I'm not about to drag him into this. He deserves the vacation time. Besides, even if he were here, I'd be loath to use his tech talents. The clearing we used last week is about two miles east. No way can Trevor, Isabel, and thirteen girls hike across that entire compound, reach the fence, and hoof it to the clearing without alerting any of the guards. It has to be through the servants' quarters. That's the only route that makes sense."

"But landing on his helipad?" Abby said dubiously.

"It could work in our favor," Kane said with a shrug. "A total blitz attack. Trev and Isabel get the girls in position, we land our bird right at the damn back door, guns blazing."

Abby was still uncertain. "It's not like we can fly in without being noticed. They'll see the chopper coming and try to shoot it down."

Kane and Morgan exchanged grins. "Trust me, they're not shooting this bird down," Kane said, looking far too happy. "Besides, this chopper has a fucking rocket launcher attached to its side. We'll blow them to kingdom come before they can even reach for their guns."

"What about the other buyers?" Abby asked suddenly.

Kane glanced over at her. "What about them?"

"You know how much I want to rescue those girls, but we can't let those sick perverts escape. They'll be speeding away in their cars the moment you start blowing things up."

To her surprise, D backed her up. "These men are trying to buy children as sex toys, for fuck's sake. We can't let them go."

Morgan gave a firm shake of the head. "We have no choice. Our first priority is those girls. We can't go running around the compound tracking down every last bidder."

"What if we involved the Colombian government?" Abby suggested. "They're the ones who wanted Blanco dead in the first place. I'm sure they would be thrilled to arrest a bunch of wealthy deviants."

"No way," Isabel said. "Blanco made it clear that he's got some high-ranking officials in his back pocket. We can't risk involving the government. Whoever he's paying off could warn him about the mission and screw everything up for us."

D shook his head angrily. "There has to be a way. We can't just let those fuckers escape."

"We have no choice," Morgan replied in a tone that brooked no argument. "If any of the buyers foolishly try to run to the helipad, feel free to take them out, but we're not risking the lives of those girls to go on a suicide chase."

Both Abby and D went quiet. She could feel the frustration radiating from D's body, frustration that mirrored her own. For once they were on the same side, but there wasn't a damn thing either of them could do to win this fight.

"Fine," D muttered. "We leave the buyers alone."

"But we get to blow things up," Luke said helpfully. He rubbed his hands together. "I love blowing things up."

"A blitz is the only way," Morgan decided. "They won't be expecting a fucking assault chopper to descend in their backyard." He glanced at Trevor. "And we'll be there to provide cover fire while you guys come out the door."

"*If* we can come out the door," Isabel spoke warily.

"Yeah, that's another thing," Trevor said, wrinkling his forehead in concern. "Isabel and I figured the best way to handle this is if she sneaks out of the room first and gets the girls ready. I'll have to stay put, so they've got me on camera. Otherwise they'll get suspicious."

"Won't they be suspicious that your wife isn't with you?" Luke pointed out.

"I'm sure we'll be able to come up with something," Isabel said with a small shrug. "I'll find a reason to leave the room and pretend to get lost or something. That's not the main issue here."

"What is the issue, then?" Morgan asked, all business.

"Weapons," Trevor said bluntly. "Isabel and I won't be able to get a weapon in there. The guards in the security booth do a search before you're allowed to go in. They confiscated my gun when we were there before."

"And I won't be able to protect the girls without a weapon," Isabel said, worrying her bottom lip with her teeth. "There are too many variables inside that house. The place will be crawling with guards, and sure, I could probably take a few of them down, but I have no idea what will be waiting for me when I try to make it to the storage room. Blanco's probably catering the damn auction, and the kitchen might be crowded with people. And if I do manage to get the girls into the storage room, what if ten guards swarm us?"

Morgan rubbed the stubble on his jaw. "So you need a gun."

"I need a gun," Isabel confirmed.

The room fell silent as everyone worked the snag over in their heads. Abby stared at the blueprint, an idea creeping into the forefront of her mind. She chewed on the inside of her cheek. "There might be a way."

Kane's green eyes studied her face. "What are you thinking?"

"The servants . . . the ones that live off the compound. They don't enter the property at the front gate." Abby pointed to the fence at the edge of the property, about a hundred yards from the helipad. "They come in from back here. There's a couple guards posted at the gate, but they don't search the servants, as far as I know."

"I'm pretty sure they'll search a servant they don't recognize," Kane replied. "No way can one of us pretend to—"

"None of us has to pretend anything," she cut in. "We can ask Inez Alvaro to help us."

"Inez Alvaro?" Isabel echoed.

"She's the mother of one of the captive girls. She's one of Blanco's housekeepers, or at least she was before she launched herself at him with her fists swinging. She's the reason I found out about the auction. After she confronted him, Blanco bragged to me that he kidnapped her daughter to punish her husband."

"If she was fired, how can she help?" D asked with a stony glare.

"I don't know." Abby shrugged helplessly. "Maybe she

can pretend she left some belongings at the compound. We'll give her the weapons Isabel and Trevor need, and she can enter the property through the servants' gate and plant the guns in the storage room."

There was a short lull.

"That could work," Kane finally said. "But are you certain the servants aren't searched?"

"I'm pretty certain." She bit her lip. "But maybe one of you can hide in the hills with a sniper rifle just in case. If the guards discover the weapons on Inez, just take them out."

"And alert Blanco to the fact that he has company, thus taking away the element of surprise, and thus no extraction," Morgan said ruefully.

"Isabel and Trevor can't do this without weapons," Abby pointed out. "If we can't get those weapons to them, there won't be an extraction anyway."

"It could work," Kane said again.

"That is, assuming Inez Alvaro would be willing to help," Morgan countered.

"She will," Abby said, confidence ringing in her voice. "Her daughter is missing. Her husband fled like a rat on a sinking ship when Blanco found out he was stealing from him. Inez is all alone, and she's desperate to get Lucia back."

"Is there a way we can contact her?" Isabel asked.

Abby slowly shook her head. "Corturo is a tiny village, where most of the villagers live in huts. Indoor plumbing is about as modern as they get." She paused. "But I think the church has a telephone." She searched her memory, trying to picture the village she'd visited. "Yes, there's a phone there. The priest uses it to contact the relief foundation that brings food and medical supplies about twice a year."

"If we could contact her, could she leave the village without rousing suspicion?"

Abby thought it over. "Blanco has men all over the area, definitely has some in the village. But . . . Inez has a sister here in the city. She mentioned her the first time we met. I'm sure if her sister told her there was some emergency, she would make the trip here."

"In the car she probably doesn't own?" Kane said with a sigh.

"She'd take a taxi. Or the bus."

Luke rolled his eyes. "And village buses are so reliable," he said sarcastically. "For all we know, she'll show up two days from now and the auction will already be over."

Ignoring the remark, Morgan pulled his cell phone from his pocket. "Then we'll just have to make sure she gets here today."

"You're seriously going to recruit the housekeeper as an undercover operative?" D said in disbelief.

"It's worth a shot." Morgan punched in a number. "Holden," he barked a moment later. "I need you to find me a telephone number."

Inez Alvaro talked like an auctioneer on speed. Kane could barely keep up with the plump, dark-skinned woman, whose words fired out of her mouth like an endless stream of bullets from a machine gun. From the moment she'd walked into the house, she'd alternated between loud sobs and hurried sentences. Didn't help that she was speaking Spanish too.

His head spun like a merry-go-round as he watched Isabel and Abby attempt to soothe the hysterical woman. They'd been at it for ten minutes, yet she still didn't seem ready to calm down. Thinking her sister had been in a gruesome car accident hadn't helped the poor woman's mood. It was the ruse Abby had used to get Alvaro to leave her village. Conveniently, a taxi had been waiting right near the bus stop the woman had raced toward, and when she'd heaved herself into the backseat, she'd nearly had a coronary when she found Kane and Abby sitting there.

Fortunately, Inez recognized Abby, and she eagerly agreed to meet with the people who were trying to get her daughter back. She'd mumbled the word *milagro* so many times that Kane had finally asked Abby for a translation. She'd quietly told him it meant miracle.

It didn't surprise him that Abby spoke fluent Spanish. It had surprised Inez, though, who'd met Abby as Erica, the American mistress of Señor Blanco. Inez had recovered quickly from the shock, though, and ever since she'd climbed into the cab, she'd been crying like a hormonal pregnant chick.

"What's she saying?" Kane said from his perch by the doorway. Only he and Luke were present at the moment; Morgan and the others had retreated to the den, trying not to overwhelm the distraught mother.

"She said she wants to cut off Blanco's balls and feed them to the goat," Isabel said with a barely contained smile.

"I hear that." Luke sighed. "I wish I owned a goat I could feed that dirtbag's balls to."

Isabel turned her attention back to the wailing woman, gently rubbing Inez's shoulders. She spoke softly in Spanish, and the soothing note to her voice seemed to have an effect on the woman. Kane noted with interest that Abby made no move to embrace Inez Alvaro. And her tone was not as gentle as Isabel's. She sounded strained, almost awkward.

His heart tightened in his chest. Opening up wasn't something Abby did easily, which made him all the more grateful that she'd allowed herself to get close to him. And not just in bed. He thought of their talk last night, when she'd quietly insisted she wasn't normal. He knew there was some truth to that. Abby Sinclair wasn't normal by society's standards. She was a warrior. A killer. A woman willing to use any weapon at her disposal to get the job done.

But she was also more than that. She cared about others, no matter how much she insisted she didn't. She'd risked her neck—literally—to try to save those girls. And when she'd clung to him after sex, she'd felt so fragile, so small and helpless. A part of him wanted to take her into his arms and never let her go. Another part simply wanted to push her away. He hadn't felt this close to a woman since Emily. But Emily had abandoned him.

And Abby . . . no matter how hard he tried to convince himself otherwise, he suspected she would abandon him too.

"You . . . help?"

Kane's head jerked up as he realized those two awkward words had been directed at him. He looked into Inez's hopeful brown eyes, and his throat felt tight. "Yes, we're going to help," he said gruffly.

"You bring Lucia to me? Take back?"

Her broken English was hard to decipher, but the emotions flickering across her face were unmistakable. "We're going to try," Kane said. "But we'll need your help."

Inez didn't seem to understand. She looked at Isabel in confusion and asked something in Spanish. Isabel answered with a nod, along with another gentle squeeze of the older woman's arm. Kane listened blankly as Isabel continued speaking, evidently explaining what they required of Inez. The woman started to nod in earnest.

"She says they don't search her at the gate," Isabel translated. She paused, listening. "And she left some clothing and photographs in the bedroom she used whenever she was ordered to stay the night."

Abby quietly posed another question to Inez and received an enthusiastic nod in return. "She says Blanco gave her permission to come back for her things."

Inez's eyes flashed at the sound of Blanco's name, which sent her on another muttering rampage. Kane picked up on the word *serpiente*—he knew that one. Snake. Yep, Blanco fit that bill.

"She wants him to suffer," Abby said flatly. "She wants him dead."

"Don't we all," Luke mumbled.

The women spoke to Inez for several more minutes. By the end, steel had sharpened Inez's dark eyes. Her tanned face became grave, intent as she listened to Isabel and Abby.

"*Sí,*" she said firmly. "*Sí* . . . I help."

"She'll do it?" Kane asked, satisfaction sweeping through him.

"She'll do it," Abby confirmed.

Inez focused those bottomless brown eyes on Kane. "Señor Blanco . . . *serpiente.*" She pointed a plump finger at him. "You bring Lucia. You save Lucia. *Ayudaré* . . . I help."

*　　*　　*

"She scares me."

Kane shot Luke a sidelong glance, grinning at his friend's ashen face. Across the room, Abby was teaching Ethan about the art of knife fighting, and the kid looked as pale as Luke did. He supposed it was an appropriate reaction when an angry redhead was pointing a blade at you.

Trevor and Isabel had left for their hotel an hour before, and D had taken Inez Alvaro back to her village, leaving Kane and the others to be tortured by Abby Sinclair all afternoon. She'd already forced them go over the blueprints of Blanco's compound seven times, quizzed them about every weapon being brought on the extraction, and when Ethan had misguidedly revealed that he didn't have much use for knives, she'd been so horrified that she'd raided the armory in the safe house and returned with a selection of nasty-looking blades, determined to give Ethan a thorough lesson.

Needless to say, she was driving everyone crazy with her preparations, including Morgan, who'd stormed off after Abby complained that it was a shame his prized helicopter didn't have more than one rocket launcher. Morgan had locked himself in the den and hadn't come out since.

Kane knew he could try to derail the obsession train Abby had decided to board, maybe seduce her into distraction, but he was loath to do so. She was already pissed about being left out of the rescue. If overanalyzing every detail and jabbing a knife around made her feel better, he was willing to indulge her. Besides, it wouldn't hurt Ethan to learn some new tricks.

Luke was right, though. It was scary, how good she was with a knife. And graceful. She looked like a damn ballerina as she showed Ethan the proper way to shove a sharp blade into someone's heart.

"No," she said in aggravation when Ethan yet again blundered the task. "You'll hit bone if you enter from there. Jeez, who *trained* you?"

Ethan's face went beet red. "The Marines."

Abby grumbled something under her breath, then tugged on the hem of her tight T-shirt and pulled it over her head. She wore a black sports bra underneath, and though it wasn't indecent by any standards, Kane didn't appreciate the way she stripped so readily in front of his men.

"Here, feel this," she told Ethan.

Kane's shoulders stiffened. Uh, no fucking way was he letting Ethan, kid or not, get his hands on Abby's chest. He took a step forward, but Abby turned to scowl at him, making him stop in his tracks. As she took Ethan's hand, Kane clenched his teeth so hard his jaw began to ache.

"You stick it here," Abby explained. "Under the sternum. And you aim upward and toward the spine. You'll usually hit the heart, but if you don't, you'll most likely connect with an artery and the guy will drown in his own blood."

She spoke so matter-of-factly that Kane found himself gulping. So did Ethan, whose hand seemed to be trembling against Abby's chest.

"If you're coming from behind, your best bet is to stick the knife here, right below the ribs." Abby offered Ethan her back, using her hand to indicate the right spot. "Hit this and you take out a kidney. Hit higher and you puncture a lung. And if all that fails, use your backup blade to slit the bastard's throat." Abby grinned. "Any questions?"

Looking terrified, Ethan shook his head.

"Good. Then let's try it again."

Half an hour later, Ethan had succeeded in earning a silver star from Abby. Kane didn't want to know what it would take to get a gold star. Abby gave Ethan a brisk nod of approval and strode off, leaving the kid standing in the middle of the room, the knife dangling from his hand. As Luke broke out in mock applause, Kane smothered a smile and trailed after Abby. He found her in the bathroom of their bedroom, and watched from the doorway as she turned on the faucet and splashed water on her face.

"You could have gone easy on him," he remarked.

She scrunched up her face, as if she were truly perplexed. "Why? Blanco's men won't."

She had a point. "True, but chances are, this won't turn into some gang knife fight. We'll have guns. Really big guns."

To his surprise, she grinned. "I know, but . . . is it awful for me to say that I have fun toying with Ethan?"

Kane threw his head back and laughed.

"He just acts like he's so damn scared of me," she said, sounding defensive. "I figured I'd give him a reason to be."

"And you also want to feel like you're part of the rescue."

"It was *my* mission," she said fiercely.

"It's still yours. But it's ours now too." He stepped into the bathroom and wrapped his arms around her from behind. "I promise you, we'll save those girls."

She met his reflection in the small mirror. "I know you will. It just feels *wrong*, you know? Not being able to go in and rescue them myself. I know Isabel can get the job done, but . . ."

"But you can't sit idle. Trust me, I know. We're built for action, you and I. It's normal to want to be right in the midst of it." Unable to stop himself, he slid his hands up her belly and cupped her breasts. "But there's another kind of action we can partake in, you know."

A faint smile crossed her lips, then faded abruptly. Disentangling from his embrace, she turned to face him, and he glimpsed the apprehension on her face. "What is it?" he demanded.

"I did something before, when Isabel and I were talking to Inez." She visibly swallowed, as if admitting it took a physical toll on her. "I asked Inez to plant another gun in the common room."

Kane narrowed his eyes. Earlier, when they'd told Inez that the girls would most likely be taken to the servants' area, the woman had said that the only room large enough to accommodate them would probably be the break room, which apparently had some couches, a crooked pool table, and a small kitchenette. "Why would you ask her to do that?" he asked carefully.

Abby averted her eyes. "So if the girls are in there, they won't be unarmed. They can use the gun to take out the guard at the door, and then—"

"Jesus," he interrupted.

Her features hardened. "Just hear me out, okay? Look, Inez used to bring Lucia to work with her every now and then. Lucia knows the layout of the servants' quarters."

"So?" Kane asked with deep suspicion.

"So maybe Lucia can get herself and the others to the storage room that leads to the rear exit. That way Isabel can meet them there at an arranged time, instead of roaming the halls and opening doors until she finds where they're being kept."

"Lucia Alvaro is thirteen years old," Kane said stiffly. "And there will certainly be a guard or two posted at their door. You can't expect a little girl to—"

"Yes, I can," she cut in, her voice cold and even.

He let out a curse. "Christ, Abby. Do you honestly think a thirteen-year-old girl is going to be able to murder a man in cold blood?"

"I think a thirteen-year-old girl will do anything she needs to in order to save her own life."

Chapter 18

"I'm really going to miss this suite," Isabel remarked as they walked through the door.

Trevor tried not to smile as he watched her gaze sweep around the room. The disappointment in her eyes was evident. "It's just another hotel room," he pointed out.

"Compared to the other rooms I've stayed in, this is a palace." She kicked off her stilettos and collapsed on one of the love seats.

"What about your home? It must be better than all those hotel rooms."

"I have a place in New York, but it's just a small walk-up. Nothing as elegant as this. And besides, I'm hardly ever there."

"Too busy pretending to be a jet-setting Brazilian heiress?"

"Sure beats my regular old life."

Trevor found himself grinning. Isabel Roma really was one of a kind. Intelligent, beautiful, and completely unaffected by the evils of this world. She took everything in stride—the good, the bad, the seriously shitty. He wished he possessed that kind of attitude.

"I wanted to discuss something with you," she said suddenly. "Abby came up with an idea earlier, which I think has merit."

Trevor frowned. "I'm listening."

Isabel quickly explained Abby's plan to arrange for the captured girls to find their way to the storage room at a predetermined time. His frown deepened when she told him about the gun planted in the servants' break room. When she finished, Trevor leaned forward in his chair and rubbed his jaw. The idea definitely had merit; he had to admit that. But he still wasn't sold on recruiting Lucia Alvaro to help them.

"Lucia would need to know about the gun, along with where to meet us and what time. How do you propose we do that? Like you said, the girls are going to be locked up in the servants' quarters."

"Blanco said we were entitled to a closer look," Isabel reminded him.

His breath came out in a soft hiss. "If there's an *item* we're interested in, he said he'd bring it to our room."

"We can ask for a closer look at Lucia. She'll be brought to our room, and we can tell her what we need her to do."

He paused, thinking. "It could work."

"We just need to make sure the timing is on our side. Bahar said the auction starts at seven. We have an hour to examine the merchandise, and that's when we'll request to see Lucia. At eight the bids go in, and I imagine it'll take about an hour for all the bids and money to be processed. We tell Lucia to move at, say, eight twenty, and arrange for the chopper to launch its attack at eight thirty."

Trevor mulled it over. "That gives us a thirty-minute

window. The girls get themselves to the storage room, you meet them at eight twenty, and I make my way over there at eight thirty, just in time for us to make a run for it."

"It could work," Isabel said. "You know it could."

"Depending on whether Lucia is able or willing to help."

"Abby says she will. And I'm inclined to agree." Confidence rang in her tone. "Lucia has been locked up in Blanco's dungeon for more than a week. The girl will fight to survive, Trevor. I know she will."

Their gazes locked, and Trevor felt a sizzle of heat course from him to her, her to him. No, not now. Not ever. This growing attraction toward Isabel wasn't something he was entirely comfortable with. Hell, he would never be comfortable with it.

"Trevor . . ." She trailed off for a moment. "You had the nightmare again last night."

Shock coursed through him. "What?"

"Don't pretend you don't know what I'm talking about," she said quietly. "You don't just toss and turn at night. You . . . you say things sometimes."

His hands clenched into involuntary fists. "What do I say?"

"That you're sorry."

Pain sliced into his gut like a dull blade as her words formed images in his mind. Gina standing over him, her curly brown hair like an angry cloud surrounding her face. Her brown eyes glimmering with fury and betrayal.

Isabel's voice was gentle as she said, "Do you want to tell me about it?"

"She always holds a gun," he mumbled. "She aims it at my heart and she yells at me for leaving her. For not being there."

Isabel sucked in a breath. "Jesus. I'm sorry."

"And in the dream, I'm always pleading with her to shoot me. To put a bullet in my heart so I don't have to feel it ache anymore. But she never does it." His voice cracked. "She turns around and walks away. And then I wake up."

A pair of warm arms wrapped around him. His head lifted in panic and surprise. Isabel was sitting next to him now. Holding him. Strength emanated from her slender form, surrounding him with heat and soothing tranquillity.

"It's only a dream," she murmured.

His muscles, so tense a second ago, turned to liquid. He found himself leaning into her, his forehead pressed against hers. "Then why does it feel so damn real?"

Isabel looked at him with shining certainty. "It's guilt. The guilt you feel haunts you at night, but you've got to start letting it go. It'll kill you in the end."

He wanted to argue. Wanted to scream at her and tell her she had no fucking right digging around in his head and yanking out painful memories. Instead, all he could do was stare into her eyes. They were Paloma green, but that did nothing to hide the sharp intelligence or deep compassion that he'd come to associate with Isabel.

He took a breath and the scent of her grabbed hold of his senses. Her skin smelled like peaches and lavender, the sweet aroma surrounding him like a warm blanket. He couldn't move. Couldn't pull back. He just sat there, staring at her, and when her tongue darted out to moisten her lips, a groan lodged in his chest.

He wanted to kiss her.

But he didn't. He couldn't. With a sudden burst of anger, he pushed her hands off his shoulders and stumbled to his feet. "We should turn in," he muttered. "It's gonna be a long day tomorrow."

Isabel didn't respond, but he could feel her bewildered eyes burning into his back as he marched into the bathroom. He shut the door, officially closing her out. She had no business making him feel things again.

No business at all.

Abby was exhausted when she finally slid into bed next to Kane's warm, naked body. It had been a long day, made even longer by all the activities she'd been determined to cram into it. She knew she'd annoyed Kane and the others by insisting that they go over every last detail and prepare for every possible scenario, but if she couldn't be part of this rescue, she was damn well going to be part of the planning. When she thought back to her time in Blanco's prison, her gut clenched with anger. The beatings, torture, questioning—all for nothing. She couldn't even finish what she'd started, thanks to a fractured wrist that made her a damn liability.

But she was confident the rescue would be a success. This ambush would catch Blanco and his men completely off guard, or at least she hoped it would. And she didn't regret her decision to try to involve Lucia Alvaro in the mission. It was clear that Kane still didn't feel comfortable with it, but he had no idea what it was like to be at the mercy of others. Abby had been fighting for her life since the age of eight. She knew what Lucia was going through right now, and had no doubt the girl would do anything in her power to save herself.

She did worry about the girl's mother, though, and she voiced that troubling thought as Kane pulled her close and tucked her head against his chest.

"Do you think Inez will be able to pull it off tomorrow?" She couldn't hide the anxious note in her voice. "What if there's trouble at the gate?"

"Luke will be there. He'll be standing guard in the hills overlooking the entrance. If the guards make a move, he'll take them out."

That made her feel better, though she wished she could be the one to go with Inez in the morning. After all, Isabel and Luke weren't the only sharpshooters of the bunch. Still, Abby knew it was safer for her to stay in this house until the extraction went down. If one of Blanco's men caught her loitering on the property, they'd surely recognize her. Erica had been a big hit with all the men, particularly the ones to whom she'd given blow jobs.

The memories brought a sick feeling to her chest, coating her throat with bile. Oh God. How . . . why had she done those things? Sex had always been a weapon for her, but now . . . now it made her want to vomit, thinking about all the things she'd done for the sake of a mission. Lying here with Kane, she suddenly felt so unbelievably dirty.

The volatile emotions pricked at her skin like tiny little razor blades, causing her to shift away, to slide to the other side of the bed, where she tucked her knees against her chest, breathing hard.

"Hey," came Kane's worried voice. "What's wrong?" His big, strong body pressed against her back, spooning her from behind.

"Don't," she choked out when he started rubbing her bare shoulder. "Don't touch me."

"Abby . . . Jesus, would you look at me?"

She blinked through a sudden onslaught of tears.

"Abby."

His fingers dug into her waist. She flinched, protesting when he forced her to turn over. His warm hands held her chin so she had no choice but to meet his concerned gaze. "What the hell is going on?" he demanded.

Abby swiped at the moisture streaming down her cheeks.

"Fuck, are you crying? Damn it, Abby, what's going on?"

"I shouldn't be here," she whispered.

"In Bogotá?" he asked, wrinkling his forehead.

"In your bed."

His eyes darkened. "Where the hell is this coming from? I thought we worked through that shit."

"Worked through it?" she echoed with a humorless laugh. "I'm a whore, Kane. A whore and a killer. I fuck men to get close to them, and then I take their lives. Why on earth would you even want to be *near* me?"

A stunned silence filled the bedroom.

Kane's grip on her chin loosened. He didn't speak, not for a long while, and she found herself looking at him. Really looking at him. He was so incredibly handsome that her throat grew tight at the sight of him. That tousled blond hair, falling onto his strong, proud forehead. The gorgeous green eyes and perfectly shaped mouth. He had the body of a warrior, hard and lean and sculpted with flawless muscles. But it wasn't just his physical features she was seeing. It was his strength and his determination, the way he touched her with infinite gentleness, looked at her without judgment, treated her like she was worthy of him.

What was a man like this doing with a woman like her?

"Why do I want to be near you?" he said, his husky voice slicing through the silence. "Do you really want to know?"

She nodded weakly.

"Because you're the strongest woman I have ever met in my life." His hands were on her face again, stroking her cheeks, touching her throat. "You're the kind of woman who allows herself to be tortured so she can save a dozen strangers. You're the kind of woman who's not afraid of challenges, not afraid of anything."

His mouth captured hers in a rough kiss. "I want you because you're smart as hell, because you're funny when you let yourself relax, and because you're the sexiest woman I have ever met. Oh, and I'm wildly turned on by you." To punctuate the last point, he pushed his groin into her stomach, his thick ridge of arousal leaving no doubt in her mind.

"You're crazy," she whispered, a tired laugh sliding out of her mouth. "You can't possibly see all of that in me."

"But I do see it. I just wish you could see it too, Abby."

She gave a little yelp as his hand moved between her legs, tugging at her skimpy panties. "What are you doing?" she stammered.

"Convincing you." His mouth found hers again, and she squeaked as he moved on top of her and drove his cock into her suddenly throbbing sex. He rolled his hips in a sensual circular motion.

She shivered. He felt so good inside her. Pleasure rippled in her womb.

"Is it working?" he murmured.

"Kind of."

"Kind of?" He made a *tsk*ing sound, withdrew slowly, then plunged back in, hard, deep, filling her completely. "Guess I'll just have to up my game."

"It's done," Luke announced, striding into the living room.

Abby looked up from the couch and dropped the

thick file folder on the coffee table. She'd been reading the dossier Morgan had compiled on Blanco, though there was nothing in there she hadn't already known. It had kept her occupied, at least. Kane and Morgan had been gone all morning, off to meet with their pilot, and Ethan and D were asleep in the back bedroom, leaving Abby bored and alone for the past few hours.

Now excitement replaced her boredom. "Inez did it?"

Luke nodded. He flopped down in the armchair opposite the couch, grinning in admiration. "I have to say, she is one tough broad. She just marched up to the gate and gave the guards a tongue-lashing that would've made Morgan proud. They let her in without batting an eye."

"Did she plant the guns?"

"Yep. She stashed three nine-millimeters with silencers in the storage room, inside a box of old Christmas lights she says nobody ever opens." He frowned. "And she hid another nine-millimeter in one of the kitchen cupboards of the servants' break room. She said you and Isabel asked her to do that."

Abby shrugged.

With a laugh, Luke leaned forward and clasped his hands on his knees. "Don't act like you don't know what I'm talking about. I heard it myself last night—you snuck in the request right before D took Inez back to her village."

Sighing, she met his knowing eyes. "You speak Spanish?"

He beamed at her. "Why do you think Morgan sent me to play sniper?"

"But you didn't say anything about it yesterday. You barely even spoke to Inez."

"You and Isabel were handling it." He slanted his head. "So why the extra gun?"

Remembering Kane's reaction, she reluctantly told Luke how they might be able to use Lucia and convince the girl to aid in her own rescue. When she finished, he whistled. "That's a lot to ask of a kid."

"Maybe, but we owe her the courtesy of giving her the choice."

"Well, if she's anything like her mother, I'm sure she'll do anything she can to save herself. You should have seen Inez back there. Nerves of steel."

"And she made it out all right, after she planted the weapons?"

"Walked out the gate twenty minutes later with a basket full of clothes and some mugs from the break room. I followed her back to the village. She's safe."

"Good." With grudging respect, she added, "Thank you."

"Hey, D's the one who's all sulky about this gig. I was on board from the start." His normally playful face clouded with anger. "Blanco needs to be stopped."

Kane's cell phone, which was on the cushion beside her, began to vibrate at that moment. She glanced at it warily, saw the private number, and suppressed a groan.

"You don't have to talk to him," Luke pointed out, sounding irritated.

"I'll take it in the bedroom," she said quietly.

Without a backward glance, she headed down the narrow hallway, flipping the phone on as she walked. "Hello, Devlin."

"Hello, luv. It's good to hear your voice."

"I'm sure it is." She stifled a sigh. "What's on the agenda for today, Devlin? More forays into the past?"

"This has nothing to do with your past. Today is all about the present." He sounded far too smug, and her guard instantly shot up. "I've decided it's time for the two of us to meet."

"Oh, really?"

"In fact," he went on, "I expect we'll be seeing each other tonight. Around seven, I presume?"

Her fingers curled around the phone. "What makes you say that?"

"Because you're going to try to rescue the girls tonight." A jubilant laugh filled the line. "And I'll be right there to greet you, luv."

Chapter 19

Abby's entire body went cold. She noticed her knuckles starting to turn white and loosened her grip on the phone, drawing in a slow, silent breath. Gathering her composure, she feigned confusion. "What are you talking about? What girls?"

"Nice try, luv. But we both know that you paid a visit to the bunker." He suddenly sounded impressed. "That's why you snuck into Luis's office, pretending to break into his files and look on his computer. You knew the cameras would pick you up. You *wanted* to get caught, didn't you?"

"I don't know what you're talking about."

"You positioned yourself in the prison to get closer to the girls. You knew what was going to happen to them, and you couldn't stand by and watch, could you?" He made a soothing sound. "Poor Abby. They reminded you of yourself, didn't they? Young and helpless, at the mercy of big, bad men."

Her hands started to shake. She decided there was no point in denying it. "You're right. I saw them," she admitted. "But you're making a very big assumption in thinking I'm going to lead some commando rescue to-night."

"But you will. You and Morgan have probably planned it to the last detail." He clucked his tongue. "I'm looking forward to seeing both of you, in fact."

"It won't happen," she lied. "I'm not even in the country."

"Save the horseshit for someone who'll buy it. Blanco's silly auction is scheduled for this evening, which means you're in Bogotá. I know you, luv. You wouldn't have been able to stay away."

Frustration bubbled in her stomach, hot and relentless. No. She couldn't let this bastard ruin everything. She should've expected this, especially after he'd told her he was back at Blanco's compound, but they'd been banking on the element of surprise, catching Blanco's men—Devlin included—unawares. Now everything had changed. Devlin had figured out her true intentions.

God, why hadn't she found a way to continue distracting him?

The rescue would fail. There was no chance of success as long as Devlin remained in the equation. For all she knew, he'd already informed his boss about the impending assault. Abby's brain kicked into high gear, working over the new information. She needed to take Devlin out of the equation. Isolate him from the other variables.

"Did you tell Blanco about this rescue you think is going to happen?" she asked slowly.

"Not yet." Devlin sounded smug. "I wanted the pleasure of making you squirm first."

She bit the inside of her cheek, an idea forming. "I have a proposition for you."

His laughter echoed in her ear. "I can't wait to hear it."

Sinking down on the bed, Abby reached up to rub one aching temple. "Don't tell Blanco about your suspicions, Devlin."

She could practically see him grinning on the other end. "Keep my own employer in the dark? Why in heavens would I do that?"

"Because if you don't, you'll never get me."

A pause. "I don't follow, luv."

"We both know you don't give a rat's ass about Blanco or his auction. I'm the one you want. Well, you can have me."

"And I will. Tonight."

"No." Her lips tightened. "Because I won't be part of the rescue team."

It killed her to say it. It *killed* her. But there was no other choice. She had to lure Devlin away from the compound. If he remained on the scene, the entire mission would go to hell.

"I don't believe you," he finally said, but his confidence seemed to have faltered. "You'll come."

"No, I won't. I do want to save those girls—you were right about that—but do you know what I want even more than that?"

His voice became wary. "What?"

"To make you suffer." A callous laugh slipped out of her mouth. "It drives you crazy, doesn't it, Devlin? Knowing I'm so close but you can't touch me. And I bet it drives you even crazier knowing that I got captured on purpose, that everything you did to me, I *allowed*."

She could hear his anger vibrating through the extension. "You couldn't break me," she finished, "and now you won't even get the chance to try."

"You're lying," he muttered. "You won't abandon those silly children. You'll try to save them."

"Morgan's team will save them," she said, correcting him. "I trust them to do it. But me? I'll disappear, Devlin. Tonight. And you'll never find me. Unless . . ." She trailed off seductively.

"Unless what?" he demanded.

"You make a choice. Me or those *silly* girls." She closed her eyes, forcing herself to continue. "Morgan and his men will ambush your employer's compound. You will say nothing to Blanco about it. And in reward, I'll come to you."

"Isn't that sweet, sacrificing yourself for those children."

She ignored the mocking tone. "You have a decision to make, Devlin. Either you stay at the compound and try to stop the rescue—in which case I'll be long gone. Or you forget about the rescue and meet me instead. It's a fair trade, don't you think? You get me; Morgan gets the girls."

He went quiet. She waited.

This was too risky. She knew that. Even if Devlin agreed to meet her, he might still tell Blanco about the rescue attempt. But Kane and the others were pros. They could pull it off even without the element of surprise. They would have a better chance, though, if Devlin were off the compound. The man was unpredictable. A sadistic asshole who would get great joy from killing every last man on Morgan's team should anything go wrong.

Luring him away was her best bet, but that meant she'd need to find a way to handle Kane. If she told him that she was meeting Devlin, he'd never let her go alone. But if she lied, faked a headache or something equally contrived, he'd know something was up. She'd fought tooth and nail with him to let her be part of the rescue, even if it meant simply waiting on a helicopter. No way would he believe she'd suddenly decided to sit it out.

"All right."

Devlin's harsh response jerked her from her thoughts. "All right?" she echoed.

"I choose you, luv."

Relief soared through her. "And you won't interfere with the rescue effort? You won't tell Blanco that his auction might be in danger?"

"Do you honestly think I give a damn about Blanco's auction?" Devlin said in a cavalier tone.

"I want your word."

He laughed again. "Then you have it, my sweet Abby. I give you my word that Blanco will not know what hit him. To be honest, I've grown rather tired of the man. Perhaps he'll have a run-in with Morgan's rifle."

He sounded sincere, but Abby didn't trust the bastard. Not one bit. She'd done all she could, though. She would warn Morgan that the team might be expected, but she would not be on that chopper with them.

"Now, back to business," Devlin chirped. "There's a little mining town about two hours north of Bogotá. We'll meet there."

"Fine," she agreed.

"There's an abandoned emerald mine in the western foothills. I'll expect you there at— When is that silly auction? Seven. Yes, we will meet at seven. If you don't show, I pick up the phone and warn Blanco."

"I'll show," she said in a low voice.

"Good." He paused. "And I don't need to remind you to come alone, do I? No backup, Abby."

"Any backup I may have brought will be indisposed at that time," she reminded him.

"Yes, I imagine so." He chuckled. "You know, I find myself almost rooting for Morgan. I've always thought of him as a worthy adversary. Not as worthy as you, though." His chuckle transformed into a hearty laugh. "I will kill you, luv. I hope you realize that."

She offered a laugh of her own. "I'd like to see you try, *luv*."

He hung up.

Shit.

Abby drew an unsteady breath, hoping she hadn't just made the biggest mistake of her life. But what other choice did she have? Devlin could not be at that compound when the rescue went down. His insane obsession with her would ruin everything, endanger not only Kane and his team but the lives of those innocent girls as well. The only way this mission had even the slightest chance of succeeding was if she distracted Devlin. If she killed him.

Exhaling slowly, she got to her feet. She had to go.

Now. Before he gets back, Abby.

Jeremy's voice in her head. Sharp and confident as always.

Right. She needed to leave. It was only one o'clock. The mine was two hours away. If she left now, she'd get there at three, four hours ahead of Devlin. It meant being out in the open, exposed, for far too long, but there weren't many other options available to her. She had to leave the safe house before Kane returned, or else he'd try to stop her.

Her mind raced as she worked over the details. She needed a vehicle. Weapons. A way out without the other men seeing her.

The sound of the front door opening caught her attention. Frustration slammed into her when she heard Kane's voice drifting from the living room.

Damn it.

Damn it.

Lucia's hands trembled as she followed the unfamiliar guard into the familiar room. Her pupils were still struggling to adjust to the sunshine streaming in from the window. It felt like they'd been locked in that cold, dark bunker for months rather than days. Blinking, she looked around in surprise.

Mamá had brought her here before. This was where the staff went when their work was finished. The other girls looked confused as they glanced at the frayed couches and the small but tidy kitchen area.

"Where is this?" Valencia whispered, sounding uncertain.

"Quiet!" the guard snapped. He stalked around and did a head count, nodding stiffly when he confirmed they were all there. "If any of you make a sound . . ." He didn't finish the rest of his sentence, simply lifted his scary-looking gun and waved it around before making a move for the door.

A burden lifted off Lucia's chest as he closed the door. A lock clicked into place, and then they were alone.

She instinctively looked at Valencia, whose tanned arm was wrapped around Sylvie's quivering shoulders. Consuela stuck close to Valencia, while Emiliana, Nita, and Gabrielle huddled together. The other six girls stood there with blank expressions, waiting for someone to take charge.

"My mamá works here," Lucia said, her voice barely over a whisper.

"Do you think she's here, in the house?" Valencia whispered back.

Lucia shrugged helplessly. "I don't know."

Valencia led Sylvie to one of the couches and urged the girl to sit. Sylvie obeyed, curling into a little ball, her head propped against the armrest. Several of the others sat down too, but not Lucia.

"I don't like this," she whispered. "I think Señor Blanco is going to hurt us."

"Is there a way out?"

The question came from Consuela. Lucia was quick to shake her head. "Only the door."

"The man with the gun is out there," Emiliana reminded them, her big blue eyes filling with tears.

"We can find a way," Valencia said, her mouth grim. "We have to find—"

Voices sounded outside the door. The lock scraped open, and then a dour-faced woman with long black hair entered the room. She was rolling in a long metal rack. With dresses. There were see-through white dresses hanging on the rack.

Fear exploded in Lucia's belly.

"Undress," the woman said briskly.

The girls looked at one another, apprehensive.

The woman glanced at the guard, who promptly lifted his gun. "Undress!" he snapped.

Thirteen pairs of hands fumbled at their clothing.

"Hey," Kane said as he entered the bedroom, his green eyes lighting up at the sight of her in a way that made Abby want to burst into tears.

Oh God, what was she going to do?

"Did Luke tell you about Inez?" Kane asked, oblivious to her distress. He crossed the room and sat next to her on the bed, one muscular arm casually draping over her shoulder.

She nodded. "Inez managed to do it. The plan worked."

"And now Trevor and Isabel have a shot to get out of there alive." Kane's lips curved into a frown. "I don't like being in the dark about how many guards there'll be or where they'll be positioned. Once Trev and Isabel are in the compound, they won't be able to contact us to let us know. Blanco will search them for transmitters."

She tentatively touched his thigh. "You're worried."

"Yeah," he admitted. "It bugs me that we won't be able to communicate with them. We're working under the assumption that they'll be in position at eight thirty. If they aren't, we'll all be screwed."

Not her, though. Of course, she could very well be dead by that time.

Kane took her hand and stroked the inside of her palm. "But let's not think about any of that now." A dimple appeared in his chin as he grinned. "We have some time before we need to leave. Wanna fool around?"

She laughed. "Are you serious?"

"Sure. It's a good way to relax before all that adrenaline kicks in."

Without waiting for a response, he flopped back on the bed, pulling her on top of him. Abby's heart raced as he cradled her head and brought her closer for a soft kiss.

An idea floated into her mind.

No. No, she couldn't.

"So what do you say?" Kane's voice was light, teasing, and his lips met hers again, accompanied by a wicked tongue that he dragged over her bottom lip before thrusting it into her mouth.

She closed her eyes and kissed him back. Tried to keep herself in check and stop her mind from turning to mush the way her body seemed determined to do. Ignoring the tiny bursts of pleasure exploding inside her, she threaded her fingers through his hair, then ran them over his neck.

You have to, Abby.

God, Kane would never forgive her for this.

"Fuck, I love kissing you," he muttered against her mouth, slowly caressing her back in a way that made her fingers tremble.

Steady hands, Abby.

Fuck you, Jeremy.

She dragged her fingers over the nape of Kane's neck, guilt and sorrow combining in her stomach, making her insides burn.

Kane's tongue slid into her mouth again at the same time she located the precise spot.

"I'm sorry," she murmured.

"What—"

She applied just enough pressure on his carotid artery, eliciting a startled curse from his lips. A second later his green eyes glazed over and rolled back in his head. And then he went motionless.

Her throat was so tight, she could barely take a breath. Pain streaked through her body as she stared down at his still form. God. A knot of raw shame tangled in the pit of her stomach like a pretzel. It had been a risky move going for his neck. It took most martial arts experts years to use pressure points safely, but she'd been taught well. Aside from a bad headache, he'd be fine when he came to in a few hours. Angry as hell, but fine.

She inhaled slowly. Okay. She'd bought herself the time she needed. Better make good use of it.

Abby left the bedroom, shutting the door tightly behind her, then made her way to the doorway across the hall. She knocked softly.

D appeared almost instantly, despite the fact that he was supposed to be sleeping. She gazed past his broad shoulders, noticing Ethan sprawled on one of the twin beds, out like a light.

"What do you want?" D said coldly.

"I need your help."

He moved to close the door.

"Please," she pleaded. "Please. Come with me, okay?"

Something in her voice must have alerted him to her state of desperation because he stepped out into the hallway. His stiff body language radiated suspicion as he followed her into the bedroom she and Kane were sharing.

"Inside," she murmured.

D entered the room, took one look at Kane lying on the bed, and spun around to face her, murder in his eyes. "What the hell have you done?"

"I didn't kill him," she said quickly. "Please. Just . . ." She took a breath. "Just dial the rage down a bit. I need your help."

D was already heading for the bed. He leaned over Kane to check for a pulse and Abby wanted to scream. Did he honestly think she would hurt Kane?

"What the fuck is going on?" he demanded when he was certain Kane's heart was still beating.

"Devlin called. He knows about the rescue, but I convinced him not to alert the other guards about it. He gave me his word, but we both know his word means shit, so make sure you tell Kane and Morgan that the element of surprise might have been lost." The words spilled out fast and urgent. "I agreed to meet with him at the same time the rescue is going down. I have to lure him away from the compound, otherwise he'll fuck everything up. I need to get out of here, D, and I need your help to make that happen."

He stared at her incredulously. "Are you serious? Do you honestly think—"

"Kane would have tried to stop me," she interrupted. "Or worse, he would have found a way to go with me, even if it meant leaving you guys in the lurch. You need him on the extraction, D. You can't do it without him."

"So you *knocked him out*?"

"I had no other choice." Desperation bounced off her words. "Devlin wants me to come alone. Kane wouldn't have let that happen. You *know* it."

D's jaw was tight, his expression feral. "I once told you that if you hurt any of my guys, I'd break your neck."

"I remember." She met those furious black eyes. "But you know I did the right thing. Kane can't be a part of this."

"He'll kill me if I help you."

"He'll get himself killed if he tries to help me. Not to mention leave you one man short on this rescue. So for the love of God, stop arguing with me and *help*."

D shook his head. "You want me to send you into Devlin's clutches? I worked with that man once, Abby. He'll tear your throat out."

"Would that really bother you?" she said, sarcasm oozing from her tone. "You don't give a damn what happens to me. But you *do* care about this mission, and making sure that everyone involved gets out of it alive. The extraction will go smoother if Devlin isn't at the compound. That's one less thing to worry about."

He didn't argue with that one. Like he'd said, he'd worked with Devlin. He knew better than anyone what a vicious pain in the ass that man could be.

D went silent. She could see him thinking, working it over in his head, and then some of the ice in his expression thawed, and she knew with a burst of relief that he would help her.

He squared his shoulders. "Follow me."

Knowing better than to ask questions, she did as he asked. The living room was empty when they entered, but Morgan's voice wafted out from the den, followed by a loud guffaw from Luke.

"Out, now," D said almost inaudibly.

They quietly moved toward the front of the house, but rather than leave by the front entrance, D gestured to a narrow door to the left of the hall. She'd assumed it was a closet, but to her surprise, it opened to reveal a metal staircase.

"Hurry," D snapped, sounding annoyed as he glanced over his shoulder to see her hesitating at the top of the stairs.

She quickly followed him down. Neither of them made a sound as they reached the landing at the bottom, which featured yet another door, this one opening to a spacious garage she hadn't known existed. Several SUVs cluttered the large space, along with a pickup truck and a sleek yellow Ducati motorcycle that made her gasp.

"Is that a Desmosedici?" she demanded.

D looked like he was going to smile. He didn't, of course. "Latest model on the market."

"Those things go like two hundred miles an hour," she said in admiration.

"Which is why you're taking it." He strode in the opposite direction of the bike, toward a metal utility cabinet. Yanking it open, he looked over his shoulder and snapped, "Get over here. Help me with this gear."

Five minutes later, she had everything she needed and D was handing her a black helmet. "The garage door is automatic. They'll hear it opening from upstairs."

Abby tucked her hair behind her ears and slid the helmet on. Flipping the visor open, she shot him a grave look. "Stall. Make something up. Give me as much time as you can. And when Kane wakes up . . ." Her throat clogged. "Tell him . . ."

D waited impatiently.

Abby swallowed hard. "Forget it. I'll tell him myself." She swung a leg over the bike and straddled the powerful machine.

D stepped toward a control panel on the wall. "Ready?" he said gruffly.

She lowered the visor and revved the engine.

D pressed a button and the garage door came to life with a grating metallic roar.

A moment later she was gone.

His head felt like someone had pounded it with a baseball bat. Lord, why did it hurt this much? Why did—? Kane's eyes snapped open.

What the *hell*?

Feeling groggy, he took a few seconds to orient himself, groaning as he tried to sit up. His temples ached. Blinking wildly, he tried to remember where he was, what had happened—and then it all rushed back with startling clarity.

"Son of a bitch!" He shot into an upright position.

Abby. Abby had knocked him out. The image of her dark yellow eyes, glimmering with regret, swarmed his brain. Red-hot fury crashed into him like a tidal wave.

He heaved himself off the bed, but a deadly voice stopped him before he made it to the door.

"She's already gone, man."

Fighting a wave of dizziness, Kane spun around and spotted D in the armchair by the window, his ankles crossed, his expression nonchalant.

"What do you mean, she's gone?" Kane demanded.

"She left. A few hours ago."

Kane swore violently. "She knocked me out. She . . . *kissed* me," he choked out. "She fucking seduced me and then knocked me the *fuck* out."

"I know," D said with a shrug.

"What?"

Sounding extremely calm, D uncrossed his legs. "She brought me in here afterward. She asked me to help her leave. So I did."

Rage congealed in Kane's blood. His body went stiff as the implication of what D had just said settled in. "You helped her? Why the hell would you do that? Where the hell did she need to go that was so damn impor— Devlin," he said dully.

D didn't respond.

"He got to her," Kane muttered. He sagged against the wall—it was suddenly hard to keep himself vertical. "He convinced her to go to him. Why? Why would she agree?"

And why wouldn't she tell me?

The question hung in the air, but neither man said it

out loud. Didn't matter. Kane knew the answer anyway. She hadn't told him because he would've tried to stop her. Failing that, he would have gone with her.

And she hadn't wanted him to come.

She hadn't trusted him to come.

His chest felt ravaged, as if someone had burned it with a hot poker. He'd actually believed they were getting somewhere.

It was a slap in the face, knowing he'd been wrong.

"It doesn't matter why she went," D said calmly. "She's gone. And all you can do is focus on the mission now."

The fury swirling through his body channeled itself at D like an electrical current. Kane charged across the room and heaved the other man off the chair, slamming him against the wall with so much force that a picture frame came crashing down to the parquet floor.

"You let her go!" Kane's vision registered nothing but a red haze. "You let her go so she could meet up with a *psychopath*! What the fuck is wrong with you?"

The bedroom door burst open. Morgan took one look at the scene in front of him and let out a curse. *"What is going on here?"*

Kane held D up by his collar, shaking him hard. "You bastard," he muttered.

It took him a moment to realize that the other man wasn't fighting back. He hung limply in Kane's grip, his face completely emotionless.

Tamping down his disgust, Kane regained his sanity. He swiftly released D and turned his back on the guy. He couldn't even look at his friend right now.

"Abby's gone," Kane said flatly. "D helped her escape."

Morgan shook his head. "I knew something was up

when you told me you opened the garage by *accident*."
He glowered at D. "What were you thinking?"

"She asked for help. I gave it to her." There was zero
remorse in D's voice.

"She went to meet Devlin," Kane said.

"Shit." Morgan reached up to rub his temples, which
couldn't be hurting more than Kane's were at the moment. "I should've known she'd do something like this.
That woman is going to get herself killed."

"Not if I have anything to do with it," Kane muttered.

"No way." Morgan's tone was hard as steel. "You're
not going after her."

"Like hell I'm not." He shot D a cold look. "Where
did she go?" When D simply shrugged, Kane had to resist the urge to attack him again. "Where—did—she—
go? And if you don't answer me, I swear to God, I'll rip
your throat out, Derek."

As if weighing the options, D finally let out a frustrated breath. "Muzo. It's a small town two hours north
of here. I put it in the GPS for her. But you don't want to
go after her, Kane. We're about to storm Blanco's fucking compound."

Frustration seized Kane's insides and twisted them
into hard knots. D was right. He couldn't abandon his
men, not when he'd been the one to convince them to
take on this mission in the first place. Anger streaked
through him, all of it directed at Abby. She'd put him in
an impossible position. Christ, how could she do this?
She'd known, when she knocked him out and ran off to
meet Devlin, that Kane wouldn't be able to follow her.
That he wouldn't desert his team.

Unless . . .

"When is she meeting him?" he snapped.

D sighed. "Right when the auction begins. Seven o'clock."

"The chopper's not taking off until eight twenty," Kane said slowly.

Morgan's tone took on a note of wariness. "Kane . . ."

Without a word, Kane marched out the door. Luke and Ethan were in the living room, shoving magazines into the pile of assault rifles on the coffee table. Both looked up in shock when he rushed past them, but he paid them no attention. He found what he was looking for in the den, and when Morgan and D appeared in the doorway a few moments later, he met Morgan's eyes with the determined set of his jaw.

"Muzo's an hour from the helipad in Corturo," he said as he closed the laptop he'd swiped from the desk. "I can make it."

"For fuck's sake, Kane—"

"I won't let that maniac kill her," he interrupted, feeling his cheeks go hot. "And I won't leave you in the lurch either."

"Kane, I know you care about her," Morgan said, "but—"

"She *needs* me." His mouth tightened in a grim line. "Whether she likes it or not."

Before either of them could object again, he sprinted out of the room, nearly knocking them both over in the process. Two hours north. Abby was probably already there, scouting the area and making sure Devlin wasn't laying a trap for her. *Damn* her. He let out a string of expletives, which only got louder and more obscene as he burst into the garage and discovered that Abby had commandeered their fastest vehicle.

He forced himself not to dwell on what she'd done as he ran around the garage like a crazy person, gathering everything he needed. But it was hard not to. She'd knocked him out. She'd run out on him. Hadn't even trusted him enough to tell him what she was doing. She'd trusted D. *D*, for fuck's sake. Biting back his anger and resentment, Kane hit the button to open the garage door and slid into one of the armored SUVs parked in the large space.

He was going to *kill* her.

If Devlin didn't do it first.

Chapter 20

"This is it," Isabel murmured.

She and Trevor were being escorted out of the car Blanco had sent to their hotel, and she was troubled to see that the courtyard of his estate was littered with other cars. Isabel counted eleven. She suddenly felt sick. Eleven sick bastards already here, eager to purchase a *human being*. What kind of world was she living in? What kind of people did these things?

Trevor casually gripped her hand as they climbed the front steps of the house. The sun was just beginning to set, filling the sky with shades of orange, pink, and yellow. Beautiful, actually. She felt even sicker, finding beauty in such an ugly situation.

At least she didn't have to do this alone. A part of her was incredibly grateful to have Trevor by her side, though she was still a tad apprehensive after last night's unsettling encounter. He'd almost kissed her. He might deny it, but Isabel knew when a man wanted to kiss her. She couldn't decide if she was relieved or disappointed that he hadn't.

No, of course she wasn't disappointed. She'd told herself right from the start that she couldn't get involved with Trevor Callaghan. He was too broken, maybe even beyond repair, and as she held his hand on their way to the house, she forced herself to push aside the troubling thoughts and focus on the task at hand.

As before, Trevor's weapon had been confiscated at the gate, and although both of them had been subjected to a thorough search, Isabel drew comfort from the fact that none of the guards seemed to be eyeing Trevor and her with suspicion. Morgan had called earlier to give them a heads-up that Blanco might have caught wind of their plan. If Devlin had told his boss about the potential ambush, then Blanco might very well suspect that the Martins, last-minute bidders, could be involved. Even though she and Trevor had been treated with indifference by the guards, Isabel prayed that they weren't walking into a trap.

She also prayed that Abby didn't lose her life. Morgan himself had sounded frazzled when he'd told them about Abby's meeting with Devlin. Granted, Abby could take care of herself, but it was difficult for Isabel not to worry.

When they walked inside, Blanco met them in the front parlor, wearing a black pin-striped suit with a bloodred carnation pinned to his left breast pocket. "Mr. and Mrs. Martin," he said happily. "It is good to see you again."

Trevor nodded. "I trust the transfer went smoothly last night?"

Blanco's dark eyes twinkled. "You wouldn't be here this evening if it hadn't."

The man seemed to be in high spirits. A good sign. Maybe Devlin had actually kept his word and left the compound without saying anything to Blanco.

With a chuckle, Trevor leaned over to nuzzle Isabel's neck. "Good. My wife and I are very excited to be in attendance."

"Then if you'll go with Gerard," Blanco said, pointing to a solemn guard holding an assault rifle, "he will take you to your quarters. You'll find a catalog of photographs in your room. As I said before, if you wish for a closer look, Gerard will be happy to take care of it for you."

"Thank you, Señor Blanco," Isabel said graciously. She stepped toward him and brushed a seductive kiss on his tanned, wrinkled cheek. "You are a wonderful host."

Blanco smiled. "Your kind words are greatly appreciated. And I hope we will be able to do business again in the future."

Hopefully not.

"I hope so as well," she purred.

Trevor took her hand again, and the pair followed Gerard as he easily navigated the many corridors leading to the west wing of the house. They reached a wide, elegant hallway with a dozen doors on each side, and the guard led them down the white marble floor to a door at the end of the hall. He unclipped a key ring from his belt, unlocked the door, then gestured for them to step inside. "The door will be locked," he said in English. "If you need something, knock."

They entered a room that was as elegant as the hallway leading to it. An enormous bed graced the center of the room, which was furnished with Victorianesque pieces and had thick velvet drapes in dark burgundy hanging at the window. A metal serving cart sat at the other end of the room, featuring a crisp white cloth and a sterling silver ice bucket containing a bottle of champagne.

Isabel rolled her eyes. "How welcoming."

Trevor unfastened the top button of his suit jacket and strode across the room toward the plush leather sofa with a rectangular-shaped glass coffee table in front of it. On the table was a black leather portfolio case.

Isabel felt uneasy as she watched Trevor pick up the heavy book. "Is that what I think it is?"

He opened the cover, then sucked in his breath. "Yeah." He quickly snapped the portfolio closed. "Don't look at it. You won't like what you see."

Despite his warning, she was curious by nature. Her satin flats clicked against the polished hardwood floor as she crossed the room. Trevor handed the portfolio to her without a word. She opened it to a random page. Her expression didn't even change.

"Sit down," she said quietly. "We need to look through it."

"I don't really feel like throwing up."

"Neither do I, but we have no choice." She gave an imperceptible nod at the ceiling. "We're not being recorded, but they're still watching. We need to do what we're supposed to."

"You're right." His face remained pleasant, but she could hear the reluctance in his deep voice.

They sat side by side on the small couch and opened the portfolio together. "You're very interested," she reminded him.

"And you're very excited."

Together, they flipped through the pages, pausing on certain photos. Trevor dragged his finger along particular aspects he found "pleasing." Isabel clapped her hands together at one point.

All the while choking down the urge to vomit. The

photographs were indecent and revolting and made her wish Blanco were standing in front of her so she could strangle the rotten bastard. Children in lewd poses meant only for adults. Naked brown skin. Private, unspeakable body parts that no one should ever have to see.

"This is her," she said suddenly, stopping Trevor from going to the next page.

He examined the photo. "You sure?"

"She _has Inez's eyes," Isabel said, her voice soft. "That's Lucia."

Lucia Alvaro had earned three pages in Blanco's dirty book. Shot from the front, the back, the side. Close-ups that made Isabel's eyes water. Oh God, that poor sweet girl. At the top of the page were the words *Item #8.*

Staying in character, she gave Trevor a sexy smile and touched his well-defined biceps over his sleeve. "I want to tear that man's balls off and feed them to Inez's goat."

Trevor responded by leaning in to nip at her bottom lip. "You'll have to beat me to it."

They resumed the show, pretending to inspect each image in great detail, Trevor pursing his lips every few minutes.

Isabel discreetly glanced at her watch. "Seven eighteen," she murmured.

He pointed to Lucia's terrified brown eyes, which practically popped out of the photo, screaming at them for help. "Shall we request a closer look?"

Isabel nodded. "Please."

Getting up, Trevor went over to the door and rapped on the smooth cream-painted wood. The door swung open to reveal Gerard's questioning eyes. "Yes?"

"We would like a closer look at item number eight," Trevor announced.

"Right away, señor."

Devlin was late.

Abby had been killing time for nearly four hours, and she was growing rather impatient.

The Colombian Andes loomed in the distance, rugged brown peaks making jagged slashes in the horizon. A weird scent hung in the air, not unpleasant but oily and earthy, which made sense since this town was apparently known for its emerald mines.

She didn't know much about emeralds, save that this area produced some of the finest stones in the world. She'd read once that treasure hunters often poached from the mines along the Muzo valley, scavenging the river-beds and even tunneling into the hillside to search for stones. As a result, the mines were well guarded, but she wasn't expecting any angry men with guns to show up and accuse her of attempted emerald theft. Devlin had said this particular mine was abandoned.

She'd ditched the motorcycle about half a mile back after the ground went from dirt to rough gray stone, and then she'd climbed a tree and sat there for hours like a damn monkey. Now her ass was sore and Devlin still hadn't showed his face. Granted, it was only 7:02, but what had happened to punctuality? The only saving grace was that Kane hadn't shown up either. She'd been afraid that D would tell him where she'd gone. Afraid that Kane would abandon the mission and foolishly come after her.

With a sigh, she shimmied down the tree and landed on her feet with a thump. She could hear the faint trickling of water in the distance. The river must be close by, most likely on the other side of the rocky hill.

For the hundredth time, Abby studied the deserted area. A shadowy opening gaped in the rocks about fifty yards away. She walked toward it, noticing as she got closer that it was the entrance to the mine. Splintered boards crisscrossed the large opening, and a crude wooden sign told her in Spanish that trespassing was forbidden. It also spoke of the hazardous instability of the tunnel ahead.

The fine hairs on her neck stood up suddenly. *Finally.*

Devlin. She could feel him watching her. Probably from the rock-strewn slope off to the right. She wasn't worried about being taken out with a sniper rifle. She knew from experience that Devlin preferred a hands-on kill. He liked looking into his prey's eyes as he sucked the life out of it.

"Stop being dramatic and show yourself!" she shouted. Her voice echoed against the rocks, bouncing back at her ominously.

His familiar chuckle rang in the air. Footsteps sounded from the slope she'd been looking at and then Devlin appeared, deftly navigating the rough landscape as he made his way toward her.

His one eye swept over her, his thin lips curling in a little smile. "You're looking well. I see Morgan and his men have nursed you back to health."

"I wish I could say the same about you." She shrugged. "That eye patch is a touch *Pirates of the Caribbean*, don't you think?"

His smile faded. "Don't think I've forgotten who put it there."

"That's why I'm here, isn't it? So you can regain your pathetic pride?"

He didn't take the bait, but she hadn't expected him to. He was too smart to lash out irrationally. He simply moved closer, until they were about six feet apart.

"So how's it going to be?" she said with a sigh. "Ten paces and then draw?"

"Nothing so dramatic." He tilted his head thoughtfully. "Throw your weapons to me."

"Who said I'm armed?"

He let out a genuine laugh. "Don't worry. I'll reciprocate. I think we'll both enjoy this more if it's all about brute strength. No distracting bullets."

She shrugged again. "Sounds good to me."

Without taking her eyes off him, she removed the Glock tucked into the waistband of her jeans and waved it around before setting it on the ground. Devlin stayed true to his word, revealing his own gun and dropping it. He kicked it away, sending it skittering to the edge of the mine's entrance. Abby did the same.

"Now the backup," he said, wagging his finger.

Bending down, she pulled the small derringer from her ankle holster and kicked it away.

Devlin did the same.

"And the knives," he said in a tone that told her he was truly enjoying himself.

Suppressing a groan, Abby lifted up each pant leg and unsheathed the knives D had given her. Chuckling, Devlin got rid of his own knife. A moment later, they faced each other, completely unarmed.

He crooked a finger at her. "Come on, luv, let's see what you've got."

Lucia Alvaro wore a filmy white dress that ended at her lower thighs, revealing the pair of tanned, knobby knees below. Her brown hair was long and straight and hung down her back like a shiny curtain. Isabel's heart squeezed when Gerard led Lucia into the room. The young girl's eyes were awash with panic, as if she thought Isabel and Trevor might jump on her at any moment.

"Knock when you are finished," Gerard said in a bored voice. He cast a firm look in their direction. "Remember, Señor Blanco says no touch."

After he left the room, Isabel gestured for the girl to come closer. Lucia's gaze darted around like that of a frightened animal.

"We're not going to hurt you," Isabel said softly.

The girl stared at her blankly, prompting Isabel to switch to Spanish. She repeated the words, and some of the panic in Lucia's eyes dimmed. "Do you promise?" the girl whispered.

"I promise." Isabel held out her hand. "Now come closer. Stand in front of us. When I ask you to, turn around." She swallowed. "And when I ask you to take off your dress, don't be scared. Remember, we won't hurt you."

Lucia's legs were trembling as she walked toward the sofa. "What is going to happen to me?"

"Nothing, if we have anything to say about it. Do you know why you're here, Lucia?"

The girl blinked. "You know my name?"

"Yes. And we also know your mother."

A sheen of tears clung to Lucia's thick black eyelashes. "Mamá? Is she here?"

"She's not here. But hopefully you will see her very soon."

"She can't just stand here," Trevor spoke up, pasting a leer on his face for the camera's sake.

"Turn around, Lucia," Isabel said. "Very slowly."

Lucia did as she was asked, while Isabel continued quietly. "Some very bad men want to hurt you and the other girls you were locked up with. Trevor and I" — she gestured to him in case Lucia couldn't figure it out — "we want to help you. But you're going to have to help us too. Slowly take off the dress, sweetheart."

Lucia's cheeks turned a bright shade of crimson, but she followed Isabel's instruction. Isabel clasped her hands tightly in her lap, resisting the impulse to stand up and wrap her arms around the girl. Protect her from this disgusting situation she'd unwillingly found herself in.

The girl stood naked before them, and even Trevor seemed on the verge of tears. Isabel could tell from the way he kept swallowing, working hard to maintain his composure.

"Can you describe the room where you're being held, Lucia?"

"It's where the servants drink coffee and talk before work. Or after work." Lucia seemed unbelievably nervous. And she looked unbelievably frail with her flesh exposed and the white dress pooled around her ankles.

The break room. Abby had been right. "Is there a clock in the room? Turn around again."

Lucia did a slow turn, then said, "Y-yes. There is a clock."

"Good." Isabel swallowed the acid coating her throat. "Now get on your hands and knees."

Next to her, Trevor's face grew pale. "Hurry this up," he said smoothly. "I'm two seconds from walking out that door and murdering every last person in this house."

"Do you want to go home, sweetheart?" Isabel asked.

Lucia nodded earnestly.

"Then at exactly eight twenty, you'll need to do something. Something very, very dangerous."

"I—I will do anything."

"There's a gun in the far left cupboard in the kitchen, the one in the break room you mentioned. Do you know how to use a gun?"

Lucia shook her head.

"That's okay. There's nothing to it. There's going to be a little button under the handle. That's the safety. You'll need to switch it off before you can use the gun. Do you know where the storage room is?"

The girl wrinkled her dark brows. "The room with the containers? Boxes?"

Isabel nodded. "Where they keep the Christmas lights. Do you know where it is and how to get there from the break room?"

"Yes."

"Good. What you need to do is gather the other girls and take them to that room, Lucia."

"H-how?"

"You'll need to get the guard outside your door to come into the break room." Isabel paused. "And then you have to shoot him."

The girl paled.

"Stand up and do another turn. I know the idea scares you, but it's the only way out of here. Once the guard is taken care of, you have ten minutes to get to the storage room. I'll meet you there, and then we're going to run outside to a helicopter that will be waiting for us."

Lucia's eyes lit up. "And then I can go home?"

"Then you can go home," Isabel said, blinking back tears. "There are a lot of bad men in this house, Lucia. If we're going to get you out of here, you need to do every-thing I just said."

"I will. I promise, I will do it." Lucia looked at her with such gratitude that Isabel's tears almost spilled over. "Eight twenty. I will . . ." Her voice wobbled. "I will shoot the guard and bring everyone to the storage room."

"Good girl. And remember, it has to be at exactly that time. If you're even a minute late—"

A knock sounded on the door. "Time is up," came Gerard's voice. The lock clicked and the guard stood in the doorway, gesturing for Lucia to pick up her dress.

Hands shaking, Lucia pulled the transparent material over her body and straightened out the hem. She gave Isabel and Trevor a hesitant smile before following the guard out of the room.

The door locked again.

Isabel wanted to bury her face against Trevor's chest and cry, but she reined in the urge. "She'll do it," she said softly.

Trevor leaned his head toward hers and made a show of seductively sucking on her earlobe. "Do you think she can?" he muttered, his warm breath tickling her neck.

"We'll just have to wait and see."

She glanced at her watch—7:36.

Trevor's tongue traced the shell of her ear. "You did good," he murmured. "You were amazing with her, Isa-bel."

Not even the feel of his warm lips on her skin could ease the ache in her gut, the sick feeling crawling up her spine like ants. She let out a pent-up breath. "Let's just hope it wasn't for nothing."

They circled each other like a pair of wary wolves fighting over territory. Neither was in a hurry to make the first move, though Abby could see Devlin's arms tensing, ready to lash out. He wore a long-sleeved black shirt that revealed the coiled muscles of his wiry frame, and he moved with a lithe grace that seemed out of character for such a cold and cruel robot.

Abby knew better than to underestimate the man. He'd once been considered for Morgan's team, which meant he had to be very, very good.

But so was she.

"You don't know how much I'm enjoying having you here with me," Devlin said as he moved toward her, then sidestepped. "I've thought of nothing but you since the night Jim Morgan stole you away from me."

She balanced herself on the balls of her feet, ready for his first attack. It came swiftly, in the form of a rapid uppercut that made a hissing sound as it barely missed her jaw. Abby danced away, adrenaline coursing through her veins. "Nice try," she taunted.

He came at her again without warning, this time with a series of jabs that she blocked easily. The last blow scraped by her wrist, and a tremor of pain spasmed through her hand. She forced herself not to wince, praying Devlin hadn't noticed the brief tightening of her jaw. She decided to distract him, launching herself at him and executing a throw that landed him on the hard ground. He recovered quickly, back on his feet and ready with a counterattack.

He was well trained in martial arts, making her head spin with everything from lightning-fast karate chops to a lethal jujitsu armlock that sent pain shooting up to her wrist. Gritting her teeth, she fought him off, locking his right knee with her legs and twisting hard. Devlin cursed as his legs gave out. He stumbled to his knees, then dove out of the way a split second before she unleashed a karate chop of her own on his carotid artery.

They separated again, circled. Abby was breathing heavily, her lungs burning. Devlin's shirt was soaked with sweat. So was his angular face. He lifted a hand and wiped away the sheen on his forehead. "Better than I expected," he said between ragged breaths. "Jeremy Thomas trained you well."

"So that one day I could snap the neck of a psychopath like you," she returned cheerfully.

His face tensed with rage. He charged, so fast, so unexpectedly that Abby found herself caught in a gear lock that nearly crushed her windpipe. Gasping for air, she unleashed a right hook, striking him squarely in the jaw. He retaliated with an uppercut that had her seeing stars.

Enough. She was getting tired of this bullshit.

Her leg snapped out, slicing into his calf and sending him to the ground again, and this time she pounced, pinning him down, jamming her elbow against his throat until she managed to get her arms around him in a chokehold that had him wheezing. He grunted as she restricted his airflow. She shifted her hold, seeking out the spot that would compress his carotid artery. The eye she'd left him with began to glaze over in its remaining socket. She applied more pressure, sweat dripping down her neck. Almost there. Almost—

The tip of a blade sank into her forearm, just beneath her elbow. A knife. The bastard had held out on her. The sharp sting of pain had her instinctively loosening her grip and Devlin pounced on the opportunity.

White-hot agony sliced through her.

His fingers dug into her injured wrist. With a triumphant growl, he twisted so hard her vision went hazy. The sound of bone splintering cracked in the air.

And then he was on top of her, pinning *her* down, *his* hands around her throat. She fought for air, batting at him with her uninjured hand. He tossed away the small switchblade he'd surprised her with and squeezed her neck tighter.

"I've wanted this," he panted, "for so long. So long, Abby."

Arousal swam in his one good eye.

Abby felt herself losing consciousness. She tried to breathe, but his grip was too tight. No air. Her trachea tightened, closed. Oh God.

"I love watching you die," he hissed.

Her vision went in and out of focus. The girls. She had to save the girls. But she couldn't. Ted was trying to hurt her and— No, Ted was gone. And she was . . . she was . . . Her lungs were on fire.

"That's it, luv," he whispered. "That's it."

He squeezed tighter, his face inches from hers, taut with intense concentration and pure sexual pleasure.

So this was it. This was how she would die.

She looked up at him, giving in to the darkness beckoning her.

And then Devlin's head exploded in her face.

Chapter 21

Abby gasped for air, wiping specks of blood and brains off her face as she tried to remember how to breathe. She sucked in as much oxygen as her greedy lungs demanded, her chest burning with each desperate gulp. Devlin's body was pinning her down on the rocky ground, his warm blood spilling over her sweatshirt, her neck, her face. She tasted copper in her mouth and spat it out, struggling to get out from under his dead weight.

Confusion and relief warred inside her. She slid away, crawling on her back until she was a few feet from Devlin's lifeless body. The metallic scent of his blood still hung in the air.

"Abby!"

Kane's urgent voice brought tears to her eyes. She blinked them back, watching as a shadowy figure emerged from the slope. Kane slowed down as he approached, like a wild animal creeping toward a kill. He wore a black turtleneck and black pants that matched the black look on his face. Concern and fury dominated his expression, each emotion growing stronger, more turbulent, as he fixed his gaze on her.

"W-what are you doing here?" Abby stammered.

"Saving your ass, apparently," he replied in a severe voice. He extended a hand, and she grasped it uneasily, allowing him to haul her to her feet.

"Are you okay? Did he hurt you?" Kane demanded.

Abby cradled her broken hand against her chest. "I'm fine. It's just my hand." She glanced at the streak of blood on her other arm. "And he nicked me with his knife."

She looked into his deep green eyes, stunned by the intensity of emotion she saw in them. Relief. Pleasure. Anger. Disgust. Betrayal.

It was that last one that made her heart ache.

Turning his back, he moved toward the entrance of the tunnel and bent down to gather the weapons she and Devlin had tossed there. He shoved everything except one gun into the canvas bag on his other shoulder, then looked over at Devlin's dead body. He made a disgusted noise, muttering what sounded like "Good riddance."

She watched him for a moment, then snapped out of her trance as she realized what this meant. What his presence meant.

"You can't be here!" she burst out. "Damn you, Kane, how could you come here?"

He stared at her. "How could I not?" he answered, his voice low and deadly. "You needed me."

"Those girls need you," she snapped. With a rush of panic, she grabbed his arm and twisted his watch around so she could check the time—7:16. The chopper wouldn't take off for another hour. "You have to go, Kane. Now."

"I plan on it," he said grimly. "Do you think I'd leave my team one man short?"

"Obviously you would," she shot back. "I can't believe you came here instead of staying with them—"

"And I can't believe you knocked me out back at the safe house!" His eyes blazed. "Did you honestly think I wouldn't come after you?"

"You didn't need to! I needed to come here alone, and *you* need to be on that chopper."

"I will be." His expression darkened. "I just have one question—why didn't you tell me about Devlin? Why the fuck didn't you trust me?"

"It was something I had to do alone," she said unhappily. "If I'd told you, you would've—"

"Tried to help?" he finished coldly. "You mean, the way I helped now?"

"I'm sorry," she said. "I know you're pissed, but you've got to understand that—"

He cut in again. "What I understand is that you don't trust me. That all the time we've spent together, in and out of bed, hasn't meant a damn thing to you."

Panic skittered up her spine. "That's not true."

"Isn't it?" His eyes became weary. "You didn't trust me to tell me why you were in the prison. Didn't trust me to tell me about Amanda Silverton. Didn't trust me to tell me about this meeting."

"It wasn't you." Her heart beat wildly, and for the first time in her life, she was actually, truly scared. Scared of losing Kane. "You know how hard it is for me to trust *anyone*. I've been on my own my entire life. Even Jeremy couldn't get me to open up fully. I've always been alone, Kane. Always."

"Then you shouldn't have any problem being alone now." He took a step back. "I have a mission to carry out. Here." He reached into his pocket, retrieved a set of car keys and tossed them into her good hand. "Take the SUV. The bike will get me to the helipad faster."

When he turned around, Abby experienced a burst of panic. "Kane, don't leave like this. At least promise me we can talk about this later."

He did a half turn, his features lined with weariness. "There is no later, Abby. It's done. We're done."

Her throat tightened. "Don't say that."

"Why the hell not?" he demanded. "Come on, Abby, give me one good fucking reason not to write us off."

Kane met Abby's yellow eyes, frustration burning in his gut as he waited for her to respond. When he'd looked into the scope of his rifle and seen Devlin's hands wrapped around her slender throat, he'd almost lost it. Almost shot that bastard's head off and taken the risk that the bullet would exit Devlin and hit Abby. But he'd forced himself to remain calm. To wait for the right moment, the moment when Devlin's head was in the position he needed it to be.

And now Devlin was dead. No longer a threat. Kane wasn't sure he even wanted to call a cleanup crew. Morgan's contacts at the CIA would probably be thrilled to dispose of William Devlin's body, but Kane wanted to leave it here. Let the wild animals gnaw on Devlin, rip him apart. Do to him what he'd done to all the people he'd tortured and killed.

It had taken all of Kane's willpower not to pull Abby into his arms afterward. He'd wanted to hold her. Comfort her.

Love her.

But he couldn't. Because you couldn't hold, comfort, and love someone who didn't want to be held, comforted, and loved.

"Give me a reason," he said again, his voice hoarse.

"Because . . . because I don't want you to go."

"Why?" he pressed. "You've made it pretty clear that you don't need or want my help. You've put up a fight with me from day one, Abby. I'm still not even sure why you slept with me—I can't help but think it was part of some plan you're not telling me about." Bitterness tainted his tone.

"It was never part of a plan," she protested.

"And I'm supposed to know that because . . . ? You haven't exactly been forthcoming. About anything."

She bit her lower lip, and for a moment he almost caved in and yanked her into his arms. She looked so small and vulnerable standing in front of him. She'd come all the way out here, alone, to battle a trained mercenary with a case of bloodlust.

"I . . ." She took a breath. "I don't want this to end. I don't know what's going to happen between us, what kind of future we could possibly have, but I know I don't want it to end."

"See, that's the difference between you and me. I know exactly what can happen between us, what the future can hold. Ten years ago I promised myself I'd never fall in love with another woman, but guess what, I fell for you, Abby."

She looked at him in shock. "What?"

"You heard me." He sighed. "And I can tell from your expression that you didn't like what you just heard."

"That's not true," she said quickly. *Too* quickly.

Kane shook his head. "You'll never give yourself to me, will you, Abby?"

"I already did," she said, sounding frustrated.

"You gave me your body," he corrected. "But you won't give me your trust. And you sure as hell won't give me your heart."

Disappointment crashed into him as he heard his own words and recognized the truth in them. Abby Sinclair was incapable of trust, and if she'd ever had a heart, it had eroded away years ago. He'd been a fool for believing he could change that. A fool for letting himself feel all these pesky emotions he'd vowed a long time ago never to feel again.

"Abby . . . I can't be with you." His voice was low and thick with defeat.

Alarm flickered in her eyes. "Don't say that. We can figure something out."

"How? You don't trust me—you'll never trust me. And frankly, I don't think I trust you, so . . ." His shoulders heaved, then stiffened as he realized he couldn't stay here any longer. A glance at his watch told him he had just enough time to make it to the helipad. Just enough time to carry out the mission *she* had asked him to take on.

"Go back to the safe house," he said briskly. "I'll call you when the extraction is over."

"And after that?"

"After that, I'll be on a plane back to Morgan's compound. I would really appreciate it if you weren't on it."

Her face looked ravaged. "If that's what you want."

"It is." His heart twisted in his chest, but he forced a cool expression. "I have to go. I'll let you know what happens."

He took a few steps backward.

"Kane."

The sad note in her voice stopped him. "Yeah?"

Abby met his eyes. She looked uncertain and scared as she cradled her hand protectively. For a moment he thought he glimpsed a genuine rush of emotion take over her beautiful face, but then she blinked, and he found himself looking at a very familiar expression. Cold. Distant.

Uncaring.

"Forget it," she mumbled.

He released a resigned breath. "That's what I thought."

It felt like hours rather than minutes before eight o'clock finally rolled around. Isabel and her pretend husband had spent the time alternating between hushed discussions over the pervert portfolio, as she now referred to it, and making out, though neither of them received an iota of pleasure from the lip-lock. A man from the catering staff had brought in some hors d'oeuvres a few minutes ago, and Isabel had made a big production out of nibbling on the delicate cheese-stuffed pastry.

Now she reached for another one and took a bite. She chewed for a moment. Pretended to savor the pastry. And then her eyes widened, she gave a sudden grimace of disgust, and proceeded to pull a long black hair out of the food.

"This is horrifying!" she hissed at Trevor, who seemed to be fighting a smile. "And it can't be sanitary."

She pretended to stew about it for a few minutes, then flounced off the couch and marched to the door, knocking angrily.

Gerard appeared. "Yes, señora?"

She held up the strand of hair as if it were a deadly virus. "I found *this* in my food! What kind of catering staff has Señor Blanco hired! This is unacceptable." She rambled on for a while, until Gerard's dark eyes seemed to glaze over.

"I will speak to them," he cut in, attempting to defuse the situation.

She shook her head. "No, *I* wish to speak to them. I would like to look into the face of the person who so carelessly prepared this food."

"I'm afraid I have orders to make sure you—"

"I don't give a damn about your orders," she snapped, her gaze flicking over him like he was a piece of lint.

"Señora—"

"I was taken to the kitchen during the tour of the house. I will go there myself," she said decisively.

His hand reached for her arm as she tried to march off. "Wait a moment. I will call someone to escort you."

Looking annoyed, she pointed to the radio clipped onto his belt. "Just let them know I'm on my way to the kitchen. I can get there myself, thank you."

He tried to protest again, but she silenced him by holding up the offending strand of hair. "*This* is not the way Paloma Dominguez-Martin should be treated." She glanced through the doorway, shooting her "husband" a determined look. "You stay put, *meu amor*. I will take care of this."

Trevor looked at the guard, giving him a what-can-you-do shrug. "Just be quick, sweetheart. Our bids have already been placed."

Shrugging Gerard's hand off her arm, Isabel pinched the black hair between her thumb and forefinger. "I will return after giving the catering staff a piece of my mind, señor."

Leaving Gerard staring after her in helpless frustration, she sauntered down the hallway, her flats slapping angrily against the marble floor. She turned right at the corridor, encountering several more guards manning their posts. One reached for his gun, but she scowled at him. "I am going to the kitchen. Señor Blanco is aware of this."

She practically flew down the hall, not daring to look back to see if any of the guards had chosen to come after her. She was extremely conscious of the cameras following her movements. She couldn't see them, but she felt them. The back of her neck prickled with unease, but she forced herself to keep going. Nobody was behind her.

Her watch revealed it was eight twelve. Lucia would be making her move soon.

Isabel let the hair slide from her fingers, the pretense forgotten. It had been her own hair anyway.

She turned into another corridor, noticing the lack of shine on the floor. The servants' quarters. Of course. Blanco wouldn't care if the marble in this particular part of the house reflected his wealth.

The sound of frantic voices came from a room to the left. The kitchen. She lingered near the doorway, peeking in to see members of the catering staff, clad in starched black uniforms with white aprons, rushing around the enormous room, pouring wine into glasses and piling food on silver trays.

She had to cross the kitchen to get to the storage room.

Isabel took a breath. It was now or never.

Eight sixteen.

"Almost go time," Morgan muttered, glancing at the three other men in the chopper.

Kane's absence did not go unnoticed. He should have been here by now, damn it. Morgan wanted to hit something. No, he wanted to hit Kane for disappearing on them when they needed him.

The Boeing Chinook chopper was idling a mile from Blanco's compound. This particular model was currently being used in Afghanistan and Iraq, and Morgan had no clue how his contact had managed to get his hands on one of these babies. But he was grateful for the coup. The machine's speed and lift capacity were just what they needed to get thirteen girls out of Luis Blanco's compound. Sam was at the helm, waiting for the green light to take off. D was absently running a hand over the rocket launcher by the door, his features hard.

Isabel would be making her move now.

And Kane still hadn't arrived. Morgan prided himself on his tolerance—he didn't play by the rules, same way the men he'd recruited didn't. But he demanded two things of his men, two things that were deal-breakers—show up and back each other up. Later, he'd have to decide whether Kane's actions were unforgivable. Whether the guy would still have a place on the team when this was all over.

In the seat across from him, Ethan muttered what sounded like a Hail Mary. Morgan tried not to snort. Right, because the rosary would get them through this mission. You could take the good Catholic boy out of the one-horse town, but old habits were hard to kick.

Eight seventeen.

The roar of an engine broke the silence.

"He made it," Ethan blurted.

The weight pressing down on Morgan's chest eased. Thank the fucking Lord. He heard footsteps, and a moment later Kane threw himself into the chopper, his face flushed, eyes glittering with satisfaction.

"Told you I'd make it," he said, sounding breathless as he grabbed the rifle Luke held out for him.

"You cut it pretty close," Morgan said mildly. "I was just practicing what I would say when I canned your ass."

"I said I'd make it," Kane repeated firmly. His face went tight with determination. "Two rules, remember? Show up and back each other up."

"Ooh-rah," Ethan murmured.

"What are you doing?" Valencia hissed as Lucia stared straight ahead at the clock mounted over the door. "Why do you keep looking at the clock?"

Lucia ignored her. Her entire body was tense with anticipation. And overwrought with terror. The black-haired woman with the kind eyes had been clear. If Lucia didn't get rid of the guard, they couldn't get rescued. She wouldn't go home.

Her palms were soaked with sweat, tingling with fear. She wanted to tell Valencia about what had happened in that room, but she was afraid it might cause an outburst. What if everyone ran to the door before it was time?

Her gaze darted to the cupboard. Was there really a gun in there?

Her fear intensified. What if the woman had lied and this was a trap? What if she opened the cupboard and the door burst open and the guards shot her instead?

There are a lot of bad men in this house.

The woman's scary warning buzzed in her brain. Yes, these men were bad. Tears stung her eyelids as she remembered the three other rooms she'd had to visit. Silent, expressionless men, sitting there and looking at her. Appraising her like she was a piece of meat.

She had to believe the woman was telling the truth.

She *had* to.

The minute hand on the clock ticked by, landing on the sixteen-minute mark.

Lucia took a breath. "Valencia," she whispered. "You need to knock on the door and tell the guard one of us is sick."

The older girl's eyes widened. "What?"

Lucia got to her feet, her legs shaking so badly she could barely walk. "We're getting out of here," she said as she went over to the kitchenette. She quickly opened the left cupboard. "Someone is helping us."

"What? Who?" Valencia's whisper was excited. "How do you— What is *that*?"

Relief rushed through her when she moved aside a stack of coffee filters and spotted the ominous black gun. It had a funny-looking pipe thing attached to the end of it, but she didn't care. It was still a gun. The black-haired woman had spoken the truth. She was helping them!

"Get the guard, Valencia," Lucia hissed. "Now."

She picked up the gun, which was heavier than she had expected.

Valencia rushed to the door.

Lucia found the little button the woman told her about and clicked it off. Her hand shook wildly as she fit the gun into it. She turned around to find the other girls staring at her in wide-eyed wonder. As Valencia began pounding on the door, Lucia moved to stand behind the older girl, breathing hard.

"What is going on in here?" came an angry shout, and then the door swung open and the guard barreled into the room.

His eyebrows furrowed in confusion as Valencia quickly sidestepped him and shut the door behind him. Leaving Lucia in plain sight, the gun shaking in her hand.

Fury flashed in the guard's eyes. "What the hell do you think you're doing? Where did you get that?"

Lucia could barely raise her arm, it shook so badly. *Do it,* she ordered herself. Her finger tightened over the trigger but for the life of her she couldn't pull her finger back.

Do it. Do it. Do it.

The guard lunged at her.

She pulled the trigger.

Rather than the loud explosion she'd expected, the gunshot made a soft little *pop!* She stared down at the gun in dismay, then looked at the man, who'd fallen to the floor, landing on his back. She'd shot him in the chest. A red stain bloomed on the front of his blue uniform shirt. He was gasping, heaving loudly. She hadn't killed him. He was still alive.

Lucia suddenly felt the gun being wrenched out of her hand. She looked over and saw Valencia pointing the weapon at the injured guard, her brown eyes hard and glittering like dark little diamonds.

"What . . ." The squeak died in Lucia's throat as Valencia pulled the trigger two more times, two more *pop*s. Right in the man's head.

A shocked silence fell over the room.

The clock above the door ticked loudly.

Valencia's voice was calm and even as she turned to Lucia and said, "Now what?"

Chapter 22

Isabel had never been happier to see anyone in her entire life. Her body shuddered with relief as Lucia Alvaro's face appeared in the doorway of the storage room. Getting here from the kitchen had been a surprisingly easy feat for Isabel; the catering and kitchen staff had barely glanced in her direction as she walked past them. It was a trick she'd learned a long time ago—act like you belong and nobody will be the wiser. She'd received a couple of odd looks on the way, but to her utter shock, not a single person felt compelled to ask her what she was doing there or where she thought she was going.

In the storage room, she'd found the weapons Inez Alvaro had planted—God bless that woman's soul. Isabel was now armed with two automatic weapons fitted with silencers, each one trained on the narrow doorway. She expected a battalion of guards at any moment. The bids had undoubtedly been placed by now, and soon Blanco would hand over the merchandise to the winners. When he discovered the girls weren't where they should be . . . all hell would break loose.

"Inside. Hurry," Isabel said in rushed Spanish, gesturing for Lucia and the others to pile in. "Close the door behind you."

She found herself surrounded by thirteen young girls, each one shooting frantic questions at her.

"Quiet," she commanded, and immediately they all fell silent. She looked at Lucia, whose brown face was swimming with terror. "Are you all right? Did you have any problems?"

She shook her head numbly. "Valencia—" She gestured to the tall, skinny girl beside her. "She made sure the guard was, um, dead."

"Good." Isabel swept her gaze over each girl, wincing at the sight of their matching white dresses, their delicate bare feet and petrified faces. "In about ten minutes, a helicopter will land right out there." She pointed to the steel exit door on the other side of the room. "When I say the word, we're all going to run toward it, okay?"

She received thirteen obedient nods. Not a single girl questioned her words. God, how desperate they were to get out of this. She couldn't even imagine how they'd held it together, locked up in the bunker for more than a week. But they were strong. Pride swelled inside her. Yes, they were very strong.

Looking at her watch, she frowned, then glanced at the door. Trevor should be here by now. Where the hell was he?

Snapping Gerard's neck took less than a second. Trevor wasn't gentle as he lowered the guard's lifeless body to the floor and took off down the hall. He was cutting it too close. He'd wanted to give Isabel enough time to make it to the storage room, and so he forced himself to stay seated and sip on champagne while the damn bids were being calculated. They'd bid on Lucia. For ten bucks.

Satisfaction tugged at his gut. He wished he could be there to see Blanco's face when he removed that particular bid from the white envelope Trevor had shoved it in.

He felt naked without a gun. Damn. There were too many fucking hallways in this place. He turned a corner, then came to a sharp halt when he nearly slammed into a guard with an assault rifle.

Eyes widening in surprise, the tall man hesitated for only a second before pointing the weapon at Trevor. But that one second cost him. Trevor lunged, knocking both the guard and the rifle to the floor. The guard fought valiantly, landing a heavy punch on Trevor's jaw. Shaking off the pain, Trevor elbowed the guy's throat, waited for his eyes to glaze over, then wrapped his arms around the guard's neck and twisted hard.

Dead. Trevor bounced onto his feet, grabbing the guard's rifle as he did so, and turned around just as three more guards swarmed the corridor.

He unloaded three shots. Three kills.

Breathing hard, he continued down the hall. This was it. Chaos had broken out. Loud voices echoed through the corridors, hurried footsteps thudding against the marble floor. The cameras must have picked up his entire adventure of the past five minutes, which meant that any second now an entire fucking army would be in his face.

He picked off two more guards, keeping a fast pace as he moved toward the other side of the house. Turned another corner, and then he was being hurled in the air, dropping his rifle as he landed hard on the marble floor. A burly guard with feral eyes jumped on top of him, fat fists pounding Trevor's face.

Deflecting a potentially fatal blow, he rolled out from under the stocky man and aimed a well-placed kick to the man's groin. The guard barely grunted as he launched himself at Trevor again, but Trevor had already grabbed the rifle. He put a bullet between the man's eyes, sending a spray of blood onto the wall behind the guard's head.

Drawing in a ragged breath, Trevor tore down the hallway. This time when he skidded to a stop, it wasn't because of another guard.

It was Luis Blanco.

Blanco's eyes filled with fury as he saw Trevor. "You!" he shouted, raising his arm to reveal a shiny silver pistol in his hand. "You did this!"

Trevor kept his own weapon trained on Blanco. "It's over," he said flatly. "There's nowhere to go, Blanco."

Blanco's dark gaze darted off to the right, toward a corridor Trevor recognized as leading to the servants' area.

"Forget it," he said. "My men will be landing as we speak. Any second now—"

A loud explosion rocked the house.

Several paintings slid off the walls and crashed to the floor. Panic flooded Blanco's face. A faint sound of doors slamming and car engines roaring to life came from the front of the house. The bidders, fleeing like drowning rats.

"You will pay for this, you motherfucker!" Blanco was livid, practically shrieking. He lifted his pistol, screaming in Spanish as he pointed the gun at Trevor's head, as his finger squeezed the trigger.

Trevor beat him to it.

He didn't even react when half of Blanco's face separated from his skull, blood spurting and spraying onto the cream-colored walls. The man's rotund body teetered, then fell to the floor. Blood spread out in a large circle around Blanco's head, a scene right out of a pretentious art-house movie as it stained the white marble floor.

Without lingering to give himself a solo high five, Trevor rushed off. The kitchen was crowded with people. Screaming, hysterical people trying to figure out why they'd just heard something explode. A woman from the catering staff screamed when she saw Trevor storm in with a gun. He ignored her and kept moving, reaching the storage room to find Isabel opening the exit door and shouting orders at a group of young girls of all shapes and sizes in identical white dresses.

"It's about time," Isabel said when he burst into the room.

He hurried toward her. It sounded like fucking World War Three outside that door. Rapid gunfire cracked in the air and the sound of helicopter rotors had the wind hissing out a rhythmic melody. Isabel got the door open, her expression calm and businesslike despite the gruesome sight revealed. Bodies littered the paved helipad, while Blanco's men shot unsuccessfully at the sleek olive green Chinook chopper. Trevor squinted and saw D at the chopper door, sweeping a machine gun back and forth, riddling the oncoming attackers with bullets. Men screaming in pain dropped to the ground like bowling pins.

Isabel yelled something in Spanish, and then dove out the door, both guns raised as she led the terrified girls toward the chopper. Kane rushed out to meet her, while Luke, Ethan, and Morgan provided cover fire as the girls rushed forward with their heads ducked down.

Trevor was about to race after them when the door flew open from behind and three guards erupted into the room. He went on the attack, lunging forward to kick a rifle out of one guard's hands and head-butting the other so quickly that the second weapon crashed to the floor too.

He lifted his rifle, only to have it knocked away by the first guard, a man packing about two hundred and fifty pounds and strong muscular arms. As the big man rushed him, Trevor got him in a leglock and both men went hurtling to the floor. The third guard threw himself into the fight, but Trevor got in a lucky punch to the man's nose that had him slumping over like a stone, unconscious.

The big one was harder to handle. Before Trevor knew it, he was on his back, with the guard's meaty hands wrapped around his throat. He shoved at the man's chest, to no avail, unable to get the monster off him. From the corner of his eye, he could see the open doorway, make out the huddled shapes climbing onto the chopper. Relief shot through him. The girls had made it. Isabel had done good.

Mr. Big's fingers circled Trevor's throat. Trevor got a hand in there too, digging his fingers into the guard's iron grip, straining to pry it away. He had a chance when Mr. Big lifted one hand, leaving Trevor to deal with only one, but then the guard pulled a knife from his belt and lowered it to Trevor's throat.

Trevor switched tactics. He grabbed the guard's knife hand, groaning as he tried to stop the blade from connecting with his throat.

Let go.

The whisper in his head was teasing. Seductive.

He let go slightly, and the blade moved an inch closer.

Mr. Big grunted on top of him, spittle from his mouth soaking Trevor's face.

This was what he'd wanted, wasn't it?

To die.

To see Gina again.

The knife moved a fraction of an inch closer.

God, he wanted to see her again. All he had to do was close his eyes and let go. Let the behemoth on top of him slice his throat wide open. Close his eyes and—

A gush of hot moisture drenched Trevor's face.

He blinked his eyes open. The guard on top of him went limp, blood spurting out of the gaping slash on his throat. Isabel loomed over them, holding a knife in one manicured hand, a knife that clattered to the floor as she bent down to help lift the dead guard off Trevor.

She'd come back for him. She'd been on the chopper, safe and sound, and for some stupid reason she'd decided to come back for him.

"Come on," she said urgently, gripping his arm. "We have to get out of here."

Anger clamped around his spine. "Why the hell did you come back?" he spat out.

Her eyes flickered with confusion. "You needed help." Without letting him protest, she hauled him to his feet and tugged him toward the door. "Now let's get on the damn chopper."

He was too stunned to argue. As he followed her out of the storage room, a rush of pure helplessness seized his insides, making him want to hit something. He'd been so close. Goddamn Isabel and her fucking compassion. How could she—

With a hoarse cry, Isabel went down.

All the air left Trevor's body as her slender body fell

to the pavement. A flash of red appeared on her pale green dress. She'd been shot. In the stomach, from the looks of it.

He saw Morgan sprinting in their direction. Heard a bullet whiz right above his head as he dropped to his knees and pressed his hands to Isabel's abdomen. Her eyelids fluttered wildly, her delicate face unbelievably pale despite the bronzed makeup she used to disguise herself as Paloma.

"Trevor?" she said with a moan.

There was too much blood, staining her dress and his fingers. Something hot and painful twisted in his chest. Swallowing hard, he tucked his rifle under his arm and scooped her up. Blood poured out of her side, soaking his suit jacket.

"Trevor?" she said again, her voice faint.

"Don't talk. Save your strength," he said gruffly. And then he cradled her body against his chest and ran toward the waiting chopper.

Chapter 23

The sun sat high in a cloudless sky as Abby killed the motorcycle's engine on the outskirts of the little village of Corturo. The village was bustling with life. A group of boys with happy tanned faces kicked a soccer ball around the dirt field near the main square. Women were chattering animatedly outside the simple wooden church, while a few feet away, half a dozen men gathered around a milk crate, shooting dice and shouting in excitement.

There was a joyful feel to it all, and the feeling grew stronger as she approached the one-story shack that belonged to Inez Alvaro and her daughter. A skinny man with a long face and a thick mustache emerged from the house with three small suitcases in his hands. He was tailed by Inez Alvaro, whose face lit up at the sight of Abby.

The next thing she knew, Inez's plump arms were surrounding her in a bear hug, and the woman spoke a mile a minute in Spanish, thanking Abby profusely for everything she'd done.

"You are an angel sent from heaven," Inez finished, her dark eyes shining.

Compliments had never sat well with her, so she shrugged awkwardly. "It was all Isabel. She's the one who went in and—"

"Señorita Isabel told me you were the reason she was involved in the first place." Tears filled the woman's eyes. "I can never repay you for what you did."

Abby shifted in discomfort. She gestured to the man who'd exited the house. He was now loading the suitcases into the back of a rusted old Volvo that looked like it had seen better days. "Are you going somewhere?"

Inez nodded. "I am taking my daughter to the city. We are going to live with my sister." Her nose lifted in distaste as she looked around the lively village. "I do not feel safe here anymore."

"Blanco is dead," Abby pointed out quietly. "He can no longer hurt you."

"It doesn't matter. We don't belong here anymore."

Abby turned her head when the girl she'd so desperately wanted to save walked out of the house. Like her mother, Lucia lit up when she saw Abby, dashing over with surprising energy despite the fact she'd been locked up in a bunker for a week. Abby endured another hug, though this one brought a rush of emotion. She clung to Lucia's fragile body, running her hands over the bumps of her spine.

"Are you all right?" she asked, searching Lucia's eyes.

The girl nodded. "Yes. Thanks to you and your friends."

"Good." She gave the girl a final once-over, making sure she was indeed okay, then cleared her throat. "I should be going. I have a plane to catch."

"Wait. I have something to give you." Lucia darted off and disappeared into the house. Inez smiled at Abby, encouraging her to wait. When the girl returned a moment later, she held out a faded photograph. After a moment of hesitation, Abby accepted it. It was a photo of Lucia, wearing a red skirt and white shirt that Abby recognized as the uniform the village girls wore in the schoolhouse. Lucia's long brown hair hung in a braid over her shoulder and her face exuded youth and innocence.

"This is so you don't forget me," Lucia said happily, suddenly sounding very much like the young girl she was.

"I don't need the picture for that." Abby swallowed. "But thanks just the same."

Inez and her daughter insisted on hugging Abby again, and a few minutes later she was back on the bike and speeding away. She had one more stop to make before hopping on the plane Noelle had chartered for her, which would take her to Noelle's home in Vermont.

The hospital, like the village, was bustling when Abby strode in. She dodged a couple of doctors and headed to the nurses' station, where she was directed to Isabel's room. Not the ICU, thank God. Apparently Isabel was on her way to a speedy recovery.

She didn't look recovered, though, when Abby entered the private room that Noelle must have paid someone off to secure. Isabel's fair face was pale, almost gray, and she looked incredibly frail in her pink hospital gown. Her blue eyes, however, sparkled at the sight of Abby. Lifting a hand, from which an IV line dangled, she beckoned for her to come closer.

"Hey," Abby greeted her friend. "How are you doing?"

"I'm okay." Isabel shrugged. "The bullet went through and through, so at least I didn't need surgery. Surgical scars are a bitch."

A smile flitted across Abby's mouth. "But puckered little bullet scars are okay?"

"They're easier to cover with makeup."

Laughing, Abby approached the bed. "I came here to thank you. You risked your life going in to save those girls and I—" Her voice trembled. "I'm so unbelievably grateful, Izzy."

Isabel looked touched. "You don't have to thank me. I did what I had to do. What *you* had to do. I'm so relieved the girls are safe."

"I'm relieved *you're* safe. I would have never forgiven myself if . . ."

"If I'd died?" Isabel said bluntly. Her eyes twinkled. "Not to worry. I'm alive and kicking. And I'll be back to work in no time."

"Don't rush yourself."

"I won't," Isabel promised.

"Liar." She paused. "Are you sure you don't want me to stay? I can hang around until you're released."

"No, I'll be fine. Hospitals are so boring—I wouldn't want to force anyone to be here if they didn't have to."

"I don't mind . . ."

"Go," Isabel said firmly. "The doctor says I can leave in a week or so, and there's nothing you can do here anyway." She grinned. "And I'm sure Kane is eager to get home."

Abby averted her eyes. "Actually, I'm heading back to the States alone. Noelle sent a plane."

There was a beat of silence.

"What about Kane?" Isabel demanded.

Abby's insides coiled into tense, painful knots. Ignoring them, she gave a little shrug. "We're going our separate ways."

"Oh, Abs. What did you do?"

Irritation spread through her. "Why do you assume I did something?"

"Because I know you," Isabel said with a sigh. "Jesus, Abby. Do you want to live the rest of your life closed off to people?"

Isabel's question sent another tornado of pain and sorrow spinning through her body. She wanted to defend herself, to tell Isabel that she was wrong, but she couldn't muster the words. Fortunately, she didn't have to, because a tentative knock sounded from the door.

Trevor Callaghan stood in the doorway, clad in the same ratty clothes he'd worn the day he'd shown up at Morgan's compound. Gone were the sleek Julian Martin business suits. And gone was that flicker of life she'd seen in his eyes only a day ago. His gaze had reverted back to empty. Broken.

Sort of like hers.

"Is this a bad time?" Trevor asked, looking from one woman to the other.

"No, it's fine," Abby said quickly. "I was just leaving."

Disappointment flashed across Isabel's ashen face. "Abby . . ." She seemed to have a hundred more things to say, but then her shoulders sagged and she simply said, "Don't be a stranger, okay?"

"I won't." With a half smile, Abby reached down to touch Isabel's arm, then left the room.

Ten minutes later, she was on her way to the airport. Alone.

Whatever he'd come here to say, it didn't look good. *He* didn't look good. Isabel bit back a sigh as Trevor came closer, then paused at the foot of her hospital bed. His

T-shirt had a hole in the sleeve and his wrinkled jeans didn't hug his legs the way those suit trousers had. Nothing about him seemed inviting. Not his shabby clothing, and especially not his dead eyes.

She remembered the way he'd looked at her right before they'd almost kissed, his face taut with arousal. Sure, there had been grief and uneasiness there too, but any emotion was better than none. It was all gone now.

"You look better," he began awkwardly. "Color's coming back to your face."

"You can't keep me down for long," she quipped.

He wrung his hands together as if he couldn't decide what to do with them. Finally he just let them dangle at his sides. "I'm flying out in an hour." He halted abruptly.

"I guess you coming to see me in New York isn't going to be in the cards, is it?"

For a second, she thought she glimpsed a burst of emotion in his eyes, but before she could begin to decode what she'd seen, he went impassive again. "That's probably not a good idea. I'm heading back to Aspen."

Right. Back to that condo he'd lived in with his dead fiancée.

She swallowed down her frustration, grounding herself in reality. She'd known from the moment they'd met that nothing could ever happen between them. He was broken beyond repair. She'd *known* that.

So why was disappointment pulsing through her veins?

The silence that descended was thick with tension. He was avoiding her eyes. Discomfort? Self-hatred for allowing himself to open up to her this past week? Both options proved to be false when he finally locked his gaze with hers.

Anger.

Isabel sucked in a breath, shocked by his expression. "Trevor," she started.

"Damn you," he interrupted, fury etched into every hard angle of his face. "Why the fuck did you come back for me?"

Isabel's palms dampened. "Because you were in trouble. That guard had a knife to your—"

"I wanted him to do it!" he roared.

"You don't mean that."

A harsh laugh burst out of his mouth. "I didn't need you to save me—I didn't *want* you to save me. But no, you had to come back and fuck everything up." He spoke with sharp, ragged breaths. "And you got *shot*. You got shot because of me, because for some fucked-up reason you thought I actually needed to be saved."

She swallowed again. "It wasn't your fault I got shot."

"Wasn't it?" His jaw twitched. "You were coming back for me."

"I couldn't just let you die," she snapped. "God, you're being a total asshole right now. No matter what you say, I know you don't want to die."

"You don't know a fucking thing about me, Isabel."

She flinched.

He edged away, his entire body vibrating with anger. She wanted to say something, anything, but her throat was too tight to get a single word out. She couldn't believe how furious he looked. Why? Because she hadn't let him die back there at the compound? Because she'd seen in him something worth saving?

Without looking at her, Trevor spoke in a raspy voice. "Send word to Morgan when you get back to the States, just so he knows you made it safely."

Isabel's gut ached, and it wasn't due to the bullet that

had gone through it. But what had she really been expecting? For Trevor to throw himself on the ground and kiss her feet for saving his ass? For him to be somehow healed from losing the love of his life?

Not the anger, though. She hadn't thought he'd be *angry* about it.

She stared at his grungy clothing, the inflexible set of his shoulders, the deep frown creasing his mouth, and his anger rubbed off on her, settling in the pit of her stomach.

"I won't apologize for coming back for you," she said in an even tone. "You can be as pissed off about it as you like, but I won't fucking apologize. I saved your life. Live with it."

His body went even stiffer. "I have to go," he said hoarsely, turning toward the door.

"Seriously? You're just going to walk away, pretend that the past week didn't happen, that I don't exist?" Her casual tone was betrayed by the trembling of her hands.

He kept his back to her. "Take care of yourself, Isabel."

There was a moment of hesitation, a brief sag of his shoulders. He lingered in the doorway. Didn't utter a word. A second passed, two, three.

Then he was gone.

"Good-bye, Trevor," she murmured to the empty doorway.

They'd been in the air for an hour before someone had the balls to come near Kane. He'd seen the other men exchanging worried glances since the moment they'd rendezvoused back at the safe house last night. Nobody commented on the fact that Kane had come in alone, though he'd heard Ethan murmuring to Morgan about Abby's whereabouts. D, in particular, had been keeping his distance, yet it was he who came over and sat beside Kane now.

The tattoos on his bare forearms flexed as he crossed his arms over his chest and said, "I'm only apologizing because you're obviously still pissed, but I wholly believe I did the right thing by helping Abby."

Kane didn't answer. The mere sound of her name sent agony streaking through his body. He hadn't felt this ravaged since Emily's suicide.

What the hell was wrong with him? How did he always manage to fall for emotional headaches?

"Look," D said, mistaking the silence for anger, "she would've tried to do it on her own and gotten herself killed, man. At least with me involved, she had some guns and a fast bike."

Kane sighed. "Would you shut up already? I'm not pissed about it."

"You're not?"

"No." He ground his teeth together. "So quit apologizing and go away. I want to take a nap."

D didn't buy it. "No, you don't. You want to sulk." He paused. "So what happened?"

"Nothing."

"Then where's Abby?"

"Probably on a plane to her next job."

"And you're cool with that?"

"Fuck," Kane burst out. "What the hell do you care? You didn't like her from the get-go. She's gone. Bust out a parade or something, and leave me the fuck alone."

A hush fell over the cabin of the jet.

To Kane's relief, D slowly got up and moved to the

other side of the cabin. In the background, he heard the others quietly talking about the rescue. Apparently Blanco's men had scattered after the death of their employer. Morgan said Blanco's entire empire was in disarray, competitors creeping out of the shadows and fighting to take over.

"The son will probably step up," Morgan was muttering.

"Blanco has a son?" Luke said, sounding surprised.

"Yeah. Lorenzo. He's studying abroad, according to Holden, but I suspect he'll be on the next plane out . . ."

Kane tuned them out. He turned to the window, staring at the gray-white clouds, listening to the sound of the jet's engine as it pushed them home.

Home. Morgan's compound. Shooting the shit with the guys and getting drunk until the next job.

For the first time in his life, none of that sounded very appealing.

"This just came for you."

Abby lifted her head as Noelle entered the enormous living room, holding a UPS package in her hands. Her boss's heels clacked against the smooth wood floor as she crossed the room that looked like it belonged in the pages of a design magazine. Abby had never been here before — Noelle usually stayed in her Paris penthouse, which seemed to suit her far more than this lavish Vermont chalet with its endless ceilings and quaint furnishings.

Abby liked this place better. It reminded her of Morgan's house.

It reminded her of Kane.

She shifted her gaze from the spectacular mountain view offered by the huge picture window and accepted the package from Noelle's outstretched hands. Her fingers moved lifelessly to pull at the string that opened the box.

Noelle perched herself at the edge of Abby's chair, her blond hair falling onto her face as she leaned over Abby to examine the contents that spilled out of the parcel. Abby had asked her lawyer to ship the box, which he'd been holding for safekeeping for the past few years. She flipped through the passport, birth certificate, and other documents, then froze when an item slid onto her lap.

Slowly, she lifted the silver chain. The small cross dangling from the chain sparkled in the sunlight streaming in from the window.

Her throat clogged.

"I never took you for religious," Noelle said, wrinkling her brow.

"It's not mine."

The shadow at the foot of the bed. The gleaming silver chain around a thick, corded neck.

The shadow cast over her, bending down, reaching for her.

She slapped away the hands. "Please . . . don't . . . no . . . no!" She clawed at him, spat at him, ripped that chain off his neck. She clasped the tiny medal attached to the chain, trying to jam it into the shadow's eyes. His hands gripped her waist.

He was carrying her away.

She took a breath. "It was Jeremy's. He was wearing it the night he broke into Ted's house and saved me."

"Abby . . ." Noelle sounded wary, as she often did when a situation bordered on emotional.

"He gave it to me in the hospital, the night before he died," she murmured. "He told me to give it to . . ."

My daughter.

Abby fell silent. *Give it to your daughter,* Jeremy had said hoarsely, *so she'll always be protected.*

But the cross was just insurance, he'd added. Because as long as Abby was around, he knew any kid of hers would be safe.

Tears stung her eyelids. A kid of hers. A kid she'd never have because she was too damn scared to let anyone in.

But she'd let Kane in.

She'd told him about her past, trusted him with her body. For the first time in her life, she'd connected with another human being, and it had felt . . . good. Really good. Laughing with him, lying beside him. Kissing him.

But in the end . . . in the end she hadn't trusted him to help her with Devlin. She hadn't trusted him, period. He was right. How could they ever have a real relationship when a part of her would always be pushing him away, just a little?

"Don't you dare cry on me," came Noelle's sharp voice. "You know I can't do tears, Abby."

Despite the warning, one tear slid out, soaking her cheek. She opened her mouth, not sure what she wanted to say, but what came out was completely unexpected. "I want out."

Noelle sucked in her breath. "What?"

"I don't want this life anymore." Her hands trembling, she shoved the cross back in the box, along with the ID papers. Abby Sinclair's ID papers. She hadn't been herself for years. It was easier that way. Pretend to be someone else, run away from anyone who gets too close. So much easier.

But she hadn't been pretending this past week. She hadn't pretended with Kane.

"Are you fucking with me here?" Noelle asked apprehensively.

She set the package on the arm of the chair and stood abruptly. "I'm tired of the solo missions. Tired of becoming a different person for months at a time. I can't keep living like this. Do you know how closed off from the world I actually am? Do you know how lonely this life is?"

Noelle occupied Abby's chair, resting her elbows on the armrests. She looked cool and collected, as always. Utterly emotionless. "You're talking crazy, honey. We both know the world has nothing but pain and heartache to offer. Why would anyone be stupid enough to embrace that?"

"Is that all there is? Is that really all there is?" she challenged. "What about all the other things?"

Noelle looked surprisingly nervous. "What other things?"

Abby started to pace, feeling on edge. "Love, for one. Family. Laughter. Hope. Those exist too, don't they?"

The other woman let out a hasty laugh. "Maybe in fairy tales. Come on, Abby, when was the last time any of those idealistic things led to something good?"

When I met Kane.

She held back the words. Noelle wouldn't understand. She only understood power. Danger. Money.

But Abby got it. She actually got it now. She and Kane had connected. They'd laughed together and held each other and when she'd needed him, he'd been there for her. He was a good man. Probably too good for her. Definitely too good for her.

Yet he'd wanted to be with her. Wanted a future with her. And like a fool, she'd thrown it away.

"I have to believe there can be something good in my life," she said softly. "Jeremy believed it could happen."

"You're scaring me."

"I'm scaring myself." She swallowed. "I don't want to work alone anymore. I want to be part of a team."

Noelle's jaw twitched. "Don't you dare tell me you're leaving me for *Jim Morgan*."

"No." She met the other woman's eyes. "I'm leaving you for Kane."

Abby had expected fireworks, a harsh reprimand, but to her surprise, Noelle simply went quiet. For the first time since she'd met this cold, calculating woman, Noelle actually looked . . . uncertain.

Sighing, Noelle stood up and gripped Abby's chin firmly, forcing eye contact. "Are you sure about this?"

Only a second of hesitation, and then she nodded. "Yes."

Noelle released her, but not before gently running her hand over Abby's cheek. It was a shocking gesture, the first hint of tenderness she'd seen from Noelle, and probably the last.

"All right then," Noelle said briskly. Back to business. Back to normal. "I'll call the pilot."

"We've got a visitor," Lloyd announced, poking his head out on the terrace.

Kane glanced up from his seriously shitty poker hand, experiencing a menacing sense of déjà vu. Last time Lloyd said that, Noelle had appeared on their porch.

He set down his cards, eliciting a groan from Luke,

whose unmistakable tell—scratching his left ear—revealed he had a ridiculously good hand.

"I fold," Kane said with a smirk.

Luke let out a curse, turning to glare at Lloyd. "Thanks a lot for that. Do you know how much money I could have milked out of him?"

Kane got up and left the patio, heading toward the front hallway. Hank, the man who monitored their security cameras, met him at the door. "Can't tell who it is," Hank said. "Tinted windows."

Shit. Not again.

"Should I let them in?"

"Might as well."

Weariness climbed up Kane's spine like a strand of unwanted ivy. He walked onto the porch. In the distance, he saw a red BMW approaching the front gate. Not the black Mercedes Noelle had driven up in, which was a good sign. Still, they didn't receive many visitors, and none of the chicks Luke hooked up with could afford a Beemer.

The gate buzzed open and the car drove through. Kane rested his hand over the Glock tucked into his waistband. No danger alarms were going off in his head, but one could never be too careful. With Morgan off on some mysterious trip he seemed to take whenever they finished a mission, Kane had been left in charge, and he was always extremely careful about protecting the compound.

The car finally stopped, parking next to D's dirt bike. A moment later the driver's-side door opened.

All the air in his lungs left his body in one fell swoop.

It was Abby.

She wore a pair of snug blue jeans, a loose yellow tank

top, and white sneakers. Her long red hair cascaded across her shoulders, and as she walked closer, he noticed something silver sparkling at her collarbone. He squinted. Was she wearing a *cross*?

"Hey," she called tentatively.

His voice came out rough. "Hey."

She climbed the steps and then she was standing in front of him. Her sweet, flowery scent floated into his nostrils and he steeled himself against it. He had no clue why she was here, but he wasn't about to let her presence affect him. So what if she looked cute and sexy and oddly relaxed? He'd meant every word he'd said to her back in Colombia. He couldn't be with a woman who didn't trust him.

"So," she started awkwardly.

"Why are you here?" His tone was sharper than he intended, but he didn't apologize for it.

"I . . ." She suddenly sighed, shaking her head in resignation. "Screw it. I was going to slowly ease into this, but it's totally not my style."

He stared at her in confusion. "Huh?"

"Here's the thing." She met his gaze head-on. "I can take care of myself. I've been doing it since I was eight years old and I'm pretty damn good at it. I can kill a person in a hundred different ways. I'm perfectly fine with being alone—it's what I've always preferred."

He drew his eyebrows together. Where the hell was she going with all this?

"I can do my job and be alone and live my life like I always have. I can live without you, Kane." She released a shaky breath. "I just don't want to."

His heart rate accelerated. Just a bit.

"I don't want my old life," she admitted. "After we

said good-bye, I went to Noelle's place in Vermont. I was planning on staying there until I got my next assignment."

"Yet you're here. Why is that, Abby?"

"Because there is no next assignment," she said simply. "There's only you."

He couldn't fight his skepticism. "You didn't want me before."

"I was scared." Her yellow eyes flickered with remorse. "I was stupid."

"Yep," he agreed mildly.

"But I've smartened up. I came here because . . . well, because there's nowhere else I want to be." She shrugged. "I'm pretty sure I'm in love with you."

He couldn't help but grin. Her careless revelation, that little shrug, didn't surprise him. Heartfelt declarations and Abby Sinclair didn't go together. This was the Abby he'd fallen for—direct, unapologetic. He loved her even more for that.

"And I want a future with you," she finished. She tilted her head. "So, is it too late?"

Was it too late? A childish part of him wanted to say yes, to punish her for the way she'd handled things back in Bogotá. But by punishing her, he'd be punishing himself. Where would he ever find another woman like her, anyway? Why would he ever *want* someone else?

"I think we could work something out," he said slowly.

The corners of her mouth curved. "You think?"

"I know." With an answering smile, he pulled her into his arms, his entire body flooding with warmth and pleasure as he breathed in the scent of her hair, nuzzled the soft flesh of her neck. "You're not going to work for Noelle anymore?"

"I'll take on the occasional assignment. But no more deep cover. No more giving up my identity, or sleeping with scumbags in order to kill them." She searched his face. "I want to use my skills for better purposes. I want to save people."

"We'll do it together." He grinned. "Morgan would love to recruit you for the team. I think he values your skills more than he does mine."

She grinned back. "Well, he'd better be prepared to let me run a serious training workshop for you pansies. Someone needs to teach Ethan how to use a knife."

Kane laughed. "If you drive everyone crazy, though, we might have to vote you off the island."

She furrowed her brows. "What?"

"You know, like on that reality show, where they—" He stopped and shook his head. "Forget it. I doubt you even own a television."

Abby seemed to hesitate again. "Do you think the others will mind having me on the compound? Coming along on missions?"

"They'll adjust," he said with a shrug. "And if they give you any trouble, you'll just scare them into submission."

"Damn right." Standing on her tiptoes, she brushed her lips over his. A jolt of desire shot through him. "They'd better get used to me, because I'm not going anywhere. I want to be with you."

They kissed again, and this time Kane slipped her a little tongue. They were both breathless when they broke apart. Abby gave him an impish grin, wrapping her arms around his neck and linking her hands together. "So, that being-with-you thing—I think I want to start now."

He raised an eyebrow. "You can't even take the time to say hi to everyone and have a cup of Lloyd's tea?"

One hand reached between them to cup his growing erection. He groaned.

"Maybe later," she said dismissively. "Right now I'm more interested in getting you naked."

He was lifting her into his arms before she could blink. "Best idea ever," he muttered, bending down to kiss her again.

Kicking open the front door, he carried her inside, the sound of her laughter echoing against the walls as he marched up the stairs with her in his arms.

"A bit overeager, aren't you?" she taunted as he took her into his bedroom and deposited her not so gently on the bed.

"You have no idea." His hands fumbled with the button of her jeans. "By the way, I plan on keeping you in here for several days at least, just to let you know."

She yanked on his collar and pulled him on top of her. "I have absolutely no problem with that."

"Good." His gaze suddenly landed on the silver cross around her neck. He slowly lifted it. "A new calling?"

"A reminder," she said softly.

"To do what?"

A faint smile spread over her beautiful face. "To do everything." She tugged on his hair and brought his mouth to hers. "Starting now.

Read on for a sneak peek at the next
exciting book in Elle Kennedy's
Killer Instincts series,
available from Signet Eclipse in February
2013.

On the roof of the low-rise across the street from the Diamond Mine, Trevor lowered his binoculars and reached for the water bottle at his side. He took a quick sip, then ran a hand through his close-cropped hair and sighed. Although he wasn't about to admit it to the others—the team leader had to lead by example, after all—this gig really was too tedious for his liking. Surveillance was boring as hell, especially after the last couple of missions the team had taken on—rescuing relief workers in Ethiopia, and a kidnapped executive in Johannesburg. Then there were the thirteen little girls in Luis Blanco's Colombian prison . . .

As usual, the memory of *that* particular assignment caused his thoughts to drift to Isabel, the undercover operative he'd teamed up with during the Colombia job. He'd been thinking about her a lot these past six months. Too much, probably. But hell, it was hard not to. He'd been a total shit for leaving things the way he had. The woman had saved his life, and instead of thanking her, he'd lashed out, blamed her for making him face his issues.

Funny, but the anger he'd been consumed by all those months ago had completely evaporated. Now when he thought of Isabel Roma, he was overcome with gratitude. He'd walked away from that mission with an important piece of knowledge—he *didn't* want to die. Once, maybe, but not anymore. Isabel had helped him to see that.

And he'd yelled at her like a toddler throwing a tantrum and left her in a hospital room to recover from a bullet wound she'd suffered while saving *his* life.

"You're a real asshole, Callaghan," he muttered to himself.

Yep, he sure was. He could still make amends, though. After this job was over, he was in line for the unwanted vacation Morgan pushed on his men to prevent them from burning out, and Trevor was thinking of sticking around in New York. Isabel had mentioned she had an apartment there, so maybe he could finally work up the courage to contact her. Unless she was out in the field, throwing herself into the latest role her assassin boss had assigned to her. In that case, Noelle would probably know how to reach her . . .

Trevor contemplated picking up the phone and calling the queen of assassins, then shuddered. Maybe he'd ask Morgan to call Noelle. She didn't seem to frighten the boss.

He was jolted out of his thoughts when Sullivan's voice crackled in his ear. "The kangaroo's leaving the Outback. I repeat, kangaroo's leaving the Outback."

Trevor grinned. He'd rather shave his legs than say it aloud, but he really had missed that crazy Australian. Missions were always more fun when Sullivan was around.

Reaching for his field glasses, he focused on the strip

club. Sullivan had positioned himself in the outdoor patio of the pub next door, directly in the line of sight of the club's entrance. Sure enough, Luke had just exited through the double doors. Trevor zoomed in closer, noticing that the dark-haired man looked a bit dazed.

He frowned. The plan had been for Luke to remain in the club until closing time, but a quick glance at his watch showed that only a few hours had passed since Luke had gone in. The eyes on the outside had no radio contact with Luke, so whatever the reason for his early departure, they had no way of finding out until he told them.

On the street below, Luke stepped up to the curb, zipping up his Windbreaker against the early-October wind. He paused at the crosswalk, then bounded across the street, disappearing into the alley separating Trevor's building from the adjacent one. Luke was coming up to the roof, then. Something must have happened in the club.

The only telltale sign of Luke's arrival was the faint creak of the fire escape. Then utter silence. Again, not something he'd say out loud, but those SEALs had definitely perfected the art of stealth. Luke didn't make a single sound as he made his way onto the roof, and when he appeared out of nowhere like a damn ghost, Trevor almost jumped.

"What happened?" he demanded.

Luke shook his head, frazzled. "I got a lap dance."

"Oh." Trevor arched an eyebrow. "Okay."

Without elaborating, Luke bent down and unzipped the backpack next to Trevor's gear, rummaging around until he found what he was looking for. Popping the earpiece in, he clicked it on and said, "Holden, you read me?"

Since they were all wired in, Trevor heard Holden Mc-Call's response. The man was watching the club's back entrance, and from the rustling sounds that met his ear, Trevor suspected the other man was up in a tree. "Yeah. What's up?"

"Call D to take your place," Luke said. "I want you to head back to the apartment and use your computer magic. Find out everything you can about one of the dancers, Livy Lovelace."

"Is that an order, Trev?" Holden said briskly.

Trevor shot Luke a puzzled look before answering. "Yeah. Do it."

There was a crackling sound, then radio silence. "What's going on?" Trevor asked slowly.

"Dane's not in that club, man. And if he is, then he's hiding away upstairs or somewhere in the employee area."

Luke reached into the pocket of his Windbreaker and pulled out his Marlboros. He lit one, and the orange tip glowed as he sucked hard and then exhaled a cloud of smoke into the night air. Huh. The guy was definitely on edge.

"I can go back in," Luke added. "Try to get past those mammoth-size bouncers and snoop around, but I'm thinking we go about this another way."

"The dancer."

"Yeah." Luke furrowed his brow, and he took another drag. "Something about her triggered an alarm. I asked her how she liked her job, and she just shut down. I swear, she even looked scared."

"That's rather flimsy."

"Look, I can't explain it, but my gut is telling me Morgan's informant was right. This dancer knows something."

"About the missing agent?"

Luke grunted in frustratration. "I don't know. Maybe. But she warrants a closer look."

Trevor snorted. "Another lap dance, perhaps?"

"No. Fuck, not that kind of look. But I think we need to find out more about her."

Trevor wasn't entirely convinced, but he'd learned to trust the instincts of the other men on the team. A soldier's gut feeling was often the most valuable weapon in his arsenal. "Fine. We'll find out more." He cocked his head. "You'll go back in tomorrow night, then?"

Luke sighed. "That might be a problem."